The Hollow Heart

...love will find a way

By Adrienne Vaughan

The Hollow Heart

How heavy hangs a heart that is just hollow?
How filled with lead the heart that knows no air?
It cannot lift with love, when spies a loved one.
It cannot miss a beat, with love to share.

The hollow heart just echoes with its longing,
Without the job of love, to keep it sane,
The hollow heart waits, unfulfilled and wanting,
Without the strength to even feel its pain.

What hollow heart could burst with love unbounded?
If the door was opened, just an inch,
And love, like light, could flood its empty chambers
And thus fulfilled the heart would never flinch.

The door to love stands proud and ever open.
The key's been found and bravely flung away.
The hollow heart has found its only purpose,
And beats with joy...for love has found a way.

Adrienne Vaughan

First Edition

Printed Edition

This book is a work of fiction. The characters and incidents are either fictitious or are used fictitiously. Any resemblance to any real person or incident is entirely coincidental and not intended by the author.

ISBN 978-0-9573949-2-6

The Hollow Heart

Adrienne Vaughan

To my parents, Harry and Marion –

for the love that binds us,
Reta my sister – the one heart and soul,
shared…
…and my husband Jonathan, my love
story.

The Hollow Heart

Adrienne Vaughan

*In memory of
Tony Poole, the man, and Spike, the cat –
two cool dudes.*

The Hollow Heart

Prologue

She stood looking up at the large iron gate, the gaps between the struts of twisted steel boarded up with blank, grey ply. No view beyond. She lifted the latch and barely making an opening large enough, slipped through to the other side. The gate swung closed on well-oiled hinges, the latch clicked into place. No escape. And drawing in the cool air, she willed her heart to still as she walked the short distance to the door, eyes fixed on the ageing enamel sign. But the letters had faded and the words were illegible.

There was nothing else to indicate what the place was about or what took place inside, no hint of activity, no sign of life. She had been here before but had never summoned the courage to go in. Now, she had no choice. Her deadline was today, no time to change her mind or have a change of heart. If she was going to do it, it had to be now. She felt a chill crawl up her spine to her neck, she pulled her jacket collar up, shivering with excitement, apprehension or something more sinister she did not know. What she did know was that by pressing this tarnished, brass door bell, her life could – would – alter for good. She pushed her shoulders back and lifted her chin, she could just see the smeared reflection of her face in the cracked paint. She blinked, caught between the girl she was and the woman she might be. And here it was, the doorway to a past she did not want, a future she could not avoid. She took a huge breath and pushed the bell; the name just a smudge but she knew what it said; what it meant.

She heard footsteps coming towards her, she stepped back, heart pounding, adrenalin pumping, fight or flight, her brain asked urgently, come on hurry up, fight or flight, which? The door swung open, a young girl in a gaily embroidered smock stood there, dark hair in braids, red ribbon woven through; she smiled brightly.

"Hello, are you the reporter?" She asked in a slight accent.

Marianne nodded, words taken away with surprise.

"Come in, Sister Mary May will be in the Chapel, I'll show you."

Adjusting her shoulder bag and taking one last look up and down the street, Marianne followed the girl into the hallway. In stark contrast to the exterior of the building, the walls were painted yellow, the polished floor a honeyed walnut and soft lighting doused the whole place in warmth. As they walked towards a set of imposing doors at the end of the corridor, Marianne could hear a faint musical murmuring, it was soothing, tranquil - disconcerting. The doors swung noiselessly open and Marianne stepped into an enclosed courtyard. She stopped to take it all in, squinting as her eyes adjusted. Above her a domed roof of sapphire glass, littered with silver stars curved across the darkening sky; before her a life-sized statue of the Madonna stood on a plinth carved into what looked like the side of a mountain; a trickle of water at the statue's feet flowed into a pond strewn with petals, as rows of fluttering candles lit a marble altar. Every hair on Marianne's body stood to attention.

There was a loud crash, a clunking of metal and then next to the altar, a door hidden in the rock, swung open and a large, elderly woman bustled in. Fiddling with keys, she raised a hand to greet Marianne, letting the door slam, the draught extinguishing the candles.

"Ah feck, I always forget to close this one first, if the other is open," She tutted, flicking on fluorescent lights. She crossed the room, hand extended, her smile exposing yellow teeth and the remains of lunch.

"You're the journalist then, what's all this about? I'm very busy you know, can we get straight to it?"

Marianne looked the woman up and down. She wore a bold checked skirt, red golfing sweater, battered gilet and carpet slippers; her crinkly hair was hennaed and twisted in a knot on top of her head.

"Are you...?"

"Yes, yes, who were you expecting, the Mother Superior from the *Sound of Music*?" She put a hand to the wall and turned off the Gregorian chant that had been oozing through hidden speakers. She stretched her mouth encouragingly at Marianne, "Well?"

"I'm investigating a very serious allegation, Sister. I have it on good authority this refuge is not what it seems. I'm told it's operating as a clearing house for

11

the illegal sale and adoption of children."

The woman didn't blink, she just kept smiling at Marianne.

"Really? And whose good authority is this?" she asked, her tone even.

"I can't tell you that, but I can tell you I've evidence. Through an internet search we have managed to reunite a woman and her daughter. This woman says she came to this refuge as a frightened, young girl to have her baby and it was stolen. She says she was drugged and told her baby had died. She said she knew that wasn't true and never stopped looking for her daughter."

The nun pulled a packet of cigarettes from her gilet, lit one and puffed on it, blowing the smoke into Marianne's face.

"What absolute bollocks! And don't quote me, no-one would believe a nun said that. It is though, complete and utter nonsense. I've been running this establishment for over thirty years, I know every woman and child personally, it's been my life's work." She moved forward to take Marianne's arm. "Come and talk to some of my girls. Yes, a few children are offered for adoption, but only when we're absolutely sure their natural mother is unable to care for them. Always the best interests of the child at heart. *Always*."

"DNA tests have proved the mother and daughter are genuine and the woman was here, she has copies of paperwork and a death certificate for the baby which we now know is fake. Will you confirm or deny this woman's story, Sister?" Marianne stood her ground. The woman dropped the cigarette and crushed it underfoot.

"You're being very stupid young lady and I'd advise you not to take this any further," Her voice barely a whisper as her eyes burned into Marianne.

"When the story breaks more women will come forward. I've spoken to some already but they're scared they'll ruin their children's lives and they're terrified, terrified of you." And for a split second Marianne wondered if someone in her life, someone she did not know yet was closer to her than anyone else in the world, had been the victim of a scenario such as this? That one thought, that single hateful wish was the one thing that made what had happened to her, bearable, forgivable.

Her brain snapped back to the present, as the nun turned on her heel, plaid skirt thwacking against her knees as she moved.

"Time you left, I've heard enough." She strode to the corridor. "Anna, the so-called journalist is leaving." The young girl appeared instantly, hurrying to open the front door and escort Marianne through it.

"This isn't the end of it," Marianne threw back as she left. "I'm going to press with what I have, I've a deadline to meet, you had your chance."

"What was your name again?" the woman called out. "So I get it right when I report this harassment to the police."

"Marianne Coltrane, Chesterford Chronicle," she replied, catching fear in the young girl's eyes.

"Coltrane? I knew some Coltranes once, nice people they were." The woman sneered after her.

13

The Hollow Heart

Marianne passed quickly through the door, pulling it tight shut behind her. The evening had become night, and as she walked into the dark, a bitter wind stung her face. She hurried on, she needed to file her report and decide upon her next move.

Adrienne Vaughan

Chapter One – An Unlikely Suitor

The runner pushed open the office door, a bundle of newspapers gripped tightly under one arm. He peeled off a copy and slapped it on her desk.

'Mother Reunited with Daughter Stolen at Birth!' screamed the headline. She read it slowly, twice; it made her want to laugh and weep at the same time. She took a deep breath, suddenly elated, she had done it again; another wrong, righted; another great story. Marianne Coltrane allowed herself the merest flush of pride. This was good work.

She checked the by-line. Jack Buchannon's name was next to hers; a nod to her boss, having unpicked the initial thread of this complicated and despicable charade. She had done the real graft though, exposing a black market in the sale of new born babies, a hideous scam masquerading as a charity helping young girls 'in trouble'. Now justice would be done and would be seen to be done. The picture told the story; two women clamped in an embrace, the years falling away, their love as fresh as if one had just given birth to the other, their new beginning shining out from the page, a ray of hope. She folded the still-warm paper crisply, putting it aside.

They say newsprint seeps into the veins, but for Marianne it was like drowning, submerged the instant she had seen her work in print; just a couple of small paragraphs and yet they were her words; powerful words. The truth hit her like a train. The pen is indeed far mightier than the sword. From that moment on, the newspaper business filled her very soul, it became her entire world, everything. It was all she had and she was sure, all she could ever wish for.

The newsroom was a goldfish bowl, all movement visible through vast panes of glass opposite her desk. Reporters flashed to and fro like minnows, the sub-editors clumped together in the middle like a puffball of tangled weed, with features, picture desk and sports spiralling out; wayward fronds in murky waters.

She could hear voices rising and although she could not yet see them, she recognised the combatants and knew what they were arguing about. She checked her watch. The glass of water on her desk vibrated, sending up tiny champagne bubbles of oxygen. Placing a hand on the polished surface, she could feel the pulse of the massive press many floors below. It was running off the lunchtime edition; pushing thousands of copies through steel rollers onto conveyor belts, to be strapped into bundles, loaded onto waiting vans and whisked through the city streets at breakneck speed. It was timed to hit the newsstands two hours ahead of its nearest rival. It had been her idea to change the print shift making this edition that bit earlier, it had helped, though sales were still on the slide. She closed her eyes, absorbing the therapeutic thrum of the machine, the life force of every word she wrote.

A door slammed, the arguing grew closer. She

ducked behind a pile of files, hoping she had not been spotted; she had been in the office for hours, checking and re-checking her notes, filing them meticulously, this story was big and just the tip of the iceberg. She always started early, avoiding the dreaded school run, when rivulets of children spilled from vehicles of all shapes and sizes, irritatingly blocking the entrance to the newspaper's car park, until the bell sounded and their relieved parents could drive away. Now she watched the two men standing beyond the glazed wall, the old dog facing down the young pup, gesticulating at each other and then towards her inner sanctum. She was in no mood for their posturing, not today, she was on a deadline, she needed to stay focused. She crouched down as they scanned the glass, hotching herself along the carpet to kneel beneath her desk, trying to make herself invisible. In her haste she disturbed some papers and the invitation to the National Media Awards fluttered past her nose to the floor. She prayed they had not seen it. She forced herself to leave it where it lay, resisting the urge to pick it up and read again the spine-tingling phrase, 'As a nominee you are invited to attend.' She could just imagine the dazzling Hollywood smile of the guest presenter, as he handed her the coveted trophy for Journalist of the Year. The voices grew louder, and deciding her presence, at least as referee, was required after all, she hauled herself up, and gathering an armful of files, propelled herself into the corridor.

As the clash between the two men heightened, she burst through the door, slicing the atmosphere, tottering to negotiate the cluttered space with her hands full, spectacles doubling as a hair band against a shock of auburn. She smiled at the younger man, who looked swiftly to the elder. She dropped the files on Jack Buchannan's overflowing desk, neither male had attempted to assist; this was a newsroom after all.

"What's up?" she asked, still smiling at her editor, Jack, a grumbling Scot with a penchant for a stiff gin at any time of the day or night. He ignored her, returning to his desk to prod at the keyboard, abruptly bringing to a close the heated discussion she had interrupted. The computer bleeped uncomfortably, he waggled the mouse, picked it up and dropped it in a drawer, slamming it shut. The network was down.

"Is there a problem? Something you're not happy about, Jack?" she asked patiently.

"Ach, look at them, no-one doing a hand's turn. You'd think their arms had been ripped out at the sockets, brains turned to slush. Can they not just pick up a pen and y'know, write with it?" He flung out an arm, embracing the disabled cluster about him, on a good day one of the most dynamic editorial teams in the country. Marianne leaned back on his desk, arms folded.

"I've seen the first edition, good work Marianne," she said, under her breath. Jack pretended he did not hear.

"I've given Paul a directive and he's being argumentative, nothing for you to worry about. Now, I need a cigarette." Jack stood up, hesitated, it was raining outside. Slumping back into his chair, he put on spectacles to bring the office clock into focus and immediately brightened. Marianne guessed what he was thinking. The Duchess of Cornwall would be just open, the public house kept odd hours, catering for the print team coming off the night shift. At least a smoke outside the pub meant a chat with someone half-intelligent, if not wholly intelligible. He made for his coat. Marianne opened her diary.

"Bit early, Jack," she said, softly. The younger man coughed.

"Have you a problem?" Jack grunted, his accent as broad as the day he crossed the border. "Alright, get it off your chest, but I'm not changing my mind, no matter what Marianne says."

"We've been discussing 'The Interview'," Paul Osborne widened his eyes at Marianne. "I think Jack's wrong to insist we run a politician and only a local politician at that. The Interview's taking off; people have started asking who we're doing next. The bag lady sleeping outside St Winifred's A & E department was amazing. I mean a war hero, on the scrapheap, living as a down-and-out, a severe failing of the system, the system she fought to protect."

"I do know the story," Jack sighed. He liked the lad. He was a promising photo-journalist, one day he could be a quality writer. He had talent. He also had a conscience, ethics and a campaigning sense of righteousness. Jack was in no mood for Crusaders. Marianne unfolded her arms, looking from one bristling bundle of testosterone to the other.

"Would you like my opinion?" She was still smiling.

"We need George Brownlow." Jack pulled on his aged Barbour.

"Not for The Interview, please, can't we write him into Lifestyle or something?" Paul pleaded support from his colleague.

"As our new MP, he needs a decent piece. He's important. Anyway, who have you lined up for the next 'Interview'? 'We're working on it' is hardly a headline." Jack was checking his pockets for cigarettes.

"It's a surprise," Marianne replied easily.

Jack guffawed, severe nicotine withdrawal kicking in.

"Okay what about this," she said, "American TV star's son, married to local beauty, living happily in that new development by the canal. You know, why Chesterford instead of Los Angeles – fors and against?"

Paul was horrified. The 'local beauty' was his sister Zara, a former fashion model. The TV star's son, his brother in law, Mike. Both kept deliberately low profiles. Paul would never use family connections as media fodder, he was aghast.

Jack fastened his coat, "And the actor's name?"

"Ryan O'Gorman, you know, good looking Irish guy, big hit series on American television, and a few arty films too, in his younger days."

Jack pulled his collar around his jowls. "Never heard of him."

Marianne looked at him, unblinkingly. Jack

shifted a little.

"Really? He's the star turn presenting the National Media Awards next week."

"I can't wait!" exclaimed Sharon, their shared secretary, as she dumped a pile of post on Jack's desk. "He's really dishy in an 'older man' kind of way. I could show him a few of the local attractions, no bother."

"Are you in this meeting?" Jack barked. Sharon exited. "I'm not sure I like the sound of this, I know we've been short-listed for a few awards but you're not hoping to influence any decisions are you?" He eyeballed Marianne, she met his gaze, he knew she would never stoop so low. He also knew she would never reveal what she was working on until it was in the bag. He recognised a smoke screen when he saw one. He gave her his 'do as I say' frown but even he had to admit the politician was not the most enthralling of subjects.

"Look this young headline hunter doesn't want George Brownlow for The Interview, but I say it has to be the MP unless you come up with something I feel compelled to run, it must be an exclusive mind. If so, you can do Brownlow as a Lifestyle piece. But not the bloody actor no-one has heard of or his son in a flat by the canal, okay? Nothing mediocre, we don't do wishy-washy, we need to keep readers not lose them."

The shrillness of the telephone interrupted them. Jack snatched at it.

"Yes, myself and Marianne Coltrane," he said into the receiver, "I took the lead, Marianne worked it up into the story. Well, she is one of my best journalists."

Marianne mouthed, "One of?" at him. He hushed her with his hand.

"I'm sure you'll find everything is in order, of course, speak to her if you like, but we do have another newspaper to get out tomorrow, so don't make a meal of it, if you don't mind!" He handed the phone to Marianne.

"Don't tell me, Legal Department?" she whispered. "Hi Lionel, how's it going? Yes all verified and checked. Yep, the forged Death Certificate has been validated by forensics. Yes, now we've hit the newsstands there is a copy of my report and relevant contacts with evidence on its way to Detective Inspector Greene. Is that all Lionel? As Jack intimated, we are on deadline here."

Jack shoved his hands in his pockets and set his jaw. Paul gazed in awe at Marianne, who was now sitting on Jack's desk, swinging her legs. She jumped to the floor.

"No, Lionel, I did not send my copy to the Legal Department first." She put her hand over the receiver. "I'm in trouble again, with compliance apparently. It's a black mark, written warning or something?" Jack narrowed his eyes. Lionel was clearly banging on.

"Well, the thing is Lionel, if I sent it to you for clearance and it gets leaked to the opposition and they publish our brilliant exclusive story and sell more newspapers than us, well there won't be a Legal Department, will there Lionel, because we'll all be out of a job." She put the phone down gently.

"Too right," Jack agreed, "Prat!" Marianne

laughed. "I hope everything is checked, treble-checked and verified," he said, glaring at her.

"Of course it is. Although we know this is going to blow wide open, so I was thinking, let's launch a website, publish the names and photos of the women who were in the home, with their written permission of course, and let those who wish to make the connection come forward. I am sure there are dozens, if not hundreds, of women who were told their babies had died, only to have them kidnapped and sold on in the illegal adoption racket."

Jack bit on his plastic substitute cigarette.

"I like it, added value. Now what were we discussing?"

"Whether or not to do our local MP for the Interview, although Brownlow would be difficult to do as a 'Lifestyle' piece, he doesn't seem to have a lifestyle," Marianne continued. "Conservative, rarely drinks, not married, not gay, spends a lot of time taking tea with community leaders of all persuasions. Not a little boring."

Paul groaned.

"Well let's see what you come up with, as I said, we don't do mediocre, who on God's earth would be remotely interested in some nobody actor's son living by the canal?" Jack called back as he left, "The Duchess awaits."

"It was a bluff." She side-stepped Paul's anxious look, "I knew he wouldn't go for it, I wasn't casting your family to the wolves, just wanted to throw him off the scent while I work something through."

Paul rubbed his left temple vigorously. "Who then?"

"A barman called Brian Protheroe, works at The Cockerel, Peatling Mill, about to be discovered as the UK's next great tenor. I hear a major audition is on the cards." She eased into Jack's chair. The computer bleeped to life.

"Sounds like a good story. Is it true?"

"Of course it's true; it's one of my stories. Buy me a coffee and I'll fill you in."

"You really are bloody brilliant you know."

She beamed at him, "Ah, only a bit bloody brilliant." She reached for his arm and then on the count of three they burst into a rendition of, '*Bring Me Sunshine*' a song they laughingly called Jack's theme tune, skipping as best their disparate heights would allow, Morecombe and Wise style toward the lift.

"Where are you two going?" called Sharon, from her work station.

"Not to The Duchess," they replied in unison.

"When will you be back?"

They let the ping of the lift answer.

George Brownlow was in a real pickle. He glared at the mirror. His reflection stared back, flustered. The overall look was pink and blotchy. His eyes were bloodshot - lack of sleep; his skin dry and flaky - too many takeaways; he oiked his trousers up, still not comfortable, far too many takeaways. Holding the hangers in front of his chest, he tried to decide what to wear. The pale blue designer shirt, tie-less, or the turquoise stripe with plain dark tie? Were the chinos too casual, too right on or the green moleskins, too county?

"I really hate this," he told the mirror.

He dropped the hangers on the floor, pulled the faded denim shirt off the bedpost where he had left it the night before and, grabbing phone and car keys, climbed into his beloved classic car. He had a meeting with a local journalist; someone called Marianne Coltrane who had suggested they rendezvous at The Cockerel in the picturesque village of Peatling Mill, about eight miles outside his constituency, heading south. He was annoyed with himself for not insisting they meet on his patch, but he had been in a rush as usual.

The mid-day radio presenter was desperately trying to co-ordinate a phone-in about teenage pregnancy. It was not going well. A vicar from an inner city Parish was being caring and constructive. A well-spoken mother of four daughters was all for reintroducing chastity belts, perhaps with digital locking mechanisms, and when the subject of abortion was raised; a young woman dissolved into tears and hung up. The presenter opted for an upbeat dance track to soothe the frazzled airwaves. George frowned, making a mental note to review his own and the Party's policy on such matters.

Roadworks ahead were impacting on his very tight schedule. He had planned to arrive at least fifteen minutes early, order himself an orange juice, nip to the loo, smooth his hair and return to his seat to sit staring at a 'very important document'. He wanted to appear calm, studious, self-assured. A loud clunking broke his reverie, the steering wheel shuddered, the engine sputtered, rallied a little with a touch of the accelerator, and then belching loudly, gave up the ghost. The Conservative Member of Parliament for Chesterford South, swore like a sailor. He did not even have the bloody journalist's mobile number. He tried the pub via directory enquiries but the line was constantly engaged. He boiled, along with the radiator.

Marianne had finished her interview with Brian, the operatic barman. Not quite as close to becoming the spectacular new star she had hoped but she would make a good enough job of it. Paul would take the photographs later, he had his brief: muted bar room background; handsome tenor in full cry; rehearsing in the gents' lavatory where the acoustics were more conducive to his falsetto. Paul was a good photographer, his pictures would add poignancy to the piece. She knew exactly what she wanted and was determined 'The Interview' maintain its quirky 'would you believe it?' character profiles, whatever her editor decreed.

She closed her notebook, looking around the pub, one of the few hostelries which had managed to avoid being 'themed', so pleasant, if a little frayed around the edges. She had hoped to kill two birds with one stone, thinking the ambience of the pub would reveal a softer, more approachable side of a man renowned for his unswerving dedication to public service. Checking the time, it appeared the MP was not going to show. She tried his mobile; it flipped to answer-phone. She could not wait, 'The Interview' had to be put to bed. She finished her drink, beamed goodbye to the singing barman and left.

A couple of miles down the road her speedy two-seater zipped past a roadside recovery man scratching his head, while a baggy trousered-bottom stuck out from beneath the bonnet of an elderly classic car. It fleetingly occurred to Marianne that this might be the Honourable Member for Chesterford South, unhorsed. She seemed to recall he drove a vintage car. She motored on, murmuring along with the radio. George Brownlow would live to be grilled another day, hopefully when she was off duty and Paul would be tasked with the interrogation. She would have to edit it no doubt but that, she considered, would be more than enough George Brownlow for her.

The National Media Awards were fast approaching, the Chesterford Chronicle had been short-listed for a number of prizes and as Jack had promised a memo about the event that very day, the newsroom was buzzing with everyone discussing the competition, what to wear, where to sit.

Sharon handed the memo and table plan to Marianne.

"I see Jack's already decided who's sitting where," she said.

The others quickly gathered round. Marianne passed the sheet of paper to Paul without comment. George Brownlow was to be seated on her left and, the irritatingly Machiavellian Jack Buchannan, on her right. It appeared Jack would not rest until she extracted some sort of story from their new MP. Great, she thought as she made her way to the lift, a real fun evening to look forward to.

Later, taking a large whiskey to her study, she flicked on the desk light beside her laptop, and sitting down, pushed aside the file she had been working on - the follow-up campaign on behalf of the stolen babies scam - and decided to go through her George Brownlow research again. Surely there was something of interest, something to give her an angle, something she would find engaging? All she could discover about their newest MP were the scrappy bits of biography from his official Conservative Party press release.

Place of birth - Chesterford General Hospital, where his father had been a paediatrician. Education - a good public school in the shires, then to Oxford and onto Leeds to read Law. He practiced briefly with a local firm and from there, moved quickly into politics, staying in the background until the seat in his home town became available. His life's ambition, according to the press release, was 'to be a true servant of the people – without cynicism or sarcasm.' A straightforward mission, allegedly like George himself, his intention was to be a dedicated public servant the whole of his working life, in fact until his dying day. Marianne groaned, *who* wrote this rubbish? She finished her whiskey, turned off the light and padded to bed, planning to share a taxi to the awards dinner, at least then she could have a few glasses of wine - she was going to need them.

As it happened, the handsome 'nobody' as Jack termed the guest presenter, never made it to the ceremony, some excuse about baggage handlers and delayed flights. So it was the aforementioned George Brownlow who was called into the breach. It was fair to say he did a pretty good job of hosting on the hoof, and rounded the evening off by presenting Marianne with the Journalist of the Year Award, for the 'Stolen Babies Scam' expose. The applause was rapturous. Paul feigned despair, rolling his eyes and grinning inanely, as she swished back to the table.

"Not another bloody award," he scoffed. "Mantelpiece will disintegrate under the weight of them all at this rate."

Marianne beamed, nursing the replica typewriter in her arms.

"Will you put it down to drink champagne?" Jack was very nearly smiling too.

She waved a free hand. "Can do both, I'm multi-dexterous."

She downed a good half-bottle before relinquishing the trophy to zealously embrace the MP when he returned to the table, kissing him so hard his lips were tattooed red. George seemed genuinely surprised to be so brutally woman-handled, but pleasantly so, and the pair immediately began an animated discussion about the origins of the first typewriter company. In fact MP and journalist seemed to have a lot to talk about and shared another bottle of champagne, or so Marianne thought, because George only touched his glass to raise it to her many toasts. Observing the banter, Jack almost smiled again.

Paul had been mortified. "You're going out with who? George Brownlow? Why? Is it for a follow-up or what?"

"Well it's because he asked me, actually. Men never ask me out, in case you hadn't noticed."

Marianne airily went back to typing notes she had been working on through the weekend, part of a training programme she had volunteered to produce for the newspaper's graduates.

"George Brownlow? Are you serious?" Paul asked again. "Looks like a St Bernard, probably smells like one too."

"Don't be rude!" she snapped.

"But I'm always asking you out," he bleated.

"Oh Paul, you don't count."

"Now who's being rude?"

After Marianne and George's first date to a smart, celebrity-chef restaurant where they agreed, once George had paid the astronomical bill, the food had been filthy and they were both still hungry, their romance rolled out quite easily. George was thrilled to have someone to share official engagements with and more than pleased this someone was not only intelligent and entertaining but drop-dead gorgeous, to boot. Very soon they were enjoying regular Sunday morning brunches, lazily scanning the newspapers, sipping cappuccino and planning the MP's media stance on a myriad of topics for the coming week, and because George had his career, he completely understood how seriously Marianne took hers. They were sitting in her neat little kitchen, drinking coffee and scanning the piles of newspapers George had gathered en route.

"I've been thinking," George said.

"You be careful." Marianne smiled.

"Cheeky. No, the story, the illegal adoption scam, there must have been quite a few homes like that which existed across the country in the 50s and 60s."

"I'd say it's been going on long before then and probably still goes on now. Maybe not telling the young mothers their babies had died, but there has always been some sort of trade in children, like slavery, it's always been there."

"Well, I could certainly help take the campaign to the next stage, get the national press talking about it, see if we can't persuade the Adoption Service to start an investigation."

Marianne laid her cup carefully in the saucer. "I appreciate your offer George, but this has to be handled very sensitively. These people have other lives, other families, they may not want to be involved in something like this at all."

"I do understand," George said, touching her hand with his, "this is not a cynical attempt at vote-catching you know – I admire you hugely for all the work you've done and how delicately you handled the story and those involved. But I agree with you, there's a bigger picture and I'd like to use what little sway I have to help."

She beamed at him.

"You know what George, you're fantastic."

He grinned back, turning quite pink.

"You know what Miss Coltrane, so are you!"
They each went back to their newspapers, smiling.
Marianne's mobile shattered the companionable silence.
She checked the caller and left the table. George could
hear mumbling. She burst back into the room.

"Sorry George, I've got to go, they've arrested
Sister Mary May, all hell's broken lose. She's screaming
the fifth amendment and demanding to see the Papal
Envoy." George was on his feet, passing her handbag,
taking his coat off the peg.

"Time to pen the follow-up, eh?"

"Where are you going?" she asked.

"I'll drive you, you might need a hand, I am a
lawyer after all."
She tutted at him as he followed her out to the car.

"I don't know why everyone thinks journalism is
so glamorous, bloody hard work most of the time."

"Is this a scoop?" George asked, squeezing in
behind the wheel.

George had nearly fainted though, when only a matter of
weeks later, Marianne turned up at his flat with an
overnight bag, dropping it unceremoniously in the
cramped hall, meeting his baffled gaze full on.

"Thought we ought to get the sleeping together
thing out of the way," she said matter–of-factly. Then
burst out laughing at the look on his face. "Well, we're

hardly teenagers are we? And I don't think we should have it hanging over us, you know - will we, won't we? Besides it's time we had a nice weekend away and we wouldn't want to spoil it by having to hide in the bathroom to put our pyjamas on."

She followed him into the kitchen. He was already pouring them each a very large glass of Pinot Grigio, and George did not drink.

"George?"

"Ah well, you see, I was hoping we could just rub along as we are for about the next ten years or so, if that's okay with you?" His eyes twinkled, "I'm not awfully adventurous in the bedroom department, not built for it." He patted his rather large tummy. "Girls tend to go off me once we've had sex, I'm afraid, usually the kiss of death." He looked dramatically glum.

"But you can't put me off George. I've seen you in your dressing gown, with a stinking cold and holes in your socks."

"So you have." He smiled and not looking a gift horse, with a glass in each hand, headed towards his shambles of a bedroom. "Follow me then, you minx and don't say I didn't warn you. Can I leave my socks on?"

Making love with George was lovely, warm, easy and all-encompassing, rather like George himself. What you saw, was what you got and if there was rather a lot of it, it was all top quality, full-bodied British male, bought and paid for. When they made love and George drifted off into a pleasant, just below the surface doze, he would stroke her hair whispering, 'My darling girl,' over and over. He performed he thought, his secret ritual every time they slept together, whether they had made love or not and the one thing his darling girl grew to love about George, even though she hardly dare admit it to herself, was how very much George loved his darling girl. Marianne was beginning to consider, very tentatively if the 'career-driven journalist' might be able to make a go of it with the 'committed to public duty' Member of Parliament. She had to admit that to be so dearly loved was more than wonderful and made it so easy to love George right back, without question. She wondered, in those rare moments she allowed herself a sliver of private contemplation, whether it was too soon to hope that George could be her second chance, her hope for real happiness? She did not have to wonder for too long.

By the time Christmas loomed on the horizon, Marianne and George had been an item for a number of months. Their relationship had nurtured gently. It was certainly no grand passion but in many ways she preferred it that way. It was lovely to have someone to talk to and walk with, and nice not to always eat dinner alone in front of the telly; or be obliged to go out with the girls because there were no boys to go out with. Her life had needed more balance, George had given her a whole new aspect, other things to think about, another person to consider. Her sex life had been non-existent for some time, and although she pretended it never really bothered her, with George around, who was genuinely affectionate and loving, she could enjoy how much or how little she needed. All things considered, even though she still dare

34

not admit it to herself, she had started to hope again.

Without thinking, Marianne put her name down for the usual skeleton staff rota over the festive period. She never bothered taking leave at Christmas, it was not that she was un-Christian but the phones were quiet and it gave her space to catch up. If the truth be told, she could not bear all the feigned jollity, or worse, colleagues feeling obliged to invite her to join them and their families. So she always worked through the holiday, only stopping to treat herself to a nice cashmere sweater or smart pair of boots to mark the occasion.

Then one morning, singing along with '*Last Christmas*' it occurred to her: what about George? Maybe George loved Christmas. Perhaps he wanted them to enjoy it together. She felt immediately guilty, she was so used to just doing her own thing; it was selfish not to consider George, especially as he consulted her about everything, always hoping they could do things together. By the time the song ended, she resolved to discuss their Christmas plans that very evening. But Marianne was way too late. George had already made plans of his own, for both of them - well all three of them, actually.

Chapter Two – Not Just For Christmas

It was the week before Christmas. She could see it was him through the coloured glass, standing large as a bear in the doorway of her small, suburban house. George, in his huge dogtooth overcoat, wearing the bright red scarf she had bought to cheer him up when he had a dreadful cold. He held a picnic basket in his arms, having pushed the doorbell with his nose. She opened the door; he seemed excited and nervous at the same time. The tartan rug on top of the basket moved. She jumped. This was not the offering of food and wine she had been expecting for their first Christmas together. It moved again.

"Have a look!" he boomed.

She lifted the fabric to reveal the pointed ears, bright eyes and shiny black nose of the tiniest puppy she had ever seen.

She gasped.

"George, he's adorable. Is it a he? Is he for me? What's his name?"

She lifted it out. The little bundle, a West Highland terrier, squirmed with pleasure. Marianne noticed a large, '*Paddington Bear*' type, brown paper label attached to a ribbon around the puppy's neck. In George's manic scrawl, it read:

"My name is Montgomery. I'm a Christmas

present from George. PS: He wants to know if you'll marry him?"

Shock rendered her speechless; she looked from the large man to the tiny animal. Her heart contracted, as both pairs of eyes radar-beamed adoration at her. She turned away briefly, as her past life and loves ran like a DVD on fast forward through her brain. George knew as much as she wanted him to know about her previous relationships. When he had pressed her for an answer about past loves, not long after they had met, she had merely recounted, "There was someone once."

"Someone special?"

"Seemed so at the time."

"Want to talk about it?"

"No, ancient history."

"Married?"

"Nearly, I thought."

"Children?"

"He has now."

"Regrets?"

"No way."

"Ah that's my gritty, award-winning career woman," he had said kindly, squeezing her knee.

"And what have you hidden in the closet?" she had asked brightly.

They had swapped early-life stories. She had spent the first eighteen months of her life in a convent in the wilds of the Wicklow mountains, while the nuns vetted various pairs of prospective parents. The couple who finally adopted her had been older than the parents of her peers. They were nice, well-educated people and she always thought of them fondly. Kind but cool, was how she would describe them, especially when compared with the parents of school friends who often invited her to stay during the holidays. Her friends always seemed to belong to big, noisy, clans who would roar their hatred of each other at the top of their voices and then squeeze each other half to death with hugs, before leaving to go back as term time approached.

She had boarded at a good Dublin girl's school while her parents travelled with their work. Her father, a marine biologist, and her mother his research assistant. Her special memories were their summers together, spent sailing off the coast of their favourite island, Innishmahon, a mile out to sea from Westport in County Mayo. Her parents, the Coltranes, had made sure she had a good education. She studied English Literature and then after a stint at a national newspaper, left for England to take up an internship at a magazine group before moving to Chesterford and the Chronicle. Her parents were proud of her, they told her, and they met up briefly whenever their schedules allowed. But they had both died relatively young, first her father with cancer and then her mother, succumbing to seemingly nothing specific, within months of each other. If Marianne were romantically inclined, she would have said her mother died of a broken heart, as she and her father had been inseparable all their adult lives.

George sighed and squeezed her hand when she had finished her potted history. Topping up her glass, he said:

"And what of your birth parents, darling girl? What do you know of them?"

Marianne flashed him a look.

"Nothing. Why would I? I was put up for adoption. No contact ever made. No mention. Weirdly, there's a black and white photo of me as a new born baby attached to my adoption certificate, which the solicitor gave to me when mother died, but that's it, that's all there is."

He handed her the drink, sitting a little distance away to look her directly in the eyes.

"Not curious? Not bothered?" He kept his tone light.

"Not at all, I'd feel disloyal to my parents. They brought me up. They are my mother and father." She lifted Monty onto her lap, wrapping her arms around him.

"But you're an investigative journalist, I wondered if you were looking into your own background when you came upon the 'Babies for Sale' scam?"

"I was just doing my job, Jack Buchannon came up with the lead anyway, his wife Isabelle knows a social worker who came across a girl who was convinced her child had been stolen. I'm not a story, George." She turned her attention to the puppy. Subject closed.

George, on the other hand, could tell stories about himself and his family ad infinitum. He adored his parents, long gone, and was part of a large, rambling, flung-across-the-globe family. He had three brothers and one elder sister, all talented, liberal and bohemian, yet differentially conservative. His parents would have loved her, he often said.

"Ahem..." He coughed bringing them back to the present. "Well, I'm sure the idea of us getting married is all a bit of a surprise, no doubt. So why don't you take your time and have a think about it? Don't want to fling everything at you all at once darling girl, but when you know something's right, no point hanging about, so to speak." He tweaked her nose and then the puppy's. Marianne kissed George on the chin and carried the little bundle into the kitchen for some warm milk. George followed, humming, '*How much is that doggy in the window?*"

Later, after supper, the three of them lay sprawled on the sofa. Marianne cuddled the little dog, burying her nose in the space between his ears. She inhaled him, a wonderful, indescribable puppy-baby smell. Montgomery and marriage? A future with George and Monty. An instant family. Someone else to think about, care about, someone to love. Marianne looked from one to the other, desperately hoping she was not being blinded by Christmas lights, yet at this particular juncture, she considered the whole idea an extremely appealing combination.

A few days later the three of them were having sausages for supper on Christmas Eve.

"Oh George, hurry up, Monty's starving." Marianne laughed watching the puppy run excitedly between George's legs as he assembled the meal.

"Well, you hurry up and jolly well give me an answer," he told her. "And then this poor little chap will know where he stands, who his folks are and won't fret so much about where his next meal is coming from."

She went to stand beside him.

"George, there's something I need you to know."

He carried on frying the sausages.

"I did want to marry someone a long time ago. It would have been a terrible mistake, I was young, foolish. It ended badly."

"I know," he replied, turning the gas off.

"You know?" she was shocked.

"Of course I know, I'm a politician, I want to marry you, if there are any skeletons in the closet I need to know about them, so we can face things together." He pulled her to him, giving her a huge George hug. "Anything else you want to tell me?"

Marianne sat down at the breakfast bar; George poked the sausages around a bit.

"It was not long after my parents died. I was feeling pretty low and my boss gave me a commission for a series of articles on young Brits living in Paris. I fell madly in love with Paris and everything about it, stepping out with a well-known celebrity photographer. You may have heard of him, Claude Dubec?" George nodded to her to continue. "Well, it was a typical whirlwind romance. My parents had left me a small legacy and my glamorous new boyfriend liked the high life, so it was fun, for a while, sort of a rebellion thing, I guess. My folks had been totally work-orientated, convinced their research would ultimately be for the good of the planet, and I had always been such a well-behaved, dutiful daughter. But they'd have spun in their graves, if they had one, if they'd known I frittered a good chunk of my inheritance on sex, drugs and rock 'n' roll and a very inappropriate partner." She smiled wryly.

"No grave?" George was surprised. "Your parents I mean, no grave?"

"Oh, the association with convents doesn't mean we're staunch Catholics, or anything like that. It just usually means things are done properly, particularly where education is concerned. My parents were eco-warriors before there was such a thing, so I scattered their ashes in the sea off Innishmahon, the island where we used to holiday when I was young."

"We should go there one day you, Montgomery and I, would you like that?"

But Marianne was not listening.

"George, my relationship with Claude, do you know everything? How it ended and everything? What it meant for me, how I can't…" Her voice cracked.

He went to her, taking her face in his hands, there were tears in his eyes.

"Yes I do, and it's you I love, you I want. If I have you and Monty I have everything I need." He kissed her softly on the mouth, "Put it this way, we don't have to make love in the dark on my account, unless that's because you can't bear to witness my man boobs and wobbly tummy in the flesh!"

"Oh George, stop it," she said solemnly, "You're

42

alright about it then? All of it?"

"Are you?" he asked. She stood up and returned his hug.

"I am now."

"Good, because we're starving." He laughed, releasing her to serve the food.

She said yes the following morning, still in her pyjamas, squeezing George and Monty together as tightly as she could. She knew she wanted every Christmas to be special from now on.

Christmas and New Year melted into spring as she, George and Monty made plans. They had a new home to find, George in particular wanted a large house, with a study for himself, and some sort of area they could turn into a library-cum-music room for Marianne. He played the piano badly and hoped Marianne would accompany him on the violin she had started to learn as a school girl but had not touched for years. Monty joined in too, making a strange yet tuneful snuffling noise.

"Watch out *Britain's Got Talent!*" George regularly pronounced.

To the amazement of her colleagues and the amusement of Marianne herself, she had taken her foot off the career accelerator to focus on building a life for the three of them, even taking owed holiday to house hunt and shop for furnishings. Sophie, one of Marianne's oldest and severely neglected friends, was thrilled at the news her career-driven chum was finally settling down to some semblance of domesticity. She was also delighted to be roped in to help, as she was particularly adept at internet research, being toddler-bound and freelance.

It was all coming together nicely, and although George was under an enormous amount of pressure at work, the three of them were having a lovely time, with Monty making the final decision about anything they could not agree on. This was achieved by Marianne laying cuttings from magazines or swatches of material in front of him and saying fetch. He would always grab something and head off to his basket triumphantly. Once retrieved, this would then be deemed their selection.

It was a fabulously bright May day. It had rained earlier, so everything looked freshly washed, the sun was quickly warming the tarmac and there were spots of glimmering heat haze as George headed north along the M1 towards home and a well-earned weekend. He was trying to put a particularly hellish morning behind him, having endured a series of very tense meetings with civil servants and academics, relating to a report he was working on, followed by a barrage of emails from locals opposed to a new Chesterford planning application. He was longing for home. The relatively new home he shared with his gorgeous fiancé and their adorable West Highland terrier. The home that smelled of fresh paint and Chinese takeaways, and stood curtain-less before the world, yet wrapped itself around him in a comfort blanket of chaos, clutter and love. As he turned the music up, his mobile rang; he answered speaking into his 'hands free' microphone beside the sun visor above the windscreen. No answer. The new-fangled instrument was always playing up. He checked his phone, it displayed the discreet code that was the Prime Minister. He grabbed it, punching the answer button.

He did not see, in the split second it took the car in front to slam on its brakes, the lurch of the juggernaut with a foreign number plate, as it tried to avoid a pheasant wandering in the slow lane. But he heard the slam, like the boom of a cannon, as the car in front plummeted into the undercarriage of the truck and, hauling at the wheel to avoid it, he swerved towards a coach that should not have been in the fast lane at all. He registered the spin of the car as the phone, flying out of his hand, smacked the dashboard, bouncing back, cracking against his brow bone, just before a large four-wheel drive hit him side on, pushing him into the rear of the coach. The steel frame of his ancient vehicle groaned piteously. George gripped the wheel and, holding his breath, rammed his foot against the accelerator, impulse telling him to get out of this as fast as he could. He hit the crash barrier as the 4x4 ploughed into the driver's door, and the coach slammed on its brakes forcing the passenger side of George's beloved car to be concertinaed inwards. He clung to the steering wheel, rigid as he gripped, holding on, determined not to let go.

All movement stopped, it was dark, the air about him filled with the thickest silence. George desperately searched for his voice inside his crushed chest, he could not move, or see anything, he was starting to panic and then he found, deep within, a tiny voice. His joy knew no bounds, he could say his words, just a few words, he would wait, hang on until someone was there to hear them. He did not know how long he had been holding on, but just as the darkness was merging to grey and there was brightness in the distance, he heard something beside him, the clunk of machinery, a shout. He groped around inside his chest for breath and found just enough to say his words, as loudly as he could.

"Tell my darling girl, always with her, I'll always be with her." Then the light ahead turned from glowing golden to searing white and George was free. He released the steering wheel, slumping backwards, a tiny slash of red on his brow, the slightest smile on his white lips.

The paramedic at his side pronounced him dead at the scene, he was sure George had felt nothing, it was instantaneous, over. Later, when he was told that the body in the unrecognisable classic car had been an MP, quite well-known, he remembered he had said something, he was sure of it. Something about my darling girl but he decided not to repeat this, it had been a nightmare of a day, the worst he had seen in nearly ten years in the job, what good would it do? The man had died, along with the others, just another statistic, a wasteful, senseless end.

Paul spotted the *RTA* report as it flashed up on a computer screen in the newsroom. He was passing through on his

way to deliver Marianne a sludge-coloured coffee from
the machine. He stopped dead in his tracks at her office
door when he heard her repeat the words 'classic car' in a
deadpan voice. She had been toying with wording for the
wedding invitation on her laptop. It was to be a small,
informal affair, with jazz, real ale and a fish and chip
supper. She dropped the phone, accidently hitting the
delete key.

Now, sometimes she woke in the middle of the night,
thinking she could feel his fingers in her hair, his breath
on her cheek, as he whispered his special goodnight. But
George had gone. His darling girl seemed to miss him
more as time passed, not less.

Jack touched her shoulder as he squeezed into the
pew beside her. George's sister, Catherine, stood
shoulder to shoulder with Marianne, Catherine's
husband, Frank, beside her. Catherine took Marianne's
hand, Marianne tried to focus, beneath the broad-
brimmed hat, almond eyes stared at her, eyes that looked
just like George's, except these eyes were dead, eyes
with the lights switched off.

The service passed over her quite gently. Frank's
address to the packed assembly was warm and anecdotal,
even raising the odd appropriate titter. A chief whip in
the Conservative Party spoke of George's generous and,
indeed, selfless dedication to duty. One of George's
oldest friends and a leading light in the Jewish
community, together with a Muslim colleague, read
funeral prayers from their respective Holy Books. The

The Hollow Heart

Reverend Pollock concluded by asking everyone to pray for George's soul and his family, sister Catherine, brother-in-law Frank and especially his fiancé Marianne.

Marianne looked up at the mention of her name, half-remembering why she was at a large, formal gathering without George. In her head she was in the newsroom, it was noisy, anxious voices, bad accident on the M1, six-car smash, fatalities, juggernaut, school bus, vintage car. Silence. The opening bars of *Stairway to Heaven* started up. It was George's funeral. She was going to be without George for the rest of her life. She felt a sharp pain in her chest, as if she had been stabbed with a knitting needle. She let out a strangled squeak and her knees buckled. Paul, in the pew behind, steadied her. Jack propped his hand in the small of her back. Together, they eased her back into her seat.

"Oh Marianne," Catherine whispered, squeezing her hand. Marianne sat perfectly still, white-faced and dry-eyed.

"Oh George," she said, desolate at the realisation of what had happened. She felt as if the life had been sucked out of her and a cavernous vacuum remained. "Poor George," she shook her head, clearing it of images. "How can I tell Monty? How will he know?" She started to sob, quietly.

The three months since George's funeral flashed by, yet Marianne seemed to be dragging body and soul through treacle in slow motion. Unsure how she had arrived there, she found herself sitting in the gloom, in the garden of the home they had shared. She had been thrilled to discover a rundown town house at the end of a Georgian terrace and, once George agreed it was perfect, they moved in and immediately started work, adding a gracious new garden room to the gable end of the house. She was sitting under the oak tree looking back at the large hole in the wall the builder had made for the French doors, still covered in thick polythene. It had been knocked-through the week George had died. It had been like that ever since. It was the beginning of September, George had died in May.

Early autumn draped the garden like a shroud. She watched motionless as Monty's constantly wagging tail and white bottom disappeared under piles of leaves hunting for anything he could chase, catch and obliterate. Even as dusk was settling, she could see the garden was badly in need of attention. A bit like herself she surmised, delicately wiping a drop of snot off the end of her nose. Monty, sensing the mood withdrew from the pile of debris and busied himself at his mistress's slippered feet, pushing at her ankles with his damp nose.

"Oh Monty stop!" she said grumpily, and then looking into his soft brown eyes, felt immediately guilty and swept him up in her arms, half-squeezing the life out of him. She buried her face in the spot between his ears, sniffing deeply. He still smelled like a puppy, like the very first time she had laid eyes on him. Monty wriggled in her arms and she smelled him again. The garden gate made a dry, rusting squeak as it pushed open.

"How long have you been sitting out here?" called Paul, as Monty jumped from her lap to greet him. It was quite dark, she could hardly make him out as he strode up the path towards her, Monty trotting merrily at his heels.

"Not sure," she answered, standing, smoothing her skirt. A couple of sheets of paper fluttered to the ground. He stooped to pick them up, she had already started back to the house.

Once inside the newly refurbished kitchen, she automatically flicked on the kettle. Paul, reaching for mugs hanging from the dresser, noticed how strained she looked under the electric light. She pulled a fleece from the back of a chair onto her shoulders, aimlessly opening and closing cupboard doors.

"We don't seem to have any biscuits…"

"You never seem to have anything these days." As soon as he said the words, he regretted them. She gripped the back of the chair, he passed her a tissue; she ignored it.

"Sorry," he offered. She turned blank eyes on him, saying nothing.

"You don't fancy Ronan's leaving do tonight then?"

She had completely forgotten they had been invited to a drinks party for Ronan O'Keefe, a star turn in the Art Department, off to pastures new. Ronan and Marianne had joined the Chesterford Chronicle on the same day.

"I just don't feel…" She sat down heavily.

"That's okay. No problem. Wish you'd phoned though."

Paul had been saying okay, no problem, for quite a

while but he considered that the time had come to suggest ever so gently, Marianne should start to get back into the swing of things.

In fairness, her work could not be faulted. She had the odd day when she just could not function, so either stayed in bed with a hot water bottle and daytime telly or took Monty for a punishing walk, drank the best part of a bottle of whiskey, and crashed. But generally, since George's death, Marianne had pulled on a semblance of a suit, dragged a comb through her hair, made a stab at the makeup and turned up at the office, still managing to meet her deadlines with a more than half decent piece of work.

Socially though, it had been far more difficult. Apart from a couple of drinks with Paul and a quick supper at Jack and Isabelle's, she had stubbornly refused to prise herself out of number seventy four Oakwood Avenue.

Even her close friend Sophie, who was totally disorganised and generally hopeless at the best of times, had tried to encourage her to attend to the ever growing pile of cards and letters on the hall table. But the suggestion Marianne respond to her phone messages, personal emails or texts was met with the same blank look. Why? The world beyond her automated performance in the newsroom, did not register, did not concern her or matter.

Paul pushed a mug of tea in front of her. He pulled out the sheaves of paper he had gathered from beside the bench, placing them on the table before her.

"Anything important?" he asked. She ignored the tea.

"Catherine phoned. Wanted to know why I hadn't been in touch, only picked the message up because she kept asking me through that bloody machine. Wanted to know when I was going to collect my things. I didn't know what she was on about. She asked me if I had heard from Snelgrove and Marshall."

Paul looked quizzical.

"You know George's lawyer. Catherine became quite insistent. I rummaged through the pile on the table, found the letter and, well, you see, George has left me everything; his half of his parents' estate, even his half of his mother's jewellery." She twisted the ruby and diamond band George had selected from his mother's treasure trove to be her engagement ring. He had presented it on New Year's Eve, the day they 'officially' announced their engagement. It was too big so Marianne had padded it out with tape until it could be properly sized, so determined was she to wear it on the night.

"Wow," Paul put his cup down. "Good old George. How does Catherine feel about it?"

"Couldn't be nicer, I called her back and apologised for being so lax. She laughed, said George knew I didn't have a mercenary bone in my body, she said that's obviously why he wanted to take care of me."

"Well he's certainly done that. You'll probably never have to work again, well not really hard anyway."

"But how organised, so sorted. He'd dotted all the i's, crossed all the t's. Not entirely George. I said to

Catherine, 'He didn't know he was going to be killed in a car crash on the bloody M1'." She stopped. The room was completely silent, apart from the ticking Grandfather clock in the hall. "But he did know he was going to die from a congenital heart condition, runs in the family, she said he'd known it was on the cards for some time. He'd only told Catherine."

"And me," Paul pulled his chair closer to her, "he wanted to assure me you'd be okay."

Her eyes flickered. She turned to look at him, pink spots of fury rapidly dotting her cheekbones.

"He told you? Why on earth would he tell you?" she spat, "why was I the last to know? Why wasn't I told what he was going through? The selfish bastard!" She threw the mug across the room, smashing it against the polished chrome range. Paul flinched, then found his voice.

"You know why. He loved you, literally loved you more than life itself. He'd have told you at some stage, but not until he had to. That was George. Why spoil things before they were going to be spoiled anyway?"

Marianne would not be placated, she was beside herself. She banged the table.

"But I loved him, I'd have taken care of him. I didn't need to be protected, not to know how ill he was, not to be allowed to help."

"Wasn't to be," Paul shrugged, keeping his tone level, bending to pick up the pieces of china, mopping the spilt tea with kitchen towel.

"But why keep it a secret, he deceived me, I can't

believe he's done this to me…" Her fury bounced off the walls.

Paul moved towards the door.

"Call me later when you've calmed down," Paul's tone had changed, he was brusque. "When you can put things into some sort of perspective, George was only doing what he thought best. No, you're right, he didn't know he was going to die in that hideous car crash on the M1, but he did know he was going to die some time soon, so he did his best to take care of the one thing he really loved, you. Turns out, George really was a good bloke, but you Marianne, you're behaving like a spoiled brat." He closed the door gently as he left.

"Well, I…" Marianne plonked herself back at the kitchen table, hands at her cheeks as if she had been slapped.

The sound of crockery smashing had long since signalled Monty to his bed. Marianne sat still in the brightly lit silence until dawn.

Chapter Three – A Stranger Calls

She telephoned Paul as soon as she thought he might be awake. He was still in bed. He had gone to the party, which had turned out to be rowdier than expected and with good reason he considered, had put himself the other side of two bottles of cheap red wine, a kebab and a very large glass of port.

"Sorry, did I wake you?"

"Hmmmm."

"Sorry… Did I really piss you off?"

"Hmm hmm."

"Sorry… I was feeling really sorry for myself."

"Erm?"

"Sorry you had to bear the brunt."

Silence.

"Really sorry."

Silence.

"Will you come round later for a drink?"

" I'll never drink again……." Said a thin voice. The line went dead.

Marianne had heard this all before, so invited Paul round for dinner anyway. As the day brightened, so did she. Her night-long vigil had helped put lots of things into perspective. Last night she thought she would never forgive George for keeping his illness a secret, feeling again that awful gall, the gnawing of deceit, the fear that she had been taken in, betrayed. Yet as a new day dawned, she knew she would forgive, had forgiven.

George had considered he was doing the right thing, for the right reasons. His was not a true deceit, just a delaying tactic while he tied up loose ends. He would have told her, in his own time, when the time was right. George had truly loved her, she had truly known love. George deserved to be forgiven, unconditionally.

She sat up in the middle of her large, lonely bed and took a long lingering look at the photograph of them in the silver frame, taken at the National Media Awards, when they had first met. There they were smiling and shiny at the very beginning of their love affair and here she was alone, at the very end. She touched George's face with the tip of her finger. Monty scraped at the door, he needed to go out. He looked at her, moving his tail steadily from side to side in anticipation. She smiled. The velocity of his tail increased, she had not stretched her face at him in ages.

Paul arrived at six sharp; fully recovered and back on speaking terms. He brought wine, smoked haddock and olives. He also brought the latest edition of the Chesterford Chronicle, presenting her with the entertainment supplement; a social life was in dire need of restitution. The aroma of furniture polish and fresh coffee mingled pleasingly, a real fire glowed in the grate. It felt more like number seventy four, more like George and Marianne's home. It felt the best it had since George died.

Marianne gave him a huge hug. He was surprised. Since George's death she had withdrawn from all physical contact, if an embrace were offered, she would just stand there, stiffly, being hugged but tonight she hugged him right back. He put his hands on her shoulders and looked into her eyes, eyes that were still sad but not as haunted. Looking into her eyes he saw Marianne, not George's ghost. He kissed her forehead, she was going to be alright; the mist had started to disperse.

Monty, sensing a lifting of spirit, snuffled carrier bags excitedly, it was a long time since something approaching delicious had been served in this house.

"We could go and see something hilarious, frivolous and irreverent, the Comedy Festival's in full swing," Paul offered.

"Great, nothing stuffy though, I don't want to have to make an effort, if we can wear jeans and drink beer, that would be perfect," she called from the kitchen.

Monty turned to face the hall. He padded to the doorway giving Marianne the one yap and twitch of nose that meant there was a stranger in the vicinity. She put the cafetière down as the doorbell sounded, signalling Monty to stay.

Marianne's former boss, the publisher, Daniel Jacobs, stood in the hallway. Marianne closed the door behind him; she had not seen him for ages. He was immaculately dressed as always, yet today he looked a little piqued, his usual sparkle diminished. Marianne was intrigued, she knew Daniel well enough to know he would never arrive unannounced.

"I wasn't expecting you," Marianne said lightly. She had always admired him, they had been close colleagues. It was Daniel who had given her the commission in Paris. It was also Daniel who had helped pick up the pieces when she returned from France. A cup was laid against a saucer in the sitting room, a soft chink.

Daniel turned to go.

"You have company, I'm sorry."

Marianne shrugged, she pushed open the door. Paul's sandy head was level with Monty's as they wrestled on the rug, Monty grumbling as Paul tugged at a rolled up magazine. Daniel nodded towards the neat bottom in faded denims.

"Paul, Daniel." Marianne announced. Paul turned quickly, upending his empty cup on the hearth. He caught it and beamed at them both.

"We've met before," he crossed the room in an easy stride, "one of Marianne's many awards dinners. I was very drunk and sang *My Way* badly after the band had finished."

"I remember." Daniel raised a brow, teasing him.

"Wish I didn't." Paul laughed and so did he.

He clocked Marianne's death stare.

"Just taking Monty for a spin in the garden, leave you to it." He left with the little dog trotting beside him, perfectly happy with the arrangement.

Marianne poured her ex-boss a glass of wine. Daniel took a sip, standing at the fireplace, taking in the room.

"You have such lovely taste, Marianne. Artistic. Where did that come from?"

"A lot of it was George, once you cleared away

58

the clutter, he had some lovely pieces." She joined Daniel in a drink, and waited.

"It's Claude."

Marianne stifled a sigh.

"He's very ill. I saw him just a few hours ago, he was asking for you. He's been trying to get in touch with all of us, to say goodbye."

Just out of range, Marianne thought she saw the edge of a blade, looked like a scythe. Oh, hi death, you still here? Always comes in threes, she heard in her head.

Marianne polished off her drink.

"Oh Daniel, Claude's nothing to do with me, hasn't been for a hundred years."

Daniel took a deep breath and put his glass down. The past divided them, yet united them at the same time. In another life, while working in Paris, Marianne had fallen for Daniel's best friend, Claude. The match, Marianne, a hungry young journalist, and he a well-known photographer, had been the talk of the town. For Marianne it had been a terrible mistake, although fun at first, Claude had quickly reverted to his old ways, spending money like water and conducting a series of affairs with a string of models. Claude had given Marianne more than just heartache.

Nevertheless, Marianne had adored him and, believing his promise of marriage, stood by him, until the evidence of his unfaithfulness was irrefutable in the form of a very pregnant, young assistant. Distraught and desperate to distance herself from the shame of a failed relationship, despite the many warnings and the inevitable pity of friends and colleagues, she left the sprawling Left Bank apartment they shared, abruptly. As a celebrity photographer, she had hoped Claude's PR would quash any leaks to the press but on hearing the news, one of his ex-conquests decided her career needed a boost and went to the media with sordid tales of drug-fuelled, sex romps. To witness at first hand the rancour of the media and see your private life sordidly splashed across the centre pages, had deeply affected Marianne. She vowed there and then to use her skills as a journalist only for good, to campaign for justice and expose wrongdoing wherever and whenever she could.

Marianne returned to England, taking the first job offered, convincing herself that sometimes it was just as easy to let go; see which way the wind blew and where fate would take you if you just let it. She had found it quite easy to reinvent herself as an ambitious, unattached, workaholic. A new career, in a new town, where no-one knew she had been the girlfriend of a glamorous celebrity. She had blotted out Claude and the memories, because when she did think of him and their brief happiness, she could not help but relive the pain of packing her possessions into boxes, remembering how she had felt, as the boxes filled and she had emptied. Now he was dying. Marianne remained untouched. The girl he had betrayed gone forever. She had moved on, developed a shell, the legacy of their relationship a half-forgotten nightmare, an echo of another time.

"I really don't think…" she said quietly. Besides it was ancient history, Claude had married his assistant and they had children now, he had another life too.

"I understand," Daniel was abrupt, moving out into the hallway. "You've been through too much lately, losing George and everything. But Claude's one of my closest friends Marianne and he specifically asked to speak to you, so I said I'd try."

The Grandfather clock chimed.

"Does he want to speak to me now?"

"There's very little time, I've come straight from the airport."

Marianne caught his pain. She called to Paul in the garden.

"I'm going into the study with Daniel, we have some important business to discuss. We'll be a while." Dusk was falling. Monty was in Paul's arms as he sat on the swing tied to the chestnut, growing precariously close to the house. He nodded and waved.

"I'll walk Monty and make a bit of supper for later, no worries, will Daniel stay and eat?"

"Not tonight." Marianne replied.

"Seems nice," Daniel said, as they made their way to the study, "young, but nice."

"It's not like that with Paul," Marianne sniped, and was immediately sorry for her sharpness. "Not like that with anyone now," she ended softly.

Daniel went to pick up the landline.

"Where is he?" Marianne asked.

"In a hospice, outside Paris," Daniel replied.

"What's it like, so I can imagine it when I speak to him, I won't know what to talk about."

"It's very pleasant, his room is filled with flowers and soft music, not in the way of funeral parlours, but more like a home from home."

"A home to die from," she said.

Daniel continued.

"It looks directly onto the garden, there's a fountain in a courtyard. His bed is large, and piled with cushions; drawings by the children are stuck on the walls and there's a cluster of some of his best photographs, in frames, on a table where he can see them. There's a beautiful picture of you."

That hurt, for some reason.

"Is there a pretty young nurse?" she asked.

"Of course," Daniel replied.

"Good, okay dial the number." She stood by the desk, fiddling with a strand of hair.

She closed her eyes trying to remember the Claude she had fallen in love with; his dark green eyes, flecked with gold; eyes that always reminded her of a majestic cat; eyes that lit up whenever he saw her. She tried not to imagine this dying stranger, this poor man she did not know or care about. It took ages to finally get through.

"You rang, thank goodness you rang," he whispered dryly, although the voice racked with illness, was not his, "how are you?" he hissed.

"Good," she whispered back.

"I bet you still look good, you always did."

She left the air blank.

"Thank you for ringing, I'm so happy to hear your voice, you have no idea what this means to me." His words were rasping; his breathing laboured.

"Take your time, Claude. I'm not going anywhere. Are you okay? Are you comfortable?"

"I'm fine, absolutely fine and happy now that we have this chance to talk. I have meant to speak to you so many times, and now there's not much time." He stopped, breathless, she heard him take a drink. She sat on the edge of the desk, Daniel had moved away, discreetly reading a book in a corner. Her hands were trembling; she had forgotten his beautiful accent; the perfect English with the hint of France.

"Claude, I'm so sorry," she said.

"No, no Marianne. I'm sorry. So sorry, you'll never know. That's why I asked Daniel to make sure I could speak to you. Please believe me. I'm really sorry, for everything," he gasped, and then silence. He took another drink.

"It was a long time ago, Claude." It was all she could think of to say.

"Marianne, I need you to forgive me," he said, louder this time, with a cry in his voice, "Say you forgive me."

She did not answer.

"Forgive me, please, I need you to forgive and then I can pass in peace," he was pleading.

She held the telephone away from her ear and looked at the handset, hardly believing what he had just asked of her. She glanced quickly at Daniel and then replaced the receiver slowly; finally, making sure Claude heard her do it.

The Hollow Heart

Daniel closed the book and came to join her at the desk.

"Thank you, he'll pass more peacefully now," Daniel whispered, touching her shoulder, imagining Marianne too filled with emotion to speak.

Marianne closed the front door softly after saying goodbye to Daniel. Paul had left candles burning everywhere and the newly fitted French doors to the garden were open to the cold night air. Marianne poured herself a drink. A yellow post-it on the microwave door bore the message, 'Ping if you're hungry' in Paul's handwriting. She kicked off her shoes and wandered into the sitting room. Paul and Monty lay curled up together, fast asleep on the sofa. Monty lifted an eyebrow and waddled off the couch to greet her. Paul stirred. A yellow post-it on his mouth, 'Please remove to kiss', another on the fly of his jeans, 'Please remove and ravage me'. He had clearly had far too much wine. She left the notes where they were, tousled his sandy head in a brief goodnight and made her weary way upstairs. Monty followed, leaving Paul on the sofa. Her feelings had altered, the grief had shifted. She had not felt so brittle or bitter in years. She cleaned her teeth, yet her mouth still tasted metallic, it was as if she had spent the entire evening chewing tinfoil.

Daniel left a message giving details of Claude's funeral a few days later. If she were ever asked, Marianne would pretend she had never received it. Claude had been dead to her for years. She erased the message and turned to Monty, who was spinning in an excited circle, anticipating his walk.

"Do you know what?" she asked him, clipping on his lead. "Just lately, I feel as if I've had enough death to last me a lifetime!" She threw open the door, striding down the pathway, leaving the gate ajar, so all the negative vibes could swirl out into the street and dissipate before her return.

Chapter Four – A World Of Difference

Marianne read the publicity blurb with mounting excitement. It was to be the grandest of occasions, combining the very best that London and Los Angeles had to offer; an awards ceremony, entertainment extravaganza and charity fundraiser to beat any that had ever taken place on the planet. It was the event of the decade, the one on everyone's lips, 'The Power 2 The People Awards', and it was to be sponsored by Global Communications Inc., the new parent company of the Chesterford Chronicle. The event was being hosted by the Baroness of Minesbourg, a minor royal with major pull. Marianne's campaign to reunite families following her 'Stolen Baby Scam' exposé had been nominated for a major 'Power 2 The People' Award. She could not quite believe it herself, this was fantastic news. If she won, imagine the publicity it would give her campaign. It would send her career into orbit. This was beyond exciting; this was earth shattering.

As usual, Marianne had the inside take, having interviewed the Baroness on numerous occasions, because the Baroness was, after all, one of Chesterford's favourite daughters. Not quite a tale of rags to riches, hers was a great story nonetheless, episodes of which, Marianne had reported at regular intervals during her time at the newspaper.

Indeed, Baroness Bailey Caulfield, the former international fashion model, was at the zenith of her popularity. The thrice-wed commoner certainly made the most of the title her first husband, an adorable old-fashioned aristocrat, had bestowed upon her. When Bailey's Baron suffered a heart attack not long after they married, the glamorous widow wed an up-and-coming rock star who, unbeknown to her, maintained a coke habit and a couple of mistresses on the side. After divorcing him, Bailey went on to marry a young American politician, who rapidly climbed the ladder to become Senator of one of the USA's most southerly states.

Sadly, this marriage too, was doomed to fail, and not twelve months after the wedding, Bailey was left with little choice but to divorce the Senator, following salacious revelations involving a junior researcher attached to his office. Seemingly undaunted, Bailey's inheritance and two divorce settlements, gave her the wherewithal to fly around the globe devoting her life to all manner of good causes. Never considered a beauty in the conventional sense, the extremely attractive Baroness, still one of the most photographed females of her generation, could certainly add credibility to any event she chose to attend, let alone host.

With the Baroness's name intrinsically linked to what promised to be a show-stopping spectacular, Marianne knew that royals, movie stars, politicians, world leaders and all manner of celebrity would be beating a path to the capital; this would be a fundraiser of monumental proportions; the party to beat all parties, and anyone who was anyone wanted to be there. She read and re-read the email aloud.

"Wow, this could be it Monty, our big break, catapulted from the sleepy backwater of journalism which is the Chesterford Chronicle, to superstardom. I could become an international roving reporter; a world commentator; a global campaigner." Monty ran around the kitchen table in delight, tail wagging. "Of course, I can't go anywhere without you, that would have to be written into the contract. Oh Monty, this could be it, this could really be it!" She picked him up and twirled him round in her arms.

With the Chronicle's parent company, the media conglomerate Global Communications Inc. one of the event's main sponsors, whispers that a handful of employees from the newspaper were going to receive invitations to the 'Power 2 The People Awards' fluttered through the city centre office block like ticker tape. By the time Marianne reached the building, she was feeling pretty smug, with her campaign nominated for an award, she was definitely on the guest list.

The gilt-edged, Royal Crest embossed invitation requesting Marianne Coltrane and Partner to attend the event, was propped against her computer screen. She immediately phoned Paul; he would be thrilled to come as her guest and was always good company, whatever the occasion.

Marianne knew exactly what she was going to wear; she chose an exquisite full-length, swirling red silk gown.

One of the most expensive items she had ever bought, a classic halter neck with plunging back that skimmed the base of her spine, highlighting her neat waist and bottom. The last time she had worn it was to the National Media Awards. The night George had stepped in and presented the prizes and she had apologised for downgrading his article to a rather insignificant 'Lifestyle' write-up. The night George told her that it could not have mattered less, and the night she won the accolade 'Journalist of the Year', drank litres of champagne and kissed him far too over-enthusiastically for so short an acquaintance. Even more importantly, it was the night George had asked her out and she had said yes, and that was it, the red dress, the Awards, the champagne, the kiss. He had fallen, hook, line and sinker. She hugged the dress, smiling.

It was not long before Marianne found herself smiling again, this time wryly. No such thing as a free lunch, she told herself when she read the email from Jack, commissioning her to write a series of articles about the build-up to the 'Power 2 The People' event. With her usual attention to detail she began her research, making copious notes and interviewing as many of those involved as she could. At first sight, she could not believe the area chosen to build the main auditorium would ever be ready in time or be large enough to hold the thousands of guests planned to make up the audience. As she watched the plan come together, she was fascinated by every aspect of this fantastic event. Impressed by how hard the team worked, and in awe, because everyone, from the humblest junior to the biggest star, was giving their time free to support charities and good causes across the globe.

The white, stretch limousine slid along Oakwood Avenue to sit purring outside the gate. Paul Osborne ran along the path and then leapt the steps to the front door, launching himself into the hallway, brandishing a corsage of dark yellow lilies.

"Are you *rea-dy*?" he sing-songed up the stairwell.

Monty appeared first, woofing softly and wagging his tail so hard his whole body wriggled. He tumbled off the first two steps, regained his balance, then charged downwards leaping into Paul's arms from a safe height. Flowers aloft, Paul nuzzled Monty's ears; a polite cough sent both pairs of eyes upwards.

"Wow!" Paul put Monty down. "You look ravenous!"

"You look rather delirious yourself," laughed Marianne, the misnomers, a tribute to Sharon's calamitous deciphering of messages. Marianne descended slowly, the crimson fish-tail of her gown swishing behind her. Paul presented the corsage. Their lips touched briefly and, thanking him, she attached the flowers to her dress. To complete the ensemble, she wore George's engagement ring and his mother's art deco diamond droplet earrings. These perfectly complemented her hair, which was swept upwards into a professionally acquired French pleat. Paul, in a borrowed midnight blue velvet dinner jacket, had managed to smooth his wayward locks, although his navy blue bow tie flopped to one side and the frill of his dress shirt had been singed, due to overzealous ironing. His eyes sparkled and, placing Marianne's golden pashmina around her shoulders, he stood back from the doorway to reveal the waiting car.

She checked Paul's expression to ensure this was a joke.

"Great isn't it? On the company, of course."

They said goodnight to Monty and, pulling the door closed, tangoed, giggling, along the pathway. Marianne laughed even louder when Ted Cassidy, one of the Chronicle's long-serving photographers, jumped from the car to open the door. Ted apologised for being inappropriately attired for his role as chauffeur but explained he had been commissioned to take some shots to accompany the article, Marianne would no doubt be writing.

"No such thing as a free Awards dinner either then?" She smiled as they posed, glasses in hand, for Ted and the neighbours, who had gathered to see who was responsible for the white monstrosity filling half the cul-de-sac.

'The Power 2 The People Awards' extravaganza was highly organised; it had to be. Marianne's invitation had come with an allotted time for her party to arrive; ensuring all guests and celebrities could be photographed and interviewed at manageable intervals along the stretch of traditional red carpet.

Paul had another surprise for Marianne. His sister Zara and her husband Mike were also on the guest list; as was Mike's father, the American TV star who had failed to make it to the National Media Awards; his actress girlfriend, and their New York agents, Leeson & Leeson. But just hours before the event, Zara called to say the New York team had to bow out and the American TV Star, a great friend of the Baroness, had arranged for Marianne and her guest to join their table. This meant Marianne and Paul would be seated in the centre of the arena, flanking the huge stage and catwalk that had been designed to bring the live action right into the heart of the auditorium. If Marianne's campaign was to win an award, she would be perfectly placed to be called to the stage to receive it.

Paul and Marianne smiled graciously at the crowds as they stepped from the limousine onto the crimson strip of runway stretched before them. She dug her fingernails into his hand, as various stage whispers of, "Who's that?" "What are they in?" flew about them. Flashbulbs popped, as they sashayed onwards, just fast enough to keep onlookers and photographers guessing, before Paul broke into an undignified canter, waving his arms madly.

"Hey sis, look it's me, we're here!" he called out.

Marianne, now stranded on the carpet, maintained her regal swish until she reached the little group and, then joining in the laughter, shared embraces and kisses all round.

Marianne liked Paul's older sister, Zara, she was warm and friendly, if a little protective of her idealistic younger brother. When they first met, Zara often hinted, despite the age difference, and the fact that Marianne was technically Paul's boss, that she hoped their relationship would develop beyond friendship. When Marianne became engaged to George, Zara graciously put that ambition aside and had telephoned Marianne personally to congratulate her. She had also been genuinely upset when George died. In fact the last time Marianne had seen Zara, was at George's funeral, although she could barely remember if they had spoken.

Zara wrapped her arms around her.

"You look fabulous, you look amazing. How are you, really?" She took Marianne's hands and looked into her eyes.

"I'm alright," Marianne held her gaze, "honestly, I'm doing okay." Zara beamed. She could not deny she was again hopeful, that once a certain amount of time had passed, Paul and Marianne might become an item. They seemed so good together. But to Marianne, Paul was, well, just Paul. The young, cub reporter, she laughed and joked with. The typical younger brother she never had, who still got smashed, went on disastrous dates and seemed to maintain a wide-eyed wonder on the world, no matter how hideous the assignments Jack Buchannon managed to fling at him. She was his mentor. He was part of her job. It would never even cross her mind that he might be someone she would have a proper, grown up relationship with, and anyway, Marianne knew her last chance of 'happy ever after' had died with George. She had her career, she had Monty, she had a lot to be grateful for.

The Hollow Heart

Unlike the effervescent Osborne siblings, Mike was a quiet, thoughtful soul; the type Marianne considered saw everything and commented on very little. On the occasions they had met, Marianne felt a connection through their shared Irishness and they would gently tease each other for becoming 'Englified', a word she recalled her Head Nun used for anything she found too Anglican for her taste.

Mike hugged Marianne in welcome. As he released her, she caught her heel, losing her balance, to topple backwards into the arms of the man standing behind her. It was Mike's father, the surprisingly youthful American TV star. He grasped her elbow swiftly and propped her back on her heels. She caught his scent, a delicious blend of wood and amber. It was Zara who took her arm, turning her fully to face him.

"Marianne, this is Ryan…" Marianne beamed upwards. Flinty eyes glinted down at her. He was tall, tanned and smiling. Marianne caught her breath, only just managing to prevent herself wobbling off her heels again. The fabulous creature beside him was equally statuesque. Marianne's gaze swept upwards. The couple were stunning, luminous and just beautiful.

"The pleasure is mine." He smiled, eyes crinkling. "But I think we should have met before. I was scheduled to present the National Media Awards and couldn't make it. I'm sorry I let you down and I'm sorry I didn't show, because I heard it was a great night."

Marianne was taken aback. She looked across at Paul, delighted but surprised he had briefed her fellow guests so thoroughly. Paul was oblivious, totally awestruck as a gaggle of soap stars hoved into view.

"It was indeed a great night." Marianne smiled, glancing at Mike. "You two look more like brothers. I can't believe you're Mike's father."

"I was a child bride." Ryan laughed and then turned to introduce the goddess at his side. "Angelique, this is Marianne Coltrane."

"Delighted, you're a journalist; award-winning too I'm told," the actress said in a sultry, Texan drawl. Marianne beamed back at them both, all apprehension dispersed, she was looking forward to a truly memorable evening. They took their seats in the middle of the auditorium, right in front of the stage.

Marianne checked the place names, Paul to her left and Ryan on her right. Ryan held out her chair, doing the same for Angelique. He took his seat when the ladies were settled. He poured wine and water, handing her a menu, passing her the order of events. He was attentive, he was easy. Marianne felt her heart miss a beat, for half a millisecond, he reminded her of...

"George said you were a very special lady and he wasn't wrong. Brains and beauty." Ryan was reading the list of nominations. He raised his glass, "Here's to him, God bless him, a great bloke."

Marianne left her glass untouched.

"You knew George?"

Ryan was immediately apologetic; he had taken her by surprise.

"I'm sorry. I thought you knew. George and I go

75

way back. We were in a band together in the early days, just after he left University and I landed here from Ireland. We both thought we'd be rock stars one day, as you do."

"No, he never said. Well if he did, I didn't register. You seem an unlikely alliance." She smiled and so did he.

"Not at all, he was the suave English gent and I was the wild Irish rogue, a fatal combination when it came to pulling girls back in the day, I can tell you."

She burst out laughing. She could just imagine them, so different, so charming, so incorrigible.

"What happened to the band?"

"Oh, a huge success, did you never hear of us? Gave some of the big names a few sleepless nights I reckon." He was teasing, his State-side twang becoming less obvious as he talked. "We did a sell-out tour of two village halls in South Devon, then fell out with our manager when the drummer was recalled to London to join the family firm, taking most of the equipment with him. George and I bummed around for the summer until we ran out of money and had to find a proper job." He grinned at the memory. "With me working in the States I hadn't seen him for ages, so when I found out he was an MP and in Chesterford, which is where my son and his wife live, it made sense to visit and do a gig while I was there. Sadly I couldn't make the Awards Ceremony in the end and asked him to stand in for me. I hope George was a good enough substitute?"

"Oh, he was! It was how we met really, but I

wasn't aware of the connection." Marianne gulped back a huge slurp of wine.

"I did make it to the funeral, there were so many people there, people I hadn't seen for years," He looked into her eyes, the flintiness softened. "You were very brave that day. I'm sure you and George were great together."

"Thank you," she said quietly, then brightly, "I never knew George was in a band."

"Hey, come on you two, it's about to start," Paul interrupted.

Ryan nodded at Paul and, touching Marianne's hand briefly, laughed.

"We were rubbish. Thank goodness we both changed careers." He turned and placed his arm lightly across Angelique's shoulders. "You okay?" he asked.

"Sure," she replied, "why shouldn't I be?"

Marianne noticed Angelique refill her empty wine glass abruptly.

The beginning of the attack was almost silent. A faint eerie hiss complemented the band's opening riff, followed by a vague rumble, gently vibrating the stage. It tripped along the catwalk, as a floor-to-ceiling streak of light lit the auditorium. The audience gasped; the effect was obviously pyrotechnic, a flash of firework genius. The lead singer turned to check the musicians were still with him and as he nodded back to the orchestra pit the explosion erupted; a loud crack, followed by an enormous boom. Then stillness, as the sound hung in the air; a malevolent hum, like a swarm of locusts. Flames burst from the stage, followed by immediate, intense heat, then swirling smoke and screaming.

Someone turned the sound off as Marianne, watching in slow motion, saw the stage implode and the Royal Box and its contents slide, arms flailing, to the floor. Instantly people were crashing against her, charging for exits as clouds of smoke mushroomed around them and the fumes intensified growing into a dense, black, suffocating smog. Someone grabbed her hand, she was spun round harshly. It was Ryan. He put Angelique's hand in hers, squeezing them together. Paul had been pushed to the floor. Ryan hauled him up and put his hand in Zara's, who was holding onto Mike. Ryan signalled them to hang onto each other, demonstrating by clamping his arms together. He tied a napkin over his mouth and nose, urgently indicating they all do the same. He pinched his nose and put a finger to his mouth, shaking his head, signalling them not to breathe. No point speaking, people and alarms were shrieking and they were all bomb-deaf anyway. He did all this in mere seconds. Then taking the lead, he began to move swiftly towards the exit. People were panicking and pushing, some were shouting, trying to barge through the crowd, others had fallen to the floor and were being trampled. The smoke kept building, blacker and thicker, people were coughing and spluttering, some were collapsing as others pushed them aside.

The area around the main entrance was a mass of bodies pressed together, the crowd banked back into the auditorium. Violent struggles were breaking out; teams of security guards in oxygen masks were trying to maintain order. A man with a camera snatched a mask off one of the guards. A colleague hit him with a truncheon, he fell to the floor. The guard tugged his mask back on.

Ryan led his crocodile of survivors towards the main entrance and then turned, pushing against the crowd. Marianne was struggling to hold onto Paul, they were being buffeted and bashed as they battled through. Paul's hand fell away and as she turned to find him, she could just make out his head as a black patent shoe crushed into his face. She yanked Angelique's hand. Angelique tugged Ryan. He slipped back and helped Mike drag Paul to his feet. Paul's left arm swung uselessly away from his body, his elbow smashed, his nose flattened in a pulp of blood. Ryan indicated to Zara to hold onto Paul's shoulder and they pushed on.

There was a large group of people at a doorway, they seemed to be passing through, not quickly but steadily when another explosion erupted deep in the bowels of the structure. Directly above them, the walls and ceiling of the marquee burst into flames, melting away to expose the night sky. The influx of air exacerbated the inferno, the smoke intensified, Marianne could hold her breath no longer, her throat was burning, eyes stinging and streaming water. She started to cough. Angelique's fingers were oily, they were slipping away. They pushed on. She cracked her knee against what appeared to be a large metal object, she was sliding as she groped ahead, sliding on water, or was it foam? She could see metal shapes around her; they were in the catering area. Ryan must have guessed there would be exits here to the outside world. It was becoming brighter. The crush of bodies was easing; they seemed to be peeling away. She looked down at her right hand, Paul's fingers were no longer there. When had she let go of Paul? She felt a wave of panic rising in her chest and then a rush of air, fresh, clean air flooded her nostrils, gushing into her face. She blinked against the light. Marianne realised she was outside. Through blurred eyes, she saw a woman in uniform, who put her face close to Marianne, feeling down her arms, touching her head. Smiling grimly, she urged Marianne into a vehicle. Marianne could make out Angelique ahead. They were wearing the same shiny, silver blankets. The vehicle lurched. Through the window of the ambulance, she saw Ryan helping Paul onto a stretcher. Her skin hurt. No-one even tried to talk. She and Angelique bumped along beside each other in silence. Marianne's shoulders throbbed where the roof structure had caught her as it fell to the floor. She could see Angelique's blackened legs, burned where her evening gown had melted onto her skin. They rattled through the streets in a daze, deposited with the rest of the ambulance's bloodied passengers at a hospital on the outskirts of the city.

Once inside the building, bursting with trolleys and wheelchairs, Marianne and Angelique were separated and Marianne found herself sitting alone in a makeshift emergency bay for what seemed like hours. She remembered a smiling, yellow-skinned man in a pale blue shirt, asking her to count to ten beneath her oxygen mask, before she faded into the luxuriant blackness of anaesthesia. Luckily, her collarbone was only dislocated, but the gashes to her shoulders and back were dangerously deep and needed surgery to remove pieces of metal and debris from her wounds. Once cleaned, patches of skin were grafted onto the largest wounds, the remainder pulled together with a variety of stitches and small metal clamps.

When she came too, she felt fantastic for about thirty seconds and then waves of nausea caused her stomach to tighten and she vomited copiously into the dressing on her left shoulder. Struggling to sit up, she began to panic as the nausea returned, terrified she would choke and die where she lay. She was just losing consciousness again when a woman's face appeared, hovering over her. She was wearing white. She looked like an angel, a beautiful, black angel.

"Up ya come me darlin'. Dere ya go. Dearie me, ya makin' a mess. Not to worry, we'll soon have you cleaned up and resting nicely." The nurse set to work. Marianne was cleaned, drugged and as comfortable as possible in less than ten minutes. Marianne stretched out her blistered fingers to touch the nurse's hand.

"It was bad, wasn't it?" she hissed through a cracked mouth.

"De worst it could be." The nurse's eyes filled, and she blinked. "Dere's evil in de world. But dere's good people too. We need more good people." She patted the coverlet and bustled away. Marianne was vaguely aware of another wave of activity across the corridor; the noise was dull but constant. She drifted in and out of sleep.

Three weeks had passed since the worst terrorist attack London had ever encountered had blown the 'Power 2 The People' extravaganza apart. Marianne had witnessed and escaped the main explosion at the every epicentre of the event. Forensics discovered the device had been secreted in a drum kit, centre stage, the kit had had been checked by sniffer dogs and cleared, it had to have been an inside job. The explosion triggered ten more incendiary devices to simultaneously ignite across the city; the bombs were placed in abandoned vehicles, shop doorways and churchyards. As the numbers of the dead continued to rise, the five fatalities in the church were among the most shocking; so too were the disturbing details of the death of the Baroness, who had masterminded the whole evening. It was reported she had been found in what remained of her dressing room, without a mark on her, in the arms of her loyal aide, whose handsome face had been blown away. She had never even made it onto the stage that fatal night.

With the emergency services stretched to breaking point, teams of volunteers, hurriedly trained in rescue and recovery by experienced disaster workers, had been flown in from all over the world. It took some time to confirm the final death toll, but the impact of the catastrophe was made all the more startling by the revelation that 2,996 people had perished in the attack, exactly the same number as had died in the 9/11 atrocity in the USA.

The tales of carnage, heroism and sheer bloody mindedness were endless, the media coverage relentless. Pages of reports, photographs, interviews, facts and figures combined with hours of TV coverage. The aftermath was both despairing and inspiring. Thousands had lost their lives pointlessly and a handful had lost their lives rescuing others. The bitter irony being the whole point of the event had been to save people, not massacre them. And every day a different story, another faction to blame, hero to applaud. Yet still the recurring question, why? Still the same answer. No answer.

The impact of the painkillers meant that, to begin with, Marianne felt as if the whole thing had happened to someone else. She was distant and removed, as if she had seen it on a screen somewhere. It was not until, aimlessly sorting through a pile of magazines and newspapers beside her hospital bed, she came across a photograph of a young Asian female police officer lying beside a large chestnut horse, the conker coloured mane mixed with the ebony gloss of the woman's ponytail. The headline read 'Beauty and the Beast; slain in the line of duty'. So the final death toll was 2,996 people and one horse; she had read somewhere a dog had died in 9/11. Grief flooded through her, seeping up from her toes as if she were blotting paper, absorbing her whole body in one continuous sweep. She had never felt so lost, so desolate. It was visiting time, the ward was full of people, friends and relatives coming to see how their loved ones were doing, willing them to get better, showing them they were loved, letting them know it was all going to be alright. Who was coming to see her? Where was her loved one? Where was George? She climbed back into bed and burrowing into the pillows, pulled the covers over her head. She must have sobbed for hours until she finally slept; the picture of the policewoman and the horse clamped tightly in her raw-skinned fist.

It was around midnight and the ward was uncommonly quiet, when the nurse whom Marianne had come to know as Sister Jackson, made a rare appearance.

"Dere you are Marianne, how are ya doin? Ya lookin' a bit peaky to me. Soon be time for you to go home. Dis place is not good for your health."

Marianne managed a half-smile. Sister Jackson propped her up, plumped her pillows and straightened the sheets.

"I'll go and get you a nice cup of hot chocolate for your nightcap. Did you eat any supper at all dis evening?" Nurse Jackson eyed the congealing bowl of stew. She whisked it away, disturbing the pile of magazines and papers on Marianne's bedside table. "You not botherin' wit' your personal correspondence either?" She handed Marianne an envelope. "It could be good news, Marianne, a well-wisher. Lord knows, we all need wishes and dreams these dark days, a light at de end of the tunnel." She flicked on Marianne's beside lamp as she trundled away.

Marianne did not recognise the handwriting. She half-heartedly opened the envelope, the same handwriting filled the page; it was on notepaper from a well-known Knightsbridge hotel. It read…

Dear Marianne,

Just a brief note to send you best wishes for a speedy recovery. I'm sorry I've not had a chance to visit, but schedules rule and we are filming the end of the TV series, so I am going back to the States tomorrow. Angelique has made a good recovery and will be flying back with me and I hear, although Paul is still undergoing surgery, he will hopefully make a full recovery too. Both Zara and Mike are fine, thank goodness, but still shell-shocked as we all are. Don't credit me with any heroics once you recover enough to write your report, I had a friend who made no secret of his association with an illegal organisation and told me what to do if I ever found myself in a particularly explosive situation. Advice I thought I would only ever need for a role, not real life! Ha!

Take care of yourself and you never know, one day our paths may cross again and I can recount more wondrous tales of the reckless rogues, the lovely George and I once were. With every good wish, Ryan.

PS: I'm sorry those bastards blew apart your dreams for your campaign, I feel sure when things settle down you'll get the show back on the road. R

Marianne stared at the missive for some time. Well, what a surprise, how thoughtful, what a nice thing for him to do. She felt quite moved by Ryan's kindness

85

and smiled again at how little she knew of him and how, what bit she did know, reminded her of George, protective, considerate and rather heroic. She drifted off to sleep, not sure if she consciously thought or dreamed that George had sent Ryan to take care of her, in that lovely, gently controlling way he had.

Chapter Five – After The Aftermath

The very next day, Jack's wife Isabelle came to take Marianne back to Oakwood Avenue where Monty, hysterical with happiness, tried to lick every inch of her as she eased herself onto the sofa. Isabelle was reading a checklist of ready meals and, once satisfied with this, busily arranged Marianne's medication in the bathroom, presenting her with a pile of books and magazines, topped off with a cluster of remote controls and a telephone.

"Supper's in the oven. I'll ring later and call by in the morning."

"How's Jack coping?"

"He's not! Grumpy as hell, without you and Paul to moan about."

It hurt to smile.

"He'll be alright, we'll all be alright," Isabelle said. It was statement of fact; she marched off.

Marianne was so pleased to be home that Monty was suffocating in her hug. As he struggled for freedom, she glimpsed the designer collar Paul had extravagantly bought him for Christmas and she missed her crusading colleague very much indeed. She could not bear to think of him going back to his student-type flat in the centre of town. She made up her mind, life is too short, it could have been even shorter, Paul was to stay with her and Monty in Oakwood Avenue while he recovered, just until he was well and back on his feet. She would buy supplies, make all his favourite things and he would feel immediately at home and start to recover properly. Marianne smiled to herself, she was not sure what his favourite things were, she was not even much of a cook, but she would take care of him, make him better and strong again. It was the very least she could do for someone who, having been through all they had together, was now a very special friend. There were not enough special people in her life, the trauma she had been through made her realise. She had no family. No close friends, only colleagues she was friendly with, she was single and yet widowed. She took Ryan's note from her bag and re-read it, taking comfort from his words.

"Time to get this show back on the road, Monty," she told the little dog who had cheekily nestled in beside her on the sofa. He had never been allowed on the furniture before.

Paul made no attempt at even a vague protest when she told him of her plan to have him convalesce at number seventy four.

"Just while you get your strength back," she explained on the phone.

"Great, thanks, sorted," came his immediate response.

She and Isabelle emptied the contents of his wardrobe into black bin bags and with his precious vinyl collection and vintage record player perched on her knees, Marianne hummed tunelessly as Isabelle drove her and Paul's possessions across the city to the edge of suburbia and Oakland Avenue.

"It will be at least three months before he'll be able to drive," Isabelle commented as they navigated the High Street.

"That'll be nothing short of a miracle then, Paul's never been able to drive." It still hurt to laugh.

After off-loading at the house, Marianne and Isabelle began the journey south to collect their patient.

Marianne pushed her nose against the window – the ward was full, beds crammed together, men sitting up in chairs, some playing cards, others talking and laughing together in small groups. She scanned the room a second time. She could not see him. Her heart lurched.

"Looking for me?" A muffled voice ventured, behind her.

She turned to find Paul Osborne swaying slightly, in a swathe of bandage.

"I've had better looks, I know," he offered.

"You look bloody marvellous to me."

They hugged precariously. Isabelle was already emptying his bedside locker into the ubiquitous bin liner.

"Come on, let's get you home, I hate driving in London at the best of times," she busied, hooshing them both out to the car.

Paul's list of injuries was pretty impressive and he did seem to take some perverse pleasure from recounting them at length. He explained to Isabelle, he had been badly burned along one side of his body, his left arm had been broken at the elbow and wrist, and pinned in both places, the smoke damage to his lungs was lingering and painful. A piece of flying metal had lodged

itself just above his right eye. The eye had been saved
and although the gouge to his forehead was severe, he
had been told it would heal to a scar in the fullness of
time. It was the shape of a question mark, he pointed out.
Marianne thought this highly appropriate, considering his
quizzical nature.

By now the terrorist attack had started to wane in
news terms. Arrests had been made, debris cleared. With
the PR machines taking up the slack, many of the
celebrities involved were busy 'telling their story'.
Marianne kept an eye out for any mention of Ryan
O'Gorman, whose calm and, indeed, heroic performance
on that fateful night would have done much to enhance
his reputation. So far the American TV star had not even
been mentioned in despatches, and far bigger names than
his were filling miles of column inches with their near
death experiences.

Angelique had been discharged the same time as
Marianne and while Marianne had sought daily reports
from the medical team on Angelique's condition, no
message was ever returned. Angelique's career rated
higher in media terms than Ryan's, but again Marianne
found no mention of how the actress was faring in any of
the glossy, gossip-column press. Zara and Mike too, had
just faded into the background. None of them had felt
inclined to divulge the facts surrounding their very
fortunate escape. It was like an unspoken covenant. It
was understandable. The whole of London was licking its
wounds, the world moribund with tension, too shocked to
mourn, too bemused to move on. It seemed each of them

needed all their strength to concentrate on healing.

Now that she was well on the road to recovery, Marianne was beginning to feel she needed someone a bit closer, someone she had shared the terrible experience with, someone she cared for. She had enough of dealing with everything, all of this, on her own, alone.

The new routine at number seventy four was welcomed. It gave the day a framework. Recovery from a major trauma is a slow process, moving on, standing still, stepping back. At times Marianne felt she was looking into a black, bottomless pit, staring into emptiness, being there just in case, waiting but not waiting, life on hold. Without ever mentioning it, Paul seemed to know this and they both knew that just being where they were, together, was probably the best place they could be, for now, anyway.

Paul's recovery programme was going well, it was the end of October and he was beginning to look and feel more like his old self. He had physiotherapy, which helped with mobility, and he had started painting again, which helped with the night terrors. Happily for the residents of number seventy four, Paul was addicted to daytime TV chefs and quickly became a competent cook – they had all grown tired of Marianne's one-pot repertoire. So a routine was set, Paul filled his days with art, food and his fitness regime and in the evenings after work Marianne cleared up, having enjoyed whatever delight Paul had prepared that day. Monty was entirely content with the arrangement, alternating between artist's model and invalid companion, especially supportive when 'air had to be taken' in the form of a wobbly stagger to the park; and also pleased with the job of 'dish of the day' taster. Life was good, being alive, even better.

Marianne realised things were genuinely on the mend when she heard a sound she barely recognised one evening, Paul's laughter. They had always had a similar sense of humour but real, chortling, tummy-hugging laughs had been absent for some time. Besides, laughing hurt Paul's chest and Marianne's heart.

Initially there had been a quaint formality when Paul moved in to Oakwood Avenue, but the fact that washing and dressing was a real struggle, meant they soon had to dispense with feigned sensibilities, particularly on the evening Paul got stuck in the bath. Marianne averted her eyes while she tried to free him, but it was pointless. As was his attempt at balancing a soggy face flannel across his private parts. As hard as she tried to haul him upwards, he just slid gingerly back towards the taps. After the third attempt, Paul had no choice but to drop the flannel and, grabbing her shoulders, tried to save himself; she slipped on a towel, completely losing her balance, and landed on top of him. She shrieked; there was water everywhere, she sploshed about, panicking.

"Ouch, you're hurting me, I can't move," he burbled, dunking in and out of the bubbles. Marianne started to giggle. Paul came up for breath laughing and pulling her hair, pushed her face under the water. She surfaced, splashing him with all her might. Before long they were howling, tears of laughter running into the rapidly cooling bath water.

"Just don't get stuck on the loo," she warned, and from then on all formality dispersed and they started to have fun again. She just laughed, when a cake she had created for his birthday, was baked so solid he suggested they use it as a doorstop, and he was not remotely miffed when she asked about the fox he was painting, knowing full well it was an attempt at a portrait of Monty. The cosy banter of their past life was beginning to return.

Though there were some things Marianne needed to keep private and would not discuss with Paul, such as her occasional habit of clunking around George's study in the small hours, slightly squiffy, berating him for his insensitive, unsupportive and ill-timed demise. If Paul ever heard her, he had the decency not to mention it. So in many ways they were all very happy together, in every way they were each very glad of the other.

It was Sunday afternoon. Paul had cooked a traditional roast; melt in the mouth South Devon beef; roast potatoes crispy with sea salt and his 'signature' vegetable dish of crunchy leak and broccoli cheese bake. Monty had been walked, the second bottle of red opened, the fire lit and newspapers spread, heaven. Marianne became aware of someone not quite concentrating on the crossword.

"Okay?" She peered over her glasses.

"Yep." He did not look away.

"Sure, you hurting?"

"No, I'm fine…well, I am a bit."

"Painkiller? Need a rub of Ibuprofen?"

He held her gaze, leaving the armchair, hotching stiffly across the space between them to kneel by her legs, stretched languidly from sofa to coffee table, glamorously clad in dog-haired jogging bottoms. She put her magazine down.

"What?" Monty had joined Paul at her feet.

"I need a kiss."

"Oh, is that all?" She leaned down, ruffled his hair with her free hand and planted her lips on his frowning forehead.

"No, a real kiss." He took hold of her arms, turning her so she fell back onto the sofa, he raised himself off the floor and perched above her, looking down, smiling but serious. She felt a flutter in her chest, desire, fear or both? She could not be sure, it was sudden, fleeting. She scanned his eyes, questioning. He brought his face next to hers. Briefly rubbing noses, breathing her in and then he licked her lips, a swift darting tongue, tasting of salt and wine.

"Whoa Tiger," she said, forcing a laugh.

"God Marianne, you must know how much I want you? How I feel about you?" he whispered, and then he kissed her, a hard needy kiss, a kiss that wanted an answer, a kiss demanding response.

"I'm not sure this is right Paul," she said, but it felt so good, a gorgeous, proper, grown up kiss. She could not deny she wanted him to kiss her again. He was so young and lovely and warm and alive. She ignored the rebuke bubbling at the base of her throat. Throwing caution to the wind, she moved to lie deeper beneath him

94

and wrapping her arms around his head, pulled him to her, kissing him back, moistening his dry mouth with her tongue, biting the edge of his lips gently with hers. He pulled back, looking straight into her eyes, his passion so fierce, she could feel it. He pushed his hand under her top, finding the curve of her soft breast beneath the multitude of layers she always wore; he began to caress her softly and then, leaving her lips, ran his tongue up and down her throat. She groaned with pleasure.

And then, "Paul, I…" She held him off, "I can't, I'm not ready, not sure." But her body belied her words. There it was again, that feeling, that rush of heat, lighting her up from inside. The tingling between her legs made her moan and she stretched beneath him. He moved to lie beside her and she could feel his hardness pressing through his jeans against her thigh. Her stomach lurched in pleasure. She pushed against him, sliding beneath him, pulling him to her. He groaned as he twisted, a pile of newspaper fell from the sofa onto Monty, who had been dozing gently beneath their fondlings. He grunted. Paul moaned again, then he screamed. Her eyes flew open.

"What's wrong?"

"I'm stuck, I can't move."

"Shit, nor can I."

"Sorry."

"Hang on, I'll see if…" She wanted to giggle and weep at the same time. She squirmed beneath him. He was locked in position, his face white, a line of perspiration formed along his lips which were turning blue. Fuelled with horror, she gave an almighty heave and

95

lifted him off her to free herself and slide to the floor. Paul slumped, face down on the sofa. Marianne retrieved her top, pulling it on. In a flash she was easing him onto his back. He squealed and slowly she began to straighten him out, his legs were numb. She pushed a cushion under his head.

"Ouch!"

"Don't be a baby. I'll go and fetch your pills."

On her knees beside him, she fed him painkillers with wine, then brought a warm flannel, drenched in lavender water, and wiped his face. His colour was returning. She undid his belt and the button of his jeans. Genitals returned to status quo, she rubbed his legs gently, he wiggled his naked toes.

"That's better," he said quietly, after about ten minutes.

"I don't know; you scared me half to death." She could not decide which bit of the past half hour had been the scariest.

He reached for her hand and closed his eyes.

"I want you so much…" His voice trailed off.

"I know," she whispered, her throat dry.

"I'm sorry."

"Don't be," she said, and headed off to clear away the lunchtime debris.

It was an unusually silent vigil in George's study during the early hours of what would become a grey Monday morning. Marianne sat in his chair, at his desk, running her fingers over the heavy glass dome he used as a paperweight. She traced the engraving of his initials with her nail.

"You know, I nearly did something very foolish today," she told the inanimate object. "I nearly ruined a friendship, carelessly exchanging something special for something trite. A quick fumble on the sofa, because he was here and it was offered. Sex with someone I don't love, not in that way, sex because I miss George and I'm lonely. So I've decided, that's it, sex is off the agenda. Because if you aren't in love with someone, what's the point and let's face it what's the likelihood of me ever falling in love again? It just ain't gonna happen." The paperweight remained silent on the subject. She straightened her shoulders and looked herself in the eye in the glass, before opening a drawer and dropping the paperweight inside.

They were sitting in the garden of their favourite wine bar. It was one of those fabulous late autumn days, the trees had all but shed their leaves and were standing stark against a streaky sky. A bronze sun hung low, skimming the rooftops and the breeze smelled gently of decay, mingling with wood smoke from chimneys boasting the first of the season's open fires. They had eaten Cumberland sausage and mustard mash with onion gravy. The week, like the remaining slice of soda bread, had lain awkwardly between them. He sniffed and cleared his throat. She gazed into her cider, amber like the day.

"Last Sunday..." He coughed. She continued to stare at her drink. "I thought I had better explain."

She touched his hand, rubbing his thumb with her

forefinger.

"No need," she said.

"Oh, but I think there is." His voice was strained, he pronounced each word carefully.

"Paul…"

"No really. I don't wish to appear rude or pushy or anything."

"Why are you speaking like this?"

"Like what?"

"Like weird."

"I'm not." He blushed slightly. "It's just that I think we should make a go of it. I think we should be a couple….that's what I think."

She flipped a beer mat.

"You must know how I feel about you," he continued.

"Paul stop, right now."

"Why not? Am I so repulsive?"

"Silly." She went to ruffle his hair.

"Don't."

"Paul, you're my friend. Probably my best friend." He took a swig of his drink, putting the glass down heavily.

"But that's a great basis for a relationship. I know all about you, all about George, your childhood, your parents, your love of Ireland and the island where you spent every summer. I know all about everything."

Marianne sighed. "No you don't Paul."

"What don't I know?"

"Lots. Anyway, I am not ready for another

relationship, maybe never."

"I can wait."

It was Marianne's turn to take an angry swig of her drink. She took a deep breath, closing her eyes briefly. He pushed his hand through his hair. Whenever relationships were discussed, usually by Sharon who was always contemplating marriage and 'happy ever after' with her latest beau, Paul was firm, he wanted a wife and the standard 2.4 kids. Despite an appalling track record of one-night stands and a few dates with colleagues that went no further. She looked up from her glass, he was staring at her, his brow furrowed, pleading. Something unseen punched her in the stomach.

"You're young, you'll want to marry, have a family. You'd make a great father and I can't give you that, you need to find someone who can."

"No!" He grasped her hand on the table. "I want it with you. The age difference is irrelevant, lots of women have careers and then have children these days."

She gave him a watery smile.

"We could work something out, there are lots of options." He was momentarily hopeful.

"No Paul, not for me there aren't. I couldn't go there. Not now. I'm sorry."

She stood up sharply, but Paul was too far in to back down now.

"If you don't want to have children, we could always adopt."

She dragged her bag onto her shoulder wearily, taking up Monty's lead.

"Paul, I was adopted. My parents were mad about each other, devoted, they couldn't have children so they adopted me, they thought I would make them complete. I didn't. They were already complete." She looked straight through him and turned to go. He stood up to leave with her.

"Stay and finish your drink Paul. I don't want to be with anyone at the moment," she said evenly.

Paul was not ready to give up on Marianne. The conversation in the beer garden had revealed a side to her he had not seen before, a side that was vulnerable, crying out to be loved, nurtured and cared for. The side that George had no doubt seen, and had been determined to nourish and protect, in whatever way he could. Paul did not want a partner from among his peers, silly girls who seemed obsessed with shoes and cupcakes and spraying their skin varying shades of tangerine. Marianne was the woman for him. He had been in love with her since he had first laid eyes on her, he could see her now, trademark spectacles perched on her nose, files piled in her arms, late for his first editorial meeting. He had watched her sit deferentially at the back of the room making notes, listening intently, nodding as ideas were discussed. He had been fascinated, as this slight little thing, with rabid chestnut hair had pulled her legs underneath her, like a pixie. Jack had turned to her.

"Marianne?"

She began, reeling off outline articles, features; ideas for photographs and graphics; reader responses and competitions. Each proposal cleverly ensuring that the editorial ethos of the publication ran parallel with commercial viability. Other contributions appeared ill-thought-out, amateur by comparison.

Jack had looked up from his notes.

"Right, we'll go with this, this and this." He had scratched three of Marianne's ideas on the white board, allocating tasks to the assembled scribes, photographers and designers. Deadlines agreed, they dispersed. Paul leapt from his chair and in a couple of strides was beside her.

"Hi, I'm Paul Osborne, I'm new here."

"I'm Marianne Coltrane, I'm old here." She gave him a grin and a firm handshake.

"Can I buy you a coffee?"

"You can buy me a beer."

It was love at first sip. He was besotted. Paul knew he was in love with her, he also hoped she was very slightly in love with him. After all they had been through together, he was sure given just half a chance, he could tip the balance.

His plan of attack for the following Sunday had been derailed. Sharon had given birth to a lovely baby girl since he was last at his desk and, in true Sharon style, had invited the world and his wife to the christening, including the three suspected fathers of the child, all very Mamma Mia. Sharon came from a large East End family, so the baby had to have a proper knees-up of a do. The christening had been a huge success and everyone had staggered home, bursting with cake and booze and humming *Knees Up Mother Brown.*

Marianne, having drunk a lot of champagne, made the stairs with surprising agility and removing her funky tweed suit, what remained of her makeup and her underwear, quickly disappeared beneath the enticing folds of her duvet. She closed an eye, which sent her giddy, so decided to read a couple of pages of her book, hoping that concentrating the mind might stop the room from spinning. Paul had been more circumspect and, having paid the taxi driver, went into the kitchen to let Monty out and pour a nightcap for himself and his slightly intoxicated landlady. Her bedroom door was ajar. He pushed it open and stood in silhouette, the landing light behind him in the doorway. She looked up from her book. He was not in the room, yet filled it, every inch the Viking, his hair like a wild halo, his eyes intense under lowered lids. The air hung heavy between them. He held a glass in each hand.

"A nightcap?"

Marianne could feel her heart start to pound.

"Lovely." She put the book down.

He walked slowly towards her, placing the glass with a chink on the bedside table.

"Thank you," she whispered, holding his gaze, unable to tear her eyes away. He looked brooding and determined. She shivered, despite the warmth of the room.

"Anything else required?" he asked. She could see he was aroused and felt her body responding, "Anything at all?"

She sat up, pulling the duvet around her nakedness.

"No thank you. That's lovely…"

He threw her a look that made her skin tingle and walked back to the doorway. He turned to face her.

"Are you absolutely sure?" He dropped each word carefully, leaving space between them.

Marianne's head was really spinning now, she could feel a rash of emotion burning across her chest. She closed the book, placed it on the table and, counting to ten, in one movement flung the quilt back, slid out of bed taking three bold strides to where he stood. His eyes were all over her, taking in the still red-raw gashes on her shoulders, her full breasts, the white scar across her belly. His hand was on the door handle. She took a deep breath, she could smell him, heat and sex. She placed her hand on his, and then determinedly removed it finger by finger, to push him gently out onto the landing, closing the door quietly and firmly between them.

"Quite sure, thank you Paul," she said as soberly as she could. She pressed her body against the closed door. He did not try the handle again, he made no plea or protest. She heard him walk slowly back to his room. She clamped her nose and mouth with her hands. She shuddered, stifling a sob of sheer, physical longing.

'No, it would be wrong, so wrong,' she tried to convince herself, climbing back into bed and wrapping the duvet around herself like a cocoon.

Autumn seeped on, oozing greyness, turning cold and

wet and murky taupe. No bronze sunsets streaked with ribbons of molten gold, no backlit iridescent blue skies tinged with purple. Grey to dark grey, to black. Winter loomed gloomily, threatening to swamp them all in a damp, pewter pit. The last of the leaves swashed against the back door, the porch smelled of decay. Number seventy four Oakwood Avenue was desolate.

Marianne and Paul remained outwardly friendly. He was in charge of housekeeping and sustenance. She was responsible for lively office gossip, reports of Jack's dourness and Sharon's madcap parenting. Despite the veneer, Monty went off his food, touted a dry nose and took to gazing into the distance for long periods of time, ears pressed against his skull. Marianne took him to the vet. A charming man with a Northern Ireland accent and runny eyes, he smiled kindly, he had known George well and in fact, had found Monty for George to give to Marianne. Monty co-operated with a full examination, which was unusual in itself.

"Has anything changed, his routine, his food? Have you moved his bed? Cut down his exercise? Taken something away?" Marianne shook her head. Monty looked pleadingly at the vet.

"He seems, well almost, depressed."

"Really?" Marianne scratched behind his ears, his tail thumped once, listlessly.

The vet took some blood for tests and suggested grilled chicken and scrambled egg, fresh air and maybe a change of scene. It was a recommendation he hoped they would both consider. She bundled Monty into her arms, his snout poked out from the tartan rug, she kissed it and he closed his eyes. The vet touched her shoulder as she left.

Carrying Monty in through the back door, Marianne was surprised to find the kitchen untidy, food wrappers, dishes and empty wine bottles littered the surfaces. She heard muffled voices, laughter. She put Monty down and went into the hall, straining to listen up the stairs. Monty was out of his rug in a flash, yapping as he took the stairs at a gallop. A door opened on the landing. She withdrew, closing the kitchen door behind her. Flustered, she started to clear up. Paul tumbled into the room. He pulled his t-shirt down at the back with one hand and tried to smooth his hair with the other.

"Hi ya, okay?" He was flushed, breathless.

"Tests. Nothing obvious."

"What?"

"Monty, remember, vet."

"Oh, yeah, good, er Marianne."

A blonde head appeared behind him.

"Hello," it beamed.

Lovely smile. Marianne blinked.

"And you are?"

"Sorry, Cheryl. Cheryl Ward," the smiling face extended its hand, "nice to meet you. I've heard so much."

"Indeed? Wish I could say the same."

The girl removed her hand from mid-air where Marianne had left it.

"I met Cheryl in hospital."

Marianne resumed wiping the counter top.

"Were you in the attack?" She thought she would have remembered such a fresh, angelic face.

"No, I'm a nurse."

"Ward Sister, Ward," offered Paul, trying to make a joke of the girl's name, Marianne looked straight through him.

"I'm just taking Monty for a walk, we could do with the air. Help yourselves to anything you like." She looked them both up and down.

It was dark when she returned. The kitchen was spotless, the washing machine on. Cheryl had gone. Paul offered her a drink. She declined, angry at Paul, furious at herself.

"She seemed nice."

"I wanted to tell you."

"Is it serious then?" She examined her fingernails.

"I think so."

"Good. I'm pleased for you, pleased for you both."

"Marianne…"

"Hey, we're friends. We've always been friends, always will be. Nothing's changed."

But everything had.

Jack Buchannan did not take the news at all well. Isabelle berated him for his selfishness. He ignored her, pouring his guest a whiskey and himself vodka. He had been told to cut down on the gin. Grouchy and discommoded, he joined them at the table. Marianne pleated her napkin. Catching Isabelle's eye, she shrugged.

"You have to let me go, Jack."

He pushed the plate away. It was Isabelle's classic Aberdeen Angus stroganoff. He had barely touched it. In the candlelight he looked more liverish than usual. Isabelle tutted as she took his plate.

"Paul's a bairn. Nay the gift," he said to his placemat.

"I'll be back. I just need some space. A break."

"But six weeks?"

Marianne was entitled. She had been with the company long enough for a career sabbatical, she was permitted to take three months leave in any given twenty-four month period.

"Well, work while you're away. What about a Travelogue? What about a series of retrospective articles about the attack. Aye, while you are away, that would be the time to write it, flashback style, contrast with return to normality. We could syndicate it."

"Maybe."

None of their group had written a single word about their experience on that vengeful night, no interview, no report, no discussion, not even between themselves. They had sewn their bodies back together, plastered over the cracks and returned battered and bruised to their respective lives. Jack was seriously pissed off that not one, but two of his own writers had the inside track on what was a world-shattering event – a bestselling story of carnage and tragedy. Yet there seemed to be this debilitating, unspoken pact and neither of them had written a damn word.

"Well, why not do some follow-ups on the 'babies for sale' scam. You have a few more reunited through the website – there must be stories there?"

"Early days, really."

"You know we're losing money hand over fist, Marie," said Jack; the shortening of her name, a sign of his affection. "More and more regional dailies are becoming weeklies. What about the Bath Chronicle? You know what happened there, a weekly after being published daily since 1760. Sign of the times, blidy internet."

"Progress, change, embrace it, Jack."

He guffawed, deep in his chest.

"Too late f'me but no f'you. You're the bridge between my era and the future. I need someone to hand over to. I thought it was what you wanted?"

She reached across the table and squeezed his clump of a hand. Calloused, tobacco-stained fingers gripped his now empty glass.

"Weren't you told to cut down on the drink?" She asked.

"Were you not told to cut down on your lip?" He replied. They grinned at each other.

Isabelle returned with cheese and fruit. Jack sliced a wedge of crumbly Stilton.

"Our paymasters are highly political. Don't be away any longer, I'm warning ye, lots of bright young things queuing up in the wings, promotions because of connections, not ability."

Marianne nodded. Isabelle sneaked some of the

cheese off Jack's plate.

"Good, that's settled then. Are we looking after Monty, while you are away?" she asked.

"No. Thanks Isabelle, but he's coming with me. He could do with a break too."

Although he had accepted Paul, Monty was still sniffing every man who came to the house, plumber, builder, electrician, in the hope that it might be George, returned. Marianne had decided the vet's advice could apply to them both. She was in the middle of packing when Paul announced his imminent engagement to Cheryl.

"I'll have moved out by the time you get back." He was over-chirpy.

"Take as long as you like, not sure when we'll be back." She gave him a stiff smile, continuing to stuff items of clothing into her bag.

"Congratulations Paul, hope you'll both be very happy..." he mumbled, as he left the room.

She could face neither Sophie's or Sharon's interrogation, so sent a cowardly round-robin text saying she was off to Ireland for an extended break and would be in touch. The new message symbol flashed back immediately from Sophie. Marianne turned the phone off, loaded the car and headed west, shielding her eyes from a watery sunset.

Chapter Six– A Star Is Born

Larry Leeson sipped a latte, pulling idly at a bagel, on a napkin bearing the legend 'Bennie's Wine and Diner, you won't find finer'. He lifted heavy-lidded eyes to the window, gazing at the murky early November swirl of New York, just visible from the nineteenth floor of Faddon Heights. He sighed, picked up a pile of paper and, rising with effort to his feet, unceremoniously dumped the stack in his waste basket which, already over-flowing, collapsed sideways spilling the sheets onto the thick, pile carpet.

He flicked the switch on the intercom.

"Mimi," he barked although, it had to be said Larry was one theatrical agent whose bark really was worse than his bite.

"Hmm, hmmmmm..." came the reply, Mimi was already exasperated by her boss's bad humour and unwillingness to be appeased this morning.

"Did you try Ryan again?"

"Yes, Mr Leeson. I tried Ryan again. I tried all his numbers, and left messages at his west coast beach house; his New York apartment; his girlfriend's apartment and his answering service. I have also left messages on his cell phone, and no Mr Leeson, he has not got back to me."

"Did you say it was urgent?"

"No, did *you* say it was urgent?"

"Of course it's goddamn urgent. Why d'you think

I got you to ring half way around the goddamn world, if it's not goddamn urgent."

Mimi remained quiet while Larry calmed himself. It was a ritual they had established over the years.

"Well, his service said they were under the impression Mr O'Gorman was out of the country at present, but couldn't give me any more information than that."

"Which country?" Larry was really irritated now; with Mimi; with Ryan's answering service, and particularly with Ryan.

"I didn't ask," Mimi offered. Then quietly, "Ms Leeson's just arrived, sir."

"Shit!" said Larry.

"I heard that," responded his sister, striding through the doorway into his office. Lena Leeson was not the door-knocking kind.

"So you haven't managed to track down Boy Wonder then?" she observed, planting her considerably-sized bottom on the edge of his glass and chrome desk.

"Not yet." He smiled, more of a grimace - a vain attempt at brightness.

Lena could see straight through her little brother; it was obvious he was unconvinced the time between now and contacting his errant client was diminishing in anyway, and worse than that, he also seemed to be, well, scared.

"There's something you're not telling me," she sing-songed at him, in her gravelly New York accent. Larry hastily wrapped the remains of the bagel in the

napkin and threw them towards the bin. Lena followed the trajectory.

"Well, what have we here?" The magenta-taloned hands bent to retrieve the discarded script. She flipped the opening pages, raised an eyebrow and slammed the paperwork down on Larry's desk.

"He's not even seen the script?" She was incredulous.

"He doesn't need to. The part's global, it's monolithic. The script mere detail, not important..." He trailed off.

"Not important? Maybe, if he were any normal, hungry, half-talented, not-too-bad looking actor perhaps. But you know Ryan. I know Ryan. He actually thinks things like the script matter, he actually believes acting is an art form; he has some mad cockamamie notion that his work could somehow be cerebral. Gimme-a-break, Larry. We're on the verge of the biggest, single deal in the history of not only Leeson & Leeson, but the whole goddamn Universe and I can tell that you – beloved brother – are scared outta your mind because there is a distinct danger that the stupid, Irish son-of-a-bitch, could actually turn this down. He might, just might, say no."

"Ah, come on Lena." The reply was unconvincing.

She pulled a pack of cigarettes from her latest designer handbag, flipping her solid gold lighter and taking a deep drag of the sweet tobacco. She glared out of the window. This building is strictly no smoking thought Larry dismally, as he played with the heavy gold chain at his throat.

"Mr Rossini has been on, himself, personally, two times. He needs an answer. We need contracts, a schedule. He has two others lined up and I know Steven Saggito has already told half of LA he has the part." She expertly flicked ash into the remains of his latte. "We need that half-baked son of a tinker and we need him now!"

Larry frowned, his stomach churning. Ryan was one of his oldest friends. They had been at drama school together before Larry decided the roar of the crowd was not for him and offered, half-jokingly, to become Ryan's agent instead. They had, by many others' standards, been successful but this was potentially the biggest deal he had ever handled. It could make them, all three of them, very wealthy and without any real need to do anything much for the rest of their lives.

"I am not flying back to Los Angeles unless I can drive straight to Rossini's office with a clutch of papers in my briefcase, ready for the great man and our two bit TV star to sign."

The significance of her presence in his office was portent, she rarely left her Californian masseur, hairdresser or plastic surgeon for longer than a weekend these days. Larry decided to come clean.

"The last time I saw him was a couple of weeks ago. He was stressed out of his mind, really strung out, said he was under pressure...needed a break. He and Angelique have split up, for good this time, said he needed to get his head round stuff, said he needed to go find himself."

Lena dropped the cigarette in his coffee. It hissed, floating to the surface.

"Find himself?" she roared, leaping off the desk with as much velocity as her bulk would allow. The intercom buzzed.

"Mr O'Gorman on line one, long distance," Mimi announced primly.

They both lunged for the phone. Lena was there first.

"Ryan, thank God, Alleluia! Where are you? We need you, come home immediately. I'll send an airplane, helicopter, whatever..."

Silence.

"Ryan!" she yelled.

The line went dead.

Lena threw Larry's office phone, complete with intercom the entire length of the room.

Chapter Seven – Stranger On The Shore

The view forced her eyes wide open. It was surreal, yet so vivid it seeped into her pores as she stared. She could feel the top of her head lifting, like a tin can opening, the lid rising up and the bright fresh air flying in like a flash of lightening; sudden and scorching. It was the most amazing sensation. She breathed deeply, eyes stinging, lips tasting of salt. She felt her shoulders drop and her fists unfurl. Looking upwards, the sky swirled turquoise and sapphire above as the sun, hidden behind a clutch of smoky cloud, streaked the blue with cream plumes. It was like a painting she remembered from the convent, The Ascension of Our Lady into Heaven. Either the artist had come from County Mayo or the Virgin Mary had taken an unrecorded sabbatical to the West of Ireland, just before following her destiny and ascending to heaven. She took another huge breath, and raising her arms screamed, and screamed and screamed. She had not felt this good in years.

Sean Grogan had been poking around with a stick in a pond when he heard the screams. He pulled the battered cap on his baldy head, to the left, to give his one good eye a little more clarity. Gazing upwards at the Christ-like figure on the precipice of the cliff, he sighed. What was it, another bloody American searching for their 'Oirish' roots? A Dubliner who can no longer stand the fact that they pay a fortune for a pint and have to stand in the rain to drink it, just because they fancy a smoke? Or worse still, a local whose holiday home redevelopment plans have been turned down by the council because of their new 'anti-Ponderosa' architectural policy?

Sean shifted in his wellies. If it jumps I'll have to go and investigate, he mused grumpily.

Luckily for him, it did not jump. It dropped its outstretched arms and walked purposefully back to the vehicle parked a little way along from the cliff edge, climbed in and, turning the engine to life, rattled down the track towards him. He splodged out of the pond, to greet the ancient four-wheel drive on the gravely roadway. It stopped with a loud crunching, the window wound down, she bent towards him smiling.

"Grand day."

He looked up. The sky had quickly closed in, grey and threatening.

"T'will change soon enough."

She continued to smile at him.

"Need a lift?" She sounded English. "I'm going to Innishmahon. Do you need a lift?" She spoke loudly and gesticulated, as if he were deaf or simple, or both. Sean tugged the front of his cap, pulled the door open and climbed in. Huge droplets of icy rain splattered the windscreen. Sean leaned over and flicked the wiper switch.

"Thanks." She was still smiling.

He recognised the 4x4, one of the vehicles Padar Quinn laughingly called his fleet, a few battered trucks, kept barely functional to hire to tourists renting holiday cottages on the island. It was well out-of-season for tourists. He allowed himself a brief speculation, giving her a quick once-over. What was she doing on the island off-season? Working? Visiting relatives? He huddled himself backwards into his ageing, tweed jacket, grunting softly.

"I'm here for an out-of-season break," she offered brightly, reading his mind, "I haven't been here since I was a child, used to come with my parents, they loved to study here, marine biology. The Coltranes. Did you know them?"

He rolled his one good eye up to heaven, frowning through the smeary windscreen as they rattled away. The bundle beneath the Tartan picnic rug on the back seat moved and a couple of pointed white ears, sharp black eyes and a soft nose poked out. It sniffed the air with interest.

"That's Monty, I'm Marianne," she said chirpily, to the other bundle in the car. "We're over from England, stopped with relatives in Dublin before heading out early this morning, boat, train and now car. We're here for six glorious weeks, rented one of the Quinn's cottages, looking forward to it, it'll be great."

He made no comment.

The rain battered the windscreen, the vehicle bumped along the track as the mist swirled about them. A few lights ahead in the encroaching twilight twinkled, flickered on and off and then all went dark.

"Crikey, the night comes in suddenly, doesn't it?" She searched the dashboard. He leaned over again and flicked another switch, headlights.

"Especially when there's a power cut." He nodded ahead, the village was in darkness.

"Ah, does that happen often?"

"Once is too often."

They continued the rest of the journey in silence.

With the 4x4 safely parked, Sean pushed open the door of the pub to allow her to enter, grunted a thank you for the lift and disappeared into the dark, leaving her standing in the half-light of a couple of fat church candles burning on the bar. A fire flickered in the hearth. There was a clank of bottles from somewhere below, the cellar door was propped ajar.

"Hello, anyone there?"

A burly, red-headed man emerged smiling, a couple of cases of bottles in his huge hands. She recognised him as the chap she had rented the car from at the petrol station earlier, hardly a petrol station, a couple of pumps and a bit of a shed behind. The whole lot looked as if it were held together with a sign advertising *Mobil Oil* on one end and a *Sweet Afton* poster at the other.

"Ah Miss, a bit of a power failure, would you credit it? And the dark rolled in like the divil. Did you find the pub okay? Sure wouldn't be easy in the pitch black." He worked as he spoke, stacking shelves with bottles, rattling the empty ice bucket. "Sit down and I'll bring you over a nice hot whiskey. Then I'll check with the wife if your cottage is ready. You'll want a wash and brush up before a bite of supper, no doubt. And sure you must be dog-tired, it's not an easy journey from Dublin, whatever the weather, and you've to come from England first..."

He did not seem to require responses to any of his many observations, so with Monty bundled under her arm, Marianne said nothing, taking a seat in an old armchair beside the fire. Padar called for hot water and after about ten minutes of bottle-clanking and fierce pump-polishing the whiskey appeared, as did Padar's wife, bosomy and bustling. She was introduced as Oonagh and once she realised Marianne was on her own, immediately came to sit conspiratorially beside her, scratching Monty's ears with her chunky, country-wife fingers.

"Now, Miss Coltrane..."

"Marianne, please."

"Marianne. I've given you the best cottage. Not the largest, but the nicest 'arse-pect', when the weather allows, and the most comfortable, the bed is a good size and the fire draws well, heating the sitting room in no time. The front garden is well fenced, so the little fella can go out and do his business in safety."

"Thank you, you're very kind."

"Not at all, I'm only sorry for the power failure, an awful business. Thank God the ole cooker is still on bottled gas. I've a lovely beef casserole on the go. Now, when would you like to eat?"

The woman looked intently into Marianne's face.

"God love you, you look done in. A deeper weariness than just the journey, I would say." Oonagh touched her hand briefly. Marianne gave her a quizzical look, but Oonagh did not elucidate. Marianne sipped her whiskey, as Monty lapped milk from a dish Padar had lain before him. Mrs Quinn took control.

"Might I suggest, Miss... Marianne, Padar goes and lights the fire. I'd put the electric blanket on, but with this..." She shrugged, turning her hands skywards. "So I'll give him a couple of hotties for the bed, you have your supper and take a hot whiskey in a flask with you. Padar'll light a few candles above in the cottage and we'll have you settled before you fall off your feet with the tiredness. Sure the weather's set fine for tomorrow and everything looks better in the sunshine."

Monty sniffed the newcomer, he liked the smell of her and her voice was soothing. With his tummy full of warm milk, and a glowing hearth, he nudged Marianne with his nose, slowly wagging his tail, he seemed to urge his mistress to accept all put before her. Marianne nodded.

"Thank you, a good plan," she conceded.

The remainder of the evening was something of a blur. She remembered that Sean Grogan and a couple of men had come in for a few pints as she ate. He had nodded goodnight to her as she left, carrying Monty and her overnight bag. She had shuffled the few, short steps from the pub to the cottage door, noticed that the rain had stopped, and was glad of it. The cottage was warm and the candlelight soft. She remembered finding the bathroom, cleaning her face, pulling off her moleskins and throwing them on the bedpost. She had put Monty and the picnic rug at the foot of the bed, bade him goodnight and then everything went dark, very dark. The dark velvet warmth of a sleep without dreams, or at least dreams which had the decency not to show themselves in the morning. One of the best night's sleep she had in many, many months.

When she woke she did not know where she was, and then remembering, she slithered beneath the covers pulling the duvet over her face to lie completely still. The weeks stretched before her, like a row of precious jewels, linked only by the fact that one followed the other. She had nothing planned, nothing scheduled, no reason for any two days to be the same. There was no-one else to consider, nothing had to be done. For once in her adult life, Marianne Coltrane was not on a deadline and this precious gift of time would be spent in Innishmahon, the little fishing village sitting on the edge of the island bearing the same name. Perhaps the smallest dot on the map, nevertheless Innishmahon rose up out of the sea boldly, staring defiantly across the Atlantic with its sweeping cliffs turned upwards, seeming to snub the vast continent of America that lay across the swathe of ocean. Marianne had always loved the place.

She sat up, contemplating the time laid out before her, six whole weeks, a delicious indulgence. She had only been here one night and was already beginning to unwind. She had never admitted, even to herself, that after all she had been through over the past few months, few years, if she was honest, she desperately needed some space, a bit of peace, time to herself. This six-week break was going to be perfect.

The Hollow Heart

The electricity had returned mysteriously in the night and, standing by the kettle, her gaze crossed the stretch of green at the rear of the cottage. The little lawn led down to the lane and then onto scrub-grass, sand dunes and out to sea; a sea which shimmered purple-blue; white crests of waves, saluting her casually, as she watched. Oonagh had been right about the weather. It had changed overnight and though a stiff breeze greeted her when she opened the stable door of the kitchen to let Monty explore his new territory, the sun had a little heat in it. Pulling on a cardigan, she sat down on the small stone wall, sipping coffee and looking out to sea. It was already a grand day and she had only been awake for an hour.

She looked along the lane leading to the pub and village shop, with its fading name painted gold against midnight blue. It read, Maguire's Purveyors of Game and Quality Victuallers and on the other side it exclaimed, Stout, Whiskey and Quality Provisions; the repetition of quality, obviously an essential element of the marketing strategy. The gate of the neat, cottage garden was a mere dozen steps from the side door of the pub, the front of which swung to the right, curving onto Innishmahon's main street. Nothing had really changed in all the years since she had been there, a few satellite dishes, a couple of properties extended and renovated, but it all looked very much as she remembered from her childhood, familiar and safe.

To her left were two identical cottages, one painted duck egg blue, the other pale pink with rich dark green doors and window frames. The buildings stood shoulder to shoulder, smiling in the sunshine, positioned slightly back from the lane as if in deference to her gateway, proudly leading onto the pathway towards the pub. Both properties were larger than her cottage but neither had windows that faced the dunes and the sea - being built sideways - shunning the view and no doubt the weather. Weathervane, as her cottage was called, had no such qualms about its stunning location, embracing it head-on with a small garden, a terrace and a glorious glass conservatory, all facing seaward to make the most of the spectacular and constantly changing landscape. The little conservatory was a jewel of an embellishment, featuring multi-coloured glass panes; it had obviously been added at a time of great prosperity. Among its treasures: a grandiose Spanish chandelier, a fine Persian rug, a tired but elegant tangerine chaise longue, a Victorian china cabinet bearing a crystal decanter – empty but none the less appealing – and an original 1950s radio, resplendent in its highly polished walnut case. The glass doors at the end of the conservatory opened out and backwards, lying flat against the glass walls, revealing a small terrace of local slate, down to a sweep of lawn, then the fence, the lane and on to dunes and out to sea.

Retrieving Monty from a very interesting sniff around the legs of an ageing cane chair on the terrace, she bundled him under her arm and closed the doors proprietarily behind her.

"Already a grand day," she announced, nuzzling

his damp nose, "we'll unpack, have breakfast and make a bit of a plan."

Monty sat on the bed, chin resting on front paws, giving him the perfect position from which to adopt lookout. The bedroom window was across from the pub and gave an excellent view of comings and goings along the main road of the village. The ceiling in the room was very low; the top of the window was only waist-high on Marianne who was not tall by any stretch of the imagination. She could only see out of the window if she lay down beside him.

She followed his eye line. "You had better check this vantage point regularly, Monty, who knows what could be going on out there, we could easily miss something."

There was a loud creaking as Marianne heaved the suitcase onto the bed. The clasps clicked open as Monty watched her empty the contents she had so lovingly packed only few days before. What was that sound? She was humming. He half- turned so he could keep one ear on the lane and the other on his mistress who, almost merrily, was taking one garment after another out of the bag, shaking it, looking at it like a dear friend she had not seen for some time, then placing it in one of the drawers in the mahogany tallboy or draping it on satin covered clothes hangers, dangling in the lavender-scented wardrobe. Marianne kept coming across Oonagh's thoughtful, feminine touches in the cottage: tissues, bath oil, a doggy placemat and special bowl for Monty, a box of dog biscuits in the cupboard, a large slab of chocolate in the fridge.

As she unpacked, Monty spotted some activity outside. He pricked his ears, but his mistress had started unpacking footwear and this could take a while, as a complete army of shoes marched from the case: dancing shoes, beach shoes, town shoes, country shoes and, finally, boots. Monty moved his tail expectantly across the coverlet when he espied the boots. He had enjoyed many a long and, indeed, winding road with his mistress and these boots were a particularly good omen. She clumped them together in time with her humming.

"These boots were made for walking, and that's just what they'll do. One of these days, these boots are gonna walk all over you." She marched the boots, one in each hand, along the bed to trap his increasingly waggy tail beneath them. He pulled free and swerved expertly round to face her, making a playful, growling noise in the base of his throat.

"Great boots Monty, great boots for walking in. We'll do plenty of walking in these boots these coming weeks, fella me lad, you see if we don't." And then she yelped, dropped the boots with a clunk to the floor and fell on the suitcase. She pulled a plastic carrier bag bearing the logo of her aunt's favourite Dublin butcher aloft, and strewed the contents on top of the bed in a frenzy of excitement.

"Look Monty, oh look, Aunty Peggy's an old dote, she's smuggled a bag of goodies into the case. Look, sausages, a ring of white pudding and a great lump of ham. Fantastic, a feast, we'll think we've died and gone to heaven." She stopped, noticing her navy, Aran jumper oddly rolled at the far end of the bag, stuffed all round with socks and knickers.

"Aha." She lunged at the roll and laughed out loud as she pulled a litre bottle of whiskey from the wrappings. "And Uncle Michael's a bit of an old pet as well," she grinned, "we really have died and gone to heaven." She pulled on the boots and, hauling up her trove, stomped cheerfully downstairs, with Monty hot on her heels.

He had worked since early morning, all day and through the night. The words just seemed to flow. It had been like that ever since he had arrived on the island, the script flying off the pen, filling pages with vibrant pictures, scenes, dialogue. It was so much easier here, nothing to interrupt him, no phone, no email, no need to be in another place. It was such a relief to be somewhere he could not be reached, somewhere he was not known and hardly recognisable anyway, with stubble and greying temples. He had come to work, under his own steam, in his own time, to his own deadline. He needed space - this was perfect - it was all going very well. He played the announcement of his intention to take a sabbatical on Innishmahon, back in his head.

"Totally selfish," she had scoffed, flouncing through the Manhattan apartment, "you tell me you want to break up, and then run away like a frightened animal. Leaving me to deal with the aftermath, the rumours, the press."

"For how long?" His agent had spat, horrified.

His response to both, quietly spoken, "I have to go. I don't know for how long."

As soon as he arrived, he got down to it, working every hour God sent. He breathed life into his characters as they leapt from scene to scene, sword fighting and sweeping up and down staircases with passion and desire. They flaunted their personalities in his face, he smiled at their impudence, relishing their right to be born, live their lives, play out their story. This was art. This was what being creative meant. He worked through the day and night. Going from pen to keyboard and back, sipping cold coffee and warm whiskey, in turn. Then finally lifting his head, he stretched, looking up to see the sky streaked with silver. A new day beckoned. He lay down his pen. This place had taken him to another place entirely.

He read through the sheets, scratched in a few notes, stacked them together and then, pulling on his battered leather jacket, lifted the latch, pushed open the half door of the cottage and strode out.

It was a raw, fresh morning, the smallest hint of heat in the sun. He stood by the water butt, three-quarters full with rain and, taking a deep breath, pushed his head beneath its cold, glittering surface. He gasped, straightened up and shook like a dog, choking slightly.

"Shit that's freezing!" Won't do that again, he thought and, heading towards the coastline, moved quickly, keen to increase blood flow before he started to shiver. He trotted off the tarmac and along the sandy track towards the beach. There was a stiff breeze off the Atlantic. He could just see the ocean. The sun was slicing through slate grey cloud, dappling the cliff that loomed before him. He followed the sandy path as it narrowed and disappeared. If you knew to keep going, it slid through a hidden ravine to reveal a sweep of bay, blond cool sand and a silver shimmering sea, breaking nonchalantly against the shore. He scrambled downwards, loose rocks and stones falling before him. Losing his footing, he tumbled, slid a little way on his backside and, grabbing a tuft of grass, steadied himself. Pulling himself back on his feet, he made his way gingerly to the beach.

Once there, he hit the ground running and, flinging his arms outwards, charged along the sand until he reached the water, and then ran the full length of the shore as fast as he could. Heart pounding, head bursting and lungs aching, he crashed to the ground at the water's edge. A small wave lapped at his feet. The second wave came up to his waist, the third over his head. He started to laugh, spitting sand; he was soaking wet; no point in moving now; he let another wave cover him from head to toe.

Monty was snuffling through the undergrowth, occasionally cocking his leg to make his presence felt. Marianne followed his wagging bottom, until it disappeared and, looking up, she realised she did not have a clue where he had gone. She called him. She could hear yapping in the distance. She shouted again, moving towards what appeared to be a solid face of rock. She spotted a trace of track and, moving quickly, was soon through the hidden ravine and out onto a ledge that looked down to a secret beach. She caught her breath, taking in the horseshoe shaped bay. She had never seen it from the shore, only ever from a boat out to sea when crewing with her parents. The discovery was thrilling, she felt like an adventurer. The sky had brightened, the sand glowed and the water sparkled up at her, beckoning. She could see Monty just beyond a grassy ridge. He was barking downwards, indicating that something required her urgent attention. She moved towards him, he was right on the edge of a sheer drop.

"What is it, boy?" She followed the sharp black eyes and gasped. There was a figure, outstretched, flat on its back at the water's edge; it lay there immobile as the waves rolled over it.

"Oh God, Monty... Is it drowning? Is it dead? Hey, hey..." She started to scramble down, deaf from the pounding in her ears. Monty slipped and slithered ahead, breaking into a gallop as soon as he landed on the beach, scampering towards the prone figure, now embedded in its own sandy imprint.

Ryan's reverie was broken with a different kind of cold and wet. He opened an eye. A shiny black nose nuzzled his. He smiled into the dog's face. The dog rubbed his chin against Ryan's stubble, tail wagging victoriously. Marianne fell to her knees, straddling him.

"Are you okay? Can you speak? What happened?"

Ryan pulled his hand to his mouth, wiping dog and water away.

"I'm fine. Nothing's happened." He struggled to sit up, pushing her weight off him. "Do you mind?" He was annoyed.

She jumped up, shocked.

"Sorry, only it looked like you were in trouble, I thought you were drowning, washed overboard or something." She tried to brush sand and water from her jeans.

He drew himself up to face her. It was his turn to be surprised.

"Well I…wait I know you, don't I? Marianne, isn't it? What on earth are you doing here?" He shook water from his hair.

"Ryan O'Gorman. Well I could ask you the same question." It was her turn to splutter.

"I'm not here to answer questions, I'm here for a break," he snapped.

"Me too, as it happens," she snapped back.

They looked at each other for a long minute, neither one giving ground to the other.

Sean Grogan's one good eye watched the whole scene from the other side of the cliff. He recognised the people on the beach. He already knew who they were; the so-called actor and the woman journalist. There they were, charging around the sand like a pair of young pups, lying down in the freezing water, fully clothed, like they had never seen the sea before in their lives. People do an awful lot of stupid carrying on trying to find themselves, he surmised bleakly. Fecking eejits, losing themselves in the first place.

An hour later they were sitting side by side outside the

pub, a pint of apiece before them, Monty lapping his now expected saucer of milk. Ryan had changed out of his wet clothes, the cottage he was renting almost as close to Maguire's, as Marianne's. He was slightly more rotund then she remembered and the longer hair, streaked with silver, gave him a wild look, enhanced by week-old stubble, fast becoming a beard.

He thought she seemed smaller, thinner and sharper than when he had last seen her; her cheekbones accentuated by the hat pulled down over her ears; mouth taut, skin pale against the stray strands of copper hair. He avoided eye contact. They chose not to speak until they were halfway down their pints. Monty, having finished his milk, sat cautiously between their booted feet.

"What were you doing down there on the beach?" she asked, finally.

"Enjoying myself, didn't think anyone would try to save me from myself."

"Well it looked a bit odd."

"So?"

"Sorry, I didn't mean to interfere. I didn't even know it was you."

"Really, well why are you here?"

"I told you, I'm here for a break too."

"Sure." He sounded unconvinced.

"Small world as they say." She hated an atmosphere.

"Sure is." There was a tinge to his voice.

"Why here?"

"Used to come as a kid."

"Me too."

"Coincidence then?"

She thought for a second.

"My groupie days are long over."

He did not get the joke. She tried again.

"Someone after you?"

"Only my agent."

"Angelique with you?"

"No."

"How is she? I didn't get a chance to see her before I was discharged. She looks fabulous in the recent photographs I've seen of her, you know, in the women's magazines."

"Looks can be deceiving. Ah, to be honest I don't see that much of her." He bit his lip.

They each took a swig of their drinks.

"Anyone with you?" he asked.

"No, just Monty, here."

Monty gave his tail a swing at the mention of his name.

"You working?" Ryan slid her a glance. The penny dropped. He thought she was either a stalker or paparazzi, she did not know which was worse.

"No, taking a break, like I said. Been through quite a bit lately." She wished she had not said that. She finished her pint with a flourish. His gaze stayed fixed ahead.

"See you around then." She was on her feet. Monty followed, looking quickly from one to the other.

"Hopefully not, if this morning's carry on is

anything to go by," he murmured.

"Charming," she said, and strode on to the cottage, annoyed that the chance meeting had brought discord to her previously perfect day.

Once inside Weathervane, she eyed the mobile phone plugged in, and charging, on the dresser in the kitchen. She checked it. No signal. Good. She lifted the receiver of the ancient *Bakelite* telephone in the hall. She listened, nothing, the line was dead. So even if she wanted to, there was no-one she could ring to announce that she had just met a self-obsessed weirdo who, scarily, was staying in the next door cottage. She flicked the kettle on.

"Arrogant tosser! And I thought he was quite nice when he wrote to me in hospital; obviously just PR at the time, probably wrote to everyone. I mean who the hell does he think he is?" she asked Monty, angrily. Monty quickly disappeared under the table, pushing his tail over his eyes, feigning a much needed sleep.

Chapter Eight – Saving Grace

Marianne was determined to put her unpleasant encounter with someone she had previously admired out of her mind. Yes, the island was small but she was sure she could manage to avoid him, and if she did happen to see him, she would be civil and nothing else. If Ryan O'Gorman was arrogant and ignorant enough to imagine she had contrived to be on one of Western Europe's most remote islands, for weeks on end, to report on the behaviour of a barely *C-list* celebrity, well that was his problem. His was not the only soul in need of solace. After the heartbreak of losing George, the injuries and anguish following the bombing, and the stress of trying to maintain a career while nursing Paul, she had more than enough reason to take refuge in this remote and beautiful place. Who the hell did he think he was, suggesting she would go to such lengths to snoop on him? Honestly, the vanity of the man!

If Ryan thought she, a mature professional woman of some standing, had nothing better to do than traipse around the wilds of Ireland in the hope of catching him kissing a colleen, picking his nose or scratching his arse, well the whole idea was so baldly bizarre, it was depressing. Even more depressing that, should such nonsense be published, some poor sad soul somewhere might be remotely bothered to read it. She shuddered with contempt and, letting Monty out into the garden, unwittingly let Oonagh in.

"Hope I'm not disturbing you? Isn't a grand day altogether. Have you settled?" Oonagh filled the kitchen with her turquoise tracksuit, spotted sweatbands and matching trainers. She had the same manner of speaking as her husband Padar; statements and questions mixed and aired, no need for the listener to comment or respond. She leaned against the work surface, exaggerating breathlessness.

"A cup of tea?" Marianne offered, taking the hint.

"I've a terrible thirst on me, right enough," Oonagh's grey eyes swept the room.

"Something longer, fruit juice?"

"Something stronger!" Oonagh rooted around in the bizarre pink backpack she had slung to the floor following her entrance. With a flourish, she produced two bottles, one of very good gin, the other a slimline tonic, and a small parcel of tin foil, which she peeled back to reveal half a lemon, sliced. Marianne, impressed with her new friend's resourcefulness, took a couple of tumblers from the cabinet in the conservatory.

"That's what you fitness fanatics keep in those backpacks." She smiled as Oonagh dug ice out of the freezer compartment of the fridge with a bread knife.

"I always enjoy a gin after me power-walking," Oonagh caught Marianne's appraising look; she would have been described as comely, in another era.

"Ach, you should have seen me before I started on the fitness programme. I was huge, the size of a house. I've lost three stone and two to go."

The Hollow Heart

They took their drinks out to the little terrace. The
sun was streaked with iridescent afternoon clouds and the
sliver of sea glinted lazily; it was pleasantly warm in the
shelter of the cottage wall. The women sat side by side in
ancient cane chairs, and chinked glasses.

"Have you heard the news?" Oonagh downed half
her drink in one. "The famous film star staying in May
cottage, here, incognito, secretly working on a project,
you know, in secret. What do you think about that then?"
She finished her drink and grinned rosy-cheeked at her
companion.

"We've met."

Oonagh took a double take.

"No... Ah, I'm raging, I wanted to introduce you.
You know, see if you could catch him off-guard, find out
a bit of goss. You know, reveal the real story. Where did
you see him? In the pub?"

"We've met before."

Oonagh plonked her now empty tumbler on the
wall.

"You're joking me? Are you serious?" Pause. "Is
this a clandestine rendezvous, I'm not supposed to be
party to?"

Marianne held her hands up.

"God, no... No way."

Oonagh's eyes narrowed.

"Pure coincidence, we met once through work,
then here, by accident on the beach. We had a pint
together, that's all. Can't say I even like him much."

Oonagh moved back into the kitchen to make

136

more drinks, returning with replenished glasses, she sat conspiratorially close to Marianne.

"You're not really interested in his story then?"

"No, I'm not."

"But you're a journalist."

"Ex-journalist at the moment, I'm on sabbatical." Oonagh shrugged.

"So you're not interested."

"Not remotely."

"Ah, well so," Oonagh eased her comeliness back into her chair. They chinked again. "He's fierce good-looking though."

"He seems to think he is, anyway."

"I wouldn't mind him giving my peat briquettes a bang of the poker of a cold winter's evening, let me tell you."

"Oonagh Quinn, you brazen hussy, it must be the drink," howled Marianne.

"Ha, Padar says I'm worse without it." And they giggled like schoolgirls, the sun slipping away behind the clouds, with the gin.

After her third gin and tonic and a hastily prepared white pudding sandwich to soak up the alcohol and absorb the slurring, Oonagh made Marianne promise she would come to 'the session' planned for Maguire's the following evening.

"Of course, I'd love to," Marianne guided her along the path. Oonagh swayed a bit. "Are you on duty this evening?"

"I'll be grand, I'll have a little lie down first, sure

Padar won't even notice I've been gone." She smiled crookedly, slinging the luminous rucksack over her shoulder.

Friday morning arrived grey and mizzly. Marianne made porridge in the microwave, sprinkled it with brown sugar and, dividing it equally, poured half over Monty's dog food. He was particularly fond of the glutinous topping, on his savoury meat breakfast. She pulled on a padded gilet, then a waterproof, counting five layers in all.

"Should be enough," she assured Monty's quizzical look. He stuck his nose out of the half door and sniffed, bad weather was coming in, it would be down for the day. His glistening eyes glanced back at her. She had pulled the serious boots on.

"Let's go." She tugged the door behind them. She had one hell of a hangover to dispel and could not blame Oonagh. Marianne and gin had never been a good mix. A punishing walk, fresh air, wind, sea spray, whatever the elements could throw at her would be the perfect antidote, de-fuzzing the brain, cleansing the lungs and purging the body. Marianne grabbed a bottle of mineral water as they left. They turned right at the gate, passed the pub, crossed the road, taking the pathway worn by holidaymakers, towards the beach, then slipped through the crevice between the cliffs. Making their way downwards, they followed the track, towards the crescent beach, swirling beneath them, a grey and white mass of spray and froth. The wind and rain intensified. Monty charged towards the shoreline, wagging his tail, yapping at the waves, the biggest they had seen since they arrived. Marianne stood for a minute, taking a couple of deep breaths. Then, shaking her head to dislodge the cotton wool, strode off along the sand, calling Monty to follow, who seemed glad of the command, the surf being too violent for even his dogged valour.

They walked beyond the beach, heading upwards over rocky shale, following a path which faded the further they climbed. The wind was coming straight off the sea and the rain hit them in sharp bursts. Marianne was finding it hard going, her calves ached. The trail turned to craggy rock and as the mist thickened, she could just make out a ridge line, probably twenty or thirty feet above. She hoped it led to the coast road. Looking down, she was surprised to see how far they had climbed, the swirl of sand below had all but disappeared from view. Out to sea, the greyness that was sky and ocean was broken only by the white surf, crashing angrily against itself. The force of the wind flattened her against the rock. She began feeling her way along the cliff face. Trying to wipe her eyes, her fingers were numb; the small of her back felt like a slab of ice - five layers were nothing against this chilling damp. She stopped, clamping her arms against herself for warmth, then taking a huge gulp of air, turned to make the trek upwards to the ridge in one attempt, fearing if she stopped again, she would be blown clean off the rocks. She stumbled, losing her grip, then righted herself against the force of the wind. Monty followed, skilfully picking his own route, stopping every few steps to sniff upwards and move steadily on.

Then, above the howling wind, they heard an ear-piercing screech, flapping and a dull thud. An injured gull landed on a ledge, about ten feet away, it squawked and tried to move its wings. Monty, his ears pricked, started sideways to investigate.

Marianne called out.

"No, Monty, leave."

He could not to hear her and carried on.

"Monty, *no*, here."

Her words were carried away on a squall. Monty jumped down to where the dying bird lay. He sniffed it. It flapped. He jumped back startled, the impact forcing a crack in the ledge, the spot where the bird had lain, fell away. Monty froze. He turned to climb back but more of the ledge crumbled, falling into the sea. He inched away trembling, perched on a tiny shelf of sandy shale jutting out from the cliff. Marianne stared down, terrified. Monty looked up at her. She heard him whimper above the gale. She held onto the rock, stretching down her fingers towards him but he was too far away. He stepped gingerly towards her hand. More of the ledge fell away. They both looked down into the grey swirl of rocks below.

"Don't!" She screamed. "Monty stay! Stay Monty!"

She felt the panic rise in her throat. She looked desperately up towards the ridge.

"Help! Help!" she roared, at what, she did not know. She shouted again, moving upwards, something in the back of her mind, hoping against hope that the ridge led to the coast road and there just might be someone up there, someone mad or stupid enough to be out on a day like this.

"Monty, stay!" she repeated firmly, to the sodden little mass of fur, petrified on the ledge. Fearful trusting eyes looked back at her. Her heart plummeted. She scrabbled feverishly, tearing her fingers as she hauled herself towards the ridge. She dragged herself upwards, the wind beating her back until she finally reached the top of the escarpment and cried out with joy. It was a road, a beautiful new but very empty road. She looked one way, then the other.

"Oh God," she prayed, "please, God." The greyness stretched across the tarmac like a cloak. And then a glimmer, a light, headlights.

"Oh thank you, God, thank you." An elderly 4x4 rumbled into view, one of Padar Quinn's. She jumped up and down, waving her arms. "Stop! Stop!"

The vehicle screeched to a halt, the window wound down.

"Oh thank you, thank you." She clung to the door.

"I'm hardly going to drive by and ignore anyone on the road on a day like this, am I?" The man grunted. Marianne's face was snow white; oh no, not him, she thought.

"Please help me. My dog, he's stuck on the cliff, on a ledge…"

He was out of the door in an instant.

"Where? Show me," he shouted over the wind, following her as she ran towards the ridge and cliff face.

He looked down.

"Shit!" He started to climb towards the trembling animal, far below. "Okay, I'm coming little fella. It's okay."

Marianne followed him.

"Stay up there, on solid ground," he commanded. "Have you rope, string, anything?" She fumbled in her pockets; she found one of Monty's retractable leads.

"Wrap it round your wrist and pass the end to me." He wrapped the other end around his own wrist and continued downwards. He had reached the same level as Monty, when a squall hit. He slipped and crashed against the cliff. Rocks fell away below. The slip and tug on the leash pulled Marianne over, smashing her back on the ground. She stifled a scream and, grabbing a branch, scrabbled to her feet. Holding her breath, she sat down next to a jut of rock. She wrapped her arms around it; the lead was taut off her wrist, all the anchorage she could offer. She started repeating Hail Marys, as she watched him inch towards the terrified canine.

"Good boy, good boy. Steady now." His voice was calm. He reached towards the dog. A blast of wind and rain hit them sideways on. The animal was lifted off its paws into the air. In the same instant the man reached out and grabbed the dog by the scruff, as the ledge he had been clinging to, disintegrated. With one almighty surge, he hurled the dog upwards, throwing him like a cricket ball back towards her. She heard the crack and crumble of the ledge as a mass of fur flew by her head. The lead went slack. She gasped. There was a thud, a yelp and then a scuffle as Monty trotted over to her, tail wagging furiously, nuzzling her, in joyful recognition. The lead loosened off her right wrist. She pulled herself up and staggered to the cliff edge. A hand appeared. She lunged at it and with one almighty yank, hauled him up. He lay still and flat on the ground for a couple of minutes. Monty sniffed him and wriggled his whole body as he wagged his tail in relief. Marianne dropped down beside them and promptly burst into tears.

"Thank you, thank you. How can I ever thank you?" she asked, pulling Monty into her arms.

He lifted his head, his hair matted with rain and sweat. He stood up and, grabbing the collar of her jacket, hoicked her to her feet in one swift movement. He held her off the ground, her nose touching his, his slate blue eyes glittering, boring into her for all their coolness. He smelt of sea and musk, she felt a sudden urge to kiss him. She could almost taste the salt on his lips. He scanned her face, the sweep of his eyelashes branded her skin as his gaze rested on her mouth. Beneath the dampness, she felt a burning in her chest. She closed her eyes. Kiss me, please kiss me, she begged silently, leaning towards him.

He let go of her jacket abruptly, dropping her like a stone to the ground.

"Ouch!" She landed unceremoniously on her arse.

"Are you a complete moron? We could all have been killed," he barked, "this is the west of Ireland, not West Hampstead, for goodness sake. For someone supposed to be vaguely intelligent, what on earth are you doing out climbing cliffs on a day like this?"

And with that he strode off towards the car, leaving her there in the rain. She struggled to her feet and, lifting Monty, tucked him safely inside her jacket, then pulling a sour face at Ryan's back, followed and climbed into the vehicle. She felt relieved and pissed off at the same time. She should be grateful. She was grateful but he was still an arrogant tosser. She could not believe she had wanted to kiss him, surely it was just the emotion of the moment? She certainly did not fancy him, not one bit. Then she felt guilty, he had taken a huge risk and she had put them all in a very dangerous situation. Ryan O'Gorman, her saviour yet again. She contritely considered his heroism as they rattled down the road towards the village.

"I really am very grateful," she said in a small voice.

"And I really am very wet and very cold, so you two must be nearing hyperthermia. You stupid woman, what possessed you?" He poked his words at her, snarling as he crashed through the gears. He was probably the rudest and the bravest man she had ever met.

Arsehole, she thought, staring blankly at the windscreen. They drove the rest of the way in silence.

When they reached Weathervane Cottage he surprised her by gallantly jumping out of the car to run round and open the door for her. Tucking a shivering Monty even further beneath her jacket, she found her voice.

"I really don't know how to thank you."

"You can buy me a pint later." He nodded towards

Maguire's.

"I'd be glad to." She said, quietly.

"Sure you're both okay?" He seemed kinder now. She nodded and he was gone.

She flung herself through the door. Putting Monty down, she ran, still trembling, to the bathroom to draw a bath, as her heart rate gradually returned to normal. Both bathed and dry, she heated soup and, dunking brown bread in the creamy vegetables, fed it slowly to Monty. He licked it elegantly off his whiskers, his gentility making her smile. She scratched the space between his ears with shredded fingernails and when he had finished eating, bundled him in her arms, taking him upstairs, breathing in his clean, freshly-washed smell.

"I very nearly lost you today, you monster. What would I have done then?" She held him at arm's length, laughing at the little white ball, soft, bright eyes and huge pointed ears. He turned his head endearingly, giving her his quizzical, 'what's up?' look.

"You little scrap." She smiled. "You lovely little scrap."

She wrapped him in her arms, rocking him gently and, without noticing, she started to sob softly. As she wept, her sobs grew louder and longer, coming from somewhere buried deep inside, her weeping became a mournful howl, the desolate wail of bereavement she had never allowed herself to release. The cottage filled with the hollow sound of loss. Weeping and rocking, rocking and weeping, gradually her mourning grew quieter, the rocking stopped, until her sobbing subsided and the bleak

145

tears had dried on her skin. Monty did not stir from her arms throughout. At last she slept, another dark and dreamless sleep in the big warm bed and when she woke, a couple of hours later, everything had changed. She felt calm, still and a deeper, stronger feeling that whatever the danger had been, it had passed, and a lot more besides.

Chapter Nine – A Hooley In Maguire's

The heat of bodies and smell of burning peat greeted her as she pushed through the door of the Lounge Bar of Maguire's. The aroma of alcohol combined with the faint whiff of excitement blended pleasantly in welcome. Oonagh spotted her first. She beckoned, chubby arms jangling with bangles, smiling through tangerine lips, painted to match her satin blouse.

"What can I get you?" she called across the crowded bar.

"A whiskey and red, please." Marianne had enjoyed whiskey and that unique Irish concoction called Red Lemonade since her student days. She loved this uniquely Irish tipple, although she also included a cube of ice, much to her Aunt Peggy's dismay.

"Sure you're watering it, girl. It'll have been watered enough already in dis establishment," Aunt Peggy would comment loudly, no matter which establishment they happened to be in.

"And mine's a pint." He had slipped in unnoticed.

"Good evening Mr O'Gorman, still a filthy night out there, but you're looking well enough," fluttered Oonagh. He wore faded denim and leather, quite well, Marianne begrudgingly thought. She was in green moleskins and an Aran sweater, in honour of the occasion, a green silk scarf at her throat and emerald studs in her ears; a gift from George.

"That's definitely on me." She smiled at him, a warm, genuine smile. He very nearly smiled back. "He rescued my dog this morning."

"Ah, sure we know all about it," laughed Padar, coming to help Oonagh pull pints, standing them in an enticing row to settle. "You were out alone on Croghan with the storm raging, it can be very dangerous there, even in the sum-ugh." Oonagh had given him a good puck in the ribs but Padar would not be quietened, "Sean told us, he saw it all. He was up on the hill watching."

"Shame he didn't move his arse and come down and help," snapped Oonagh. "Two packets of crisps, was it?" She cooed at another customer, passing Ryan his pint, as Marianne handed over the euro.

"Slainté," she said.

"Cheers." He returned, nodding to a faraway corner. She followed. Oonagh raised an eyebrow at her. Marianne pretended not to notice.

The band was tuning up, an electric fiddle, guitar, accordion and drum kit were cluttered together on the makeshift stage. The bass drum bore the legend, The Finnigan Twins, though it was hard to see any family resemblance between the gathered ensemble. There was the obligatory ruddy, redhead with beard and beer belly; a reed-thin middle-aged man, wearing a pony tail and a bit of a hump, and a young, elfin-faced boy, beneath a flurry of blue-black curls who reminded Marianne of a long ago pop star, Stevie Saffron. Momentarily lost in thought, she remembered when, as a young girl, she had seen a recording of the pop idol on *Top of the Pops*, and as she watched him, feeling for the very first time, the deep, fluttering stirring of teenage lust; the seeping dawn of sexual desire. Delicious.

"That young boy reminds me of Stevie Saffron," Ryan broke into her reverie, nodding at the gaggle of musicians.

"I was thinking just the same."

"Really? You must have been no more than a baby when he was around. I met him once when we were in the band, charming, handsome and a wicked sense of humour."

Marianne smiled. "I'm envious. The older girls at the convent loved his music. He was my first proper crush. I really fancied him."

"Everyone did." He laughed, eyes twinkling, and watching him as he bent to lift his pint, eyelashes so long they shone, Marianne felt again, that long hidden stirring deep inside and gave herself a little inward shake. Enough of that, thank you. She took a sip of her drink and looked back at the members of the band tuning instruments, putting microphones on stands.

The boy was smiling a half-grin at a girl, about his age but taller and fairer. She wore a purple smock over stonewashed jeans; the smock was worn where her bony elbows threatened to break free. Her hair was roped in a plait to the side and threaded with purple ribbon, highlighting the violet of her eyes and the veins in her translucent skin. They were both beautiful and clearly in love. Marianne was not sure whether it was the whiskey or the young couple giving her a warm glow.

"Who are the twins, I wonder?" Ryan asked, as he sipped his pint.

A woman with a perm and a low-cut t-shirt squashed up beside them on the bench.

"Sure, don't you know the Finnigan Twins?" She oiked a finger at the two men. "Sure everyone knows the Finnigans. You're in for a real treat if you've never heard them before."

"Did you never hear of the Finnigans?" a round-faced man chipped in, squeezing in beside her, pint in each hand. "Where've you been? You've never heard of them!" he exclaimed. Ryan blinked. They had both looked straight into his face and neither gave the remotest sign they had any idea who he was, or had ever seen him before in their lives. Ryan looked at Marianne, he seemed surprised not to be recognised. She could not tell whether this pleased him or not.

"I work abroad a lot," he said, hopefully. They looked back blankly.

Marianne smiled. "Oh, the Finnigans, those Finnigans, sure they're great altogether." She laughed, loading the accent and pulling a face at Ryan.

The place fell hush, the first strains of an air started up as the snare beat them in, the accordion and guitar followed and then the boy on the fiddle. The jig started softly, easily and flowed over them with a light, dancing beat. Fingers tapped glasses, toes tipped off the floor and heads nodded in time with the lift and fall of the tune, light and lovely, like a sunlit meadow of wild flowers. The band was tight, they finished as one, and as one, the packed pub erupted, roaring and clapping and calling for more.

"Told you they were good," teased Marianne.

"Wouldn't miss this for the world," Ryan acknowledged, "I was only having the one, but looks like I'm here for the night. Want another one?"

She hesitated. He sat down abruptly.

"I'm sorry, where are my manners?" he said. "I'd be delighted if you'd join me for a drink and we could listen to some more of this fantastic music together."

She flushed, and drained her glass.

"Why not?" She smiled and this time he smiled back and the smile reached his eyes.

The Finnigan Twins, a mismatched bunch comprising unlikely looking twin brothers in their forties, various cousins and friends, and the handsome young couple, were the purveyors of the type of magical gatherings the west of Ireland could still produce at the drop of a hat. Each musician selected pieces highlighting their talent, and the one featuring the boys' feisty interpretation of *Whiskey in the Jar* had the place rocking. The girls' haunting vocal of *Ride On* made the hairs stand up on the back of Marianne's neck, and the audience was so still, only the groaning of the gale, building to a crescendo outside, could be heard along with the youngster's spellbinding voice. The rafters rattled with applause again as, without signal, tables and chairs were pulled from the room, so those who had been jigging in corners and generally straining at the leash, could get up and let rip in whatever style they fancied, for however long the band had the wherewithal to play.

Padar and Oonagh kept the drink flowing and then with the help of Kathleen MacReady, the postmistress and one of Padar's many relatives, they passed around plates of ham and chicken sandwiches, piled high with delicious sticky-skinned sausages.

In what seemed like the blink of an eye, the Finnigan Twins announced the next number had to be the last, nothing to do with licensing laws, Sergeant Brody and Garda O'Riordan were in the audience, but they had played for nearly four hours and there was a hell of a storm kicking up its heels outside. The whole place rose to its feet for *Brown Eyed Girl* and because it would have been churlish not to, they rolled it into *Dark Side of the Street* for the grand finale.

Marianne found herself dancing with Padar, then Garda O'Riordan, who politely introduced himself over the music and enquired if she was enjoying her holiday, and eventually with Ryan, who had been swirled away by Oonagh and a variety of Innishmahon's womenfolk. Ryan danced in a very un-thespian-like manner, he looked more like a scarecrow than an actor, holding his arms out so that they hung and swung at the elbows, nodding his head in time with the music, placing his feet oddly around himself and his partner, in a quirkish clodhopper style. Marianne swished around him, lifting her arms and waving her fingers in a fashion she considered, being at this stage rather intoxicated, engagingly exotic.

"Hah, hah," he guffawed overacting dreadfully, throwing his head back and catching her by the arm, twirling her into his side. "You're trying to seduce me with your womanly wiles, I surmise." He used a mock-dastardly voice, pretending to twist the end of a moustache with his fingers.

"Unhand me, sir. I do declare, I mean no such thing," she flipped back at him in her best Southern-belle drawl and, unfolding herself, nearly fell across a stranded chair. He leaned quickly forward and put his arm around her waist as she stumbled.

"Then let me save you from yourself, Ma'am," he countered, melodramatically.

"You're always saving me." She leaned back as he held her tightly. It was the first time they had looked at each other directly since they had met on that fateful night in London. It was like an electric shock, the tip of her nose started to tingle, she could not tear her eyes away from his. The music stopped and they straightened up, breaking away from each other quickly, not easy, as they were both a little drunk.

"Can I walk you home?" His voice returned to normal.

"All that way? How kind."

The gale nearly blew them both back into the pub as they battled against the wind to the cottage door. Monty pricked his ears; he had been waiting for her return.

"Now, don't ask me in for coffee. I have far too much work to do tomorrow."

"I wasn't going to." She pushed her hands further into the pockets of her jacket. "Good night and thank you. I had a great evening."

"Me too," he said, leaning forward and speaking softly into her hair. "Night, night, Marie." He strode away as best he could against the squall.

She closed the door behind her, leaning against it, smiling. Monty appeared, tail wagging. She slid down the door to the floor to kiss him.

"Oh Monty, I've had the most fabulous night, really fabulous. I've changed my mind, he's gorgeous and he just called me Marie, only people really close to me call me that, as you know, but he just said it as if it was the most natural thing in the world," she slurred, and started crawling up the stairs, humming. This is good, surmised Monty, wisely bringing up the rear, this is happy-pissed, happy-pissed is a good thing. She stood up when she reached the top, missed the last step completely and, losing her balance, went flying. Luckily the door was open and she landed flat on her face on the bed.

Chapter Ten – Stormy Weather

Monty was restless. He had been all night, moving from the rug at the side of the bed, to the chair in the corner and finally to the eiderdown near the footboard, where he could rest his chin and peer out of the bedroom window as dawn broke. The storm had howled and railed against the building unceasingly; roof tiles lifted and thrown to the ground; the gate at the end of the tiny garden ripped off its hinges and Marianne's underwear long since disappeared with the washing line, into the dark.

His ears twitched at muffled voices, drowned to murmurs by the wind, the odd shout signalling an instruction. His black eyes flicked from the window to the bundle under the duvet, which had flopped and twisted a few times but had not acknowledged any of the impact of the storm. His mistress had to all intents and purposes, been dead to the world. Monty on the other hand had spent most of the night fretting. He stretched his chin further to watch, beneath the grey swirl of water spiralling off a broken drainpipe, a gaggle of sou'westers and sailing jackets, bent in formation, as the inhabitants sandbagged doorways and portals against the water rising along Innishmahon's main street. An alarm was wailing intermittently, the warning light flashing as it outlined feverish activity further along the road towards the Post Office. Everywhere else was in darkness. Monty growled. Someone was banging on the door. He placed his cold wet nose in his mistress's left ear and sniffed loudly. It always had the desired effect.

She groaned. The banging continued. Monty snuffled her hair. She reached out from under the duvet.

"What the..?"

He yapped, nipping sideways to avoid her upwards serve. The banging persisted. She opened an eye.

"If that's in my head, I've had it," she surmised, then twisting to place her feet on the floor, she hoisted herself upright to stagger towards the stairs. Monty led the way, unsure if she would remember where the front door was. It flew open and a bundle in a blue and yellow Musto fell in. Padar emerged from under the hood, his eyes swept over her.

"Don't tell me you've bloody well slept through this lot? The bridge is down. No power and the water's rising. Are you alright? I need to check everyone is okay." The blast of rain that hit her in the face as he burst through the door, brought her round a bit.

"Fine Padar, we're fine. What about everyone else? Anyone injured? Anyone on the bridge?" She struggled to get a grip on the situation.

"Don't know yet. They're trying to sort the power out. In the meantime, Oonagh's got the old stove on the go up at the pub. Soup and sandwiches. The men are bringing anyone down who could get into real trouble if they stayed put. Could you go up and lend a hand?"

"Of course." She took her shoulders back and smoothed down her hair. "Shall I go now?"

"Well it is sort of an emergency." Padar turned to leave.

"Has anyone checked on Ryan? Is he okay?"

"He's out here with us, has been since this thing started to take hold."

She felt wretched. Wretched with a humungous hangover and wretched that she had slept through what seemed to have been a devastating storm, and so far she had been neither use nor ornament to man nor beast. With pounding head, she ran upstairs to dress.

Oonagh was working like a demon. The debris from the previous night's revelry a mere echo of the music and dancing that had rattled the rafters in quite another way. The inside of the public bar was lit with candles and every surface shone. The huge oak door to the private quarters was propped open with a stone flagon on the quarry tiled floor and Oonagh appeared to be stirring soup with one hand and buttering soda bread with the other. She managed a half smile of acknowledgement as the street door opened and a gale force blast of air swirled Marianne through the portal. She pointed the bread knife at a large, metal tea pot.

"Make tea will you, Marie. They'll be here soon enough."

"Was this forecast?" Marianne asked, as she filled the kettle.

"Bad weather was predicted alright, but nothing like this. We've had some storms, but never lost the bridge."

True to her word, Marianne was just setting mugs

and a variety of cups and saucers on the scrubbed table, when the door opened and a steady stream of bleary eyed locals, attired in an array of wet weather gear, overcoats over pyjamas and raincoats over housecoats filed in. They shuffled in wellingtons, stout Sunday shoes and trainers to huddle by the log burner Oonagh was enthusiastically feeding with fuel. Laying down the bizarre assortment of belongings they had quickly gathered: pillows, cushions, a blanket, toothpaste - one elderly gentleman was still clutching a remote control - they stood in a bemused queue while Marianne and Oonagh served them. With a couple of sips of tea and slurps of soup inside them, the murmuring started to become discernible.

"Have they gone as far up as Mrs Molloy yet?" one elderly lady with hair in pins under a rain hat asked.

"God, would be a struggle up to her in this," commented a young woman, with a sleeping infant wrapped in a blanket against her.

"Padar and the film fella were taking the best truck up to see if they can get to her. Sure she's little enough up there, without this," said a frail looking man with a shock of standing-on-end white hair. He nodded at the baby. "Sleep through anything." Marianne looked up from her tea pouring, relieved he had not meant her.

The pub door opened again and a family of six poured in. Joan Redmond and her five children, two girls and three boys, aged between five and nine. The Redmond's had two sets of twins. The nine-year-old boys were each holding a mongrel puppy. The eldest girl, seven-year-old Cicely, had a basket with a cat in it. Both

158

the five-year-olds, Molly and Milly, were sobbing softly.

"What's wrong?" asked Oonagh of the girls; gently feeding them cheese and pickle sandwiches. "Come on now, don't be crying, it'll be alright." She put her spare arm around them.

"But Mammy won't let us bring the ponies," snivelled Molly, "and they'll be swept away and drowned."

Oonagh caught Joan's eye.

"Not at all, sure they'll have gone further up the hill till the storm's over."

"Mammy said you won't let them in the pub." Milly glared.

"Ah sure, ponies hate the pub, it makes them very claustrophobic, no they'll have gone further up the hill, you see."

Joan smiled at her frowning daughters, who seemed to have jointly decided that the big word Oonagh used sounded far worse than being drowned. They sat down and ate their sandwiches in silence.

"How bad is it?" the white-haired man asked Oonagh. She turned the corners of her mouth down, though she had still managed a flash of tangerine lipstick.

"Ah sure, we couldn't know yet," she said. "No electricity anywhere, but Kathleen MacReady has the Gardaí and the Coastguard on the radio, so she's told the mainland anyway."

"Sure they couldn't get across in this. The 'copters couldn't even fly. Where is she?" The man asked.

"Ah, you know well enough she wouldn't leave

her post for the Second Coming! She told Padar she'd a bottle of whiskey and she'd be grand till that ran out. The worrying thing is, if anyone is injured or sick, they'd have to be airlifted out of it."

"What about the Lifeboat?" He asked.

"Too far from us and stretched to capacity along the coastline, I shouldn't wonder." Oonagh said.

"Should never have closed the surgery," grumbled a woman in curlers, "Bloody holiday homes, I ask ya?"

Marianne raised an eyebrow at Oonagh.

"I didn't realise there's no doctor on the island, but I suppose with the bridge that's not too much of an issue?" They were in the kitchen, washing up at the old Belfast sink.

"If we had a bridge," Oonagh said grimly, "Padar always says Innishmahon has a lot in common with seaside towns everywhere, not quite a holiday resort and a barely functioning fishing village. That's why the bridge is so important to us, it makes it easier to get to and away from, for locals and visitors alike. The doctor's surgery was that fine double fronted house, above the main street, you know the one with the big gates." Marianne nodded. It was the grandest property on the island. "Well, three generations of Dr Maguire's lived there. The family originally owned the pub too but Padar's father bought it when he came back from overseas and wanted to settle down. Anyway, the last Dr Maguire was a bachelor who mysteriously left the island without so much as a 'by your leave'. Not long after that, the property was sold to an English stockbroker. I've only seen the stockbroker twice.

It's such a shame, that beautiful house just stands there on its lonely hillock shuttered and closed." Oonagh was gazing wistfully into the washing up bowl.

"So what happens if anyone needs medical attention urgently?" Marianne asked.

"Ah, we're very lucky Phileas and Sinead Porter have the pharmacy attached to the main shop. Phileas is a pharmacist and Sinead's a midwife. I believe they met at medical college, Sinead still works three days a week on the mainland, at the cottage hospital in Newtownard. They moved here from Cork a few years ago. She's lovely, but he can be a bit moody at times. When they've had a row, Sinead comes in on her own for a few glasses of wine, God love her, and her job must be very stressful at times."

"I hope there are enough medical supplies on the island for what we need at the moment." Marianne was folding tea towels.

"We can't do without the bridge, not now," Oonagh said firmly, as they headed back into the pub to see what else they could do for their gaggle of guests.

Marianne was making the third pot of tea when the three men came in, climbing over sandbags in the doorway. Padar pushed the hood of his sailing jacket back. Ryan's baseball cap was sodden and rammed onto his head, but the last man, the tallest, was hatless. His short greying hair sent drips down his forehead and along the sharp line of his nose, bright blue eyes darted around the room as he moved swiftly among them, nodding and smiling reassurance.

"Gregory, a cup of soup?" Oonagh pushed a mug into his hand. He unzipped the top of his jacket to reveal a clerical collar, his badge of office. Oonagh took a step back, it was unusual for Father Gregory to wear it, everyone in Innishmahon knew who he was and his modern, laidback style when performing his priestly duties was like a breath of fresh air after the hell and damnation of the previous incumbent.

"Official business?" Oonagh whispered, concerned.

"Mrs Molloy's in a bad way. Fell down the stairs in the dark. Padar fetched me and Mrs Walsh, while Ryan resuscitated her. Mrs Walsh is with her, but when she first came round she wouldn't have a man near her. She's very distressed, but neither of them should be left for very long. Sinead's on her way, Padar'll take her and see if we can make her comfortable till Miss MacReady has news of the Coastguard."

"She needs the hospital?"

Gregory nodded, relieved it was not the undertaker required at this stage.

Sinead arrived, swathed in waterproofs, a doctor's bag clamped under her arm. She moved quickly among those gathered and once assured no-one needed immediate administration, nodded to Padar and headed for the door. Ryan put his cup down to go with them.

"We should be okay," Padar said.

"No way, what if you get stuck, the road's nearly washed away."

In a flash, Father Gregory was at Ryan's side.

"C'mon, the more the merrier."

Ryan grabbed the basket Oonagh had prepared for Mrs Molloy.

"Good luck," Marianne whispered, as he passed.

He touched her arm. "You okay?"

She smiled, relieved for some reason. "Absolutely fine."

"The little fella?"

"Over there with the rest of the menagerie." She indicated the pile of puppies and children on the floor in the corner, Monty in the midst of them, having the best of times.

"You take care," she told his back, as he left.

Father Gregory turned at the door.

"In the name of the Father, and of the Son and of the Holy Ghost, God bless us all. Amen."

"God Bless, Father. Amen," they murmured back at him, crossing themselves as the makeshift rescue team disappeared.

There was no let up. Even the oldest resident had never seen anything like it. The torrential rain coupled with gale force winds had not eased in nearly twenty-four hours. The roads in and out of Innishmahon were impassable. The new black tar of the European Union funded thoroughfares, awash, as the land alongside, unable to bear the force of the water, broke banks and gave way; rocks, trees and livestock were swept down towards the village, which clung precariously to the sea wall. A section of the new bridge, only two kilometres from the village centre, had cracked and split in the night

163

and crashed, hardly discernible above the howling of the storm, into the bay below. The last non-residents leaving after the session at the pub, had driven over it, barely half an hour ahead of its collapse. It was a miracle no-one had been killed.

Ryan watched as Sinead made Mrs Molloy as comfortable as possible, but diagnosed the old lady had fractured both her hip and collarbone in the fall. How bad the breaks were, was impossible to tell, but the old woman was in excruciating pain, the merest movement, agony. Sinead spoke softly to her, administering a pain killer.

"This will ease things a little, Mrs Molloy. Try not to move." The old woman barely felt the needle. As Sinead withdrew it, she flashed a look at Padar. He nodded. The old lady started to cough, the very act unbearable. She whimpered, pitifully.

"It'll be alright Mrs Molloy, we'll get you to the hospital just as soon as we can," Padar said reassuringly. The woman's eyes pleaded back at him.

"God love her," he said to Ryan, as he closed the bedroom door behind him.

The men set to work. Father Gregory was sloshing about downstairs, passing items of furniture and bric-a-brac up to Ryan on the landing.

"She'll have to be moved; Sinead's concerned pneumonia will set in," Ryan said. Gregory looked up.

"This place won't hold much longer. We all need to get out." As he spoke, there was a loud groan and a beam at the gable end of the cottage eased away from the wall. "Let's go. Now!"

The 4x4 barely made it back down to the village. Two converging waves pushed it off course and at one point it stuck in a landslide of mud, wheels spinning.

"Keep it going, Padar. If it stops we've had it," roared Ryan over the storm. As he and Gregory heaved the vehicle over into a slipstream, it freed the backend and they were away again. The vehicle slid into the pub yard. Ryan and Gregory carried Mrs Molloy inside, while Padar chained the vehicle to the building.

"It could get worse," Padar told Sinead, as she pushed the precious bag of medicine under her coat and made for the sandbagged entrance.

Kathleen MacReady had managed to make contact with the Coastguard about Mrs Molloy. She was sipping out of a bottle of stout up at the bar. It was a trend she had noticed the youngsters favoured with foreign lagers, although lager was not to her liking, she could never miss out on a trend. Her spindly legs clad in laddered black stockings were crossed in wellington boots, a scarlet French beret was flattened on her russet curls. She wore dangling diamante earrings, her Friday earrings. Things must be bad. Today was Saturday.

"We've a bit of break in it coming this afternoon. Not long. The air ambulance will try to get in then. She'd need to be down at the pier though." Miss MacReady addressed Padar. The pier to which she so grandly referred, was a fifty foot stretch of stone and wooden jetty tacked onto the bay at the edge of the village, just beyond where the road turned to a sandy track.

"It'll be under water." Padar glanced out of the window. The water was rising steadily in the yard. The street which had become a stream, was turning into a river. He and Father Gregory had the same thought. Not ten minutes later they were launching the boat into Main Street. Ryan went with Joan Redmond's husband, Paul, to commandeer his, and with three other men, they loaded the sturdy fishing boats with lump hammers and pickaxes.

"What's the plan?" asked Miss MacReady, puffing on a cigarette, despite the ban.

"We reckon if we break a hole in the sea wall to release some of the water coming through the town, we'll at least be able to get down to the jetty with Mrs Molloy."

"And save half the village from following the bridge into the ocean," added Father Gregory.

"You have a couple of hours. Then it's back, maybe worse." Miss MacReady dropped the stub of her cigarette into the beer bottle. It hissed.

"Please Padar, she's only one old woman. You'll all be swept away," Oonagh pleaded. Mrs Molloy groaned in the corner.

"Has to be done," Padar answered. And the men left.

After about an hour and a half, the water which had been rising rapidly in the street, started to subside and drain away. The men had managed to make a hole at a pressure point. The water began to spill through the gap down the cliff face and, as the wind dropped back, the driving rain dissolved into a swirling, damp mist.

"Right, let's go," commanded Sinead, as Marianne

and Oonagh lifted the frail old lady, strapped in a sleeping bag, onto the lightweight stretcher that Phileas had brought down from the pharmacy.

"I'll drive," said Oonagh, unchaining the 4x4. "I understand her temperament." She nodded at the car.

In minutes, they were at the pier; the reassuring whir of the helicopter blades a little way out to sea. The men had moored the boats to the jetty, the waves crashing them against the wall. Oonagh counted, to be sure they were all still there. She blessed herself. The women edged the vehicle as close to the sea wall as they could. The men hauled one of the boats, hanging onto the mooring chain, towards them. The women passed the shrouded parcel across. The old lady was as light as a feather, her only bulk, the sleeping bag. Sinead had dosed her with morphine and although her eyes were open, she was out of it. Padar and Ryan took her into the boat, while Father Gregory and the others began hauling it back down the jetty, the outboard motor struggling against the tide to give any direction or support.

"Alright?" Oonagh called to Padar.

"Nearly there, love." The wind whipped the words back.

They did their best to keep it stable, pushing it as far out into the bay as possible. The women huddled together at the wall, watching the scene as if it were in slow motion.

Then, in what was the briefest of movements, the sea rescue helicopter appeared, hovering hawk-like over the little vessel bouncing in the swell. A member of the crew in high visibility garb descended and the bundle that was Mrs Molloy was quickly strapped to the helicopter's stretcher. With a flick of his hand, she was lifted away. The man followed, and while those below held their breath, there was the merest swoop of acknowledgement, and the aircraft flew back towards the mainland. Even the sea seemed to breathe a sigh of relief, as momentarily, the waves flattened and the wind dropped. The men turned and headed back towards the shore, the threatening sky following close behind.

"We'll chain the boats up in the yard at the pub. There's probably still enough water to float them," Padar called over the wall to Oonagh.

"Will we need them again?"

Padar eyed the sky beneath his hood. She had her answer.

"We'll punt back up the lane," laughed Father Gregory, already making headway, pushing the boat along with the oars.

"Last one back's a poof," challenged Ryan, standing up in the other boat. "Sorry Father."

"Sorry yourself," quipped Gregory. "You're the thespian!"

They raced, as best they could, punting back along the lane towards the village. The women looked at each other.

"Adrenaline or Testosterone, I don't know which?" sighed Sinead, climbing into the vehicle.

Oonagh grimaced as she pulled herself up behind the wheel, her face ashen.

"I'll drive back," Marianne offered, making for the
door.

Oonagh gripped the wheel.

"No sure, I'm grand."

They too, raced all the way back to the pub.

Chapter Eleven – The Yanks Are Coming

The first thing a visitor to Knock Airport will notice, even after the biggest terrorist attack the Western World has ever seen, is its relaxed, gentle intimacy. The sprawling airfield in one of Ireland's most westerly counties is only a few miles from Knock, the tiny village where the Virgin Mary miraculously appeared to a gathering of locals on 21st August 1879.

Passengers, airport personnel and even security staff, of which there are scant few, communicate in a civilised and cheery tone, talking of whence they had come and where they were going. They sit around the bar in the centre of the general lounge, travellers together, chatting and laughing, drinking beer and taking tea. Knock Airport feels like the beginning or the end of a very pleasant adventure, the place has a tangible sense of wonderment, a most unusual atmosphere for an airport, miraculous even and, given its history, perhaps not surprising. Of course, it did not appear that way to everyone.

Larry Leeson strode out of the lavatory marked 'Fir' – Gaelic for man - his fist taut around the handle of his holdall, his eyes smarting as they always did after he had spent more than five minutes on an aircraft. The flight from Shannon to Knock had been particularly harrowing, the little plane had been bumped and buffeted during what the captain said was a welcome lull in a particularly severe weather front.

"A lull?" Larry had asked incredulously of the lone air stewardess, who having served coffee, hastily took her seat and strapped herself in.

Now safely on terra-firma, Larry took an inhaler from the pocket of his Donegal tweed overcoat, bought in a hurry especially for the trip. He had been concerned he would look conspicuous; the collection of cagoules, hoodies and fleeces modelled by his fellow passengers did little to assuage his fears. He returned the inhaler, sniffing to clear his head and, wiping horn-rimmed spectacles on his scarf, squinted at a large, roman-faced clock. Had he gone back in time? He was half expecting to find a horse and cart at the taxi rank.

A blond man, in a blue blazer and spotted handkerchief was leaning against the door of a battered people carrier. He wore jeans and cowboy boots and was seriously underdressed for the weather. On closer inspection, the ensemble had seen better days, frayed cuffs were revealed as he put a roll-up to his lips, trying to shield the lighter from the wind.

"In-is-may-hon?" Larry asked, hoping the man could only speak Gaelic and he would fall at the first hurdle and have to return to the sanctuary of the airport, the next flight to Shannon, and home. The man clipped his cigarette, beamed at Larry and threw open the rear door; in the same movement, slinging Larry's holdall and briefcase into the boot. Larry had no choice but to follow his luggage into the vehicle. The man jumped into the driver's seat and, revving the engine as if it were Formula One, flung the car down the sweeping driveway and out of the airport.

"Where was it, sir?" he barked, fixing Larry with a bloodshot eye through the rear-view mirror. Larry looked blank.

"Is it the Shrine you're after, sir?" The words were spoken very quickly, sliding into each other in a slur.

"The Shrine, sir, is that it? Knock d'ya want?"

Larry realised the driver was asking him where he wanted to go. He was getting the hang of this Gaelic alright, he was sure he had understood a couple of words here and there. Larry fumbled in his inside pocket and pulled out a sheet of notepaper bearing the words: 'From the desk of Lena Leeson.' He could almost hear her adding, 'And don't you forget it." He handed it to the driver, who mercifully slowed down a fraction to read.

"Can you understand?" Larry said very slowly. "Do you know it?"

"I do, sir. It's a good way though, will cost a bit. Is that okay?" Larry did not answer. "Many dollars," said the driver.

"How far?"

"Nearly an hour."

"Okay." Larry gripped the door handle as the car bounced over another pothole.

"Is this the best road?" he asked, after half an hour of torture.

"Well, it sorta is."

"How come?"

172

"It's the only road," replied the driver, swerving to avoid a hefty boulder.

An hour later, Larry was nauseous and no amount of inhaler could ease his discomfort. The windscreen wipers were useless against the driving rain and Larry could not tell if the headlights were on.

"Is it much further?" He had long ago given up any attempt at conversation with the driver, who was listening to what sounded like an interminable and explosive diatribe on the radio. It was in fact, a hurling match commentary.

"Nearly there, sir," quipped the driver, as they veered around a bend, swerved a bit and then, with brakes screeching, came to a shuddering halt before a bank of flashing blue lights, a red-and-white-striped barrier weighted with sandbags, and a couple of police cars parked nose to nose.

"Mother of God!" exclaimed the driver. He leapt from the car, almost into the arms of a large police sergeant who was wearing a high visibility vest and cover on his cap. Larry wound down the window. The wind carried their voices to him.

"Howaya Pa'?" The sergeant greeted his cousin, recognising the taxi immediately.

"Michael. What happened? What's wrong?" asked the driver.

"The bridge is down. Did you not hear it on the radio? Came down last night. Fierce damage. No access, I'm afraid. Innishmahon is out of bounds."

"Lord, God! Anyone hurt?"

"No. Thank God. No-one was on it at the time."

"And across the way? Anyone hurt over there?"

"We don't think so. But the lines are down, and you can never get a signal there unless you're half a mile out to sea or up on the cliffs."

"My sister Kathleen? Any word?"

"Ah, sure leave it to Kathleen MacReady, typical postmistress, she had the radio working in no time and got through to Inspector O'Brien when it was discovered at first light. Sean Grogan was heading across to check his sheep above in the field."

Larry Leeson groaned and sunk lower into the seat. The driver stuck his head through the window and started to explain the situation, spitting softly onto his chin through the gaps left by his missing front teeth. The policeman gently moved him aside.

"I'm sorry sir," he said to Larry. "The bridge is closed. What business have you over there?"

Larry blinked.

"Oh, no business." He sat upright. "Just looking someone up; an old friend."

The Garda eyed the shiny brogues, bought to go with the coat.

"We can't do anything till the storm dies down a bit and we can get the machinery in and inspect the damage. Have you come far, sir?"

"Not really," sighed the exasperated New Yorker.

By miraculous coincidence, Pat the taxi man had another sister close by, who was not a postmistress but a landlady, running a small bed and breakfast establishment.

"It's off-season, so shouldn't be a problem," Pat told him. He punched a number into his mobile. Not ten minutes later, they pulled up outside a small, but elegant, farmhouse, a little way down a drive off the main road. Larry was relieved to see lights on, curtains at windows, and a womanly figure at the door. He heaved himself out of the car. A portly lady with pinned-up hair and stout shoes ushered him in. He caught sight of himself in the hall mirror. He looked the way he felt; grey and shrivelled. The woman shook hands firmly, introducing herself as Joyce MacReady, Patrick's eldest sister.

"Well," she said, matter-of-factly. "It's a terrible business the bridge being down. Hasn't happened since the Emergency, it was blown-up back then. Some say the islanders did it, so if the Germans invaded they couldn't get to them." She looked wistful and then, smiling, tutted for forgetting her manners.

"Forgive me, Mr Leeson." Larry was impressed; she had remembered his name straight off. "Come into the drawing room and let me fetch you a drink and a seat by the fire. You look half-frozen and dead with the tiredness."

She took his coat and led him through a large door off the hall into a stylishly-furnished room. Two sofas faced each other, as a huge turf fire blazed in the grate. A tall, slim man with a boyish air stood admiring an oil painting above the mantle. He wore designer jeans and a pale blue cashmere sweater, his sandy hair was well cut and gelled to lift it from his skull, in the way that was fashionable.

"Mr Leeson, may I introduce my other house guest, Mr Osborne. Only arrived half an hour before you, so you can have a bite of supper together if you wish. Mr Osborne was heading for Innishmahon too. Going to look up an old friend, I believe."

The young man turned and strode easily across the room to greet the American.

"Hi, I'm Paul. Nice to meet you. What a night. Come far?"

"Nah, only New York." Larry managed a weary grin. They shook hands.

"Don't tell me you're looking up an old friend too?" Paul took a large swig of Joyce MacReady's extremely robust gin and tonic.

"Yes, I am." Larry nearly smiled; relieved the other man's accent seemed easier to understand.

"Bet you're ready for one of these then." Paul indicated his drink.

"Yes I am," Larry repeated, twitching his nose. His nasal passages must be clearing, he could smell the peat. The colour was returning to his lips.

"Hope she's worth it," said Paul, raising his glass.

"It's a *he*."

"As you like." Paul smiled without innuendo. This was lost on Larry, who had just taken a huge gulp of the drink Joyce MacReady had prepared and was starting to gag as the neat alcohol hit the back of his throat.

"That'll perk you up a bit," Paul advised.

In less than twenty minutes, Larry was

unconscious, fast asleep on one of the sofas by the fire. Joyce MacReady put a small velvet cushion under his head and tucked an eiderdown around him.

"He'll wake later and find his way to his bed. I'll leave a light on and the door open." She put the guard against the fire.

When she came down the next morning to begin breakfast, the human-shaped heap under the eiderdown in the drawing room had not moved an inch.

Chapter Twelve – Near Disaster

The little community gathered in Maguire's, breathed a communal sigh of relief at the news of Mrs Molloy's airlift and the safe return of the rescue team.

As the second front of the storm moved in, Marianne watched those assembled make themselves comfortable and settle in for the night. She helped cover up the children as they curled together on benches, her heart wrenching as the little ones held up their faces for a goodnight kiss. Some of the men sipped beer as a few of the women chatted over a glass of wine. A card game was in progress in a corner. Joan sang a lullaby to the baby. People were trying to behave as normally as possible, trying to stay calm, trying not to let the terror of the night take hold. Marianne worked alongside Oonagh to feed them; Sinead and Phileas served drinks. They were all dead on their feet but quietly pleased with their efforts, as the storm lashed mercilessly around the building.

"Time to batten down the hatches," Padar announced, as he strode over to let Monty in, before he threw the bolt on the door. Opening it a half inch, a wet nose poked in. "Come in little fella, will ya? That's no night to be out in."

Monty straggled over the sandbags, trotting around ankles, sniffing for his mistress. Ryan spotted him and swept him up; the dog's bright black eyes searching the bar until he found Marianne, piling plates with stew.

He yapped at her.

"Hello monster!" she called. Monty's tail started to wag.

"Me or him?" asked Ryan.

"If the cap fits." She handed Ryan a dish of food. The colour was returning to his cheeks.

"You're turning into a very bad omen, Marianne. Every time we meet it's near-disaster, natural, or otherwise. I bet you're sorry you followed me from Dublin," he said, half-jokingly.

"Come again?"

"In Dublin, I saw you in the pub pretending to read the paper. I didn't think you'd bother tracking me down all the way out here. I mean, what kind of story were you after?"

She laid down the ladle, fearing if she understood what he was intimating, she would club him with it.

"You saw me, in Dublin?"

"Indeed."

"And you think I followed you all the way here for a story?"

"Can't be my charismatic charm can it?"

"No, it bloody well can't. It can be a simple coincidence though. For your information I've been drinking in that pub since I was legally old enough and I always call in when I'm in my home town. You vain, up-your-own-arse, gobshite."

She did not change her tone, or even raise her voice a fraction, but she meant every word, amazed how the vocabulary returned, when riled. He held the plate of food aloft, eyes widening at her in shock.

"I was waiting for my uncle Michael to take me to lunch, which has been his habit every time I return since I left many years ago. So, no, I didn't notice you. The fact that we are both here is, I assure you, pure coincidence and that, 'Mr World Revolves Around Me', is the truth. I came here for a break, not a compound fracture."

She pushed out from behind the bar, flustered and furious, only to stand on Monty, who yelped, making her jump. She accidently elbowed Ryan, upending his plate of stew, which landed on the stone flags, with a clatter.

"Serves you right!" she snapped, turning on her heel to follow a slightly wobbly Oonagh who was heading for the stairs.

Miss MacReady looked from one to the other.

"That told you," she said, good-naturedly.

"Well, I only thought," Ryan offered, "as a journalist, and me being a bit of a celebrity, only…"

Miss MacReady interrupted, "Is that right? You're a celebrity? What did you do, win the Lotto or something?"

Ryan gazed into her shrewd blue eyes, checking if she was teasing. He turned for her to view his stunning profile, then gave her his biggest Hollywood smile.

"I'm an actor."

"Really? I've done quite a bit of drama myself."

"I seem to have upset her." He watched Marianne disappear.

"Yes, I'd say that's a definite. Marianne's a serious journalist, a campaigner, rights wrongs, names the bad guys. Celebrity tittle-tattle's not her style and you did more or less accuse her of stalking you." Miss MacReady ferreted in a packet of crisps. "And of causing any amount of disaster every time you meet," she emptied the dregs of the bag into her mouth, "I didn't hear you say thank you for the food she's been slaving over either. No, I'd say you're well in there, alright."

Ryan glared at the gooey splodge on the floor. He felt how it looked.

Marianne's anger dissipated immediately, when she found Oonagh leaning against the banister, beads of perspiration on her forehead, top lip drawn tight over her teeth.

"Oonagh, what is it?"

Oonagh groaned, clutching her abdomen, as she crumbled slowly downwards to the step, a dark stain spreading from her groin through her jeans.

"Fetch Sinead," she hissed.

In no time, they were in the bathroom. Marianne had pulled off Oonagh's sodden clothes. Sinead had given her smelling salts.

"I'm not sure what we are dealing with here," she told Marianne, under her breath.

Oonagh was crouched on the lavatory, groaning. She doubled up in a spasm of pain.

"Oh no." She reached for Marianne's hand. "I'm losing the baby."

Sinead dampened a facecloth to wipe her forehead.

"Take deep breaths, there's a good girl. Take it steady now."

Oonagh groaned again, then whimpered piteously. Marianne looked across at Sinead over Oonagh's bent head. The midwife frowned.

"Let's clean you up love, and get you into your bed. It's a good night's rest you're needing."

Oonagh lifted her chin, her whole face fallen and hollow.

"Don't tell Padar," she pleaded, looking from one to the other as they helped her up.

"Don't tell Padar what?" asked Padar, in a tight voice from the doorway.

The whir of the bar pumps coming alive was the first sign that electricity had been restored to Innishmahon. A flicker of lights and Maguire's was back in business, saving the fact it was only six thirty on Sunday morning – but that would not be a first either, Padar considered, remembering his father's heyday. The gathered souls began to murmur and stir.

Father Gregory was up first.

"I think it's best we split, go with a household at a time and see what damage has been done and what emergency repairs are needed."

Ryan and the other self-appointed members of the rescue team agreed. Sergeant Brady arrived with a couple of young Gardaí. The Coastguard had brought them, managing to land a dingy and put them ashore. Garda O'Riordan was stationed at the entrance to the now-derelict bridge, but the only vehicle he had turned back, had been Pat MacReady's taxi, with an American in it, dressed like an Englishman in an old film. Kathleen MacReady had the radio back on though, so he had a fair idea of what was happening across on the island.

Pat told his sister Kathleen, the flooding had been even worse in Newtownard. A couple of vehicles had been swept away with people in them. The new roof was ripped off the school only minutes after the children had been evacuated, and the rescue services were stretched to breaking point. A fire officer had been seriously injured when a hotel balcony had given way, and his colleague below had suffered a broken arm. It had been a terrible night.

Garda O'Riordan was sucking a mint, listening intently to Miss MacReady's account of Mrs Molloy's airlift to safety, when the television crew hoved into view.

"Ah, here we go," he informed his listener. "Fecking Kate Adie's arrived."

The news editor was only marginally happy. The report from the edge of the derelict bridge was okay, but it was not what he really wanted. Not edgy enough – he smiled wryly at his own pun – no real drama, and Garda O'Riordan was a lousy interview. He made everything sound like a routine traffic report, not a word of it remotely life-threatening.

The reporter hurried back to the officer, who was opening a fresh pack of mints.

"Any way we can get in among it?" she asked.

"The boss wants it a bit more out there." She pushed a blonde curl behind her ear, gazing at him intently through designer spectacles.

Miss MacReady overheard.

"There's a journalist on the island and a webcam up at the marine research unit," she said. "Will that do him?"

Garda O'Riordan looked from the radio to the reporter; he had no idea what they were talking about.

"I'll check if we can hook-up through the OB unit. Can you line it up?" It was the first time the girl had sounded enthusiastic, but it was all still double Dutch to the Garda.

"I'm the postmistress for God's sake. Isn't communication my job?"

In less than half an hour, Marianne was interviewing Padar about the whole episode, with Ryan on webcam, panning in and out to get the full effect of the dereliction.

"And were there any fatalities, Mr Quinn?"

"No. Thank God. We got Mrs Molloy away, and I believe she's in a stable condition in Newtownard Hospital."

"So, no loss of life then?" Marianne bit her lip.

"We've all been very lucky." Padar looked steely-eyed, straight into camera.

"This is Marianne Coltrane live from Innishmahon."

"And cut!" Ryan could not help himself. He smiled at Marianne who ignored him, now her professional persona was no longer required. They turned to witness a clatter of heels coming down the main street. Miss MacReady was running towards them, stylishly turned out in a tartan kilt, with a large diamante brooch in place of the traditional pin. She wore a matching tam o'shanter, tilted over the left eye, her trench coat flapping wildly, as she raced towards them.

"Excellent, excellent, the producer said that was perfect; it will go out on the lunchtime news and bulletins throughout the day," Miss MacReady said. The producer had relayed his approval via Garda O'Riordan's radio.

Back on the mainland, Paul Osborne and Larry Leeson watched the report with more than cursory interest.

"Well, that's my long lost friend found!" Paul sipped his tea and turned to Larry. "What about yours?"

"Intriguing," said the New Yorker. "If he's not in front of the camera, he's usually behind it."

Paul passed Larry a huge slice of Joyce MacReady's porter cake. They made a pact to leave together for the island as soon as the emergency services would allow. The next day dawned altogether calmer.

Chapter Thirteen – Truth Juice

Innishmahon was battered and bruised from the worst storm it had seen in living memory, yet the next day belied the turmoil, as the sun rose, spreading a golden glow over the eastern cliffs. The Atlantic swirled easily below the headland; the air moist and gentle on the skin. The breeze ruffled Monty's fringe as he snuffled seaweed strewn in the corners of the cottage garden. Marianne stood at the half door, sipping coffee, staring blankly ahead. She could hardly believe she had only been here a week, with the dramatic events of the past few days, she felt as if she had been on the island for months.

He marched through the gap where the gate had stood before the storm swept it away. Monty looked up, swishing his tail in delight. Marianne groaned, pushing her hand through cockatiel bed hair. A confrontation with 'Superman' was the very last thing her strained nerves could stand this morning. He stood before her, smiling crookedly and, taking his hand from behind his back with a flourish, presented her with a seriously 'past its sell by date' cauliflower.

"The only flower I could find." He gave her his very best beam. "Improvisation. A handy skill for an actor."

She unlatched the bottom half of the door, busily avoiding the smile.

"Come in, boy," she called to Monty. Ryan also

accepted the invitation. He seemed to fill the small kitchen. Marianne was irritated and annoyed with herself for still being angry with him. He was an actor after all, an ego the size of an elephant was his stock in trade, the fact that he made stupid assumptions about people was infuriating but he was only an actor, hardly the sharpest knife in the drawer. The other thing that really irritated her, was whenever she was in close proximity with this man, she experienced a strange mixture of anxiety and excitement and, without even trying, he seemed to entice and exasperate her at the same time. She had come to dread meeting him, yet lit up when he smiled at her. Did she like him or loathe him? She really could not decide which. She flicked on the kettle. Then changed her mind and took the remaining half litre of whiskey off the dresser, placing it before him. She put the glasses down with a thud. He raised an eyebrow. It was nine thirty, Monday morning.

"Truth juice," she said, placing her jogging-bottomed bum in the chair opposite. "We'll finish this, or it'll finish us, as my Auntie Peggy used to say." She poured two hefty measures, took a swig and sat back, arms folded. "Let's talk."

And so they talked, starting with the night of the 'Power 2 The People Awards', the night they had met and the world had been blown apart. Marianne told Ryan how she had nursed Paul back to health and very nearly made two major life-changing decisions she now knew would have been disastrous; the first, accepting promotion at the Chronicle and the second, taking Paul as her lover. Thank goodness, she had taken a step back on both counts. Even as she spoke, hearing her own words, she was amazed at how frank she was.

Equally honest, Ryan explained that the 'Power 2 The People' bombing had made him reconsider his life too. He had been moderately successful as an actor, was well connected, had a good lifestyle, but something was missing. He had been horrified when his girlfriend, Angelique, had been seriously injured in the attack, and was pleased to help nurse her back to full recovery, but the whole thing had made him question their relationship. Angelique had always been considered a 'wild one' yet after the bomb blast she had wanted more from the relationship, and Ryan had felt the opposite. He had felt less ready to commit, less sure of his feelings.

"Although I think the world of Angelique, she's a lot younger than me, and what she wants is not necessarily what I want," he said.

"Does she want marriage? A family?" Marianne asked tentatively.

"She says she does, but I'm not so sure she could hack it. Anyway, I have a son, and although Mike was the result of an affair when I was very young, and I wasn't around, we've grown close over the years. We're good friends. I'm getting a bit long in the tooth for babies."

They laughed. Marianne reckoned Ryan was about the same age as George, old enough to know better, young enough to give it a go anyway.

"It was a bit like that with me and Paul. I felt as if

I'd be choosing him at the right time but for the wrong reasons."

"Exactly," Ryan agreed. "And being honest, my career is in the doldrums. I've been doing these TV mini-series for over ten years now. Don't get me wrong, the money's good and the work is regular. But you know, sometimes I catch sight of myself on a late night channel, dressed in a ridiculous outfit, usually a surgeon or a barrister - the roles are interchangeable - spouting some rubbishy script and I think, do you know what Ryan, you look a fucking eejit, sound like one too. I don't want to feel like that about my work anymore, do you get that?" His voice caught in his throat.

"I so do." She squeezed his hand on the table.

He coughed. "Then after the bombing, people kept asking me to write the 'inside story' on the attack that night. Not interested, I said, much to the chagrin of my agent. I mean, there was enough to deal with, without trying to make a fast buck out of all that misery. Did you think that?"

She nodded again.

"They've no idea." He shrugged and drained his glass. "You ever been married, or always the career girl?" he asked, as she refilled their glasses. Marianne took a deep breath.

"Thought I was going to marry someone once, I was very young. It would have been a big mistake." She bit her lip. "I had my career, so it wasn't as if I was hanging around, desperate for a relationship, and then George appeared, out of the blue, just like that and I

189

thought, why not? He was the nicest person ever to come into my life, and he loved me so much, it was just easy to love him right back."

"You're so right, why do all the good ones go first?"

When she looked up from gazing into her glass, she was taken aback to see his face wet with tears.

"So we're here for the same reason?" She drained the last of the bottle into the glasses.

"Yes and no. You see I'm here to write a screenplay, time for a change of direction, time to try and save my arse, I've been living beyond my means for years."

She laughed out loud. She liked this under-achieving, never-quite-made-it, 'don't believe the press release' side of him.

"Tell me more." She smiled.

He flung his jacket to the floor and, as he started to tell her the storyline of the script he was writing, he looked, just briefly, less like the world-weary, jaded TV actor she had first met, despite the tan, bright blue-grey eyes and white movie-star teeth.

"It's my take on the movie business. Our hero is an actor, a good actor but he's trapped in a going-nowhere career – he sold out in the early days, always going for the big bucks and regrets never taking roles that would show him for the actor he is. It's a comedy but it has pathos. The story is where he hits crisis point, he is starring in the most dreadful dross known to man and he can't see a way out. His agent, an ageing alcoholic, has totally lost the plot, so he's getting no help there, when a cranky female photographer – she thinks she should be working for an international fashion magazine, he thinks she's a lesbian – comes on the scene to do a piece. Despite them hating each other at first sight, they eventually fall in love, and realise that that's what's been missing from their lives all along."

"I love it. So what's wrong?"

"The scenes of the film he's starring in, it's a swash-buckling pirate adventure, and although it is a bit tongue-in-cheek, my dialogue sounds dreadful, too trite to be believable. It needs to be a bit naff, but I can't seem to make it real."

"Tricky," she said, taking a pencil from behind her ear. "Printed it out?"

"Yes, as a matter of fact."

"Lead me to it – I'm the best editor on the planet – well the island, anyway."

"Honestly? I love you, adore you, I worship the ground you walk on."

She looked him up and down.

"Trite isn't the word." She grinned at him.

Oonagh Quinn was sitting menus in little silver holders, ready for lunch. Sean Grogan who, immediately after making it known the bridge to the mainland had been destroyed, spent the whole of the storm holed up in his fisherman's cottage on the other side of the bay, was at the bar complaining as usual.

"Where's Padar?" Sean did not like women behind

the bar; their place was in the kitchen or serving food.

"Above, helping Phileas sort out his cellar, they were lucky they got most of the contents of the chemist's upstairs."

"Ah, he does too much. He won't be thanked for it. That Phileas Porter's a tightwad."

Oonagh carried on with her work.

"I believe there'll be terrible trouble trying to get compensation off the insurance companies for flood damage. There's people in England were flooded years ago and are still in mobile homes over there. It's a right rip-off."

Oonagh sighed.

"Sure, you'd know all about it, Sean?"

"Not at all, never paid a penny insurance in me life. I'm no eejit. And look at poor Mrs Molloy, sure she can't come back, she's homeless. She'll get nothing off no-one, God help her."

"She'll not be homeless while there is a community here," Father Gregory called, as he closed the door behind him. "And how are you, Sean? Nice and safe and dry up in your cottage?"

"Indeed, Father," Sean touched his cap at the priest.

"Good man, that's the way." Replied Gregory. Oonagh passed the priest a bottle of his usual tipple.

"We're starting a community restoration fund, Sean. You'll be involved, no doubt."

"Ah, I will Father," Sean grunted, "but I think the Government should pay for a new bridge."

"They didn't pay for it in the first place." Kathleen MacReady swept in. She was referring to the EU funding which had paid for most of the improvements in the area over the past ten years. Sean pursed his lips and averted his gaze. Today's ensemble was a full length gown in peach crushed velvet. She had draped a man's pinstriped jacket over her shoulders. A lace handkerchief flounced out of the breast pocket. Her hair was piled high under a pearl and crystal tiara. She hurried to the bar, hauling herself up onto her usual stool.

"A stout is it?" asked Oonagh.

"Not at all," snapped Miss MacReady. "Tequila Sunrise. I always have cocktails on Mondays, Oonagh, you know that."

Oonagh sighed again, making a complete hash of the orange juice, grenadine and tequila mix. Kathleen MacReady failed to notice as she reached for the glass and drank it greedily back, slave bangles clinking on scrawny arms.

"Well," she announced, when she had finished wiping her mouth with the lace handkerchief, which was in fact, a doily. "The ferry's back on, Tuesdays and Thursdays to begin with, passengers only. No vehicles or livestock, till they reinstate the jetty."

"That'll cost a bit. And what about my sheep for market?" asked Sean.

Miss MacReady sipped her second cocktail.

"There's an emergency fund for the jetty. And Sean, I can't remember the last time you sold a sheep; sure them yokes of yours are only ole pets."

Sean sniffed indignantly.

"There's many would say the bridge would be better left down."

"Ah, good man, Sean." Padar had arrived back. "Always the one flying the flag for progress, moving with the times, keeping up with the rest of the world."

"I've satellite TV, I'll have you know." Sean was put out.

"Yes, and I've a business to run." Padar pushed by down to the cellar. He touched Oonagh on the shoulder as he passed. She patted his hand but kept her gaze lowered. Miss MacReady did not miss much.

"Well I think the Quinns here, deserve a medal. No-one would have survived a minute of the damn storm, beg your pardon, Father, without the pair of them. Here's to you." She lifted her glass and beamed.

Oonagh called to Padar to take over, and left the bar quietly. There did not seem much call for lunch today.

Chapter Fourteen – The Uninvited

Marianne and Monty followed Ryan back to April Cottage after they had finished the whiskey, shaking hands good-naturedly and agreeing they had cleared the air. She sat at the table, reading the script, punctuated with Ryan's embellished set descriptions and occasional enactments, as he made coffee and cooked bacon and eggs. When they had eaten, he flung the plates in the sink, and deciding a breath of fresh air was called for, they headed out to the beach.

The couple on the sand with the little white dog were laughing and animated. Ryan was totally immersed in his storytelling, describing the climax of the tale and the ramifications it had on the main characters. His plot-telling was highly animated, particularly the action scenes of his hero's dreadful movie; a combination of *Pirates of the Caribbean* and *Shrek*. He was sure that once it made it onto the silver screen it would be a smash hit, he only seemed concerned that he might not be able to finish it before he was called back to the day job, and if he dropped it now, would it ever be made? Would he always be chained to his role as a jobbing actor and never make the transition to screenwriter, the career he felt he was destined for? When Marianne confirmed her offer of help, he jumped at it.

"Come on then, I'll buy you a pint in Maguire's and we'll seal the deal."

"One pint." She wagged a finger at him. "And then we start work."

"Okay, okay." He shrugged, and he and Monty ran ahead of her the rest of the way back.

The atmosphere in Maguire's was a strange mixture of relief and despair. Relief that the worst of the storm had passed, and regret at the devastation it had wreaked. The debate whether the resurrection of the bridge was a good or bad thing was to rage far longer than the storm itself, and probably cause as much damage to relationships as the storm had to properties.

Father Gregory was drawing up a plan for the Community Fundraising Initiative on the back of one of the many envelopes Miss MacReady kept about her person.

"We'll need a committee," she informed Marianne and Ryan as they approached.

"Sorry, but we're not here for very long," Marianne replied, referring to herself and Monty. Miss MacReady raised an eyebrow, taking in the threesome. She was pleased the humans seemed to have settled their differences, as she fussed Monty in greeting.

"That's a shame, we could do with a couple like you around here, a bit of gumption goes a long way, and we're going to need shedloads of it." She gave Marianne one of her burning 'do you think you could change your mind?' looks.

"Anything I can do to help while I'm here, count me in," said Ryan, immediately taking a seat in the midst of things.

196

"Oonagh?" Marianne asked. Padar indicated upwards. She told Monty to stay, and left to find the landlady sitting at a window, gazing down at the pub car park, filled with boats of all shapes and sizes, now aground on the shale.

Marianne sat softly beside her.

"How are things?"

"Ah, alright, you know, not too bad."

"Everyone's saying it could have been worse. Don't think it could have for you. You never said anything."

"Ah, it was very early." Oonagh wiped her eyes with the back of her hand.

"Not the first time, though? You seemed to know the signs."

"No, the third. I just don't think I can hold onto a baby, Marie. And it's my fault, I've left it too late." She was referring to age, having ran off to Dublin, as she put it, when Padar proposed to her as a teenager, only to return nearly twenty years later to find him unmarried, still waiting.

"I've been so selfish. It's not fair on him, on either of us. I don't think I can bear to try again."

Marianne put her arms around her and hugged her tightly.

"You will. You will try again and it'll be fine, you'll see. It wasn't right that time, you'll get another chance."

Voices were raised below in the bar.

"It'll be that Sean Grogan giving out again. He's

never happy unless he's moaning."

"Come down and have a drink with myself and Ryan. Just one, then we're off to do some work together this afternoon."

"Is that what they call it now?" teased Oonagh, pushing Marianne ahead of her down the stairs.

Now flooded with sunshine, April Cottage was an absolute tip. Ryan had obviously been holed up like a hermit since his arrival on the island three weeks ago. Empty beer cans, whiskey bottles and dirty crockery littered every surface, a mismatch of shirts and jeans draped across chairs and hung from banisters. A table by the window was strewn with paper, the waste basket overflowing with screwed up pages of rejected script. A laptop lay abandoned on a fireside chair, a glass on top of it. He made no excuse for the mess. He put the bottle of whiskey he had purchased from Maguire's on the mantelpiece, found a couple of relatively clean receptacles, poured them both a drink, and launched straight in.

"Right, the next scene is actually on the set of the movie he's making, *Christophe the Highwayman knows he will be hanged, he has to escape the dungeon of Lord Rothermere, of course he's in love with Rothermere's daughter.* This is where Fliss the photographer starts taking photos and notices Rory, my hero, has his lines written all over the place as a prompt. She starts taking photos of that. Can you see if you can get that thing working? I think it's faulty." Marianne found the charger for the laptop and the machine bleeped to life.

"First things first, you light the fire, I'll clear a space and see where we are up to. Are you putting this on a memory stick?" she said.

"What's a memory stick?"

Marianne gave him a considered look; she had her work cut out. She pushed her spectacles further up her nose and began.

They worked like Trojans straight through the afternoon and evening, writing and rewriting, acting out dialogue, cutting scenes and editing others. They teamed effortlessly, Ryan toasted sandwiches for supper, Marianne made tea and Monty tried to catch the balls of screwed up paper as they were tossed at regular intervals into the basket by the fire.

They started work on the battle scene, which turns into a blazing row between Rory and Fliss.

Monty was fed a tin of tuna, but could hardly eat, he was so distracted by Ryan's dramatic leaps from stairs to sofa.

Dawn broke as they were reading the final act.

"Mean it, for god sake!" Ryan implored.

Marianne repeated the lines, overacting dreadfully.

"Okay, the movie is finished," he said "and it really is the most dreadful load of old tosh. Rory is ready to give it all up and disappear into a bottle of bourbon. He watches the unedited film through his fingers, his hand clamped over his eyes, squirming with embarrassment. The camera cuts to Fliss on set, who is watching Rory and his leading lady in the final scene. She's transfixed. He

199

moves in for the kiss and unconsciously she lifts her mouth to be kissed too. He looks from the screen to the real Fliss, sitting in the movie theatre also watching the unedited film. He knows he wants to kiss her too. The penny drops, she is his leading lady and they have fallen head over heels in love. Realising this is a chance he cannot miss, he sees an embarrassed Fliss making for the exit, and hurdles the seats, flying down the stairs to stop her at the fire exit. Or should it be in front of the screen, so they kiss at the same time as the hero and heroine in the film?"

"God, I hope he gets the girl in the end." Marianne sat down on the floor beside Monty who curled up on her lap, exhausted.

"Who?"

"Rory, obviously, but we need another love interest for Fliss, someone she nearly goes for."

"You're right, we need a twist. It can't be same old, same old."

"That's what the public wants, boys meets girl, boy nearly loses girl, boy gets girl in the end, although we do appeal to everyone with Christophe's handsome sidekick and aide de camp, being precisely that!" She closed the laptop.

"Indeed, nice touch, Miss Coltrane. Let's sleep on it then and see what we come up with later."

Ryan was too late with his final direction. Marianne had left the desk and she and Monty were snuggled together, out for the count in front of the fire's dying embers. He pulled the throw from the sofa and draped it over them, then turning to head upstairs to bed, changed his mind and joined the bundle on the rug. Nestled together in front of the fire, he too was asleep in a second.

Marianne thought she was dreaming, having a nightmare, or both. She opened one eye slowly, there was a commotion; the room was full of people. She could see a smallish man with glasses, in a tweed coat, severely belted around the middle, and a tall, sandy-haired chap in a leather gilet and faded denims. Where was she, in a film? Then, as her eyes focused, she recognised Padar, in his sailing jacket, coughing loudly, as he closed the hall door behind him. She shook her head and attempted to sit up but she was pinned to the floor by a large, hairy arm and the entire body of a white, furry beast still asleep in her left armpit.

"You have visitors," called Padar, through the letterbox as he left.

"Who would call at such an ungodly hour?" asked Ryan tetchily, in her right ear.

"Only your agent." The accent shot through the smoky atmosphere like a laser.

"Heaven help us, is that who I think it is? It can't be; he gets neuralgia, hypothermia and claustrophobia if he takes one step outside his office." Ryan stirred, propping himself up on his elbows.

"And I'm…remember me?" Larry's companion shoved a hand at them. "Paul Osborne. The night of the bombing. I was on your table. Zara's brother."

Ryan used Paul's extended hand as a hoist.

"Of course, Paul, and you're with Larry. Strange bedfellows?"

"I could say the same."

Ryan ignored Paul's observation.

"What brings you guys to this little island off the coast of nowhere, which has been pretty much inaccessible for days?" He scowled at Larry, who was already clearing plates and opening windows.

"Go ahead, guess," Larry called from the kitchen. Ryan hauled Marianne to her feet. Monty, dismayed that guests had arrived without his usual announcement, gave Paul a brief welcome and retreated under an armchair, abashed.

Marianne, regaining her focus, started bombarding Paul with questions, convinced there was a very serious reason he had come all this way to find her.

"What's wrong? Why are you here? Are you okay? Is it Jack? What is it?"

Paul looked vague and seemed more intrigued as to not where he had found her, but with whom.

Larry returned with a tray, having unleashed himself from the constraints of the tweed. He had rolled up his shirt sleeves and perched his spectacles on his head. He pulled a tea towel out from under a cushion with a disgusted flourish as he busily collected abandoned crockery and glassware.

"Okay, spill the beans, big boy." Ryan was nonplussed. Larry ignored him.

"And you are?" He turned a beaming smile on Marianne.

"Forgive me. Marianne Coltrane, my co-writer, editor, known each other forever," Ryan interjected. Larry arched an eyebrow.

"How nice to meet you, Mari-anne." He stretched her name out. "Surprised we haven't met before? Now you, I could fall in love with!" Larry directed this comment at Monty, who tentatively poked his nose out from under the chair. "It might take a little time, but I'm worth the effort, believe me," he told the canine, who at that particular point, remained unconvinced, "Do you have a shower?"

Ryan nodded.

"Then please use it. You two have obviously been working extremely hard but there's no excuse for poor hygiene, surely?" He bustled away. "We need to talk Ryan".

"So do we, Marianne," Paul said quietly.

"Well," said Larry, returning with the vacuum, "let's do supper in the pub later. That charming man said it's only half an inch from the cottage, and we can all catch up properly." And then he somehow managed to scoop up Paul, Marianne and Monty and deposit them outside in the porch. Marianne wrapped her jacket around herself against the wind, nodding goodbye to Ryan, who just shrugged and rolled his eyes. Paul slung his bag over his shoulder as Monty bowled on towards Weathervane.

"Staying long?" Marianne ventured.

"That's entirely up to you."

The Hollow Heart

Chapter Fifteen – Small Worlds

The life-changing announcement that Ryan O'Gorman had landed one of the most iconic roles in movie history was initially greeted with stunned silence. Followed by a sharp intake of breath as Larry, incongruous in striped apron and yellow marigolds, had chosen to impart the news at the precise upsweep of his client's razor.

"Are you serious?" Ryan studied him through the mirror.

"That's why I'm here. Contracts need signing, schedules planning and the press conference, well it's all gotta start rolling, and soon."

Ryan emerged from the steam, wiping soap from his throat with the tea towel Larry was holding.

"Are you sure? No bullshit now, Larry. This isn't a ploy to get me to toe the line, go back to the States and find myself playing an ageing Lothario in one of Lena's God-awful mini-series, is it?" He sat down on the bed, the beginning of a paunch just evident.

"No way, this is the real deal, and as you can imagine, Lena... er, I mean, we've, been going crazy trying to get hold of you. No-one knew where you were, what you were doing. I mean, you've taken off before but never for this long or this far. No message, no nothing."

"I dropped the cell phone in the sea."

"Good work."

"No signal here, anyway. I wrote though."

"Is that the envelope addressed to me sitting on the table under a pile of newspapers in the hallway?" Larry sighed. "Funny, never received it."

"You knew why I had to get away."

"Maybe, but this soul-searching ain't good for a man of your age, it's time to get back on track." Larry gave Ryan's torso a cursory nod. "And you're drinking again."

"Hardly."

Larry started picking clothes off the floor.

"You're an actor, not a writer. Come back with me and be mind-blowingly brilliant at the one thing we know you're good at. Be a writer when we've all made so much money, we won't give a shit what you do!"

"Thanks."

"Don't you dare mess this up, you Irish halfwit. This is what we've all been working towards all these years. Everything's riding on this."

"No pressure then." Ryan started to dress. "How did you find me?"

"Lena got a private eye on the job, didn't take long to find out you took a flight from Dublin to Knock. Of course I made the Innishmahon connection; you always called it 'your spiritual home.'"

"I always told you too much!" Ryan said grumpily.

"Jeez, I hoped you'd be pleased. The package is amazing. The part's global. A minimum three-movie-deal with options, the film will be translated into a zillion languages – it will take you the best part of a year to do the pre-movie and post-movie promotional tour. There won't be any city in any country on the planet where you won't be recognised."

"Exactly!" Ryan combed his hair; he had become accustomed to the greying temples. "How long before I have to make a decision?"

"What's to decide?" Larry was beside himself.

Ryan flashed him a look.

"Okay, okay, I'll see what I can do time-wise, but I have to tell you there's an awful lot of pressure out there and Lena's got her finger in the dam right now. It could blow any minute."

Ryan started gathering sheets of script from around the room, pointedly placing them in a neat pile by the bed.

"Enough! Let's go eat," Larry acquiesced, pulling off the marigolds.

The atmosphere, not five minutes away in Weathervane, was equally tense. Paul was using a game of tug of war with Monty as an excuse to avoid eye contact with Marianne.

Marianne was hoping that her all-engrossing tea-making might give Paul enough time to decide which words to use and in which order to use them. She gave up.

"How did you know where I was?" she asked.

"I remembered your Aunt and Uncle in Dublin. I

rang them, they said Innishmahon."

"You could just have phoned, no need to come all this way." She indicated the ancient telephone on the table in the hallway.

"I needed to see you."

"Obviously."

Silence.

Marianne was saddened. When had things become so strained between them? They took their tea out to the garden. Marianne perched on what was left of the wall. An old pallet stood where the gate had been, to prevent Monty from wandering. Paul surveyed the devastation.

"Of course," he said, "the storm. Wow! Amazing. You were lucky. Everyone was, really."

She looked at him over her cup, raising her eyebrows.

"Well, the thing is, I'm getting married."

"Congratulations, again."

"No, no, that's not what I meant. I meant, well, it changes things."

"Of course." She nodded, encouragingly.

"Well, you know, the wedding, honeymoon, deposit for a house, that kind of thing."

"Paul, what is it? Do you need money? What?"

"No. Well, yes. Well, anyway, I've written a book. It's a series of articles, really, and I've sold it. Well, I'm about to sell it."

"You want me to edit it, is that it?"

"Yes. Well, no, not now. But I wanted you to know." He was turning a box of matches, repeatedly, between finger and thumb, the rattle of the wooden sticks inside the cardboard driving her to distraction.

"What's it about, the book? These articles?"

He pushed the innards of the box too far and the matches spilled over the ground.

"The 'Power 2 The People' Awards, the terrorist attack, the escape, rebuilding lives, you know, that sort of thing."

"Interesting. Well, I suppose your account would be as credible as anyone else's." She folded her arms. "There's been some rubbish written, over-dramatised, sentimental tripe, a lot of it. What perspective?"

"Just personal, my own account."

"I get a mention?"

"Of course, but not much, not lots of detail about you, you wouldn't want that."

"And Ryan, he gets a mention?"

"Well, yes, sort of. Again, not loads."

"Fair enough, is that it then?"

He avoided eye contact. Marianne took the cups into the kitchen.

"I need to shower before we go and eat."

He stood in the doorway.

"Not quite it," he said. "I've been offered a new job. Your job, really."

"Really? Jack never…"

"Jack's off the scene. Sick leave. The new boys have moved in on the top floor. Big changes. I've a letter for you. I believe they've put you on garden leave."

She ignored the pale blue envelope he put on the

table.

"You *believe*? And the series of articles about the bombing? Is that part of your promotion package?"

"Sort of."

"They didn't waste any time."

"The newspaper's losing a lot of money. They're restructuring."

Marianne turned to look at him; she considered aliens had taken over her former colleague.

"Like I said, I need a shower." She left him retrieving the now-useless matches from the sodden grass.

Oonagh had rallied, resplendent in a frilly yellow blouse and peacock blue eye shadow. She was almost as technicolour as Miss MacReady, who wore a scarlet and purple gown; layers of tulle swirling around her knees, and American tan tights, teamed with a sensible pair of brogues, it was a wet old night, after all. The Donegal tweed cap, slapped on the back of her head, matched Larry Leeson's coat, perfectly.

"Perhaps you'd like to make me an offer?" Miss MacReady asked clipping and unclipping huge hoop earrings to her lobe, flirtatiously.

"One you can't refuse?" joked Larry.

"God, who could refuse that accent?" She pushed her empty glass into his hand, as she swished off to the ladies.

The pub was fairly full and there was a buzz to it. Quite a few people had taken the first ferry back to the island that morning to seek out relatives and friends, and to gauge the impact of the storm on the small community. There was a general sense of relief, things could have been a lot worse and, at times, the mood was bordering on celebratory, especially as no loss of human life had been recorded. And yet a tangible air of gloom seemed to hang over one particular table.

"Alright here, are we?" Oonagh could see this was far from the case. Miss MacReady had given Oonagh every detail of the telephone conversation with her sister earlier that day, the sister who owned the bed and breakfast on the mainland and who had in turn recounted Larry and Paul's sojourn at her guesthouse. Oonagh was intrigued. Marianne did the introductions.

"Isn't it great that you all found one another?" said Oonagh. "I mean, you coming all the way from England and America, looking for the other two." She indicated Ryan and Marianne. "And you two here, and didn't know each other were here at all. Even though you knew each other, if you see what I mean?" She served grilled fish and fresh salad. The ferry had brought supplies and the fish had been caught that morning. "Imagine that. What a coincidence?"

"Sure is," Larry agreed, "small world."

"And it's about to get even smaller," Ryan mumbled under his breath.

Marianne surmised his news had been as disturbing as hers.

The conversation during the meal started off innocuously enough. Marianne assured Larry she and Ryan had not planned to meet up on the island, despite how it looked. Ryan quizzed Paul about his book, until he asked why he had come all the way to Innishmahon to effectively tell his boss he was taking her job. Paul was put out.

"Well, that's what it sounds like to me." Ryan had barely touched his food, and was on his fourth glass of wine.

"It's not really Marianne's job," said Paul, "the column needs more of a high profile, celebrity focus. With Jack retired and Marianne on unauthorised sabbatical, the new directors had no choice."

"I think you'll find Jack authorised my sabbatical," Marianne said quietly.

"No Jack, no authority." Paul looked at the table.

"What will you do?" Ryan asked Marianne.

"Not sure. It's probably time for a change anyway." She had not eaten very much either.

"Well, be cautious, Paul, if you have decided to take on the mantle of a celebrity-gossip column reporter, any I have ever known – and I've known a few – were both reviled and adored at the same time," warned Larry, busily piling Ryan's abandoned potatoes onto his plate.

"That's good advice, Paul. You'd have few friends and many enemies." Ryan looked him in the eye.

"But plenty of money," Paul tried to make a joke of it, "I have a supermodel fiancé, who is – how do you say? High maintenance."

Marianne put her glass down. "Not the nurse?"

"Times change," Paul offered.

"Ah, why didn't you say? I know what that's

212

like." Ryan sounded bitter.

"And what of you, and the new role? Fantastic news! You'll be an instant superstar!" said Paul. Larry beamed with pride.

"Yeah, just when I thought I'd missed the boat." Ryan was unenthusiastic.

"I don't know, you rescue us from a bomb attack, save this island from disaster and now you're off to be a superhero – life imitating fiction!"

Ryan leaned across the table and gripped Paul's hand as it held his fork.

"That's all absolute bullshit and you know it. If I ever discover you've written anything so crass, I will find you and rip your heart out, Zara's brother, or not." And releasing his hand, he gave Paul his most dazzling smile. "It's people like you, who make people like me, want to go and live down a hole or, sometimes, even blow our brains out."

Paul was ashen. Marianne squeezed Ryan's hand. She knew he was referring to one of his oldest friends, an acclaimed Shakespearean actor, who, in the 1980s, following a scandal revealing his, up to then, secret homosexuality, had shot himself.

"Hey, don't tar us all with the same brush," Paul said weakly.

Ryan blinked, remembering where he was. He gave the lopsided grin he saved for apologies.

"I think we could all do with an early night," announced Larry.

"Why? When have we got to go back?" Ryan

asked.

"First thing in the morning, the sooner we get this show on the road, the better."

"Oh." Marianne and Ryan said together.

The couple on the beach with the white dog matched each other stride for stride as they strolled along the shoreline. The waves, the final breath of breakers out to sea, merely shushed towards their feet. Monty trotted in the wet sand beside them, nose in the air, studiously ignoring the playful call of the ripples at his paws. He sniffed upwards. The wind was changing.

She viewed Ryan, sideways, the bluish grey of the sea reflected in his eyes, as the breeze lifted the hair from his brow. He was frowning, he was also clean-shaven, freshly showered and smartly turned out. Casually elegant, she would have said, if she were writing a piece. Designer jeans, classic deck shoes, mushroom-coloured nubuck jacket, pale blue chambray shirt, ready for the city, but still a little at sea. His mouth let him down, the lips pulled taut in a thin, purple line, no movie star smile today. He shoved his hands deeper into his pockets. She nudged him hard, knocking him off balance. The purple line collapsed and a smile broke free.

"God, it can't be that bad. It's amazing news really. It means everything, surely?" She poked him. "I'm thrilled for you, I really am, you deserve this success and you'll be great in the role."

He smiled and gave a little shrug.

"It's been one hell of a long apprenticeship and,

don't get me wrong, I know I'll probably never win an *Oscar*, and besides..." he bent down and pointed at the top of his head, "how long do you think I'm going to hold onto my hair?"

She started to laugh. He pointed at his scalp again.

"Come on, how long? Serious question," he was smiling, not a serious question at all.

"I don't know. But can't they do weaves and transplants and all sorts of things these days?"

"They can, but that's just so much bullshit. I hate that about this business, a hairpiece here, a tuck there, and then a complete new body and your own mother wouldn't recognise you."

"Surely you exaggerate?"

"No way, that's why I've agreed a three-year deal, and I'm out. I'll do something else, something where I can be me, just me, how and with whom I want." He stepped forward and wrapped her in his arms. "With the woman of my dreams. The love of my life." He gave her a sideways look.

Marianne turned away, embarrassed. He released her.

"What utter bollocks!" She laughed, the wind whipping her hair and making her jacket flap. She skipped ahead of him. Monty took her cue and joined in the jig. Ryan strolled on.

"It's not the end, you know, the end of our screenplay. In fact, it's even better if I am a world famous movie star, because they'll make the film of my script even if it's shite."

She stopped and faced him.

"You wouldn't want them to make shite. Not with your name on it. It's not shite anyway. I'll make sure of that."

He was laughing now, hands on hips, the surf rising as he laughed out to sea.

"We'll see," he told the ocean.

They walked on towards the opening in the cliff that led to the cove. He put his hand out to shake hers and, as she took it, she leaned forward to kiss him goodbye. She somehow missed his cheek and caught his nose with her front teeth. He jumped back. She dropped his hand. Monty leapt up to lick his fingers. Ryan tried to pat him down with the other hand, caught it in the hood of Marianne's sailing jacket and, tripping over a rock, took them all with him as he fell, hitting the sand with a thud, writhing on the beach, in a pile of smart clothing, old sailing gear and white dog hair.

That weird crowd carrying on again, Sean Grogan thought to himself, from his usual vantage point.

Ryan clambered free and pulled her upright.

"For god's sake woman, there is always some sort of disaster underway when you are around." They brushed sand off each other. "Larry will kill me if I get messed up. The image, you know, smooth and sophisticated from now on."

"I know." She smoothed his hair back. "It is only an image though, remember? Keep it like that, and you'll be fine."

He caught her hand and kissed her wrist.

"Thank you," he said into her skin.

Pat MacReady's taxi pulled into the lay-by above them on the road. The ferry was waiting to leave. The horn sounded and Larry appeared, making hurry-up gestures with his arms. Paul was already in the taxi, he had spent the night in the pub, managing to avoid Marianne, completely.

"I'll call you," said Ryan. "We'll meet up, get the script finished, we can do that, can't we?"

"Of course, love to. Now go, before Larry gives himself a hernia and has to be airlifted to hospital."

"Goodbye, fair maid, until we meet again." He put his fist to his heart, in salute, and strode dramatically away.

"Er, Ryan?" She called after him. He turned. She was pointing at his head.

"Looks like it's starting to go already," she said, patting her crown. His hand flew to his hair.

"Feck!" he said, running towards the car, "no time to lose then. I would have liked longer," he called back, heading towards what looked like a demented dancing earwig in the distance.

"Me too," she shouted, but the wind took her words away.

Monty sat down at her feet and watched him go; Ryan waving through an open window as the car sped away. He busied himself with some seaweed and, finding a stick of driftwood, took it to his mistress for a game of throw and fetch. She lobbed it half-heartedly into the water. He lunged in to fetch it and charged back to her,

217

tail wagging, but she had turned away and was making for home. He dropped the stick and, giving himself a good shake, headed after her. The wind had quickly turned quite bitter.

Chapter Sixteen – Light At The End Of The Tunnel

The period following the storm was a strange time to be cast adrift on the island with its inhabitants. Although still an outsider, Marianne felt her survival of the disaster and the role she played in the rescue operation, had given her some standing in the community. She and Monty were a regular sighting on the beach, in the village, in the pub, and popular with everyone. Well, nearly everyone.

Marianne embraced this new sense of belonging, it filled a hollow, a dull emptiness she had been vaguely aware of since George had died and, was even more acute, since Ryan had left the island. She joined teams of residents helping to dry out the cottages of those less fortunate; she took her rota as one of the Handy Hot Meal Crew, Oonagh's brigade of cooks, preparing wholesome meals for those without a kitchen. She also found herself behind the bar, doing regular afternoon shifts while Padar took a nap and Oonagh prepped the evening menu.

Padar had assumed a daily check-run of all the elderly in the village who had been able to return to their homes. With power still intermittent, he made sure they had paraffin for heaters or peat for the fire to boil a kettle. A few were in a sorry state, but would not hear of taking up residence in the community hall with those whose homes had been destroyed, terrified that if they left again they would never return. Marianne thrived on the busyness, filling every minute of the day supporting the community, then falling each night into an exhausted dreamless sleep with Monty snuggled at her feet.

Padar was unpacking boxes of peanuts when Marianne arrived in for a pint and a chat, having enjoyed a long walk with Monty.

"Peanuts? We haven't had those for a while," she said.

"Thank God supplies are beginning to filter through, but it's a slow business. Small wonder though, with the storm hitting a thirty mile stretch of coastline and so many other towns and villages ravaged, a little community like ours can't be considered a priority," Padar mused. "I don't know how we're going to survive without the bridge."

"I know how we're going to survive. We're going to rebuild that bridge," cried Miss MacReady, as she sailed through the door. "We need publicity to get things done. Sure we'd be easily forgotten, flung all the way out here in the sea."

Miss MacReady and Father Gregory had already had an in-depth discussion about people's pensions. Many of the elderly honoured the age-old Irish tradition of stashing money under the mattress and, with mattresses and slush funds literally washed away, pecuniary considerations were a further worry for his flock.

"You're dead right, Miss MacReady. Sure, our lives have been transformed over the past decade by the new bridge and the upsurge in the tourist trade, we should not be prepared to accept any inertia; we've already managed to attract the attention of national telly, we need to keep the pressure on." Father Gregory was eyeing a clipboard. It all looked very official. Padar and Marianne were intrigued.

Immediately after the storm, their efforts to keep the media interested in the island, paid dividends. Marianne had given a follow-up report via the video-link, ingeniously hooked up by Miss MacReady, and once the danger had subsided, a reporter and cameraman arrived by boat to carry out a series of interviews. With Marianne as acting editor, they made sure the news team focused on areas where the community needed urgent action and, between them, managed to keep the national spotlight well and truly on the villagers' plight.

That very day, the full power supply to Innishmahon was reinstated. The whole town breathed a huge sigh of relief, things were slowly returning to normal. There literally was light at the end of the tunnel. The return of electricity though, only ignited the debate surrounding the reinstatement of the bridge to the mainland. Unconfirmed estimates for the repair of the damage, ranged from ten million to twenty-five million euro. Innishmahon's local councillor, Bryan Crosbie, who had been at his holiday home in the Canaries throughout most of the crisis, realised this was a vote-winning scenario and busied himself with public meetings and local consultations. Miss MacReady was unimpressed, whether he was for or against the rebuilding of the bridge, depended on who he had been speaking to immediately prior to his opinion being sought.

"We need a committee, a campaign," Miss MacReady said to Father Gregory, who was already writing a list of names on his clipboard. Marianne and Monty finished their drinks and slipped quietly away.

"What do you think, Marianne, as an outsider?" Oonagh asked her friend, as she watched her pack her bags to leave the following day. "Bridge or no bridge?" Marianne was shocked by the comment, she did not feel like an outsider, her six week stay had been so full of drama, and she had become so close to people in such a short time, that she felt she belonged.

"I don't think the bridge made Innishmahon any less charming or desirable a place to visit. The twenty-first century will find you anywhere, there's no point in doing a King Canute. Though I can understand people wanting any funding to be spent on other things they consider more important. The storm was a disaster on a grand scale, Oonagh. The sums required are colossal. No Government will have that sort of revenue in reserve, it will have to be borrowed and essentials paid for first. It could take years to re-establish the bridge, even if it were decided that's what's to be done. You might get used to not having it, mightn't want it back."

She watched Oonagh thinking this through.

"No, we'd be too dependent on the weather for the ferries bringing visitors and supplies. If the sea is rough, they don't come. We're too used to having things handy. Mine and Padar's fathers fought long and hard to get that bridge built."

Marianne remembered the picture of the men in their Sunday best, laying the ceremonial foundation stone. It hung in pride of place, over the bar.

"We need the bridge back for business. Padar says the romantic notion of the island community unconnected to the mainland is a load of ole bollocks."

Marianne smiled. Padar had a point, he was at the sharp end and, in today's economic climate, how could Innishmahon survive if it were not a thriving, tourist destination?

"Talking of romance," Oonagh patted the bed beside her for Marianne to sit.

"Any word of himself at all?"

"Who?"

"Ah go and shite, who? You know who. The film star, that's who."

"No." Marianne ignored the offer of a seat and busied herself in the bathroom, throwing creams and lotions into her toilet bag. "Didn't expect to. Don't expect to."

"Really?" Oonagh was incredulous, "Miss him though, don't you?"

No response.

"Sure that's why you've been running around like a thing possessed helping everyone, and doing masses to keep your mind off him and fill the hole he left in your heart."

The chestnut head popped back into the bedroom, she flashed her friend a look.

"Is it? Is that what I've been doing?"

"Isn't it?" Oonagh's eyes met Marianne's full on.

They say fortune favours the brave and this was certainly true for Paul Osborne, aspiring biographer. It was Mary, from the local supermarket, who spotted the story in the English Sunday newspaper first, and mentioned it to Miss MacReady, who had called in for a tin of tobacco and some 'skins', as she called cigarette paper. Miss MacReady swung by the pub, to be nodded on to Weathervane, by Padar.

Monty greeted her enthusiastically. Miss MacReady was always a heady concoction for the canine's sensitive nose. She picked him up, rubbing her chin between his ears as she carried him upstairs, following voices coming from the bedroom.

"Your friend didn't waste much time," she announced, dropping the Sunday Globe on the bed beside Oonagh, "the real life drama of an all-action hero, I ask you?"

Marianne picked the newspaper up, a huge photograph of Ryan covered nearly half the page. He was resplendent in a white tuxedo, perfectly styled hair, lightly tanned skin, slightly arrogant chin tilted at the camera, his super-sleuth scowl captured perfectly, glinting out from the page, revolver in hand, aiming straight at her. The article, a mere couple of paragraphs, announced the Irish actor's new role as the leading man in one of the world's most popular film series. He was to step into the shoes of a huge star, who had bowed out gracefully after making the role his own over many years. Ryan had beaten off tough competition for the part and was preparing to start filming at an undisclosed Indian Ocean location that month.

Miss MacReady pointed further down the page, "Read that bit. Not a mention of that while he was here."

Marianne read out loud, "Ryan's long-time girlfriend, American actress, Angelique de Marcos, had an announcement of her own this week; she is pregnant with the actor's second child. Ryan, who has a grown-up son from a previous relationship said: "It certainly has been an amazing year so far. This latest news has made everything just perfect." Ryan and Angelique were survivors of the 'Power 2 The People' bombing attack in London last year." Her voice trailed off to a whisper, she gave the paper to Oonagh, letting her hands fall to her lap.

"And then it advertises Paul Osborne's series of articles, starting next week. Excerpts from his, no doubt, hastily completed book," said Oonagh, reading on. "I hope he's cleared it with Ryan's agent, the Larry fella, or there'll be hell to pay."

"You're very up on all this Hollywood stuff, Oonagh," Marianne said quietly, picking at a fingernail.

"Huge fan. Addicted, Padar says. All the mags, online stuff, love it. Sure anyone'd need an escape from this place."

"Wasn't Paul what's-his-name at the Awards with ye all too?" asked Miss MacReady.

"Yes, Paul and I took Larry's place at the table. We were all together." Marianne sounded distracted.

"Paul's sister is married to Ryan's son. That's the connection," Oonagh confirmed.

"So, he'll have insider knowledge then, having the family connection, know all about it, so," said Miss MacReady.

"Not necessarily." Oonagh was authoritative. "Ryan was only twenty when Mike was born. Mike was brought up by his mother, an American, in the theatre. He and Ryan only met up again about ten years ago. But that Angelique one, she's a real piece of work, I'm led to believe. Still, the book will be a bestseller no doubt and rattle a few cages, official or no. Don't you think, Marie?"

"And how do you know so much about it all?" asked Miss MacReady, expertly rolling them each a cigarette, whether they smoked or not.

"Research," said Oonagh emphatically. The others were intrigued. "You know I take *all* the celebrity magazines every week – never miss an issue. Then there's all the online stuff, blogs and things."

"Pure tosh, Oonagh Quinn," barked Miss MacReady as she lit up.

"What do you think, Marie? Are you disappointed?" Oonagh looked into Marianne's face.

"Not really. Paul told me he'd written the articles and was turning them into a book. I suppose running into Larry, and what with Ryan's new role, it would make sense to publish now."

"She didn't mean about the book," Miss

MacReady inhaled languidly.

"Miss MacReady, you're as bad as Oonagh. There's nothing between Ryan and me. I'm delighted for him, all of them. Perfect timing, I'd say."

"Good timing for all concerned." Oonagh was re-reading the article. "Especially for Angelique, put her right back in the spotlight, hasn't it?"

"And a baby, sure a baby changes everything," Miss MacReady was wistful, blowing smoke rings over the bed.

"If it's his." Oonagh waved the smoke away. "The Angelique-one is a bit of a girl, so they say."

"Were you close?" Miss MacReady asked gently.

"Yes, we were," Marianne answered, not really sure who she was talking about. Then she grabbed her bag and started downstairs, Monty hot on her heels.

"Come on. It's my last day let's have a drink together at least."

The two women jostled at the doorway.

"Age before beauty," Miss MacReady pushed ahead, puffing like a train down the stairwell.

"You shouldn't smoke in the holiday cottages, Miss MacReady. What about the visitors?" Oonagh coughed.

"What fecking visitors?" The older woman replied.

They piled down the stairs and out into the lane.

Chapter Seventeen – The Honeytrap

Marianne gazed through the French doors of the garden room at seventy four Oakwood Avenue. The preened Chesterford landscape was in sharp contrast set against the wild, unfettered hinterland of Innishmahon. The room, which was meant to open the house to the changing seasons, only seemed to reinforce her claustrophobia. Beyond the boundary of the oak tree, Georgian railings blended into Victorian terraced houses, which faded in the distance like rows of uniformed soldiers. She had always loved Oakwood Avenue, the garden and the tree lined cul-de-sac, but now it looked bland, uninteresting, somehow it disappointed her.

Clipping his lead on distractedly, she took Monty on their daily constitutional to the park. The weather was unseasonably mild for December. Marianne sat on a bench, re-reading the letter suspending her from duty while the Board decided whether she had broken the terms of her contract by taking six weeks consecutive leave. It was a vacuous ploy to be rid of her. She grumbled under her breath, she had never been a day out of work since leaving college, and although it had not been a conscious decision, she could certainly be called 'a career girl', even if that definition just meant a female without the demands and needs of a family to impact on her professional life. She was, as her CV stated, diligent and loyal; creative yet practical; willing to learn from those who were more experienced and a fine example to up and coming professionals. How dare they?

"I don't deserve this." She stood up abruptly, beckoning Monty to abandon the rear of a friendly spaniel, and follow her homewards, as she waggled her disabled mobile in the air. She dropped the phone on the hall table and grabbed the landline to dial Jack's number. Isabelle answered.

"Oh, Marie, it's so lovely to hear you. We've been worried. Are you alright?"

Marianne assured her all was well and asked to speak to Jack. Isabelle hesitated.

"You'd better come and see him yourself. He's not the best."

"Not ill, is he?"

"No, not ill. No more so than he has been these past years. Just not the best. Not himself, but even more himself, you'll see what I mean."

Marianne caught Isabelle's anxiety.

"Come and eat with us. Come at seven."

Marianne went to hang up.

"Is it just yourself coming?"

"Monty's free too," Marianne replied, lightening the tone.

"That's good. Just yourself and Monty, then." Isabelle hung up quickly.

Jack was clearly depressed, morose, grouchy and more crotchety than ever. He barely rose out of his armchair as Marianne entered, looking briefly up from his glass with liverish eyes. He had a tartan picnic rug around his knees. Monty saw this as an invitation and pushed his nose at his legs, asking to be allowed onto his lap. Jack acquiesced, giving the dog a cursory stroke. Sensing a brief respite in Jack's demeanour, Monty settled quickly. Isabelle sighed. It was the kindest Jack had been to any living thing for months.

"Hi Jack, how's things? Can't say I'm that thrilled to be back." Marianne knelt down beside his chair.

Jack seemed to have forgotten Marianne had been away in Ireland for a month and a half. He eyed her suspiciously.

"Well, I'm not really back, as you know. They've suspended me," she continued.

He looked straight at her, as if to check if she was lying.

"What? What the hell is going on there? Do you need a lawyer? Isabelle fetch me my contacts book." He twisted in his chair, looking for the telephone.

Marianne took his hands in hers.

"No, no, Jack, I'm fine. I'll sort it out. They're in the wrong, don't you worry about it."

He took a deep breath and seemed to calm a bit, momentarily looking off into the distance.

"How are you Jack?" she asked softly.

"Furious. Fucking furious, if you want to know. I've been shown the door by a piddling pipsqueak no bigger than this fella and with none of his intelligence."

Monty, now squashed on his lap seemed unable to decide if this was a good, or a bad thing, so just eyed Jack cautiously.

"It's up to me to decide when I stop. Not them, faceless bastards on the top floor. Couldn't manage a piss-up in a brewery, as we well know. No hope managing a newspaper. And what are you doing? Why have you been so backwards in coming forwards? Up to no good, I'll be bound."

"Marianne's been away, Jack. You know that." Isabelle and Marianne exchanged a look. Jack glared at them both.

"I was just telling you, I've been suspended, something about my contract. Didn't know I had one, did you?" Marianne smiled.

Jack grunted.

"Didn't know I had a retirement plan until they told me. Now I'm living it."

"But we'll not want for anything," Isabelle called from the kitchen.

"Not the blidy point; blidy dictatorship." Jack drained his glass.

"Paul's written a book." Marianne tried to change the subject.

"So I believe. Shame he wouldn't put pen to paper when I asked him to, asked you both to, we might still be in work if you had. Could have sold the world rights for a decent series of articles - an inside take on the bombing. Might have saved our bacon, but no, too highly principled for that, too sensitive, too bullshit. Made me look foolish, weak. I can't even get a decent story out of my own team, who were there on the night. Really helped circulation, that did!"

"Jack, it wasn't like that. Not meant anyway."

"It blidy well was like that. Nail in my coffin. And now he's nailed yours. Blidy disgrace."

Isabelle came into the sitting room, making soothing gestures.

"Ah, stop woman," Jack barked, handing her his glass to refill, "you know it's the truth. Betrayed by two of my own. And now the Irish story, don't suppose you're going to write that one either?"

"What's to write? I was on holiday. There was a storm. Plenty of reports on TV, you must have seen them."

"There's more to tell," Jack replied. "More to tell in a different way, there always is."

"Maybe, but not right now."

"Humph," Jack replied, taking a long swig, which seemed to soothe him.

"Anyway, I thought you'd be happy to retire. Hand over. You were always saying you'd had enough. I could have your job if only I was half as good as you, but I wasn't, you were always saying that."

"True." He patted Marianne's hand, relenting. "But in my own time, not dancing to their tune. Suits and calculators, I ask ye? And they've even chucked you out, and you're a shining star, that's what you are, well, on and off, anyway." They chuckled together, then Jack gripped her hand. "You better get something else straight in your head. That lad's ambitious and he's changed. He's ambitious and he's angry. I don't know why, and I don't know what about. But he's a blue-eyed boy with the new regime and they don't take any prisoners. None of us will escape, you mark my words."

"Now, now Jack. Come and eat some supper," Isabelle pleaded.

"You watch, there'll be the book about the bombing – the inside story; then the storm in Ireland, all featuring this newly world-famous movie star, who is supposedly more of a hero off screen than he is on. Paul will make a fortune for himself, when he should've made it for the paper, he'll toss the likes of us aside in his stampede to become a global media magnate. Ye gods!" He pushed Monty off his lap and hauled himself up out of the chair, shuffling towards the door in carpet slippers.

"Jack... Supper!" Isabelle insisted.

"And what about the latest rumour? The notion that the movie star, has a love interest in Ireland, while his girlfriend back in Hollywood struggles with a difficult pregnancy. Who started that I wonder? What happened to news, decent features, integrity?"

"What?" Marianne too was on her feet.

"Jack! Supper!" Isabelle called.

"I need a lie down. Goodnight Marie." He closed the door behind him.

Marianne turned wide-eyed to Isabelle.

"More like himself than he ever was? I see what you mean."

The women ate in silence.

Isabelle was washing up, Marianne drying, and Monty gnawing the bone of the chop that would have been Jack's.

"He's too much time on his hands, looking at daytime telly and surfing the internet, usually both at the same time. He feels he has every right to be angry," Isabelle spoke quietly, "he feels betrayed."

"I can see that," Marianne was putting cutlery away.

"You and Paul were once so close. Did you know about any of this?"

"No way." Marianne let the knives clatter into the drawer. "He came to tell me about the articles, the book, but not to ask permission. He seemed to want me to hear it from him. But that was all. The deal was struck. Paul told me I'd been suspended and Jack was 'off the scene' as he put it."

"So he is just looking out for himself, making a fast buck, a name for himself."

"He said he needed the money, getting married and all."

"Really? I'd heard he'd called it off. He's running around with a new bit of fluff these days, a model or some such," Isabelle said, as she released the plug and let the water gurgle away.

"I think he's planning to marry the model now. You can't blame a young man hankering after the lifestyle."

Isabelle shrugged.

"When did he tell you about the book?"

"In Ireland."

"He came to Ireland then? Did he stay long?"

"No, it was after the storm had hit, we'd been cut off, he came by boat. No he didn't stay long."

"Last ditch attempt to woo you back?"

"We've only ever been friends, Isabelle, whatever others and indeed Paul might have thought. He was a bit strange, though. It was an odd time, for all of us."

"All of us?" Isabelle asked, intrigued.

"Is that the time? I'd better get a move on. Not even unpacked properly yet and Monty needs a walk."

Isabelle went to fetch Marianne's coat.

"Was it Innishmahon, you stayed? The island that was cut off?"

"Er, yes, lots of places were cut off. It made a mess of a thirty mile stretch of the coast."

"It said in one of Paul's articles about the movie star's early days, how he'd spent many summers there, on the island. I'm sure it was that island."

"Really? Nice place, though."

Isabelle wiped down the draining board, then stood looking out of the window, holding onto the side of the sink.

"Marie, be careful. I don't mind about the newspaper, Global Communications, or even Paul Osborne making money from a little bit of fact and a lot of fiction. But a broken heart? That's a much bigger issue. You can't see the damage, or feel the pain – but it's still excruciating, you should know, you've been through it before." She touched Marianne's shoulder in parting. "And a heart broken in public view is even harder to bear. I know, I'm living with it every day. Jack thinks the whole world is laughing at him. I don't know which is crueller, letting him go on thinking that or telling him the truth, that no-one really gives a damn."

Marianne left the Buchannans with a heavy heart and an even heavier stomach. Isabelle really was the most awful cook. Monty, on the other hand, considered Isabelle's culinary skills exemplary, everything swimming in grease and always generous leftovers congealing gently in cling film for him to consume later. Back at Oakwood Avenue, once he had devoured Isabelle's treats, Monty sloped off to bed while his mistress pulled things out of bags, pushing them into drawers before slamming the door of George's study, to engage in a lengthy discourse with his paperweight.

Half the week had gone by the time Marianne had dealt with the washing, a pile of post and a dodgy boiler. She was about to go out of her mind with boredom, when both Oonagh and Miss MacReady emailed.

Oonagh brought news that plans to reinstate the bridge had been agreed at the Parish Council Meeting. And news of her own, she and Padar were going to try IVF. They knew it was risky and expensive, but it was worth a chance, their final chance. If the storm had done anything positive, it had made them realise that they wanted a family more than anything. She asked Marianne to say a prayer and in the same sentence, asked if she had heard from the film star, because the latest online blog said filming was going well but that his personal life was not. His agent, Lena Leeson – not that Larry fella at all –

Adrienne Vaughan

had commented that Ryan wanted to be left alone to concentrate on his work. There had been no recent mention of the girlfriend or the supposed pregnancy! What did Marianne make of that?

Marianne laughed out loud. Oonagh wrote exactly as she spoke, and it amused her to think that this woman, living on a remote island off the west coast of Ireland, could be so bewitched by an industry operating from a town halfway round the world. She was pleased about the IVF treatment. The Quinns' disappointment, following Oonagh's miscarriage, had been heart-rending. Marianne said a quick Hail Mary for a happy outcome as she opened the postmistress's email.

News of the battle for the Innishmahon bridge, as Miss MacReady referred to the now monumental debate, was also positive. Miss MacReady agreed with Padar and the other business people on the island, the bridge needed to be rebuilt, but with so much widespread devastation following the storm, it would be hard to justify such enormous non-urgent expenditure for the benefit of just one small community. Miss MacReady wondered if Marianne could think of anything that might help the cause. Since she had looked her up on Google and saw she was a bit of a campaigner herself, she thought the website reuniting mothers with babies stolen in the charity scam, was brilliant. Could Marianne do the same for Innishmahon?

Marianne made coffee and pondered. She had more than the plight of the Innishmahon villagers on her mind, she had to decide what she was going to do with her own career. Were bridges to be built there, or left abandoned and a new direction taken? It was a strange feeling, this time on her hands. She felt becalmed, the internal wind that whipped her up and drove her on had dropped. She felt as if she never had time to think things through, always acting on instinct, taking a chance, hoping that wherever she ended up was where she was meant to be. Now all was quiet, the whistling in her ears silent, the whirring in her head stilled.

"It's quite liberating, you know," she told Monty as he followed her out of the kitchen into the study, "this thinking time."

She absent-mindedly picked up her mobile, checked it had charged, and flipped it on. There were two new answer phone messages, the first from Jack, half-heartedly apologising for his behaviour the previous evening.

"Sorry, Marie. Isabelle says I came across as rude, didn't mean to. Not in the best form. Come over and see us again soon. It's Jack, by the way." As if the gravelly tones could be anyone else.

"To listen to your next new message, press one."

"Hello, this is a message for Marianne Coltrane. Ryan O'Gorman's PA, Lisa here. I'm trying to organise an update re. the script you're editing for Mr O'Gorman. He's in the UK next week. Could you possibly call me back with your availability and we'll fix something up? Thanks."

Marianne nearly dropped the phone.

Adrienne Vaughan

It was one of those freak snowstorms which often appear in the middle of a mild stretch, warning of severity to come, a flash of frost and ice and shivering. The earth suddenly covered in a hurried blanket of white, the whole landscape, a confusing blur of softness and silence, holding the world suspended in a brief winter wonderland, a fabulous tease of the highest order, and quite beautiful. Marianne marvelled as the humongous false-eyelash snowflakes threw themselves on the windscreen of the car, blinking flirtatiously before melting clean away. She had no clue where she was going, and trusted the newly purchased SatNav implicitly. All she had picked up from the Internet was that she was heading for a small, yet fabulous, country house hotel called Meredith Lodge. Not far from Newbury, in Royal Berkshire; it had been the hunting lodge of a Tudor prince who had gifted it to his mistress on his untimely death.

Lisa confirmed the date and time in a voicemail: 'Please arrive dressed for dinner, this will be a two-day editorial summit, all expenses will be taken care of, after dinner on the first evening, relaxed and informal work wear will suffice. Ask for Mr Pickering's suite, he will look after you.'

That was it. Nothing in writing. In fact, no further instruction at all. No mention of Ryan. Would he even be there? As Marianne drove, she became aware of a gnawing in the pit of her stomach, a strange fluttering, a touch of anxiety and the merest smidgen of fear. She could feel it building quite nicely, higher and higher it

239

broiled inside her. What was it called now? Ah, there it is – excitement! What a glorious feeling you are, she told her tingling fingertips as she swung into the swirling, white oblivion that was the car park of Meredith Lodge.

Lamps burning either side of the studded oak doorway beckoned her through the blizzard, and if she had looked up from beneath the hood of her voluminous velvet coat, she would have seen, through the golden glow of a leaded upstairs bay, a figure standing perfectly still, a glass of amber liquid in hand, as he scowled the snow-covered driveway for her arrival.

The liveried porter rushed out to take her bag and escort her in, and as the door closed behind her, the figure in the window stood back, putting his glass down and breathing a small sigh of relief. He clasped his hands together, his fingers too were tingling and, though he had meticulously set this honeytrap of seduction, scene by scene, he was trembling with anxiety and as nervous as a schoolboy. Ryan O'Gorman took the handkerchief from his dinner jacket pocket, and dabbed his upper lip. His armpits were prickling. He went to knock the whiskey straight back but the door opened behind him and he froze, staring out across the glittering snowstorm, desperately trying to think of something cool and witty to say.

Marianne had taken the sweep of staircase up to 'Mr Pickering's' suite two steps at a time. She recognised Ryan's large loopy handwriting in the hotel register and her heart leapt, she longed to see him and prayed with every step, holding the folds of the full length fabric up to her knees, that the aforementioned 'Mr Pickering' was really the actor, Ryan O'Gorman.

"Shit, shit, shit," she hissed, as her heel caught the hem of her coat and she hopped inelegantly into view. "Bugger!" She tried to enter the room but the fabric had trapped as the door closed.

"If you are going to cause trouble as usual, I will send you back out into the snow." The warm Irish-American lilt surprised her, she had not noticed him standing at the window, half-hidden in the flickering shadow thrown by the many candelabra scattered around the room.

"Well at least give me a hand," She struggled to free herself from her coat and the doorway. He moved across the room, opening and closing the door to release her, then eased the heavy fabric off her bare shoulders.

"Always making an entrance." His eyes twinkled as he pushed his nose against hers in greeting. "Great to see you."

"And you." She grinned at him and, for a moment, they were back on the beach at Innishmahon, the time that had elapsed, dissolved, and they were, once again cohorts, compatriots, brothers-in-arms.

"Well," she said, as his eyes swept appreciatively over the dark green off-the-shoulder velvet gown, cut daringly low to the back; an investment piece the sales assistant had said. An investment in what, she had wondered at the time. "Who else is joining us for this editorial conference?" She took in the fabulously appointed suite, blazing fire in the baronial fireplace, flanked by large curved sofas, strewn with fur throws and velvet cushions; the table in the bay window, with only two place settings. In the far corner of the room was a desk littered with paper. A laptop's standby light blinked intermittently. A huge carved bureau stood in another corner, housing a flat screen entertainment centre. Soft jazz oozed from invisible speakers.

"Just us," he said softly.

"Lovely." She took the flute of champagne he offered, feeling the blush of excitement on her chest. If she were to be seduced, this is how she would want it to be. This would be how she dreamed it. She put the glass down. He did the same.

"Okay?"

"No. Sorry, can you excuse me for a moment? I've left something behind, er, in the car."

"Of course." He opened the door and she charged through it, picking up her coat as she left, flying down the stairs as fast as her heels would allow. At the bottom, she caught sight of herself in a huge gilt mirror. She stopped. Her skin was flushed, her eyes bright, heart pounding. I can't do this, she told herself, I can't let this happen, be seduced, allow myself to be swept off my feet, fall in love. She watched as her eyes glittered. Anyway, how dare he? How dare he assume I am interested, that I will fall for his undoubted charms, that I am his for the taking. Oh shit, but I so am.

A porter appeared from nowhere.

"Madam, can I help you? Is there anything you need?"

She took a deep breath, yes there is, she thought, and it is waiting for me up those stairs.

"No. No, thank you," She took another deep breath and, smiling at her reflection, turned to slowly mount the staircase.

He was standing in the window when she returned.

"Okay? You didn't go out to the car?"

"No, silly, I had it after all. By the way, which is my room?"

"Straight across the hall, shall I show you? I've asked them to light the fire and put your luggage there."

"No, not now. That's fine. Just so I know for later," she said, more to herself, pleased there was an exit strategy, glad he had not taken anything for granted. She took up her glass, visibly relaxing. She noted his beautifully manicured hands, expertly cut hair, the grey disappeared. His *Savile Row* dinner jacket fitted his frame to perfection, all hint of paunch toned away.

"You really do look like an International all-action spy hero, you know?"

"Of course I do." He twirled, preening. "But that's only the day job and it's not long term either, three movies, then I'm out."

"Will the three-movie deal fulfil all your heart's desires?" She sipped her drink, the bubbles tickled.

"I'll be very well-heeled at the end of it, anyway. Heart's desires? Well, that's a different subject altogether."

He showed her to a seat and rang for room service. He had pre-ordered their dinner of lobster, fresh asparagus with wild mushroom risotto, and a Belgian chocolate sour-cherry mousse.

They chatted easily as they ate; Marianne was fascinated to learn how a major movie is made, the sets, the costumes, the scheduling. Ryan's stories were captivating, animated, scurrilous, hilarious. Laughing, she lifted her napkin to her lips to dab away drips from the butter-drenched asparagus.

"May I do that?" he asked, and before she could answer, he leaned across the table, his mouth hovering millimetres from hers, and proceeded to lick her lips clean of the warm oil. Shocked, she drew back, staring at him. He calmly returned to his seat and continued his meal. He looked up then, eyes questioning. She struggled to regain her composure, stilling the butterflies in her stomach. There was only one course of action.

"Like to taste the wine?" she asked. And before he could answer, she took a drink and, putting her mouth against his, pressed the wine through his lips. He sputtered, as the liquid dripped from his chin.

"Good vintage." His eyes were fixed on hers.

"Like some more?" she whispered, leaning towards him. He dropped his napkin and, rising from his chair, walked round the table to take her by the hand. He pulled her gently to her feet and, clasping her shoulders, drew her mouth to his. They kissed with every fibre of their being. She had never been kissed like it, ever. He had never given so deep and loving a kiss.

"Please let me make love to you, Marianne. I've wanted you ever since I first laid eyes on you. Please," he whispered hoarsely.

Heart thumping in her chest, Marianne stood back and slowly unzipped the back of her dress. It fell to her waist. She stepped out of it and threw it aside. She stood before him in the most beautiful lingerie she owned, silently delighted that she had not opted for the comfort of her big pants. He stripped quickly down to his dress shirt and boxer shorts. Pulling her to him, she slowly un-buttoned his shirt, pulling it back from his strong shoulders and broad, smooth chest. Then naked in the candle light, they fell upon each other. Collapsing to the floor, they rolled together before the fire, kissing and laughing, pushing each other away to feast on their nakedness in front of the flames and then pausing briefly, they locked eyes and silently agreed their desire.

He took her quickly and urgently, until she shrieked with delight and he groaned with ecstasy into her hair as he pushed hard inside her. Sighing and kissing each other repeatedly, until their mouths and tongues were sore, they finally lay glistening in the candlelight, their breath slowing in unison, as the sweat dried on their bodies and their skin cooled.

After a time, Marianne stretched out and, taking the remains of the champagne, unceremoniously poured it over him, laughing as he squealed. Then pushing him onto his back, she licked him back to fullness before climbing astride, tearing strips off the abandoned lobster and feeding it to him piece by piece, rocking rhythmically backwards and forwards, until he exploded inside her again.

The Hollow Heart

Dessert was eaten off her breasts, the chocolate mousse coating her nipples as he sucked her clean, stroking softly between her legs, teasing her to such a shuddering final climax with his fingers, she almost wept with pleasure.

With the feasting over and all desire spent, he took a wolf-skin throw from a chair and wrapped it around them as they nestled together in front of the dying embers, softly dozing in each other's arms.

"You okay, my darling?" he asked her, holding her tightly.

"Mmm..." was all she could manage.

"Sleep tight, my heart's desire," he whispered, as she slept.

Dawn was breaking when Marianne woke. The fire had been rebuilt and was blazing. She pulled the throw about her as she went to the window, the snow storm still swirling outside. She pushed open a door, a huge four poster bed draped in red tapestry and silken fringe dominated the room, a smaller fire burned in an elegant hearth. She could hear water running. She followed the sound to a white marble bathroom the size of a ballroom. A former chapel, it featured paintings of saints and bible stories along the walls, sealed in glass frames against the moisture. The roof was a dome of sapphire blue adorned with faded silver stars. She could see his body outlined through the glass of the shower. She hesitated, the only thing assuring her it had not all been a dream was the soft burning between her legs and the sweet soreness of her nipples against the throw.

He saw her and stepping out pulled her to him gently, letting the water spill over them both, as he carefully began to soap her hair and wash her body, kissing her throat, moving down to the scars on her shoulders and back, as he worked his hands all over her. He pulled away the arm she held against the scar that dissected her lower torso, and ran his fingers along the fine white line.

"You're the most beautiful woman I have ever seen," he whispered, and she responded, taking him in her hands and stroking him until he was hard. He made love to her again, softly, smoothly, and with such tenderness, she was moved near to tears. They clung to each other under the water until it ran cool and then he wrapped her in white fluffy towels and carried her to the bed, placing her between clean linen sheets.

"I bet you're tired my darling," he said, smiling down at her, "tired but happy?"

"Happy, yes, but a little bit sleepy too." She smiled back at him.

"Okay, I'll make a start on the script, you doze awhile. See you later." He kissed her forehead and then, dimming the lights, padded out of the room to begin work on the final scene of the screenplay. She drifted off into slumber, too happy to care if she were dreaming, to dreamy to care if she should wake.

Marianne was up and dressed in suede jeans and Ryan's evening shirt when room service came to clear away the evidence of last night's passion. The butler brought coffee, croissant, scrambled egg and smoked salmon. Ryan grinned at her as she entered the room.

"Good morning, Muse. Hair of the dog?" He poured Bucks Fizz, skilfully ensuring the fresh orange juice did not cause the champagne to overspill.

"Don't really need one, but that looks delicious."

"Talking of dogs, how is the little fella?"

"Staying with my ex-boss and his wife, but in fine form. What about Larry?"

"In fine form also. Delighted with the film deal, he and Lena will do well out of it – it's all good."

"And Innishmahon, heard from anyone there?" She took the irons to poke the fire.

"Gregory, the priest emails from time to time and, Miss MacReady, she keeps me up to speed."

"Me too. And Oonagh from the pub, I'm very fond of her and Padar."

"Everything happened so quickly, I didn't have time to..."

She shrugged. He took her by the shoulders, turning her towards him.

"Because I left in such a hurry I asked Lisa to track you down. Miss MacReady came up trumps. I'm sorry."

"What for?"

"Abandoning you, rushing off, full of big plans. Not letting you know how I felt…how I hoped you might want me to feel."

"It's not up to me to dictate how you feel. But I'm

not a home-wrecker – I know what that feels like. It's not surprising I don't want a relationship with a man who already has a partner." She sipped her drink. "So, truthfully now, how is Angelique?"

"Over. Definitely over, but like these things often are, messy. Well, the thing is…" He looked away, the atmosphere shifted.

She put her hands to his face, bringing him back,

"Hey, it's okay. Come on, let's get to work, looks like you've written loads."

He smiled, relieved.

"There's a lot of waiting between takes."

"A lot of waiting when you're out of work, too."

"Really?"

She ignored the question, taking spectacles out of her bag and arranging the pile of paper in order.

"Missed you." He kissed her on the top of her head as she bowed over her work. She started to make notes. He joined her at the desk. They did not look up until the butler returned to re-lay the fire and enquire if they wished to make a reservation for dinner in the restaurant.

"Have you boots?" he asked her. "We need some air."

The sun was gold and glorious against the ivory of the winter sky, trees turned black against the backdrop of early evening iridescence. They walked hand in hand, silent footprints of powder soft snow in their wake.

"And what of Paul Osborne's book? The series of

articles? How does that sit with you?" He gave her a sidelong glance.

"For goodness sake, Ryan, I'm not an undercover agent, any more than you are. Trust me, I mean it. I'm not party to his work, or secretly researching you on his behalf, or indeed, anyone else's."

They walked on in silence for a while.

"There's been a bit of a family rift to say the least," he said.

She nodded, encouragingly.

"Paul is persona non grata as far as Zara and Mike are concerned, you can imagine. Although Lena likes the added value the frisson brings to the whole scenario, she thinks the publicity can only help the movie. Me? I'm disappointed he's written such rubbish about me. Seems I rescued all the survivors of the terrorist attack single-handed, and the sequel is me salvaging Innishmahon after the storm. He's the one over-playing this All-Action Hero stuff. It's all unauthorised and every now and then my PR has to issue a statement refuting the more ridiculous claims, but beyond that I am not too worried, just disappointed."

"More sales when you get round to writing the authorised version though."

He frowned.

"There is that. Don't turn into a Lena on me now."

"Just an observation, I'm opting out of the world of commerce and journalism – for a while anyway."

"What are you going to do?"

"Not sure. I still feel strongly about the stolen

babies' story. I'm sure there are lots of mothers and children who would love to be reunited, if not reunited, just told what happened, told the truth. Every woman I interviewed said something was wrong. They knew deep down their babies had not died. It feels unfinished to me, maybe this is the space and time I need to finish it, do something positive. I don't know yet, and won't make a decision until I have to."

"That's admirable, and I understand what you mean about unfinished business and not making decisions until you have to. But what about me? Have you decided about me?" He gave her that look again.

"What's to decide? Film star, fantastic lover, gifted writer, excellent company. You tick all my boxes."

"But do you like me, Marie? Are we friends?" He stopped, his eyes burning into her. She blushed.

"Ah, come on." She laughed. "That's going a bit too far now."

They kept to the roadway until they found a stile. He brushed the snow off, helping her over.

"Race yer," he called, and was away, taking off as fast as he could up the hill. She followed, failing hopelessly to make any ground. He reached the top of the hillock and started sparring Rocky-style. Marianne tried to run, breathless and laughing, but her feet could not take hold in the new snow. He held out his arms and then, as if in slow motion, her foot caught a rock and she fell, head first, arms flailing, to glide gracefully down the slope on her front, her chin leaving a small trench in the snow as she went.

Ryan headed after her, but he too lost his footing and ended up on his bottom, sliding at speed towards her splayed figure, now stuck in its own little snow drift. She was just setting herself right when he ploughed into her. Throwing her back to the ground, he seized the opportunity to pin her down with a full body dive, pushing her hair off her face, to kiss her passionately in an old-fashioned teenage snog. Eventually gasping for breath, she wriggled free, laughing.

"Stop it, I can't breathe, nutcase."

"I can't help it. You really turn me on. I feel like a kid with a crush, I'm mad about you, can't stop thinking about you. It's driving me crazy."

"Now that sounded like a script."

He pulled his mouth down, like a clown. Marianne kicked at the snow as he made snowballs and, within minutes, a battle ensued ending when Ryan, with an overzealous throw, slipped again and Marianne took the opportunity to climb onto his chest pinning him down to claim victory.

"Call yourself an All-Action Hero?" She laughed, helping him to his feet.

"It's only acting." His eyes grew dark.

"I know that." She took his hand. They walked on for a while in silence.

"Do you fancy the restaurant tonight? What about roast pheasant and a nice bottle of Bordeaux in front of the fire. That final scene needs some more work, doesn't it?"

"Are you on the menu for dessert?"

"Could be," he teased.

"That's a yes then. Ryan O'Gorman, you're such an easy lay."

"I'm not really." He was serious.

"Yeah, right." She reached up and bit his earlobe.

"Ouch!"

"Race you back."

Marianne packed quietly the next morning and then stood at the foot of the bed watching him as he slept. The long eyelashes on his still boyish face, the curve of his chin, straight nose, plump bottom lip. His arms were spread across the sheets, dark brown nipples like velvet against the light brown skin of his torso, a stretch of gold against the stark white linen. He looked like a god. She closed her eyes to hold the image, a picture of perfection. He stirred, searching for her in the bed.

"Marie?"

She bent to kiss him.

"I have to go. Snow's nearly melted and the roads are clear. Isabelle and Jack are leaving for Scotland this evening, I need to collect Monty."

"What time is it?"

"Eleven."

"What day is it?"

"Monday."

"Shit!" He leapt out of bed. "I've three interviews today. Lisa should be here, I should be ready."

"She is here. She called the room, your mobile is switched off. I answered, she thought I was Angelique."

He stepped back out of the bathroom.

"No way." He took her hands. "That's over. We've separated. Seriously, Lisa made a mistake, that's all."

"And the baby? I've heard Angelique's pregnant?" Marianne did not want this conversation now, he had not mentioned it all weekend, she wished she could keep her tirelessly investigative mouth shut.

"I'm not sure about that. She's said she's pregnant, she's said it's mine but she won't even talk to me. So I don't know what to think, and now the gossip columns are speculating and Angelique's PR machine is in full flow. You know what it's like."

"Sure I do." She started towards the door.

"It is over, Marie, believe me please, and I don't know about this, us, but it feels pretty special to me." He was standing before her. He took her hands in his.

"Ryan, it's okay. *Really.* I had the most lovely time, thank you."

"Oh, so did I, the best of times."

She half-smiled.

"We have each other's personal numbers, we'll stay in touch, see each other again, I do so want to see you again. I'll call, I promise. I know the coming months are going to be busy…"

"I can imagine." She tried not to sound cynical.

"Don't, Marie. This was special. You're special." He held her shoulders, searching her face.

"And so are you. *Very,* " she told him.

They kissed and she left.

Adrienne Vaughan

He moved to the window where he had waited for her to arrive and watched her go.

She started the car, and looked up. She could just make out his silhouette. She willed coldness into her heart as she gripped the steering wheel. She would not miss him, it was just an affair, a glorious brief encounter, but only that. She would never have her heart broken again. He raised his hand. She turned the wheel; the car park had turned to slush as she drove cautiously away.

Chapter Eighteen – The Phoenix Fights Back

Jack Buchanan never returned to England. He was taken ill shortly after he and Isabelle had arrived at their holiday home near Kelso and, following a brief stay in Borders General Hospital, died peacefully in his sleep in the croft Isabelle had lovingly restored ahead of his retirement.

Isabelle was stoical as ever when she spoke with Marianne on the telephone; she was having a private burial for Jack and hoped Marianne would stay in touch.

After their conversation, Marianne sat down at George's old desk and wrote out her resignation, in long hand, using her fountain pen. She was not even going to go and clear her desk. She took her laptop, mobile phone, and the letter to the Post Office and mailed the whole lot back to the newspaper's new managing director. She signed the docket for the recorded delivery with a flourish. A terse finale to her years at the Chronicle, she mused, but the empire she had hoped to one day rule was no more. The ambition which had driven her on had been driven away, and Jack's demise felt like the final nail in the coffin of her own career. She felt no loyalty to Global Communications Inc. Most of her colleagues had left, and when she heard that Paul Osborne had been made editorial director, it came as no surprise at all. Even with the news of Jack's death, a couple of paragraphs on page nine and then a brief, humourless obituary the following day, Paul did not contact her. There had been no communication between them at all and, in spite of everything, this saddened her.

Oonagh, on the other hand, liked to keep in touch with everyone, constantly, and it was while listlessly re-filing her emails on her new laptop, that Marianne received a message from her favourite Irish landlady. She was thrilled to read Oonagh cautiously announce that she had fallen pregnant. This was one conversation Marianne did not want to have via email, she wanted to hear the joy in Oonagh's voice and share in the excitement. The news touched her deeply, she was near to tears as she telephoned her long-distance friend. Within minutes, Marianne was assuring her everything would work out this time, lecturing her about looking after herself and taking things easy. Oonagh took it in good part; with Padar's help they were going to do everything they could to ensure this pregnancy had a happy outcome; they were both nervously yet deliriously delighted. Then, having discussed the well-being of their mutual acquaintances, Oonagh launched into her unofficial 'Ryan O'Gorman' fan club update: the sets; the stars; the locations; she had all the latest gossip, until finally stopping to draw breath, she said:

"He's in England promoting the film at the moment, you know. Have you seen him? Has he been in touch?" She waited, "Marie, are you still there?"

"Sorry Oonagh, I have to go. Other line's ringing. Business. Catch you later."

Marianne put the phone down quickly. She did not want to have to lie, but if she told Oonagh she had seen Ryan, the barrage of questions would have been relentless, and to reveal any detail of their recent rendezvous would be a huge mistake. Marianne did not imagine Oonagh was malicious in anyway, but she also knew Oonagh would find it impossible to keep any detail of her encounter with Ryan, romantic or otherwise, confidential. She would be straight onto Miss MacReady and between them they would be busy broadcasting the 'Romance blooms for super spy star on Innishmahon' story to the world, and although Marianne was bursting to tell somebody, anybody, of her tantalising yet fleeting love affair with currently the most popular film actor in the Universe, her lips were sealed. The ramifications of such a revelation were incalculable.

"It was a glorious fling and everyone should have one, at least once in their lifetime. And in media terms, yes it's a great story; 'Super Spy' in secret love tryst," she explained to Monty, shuddering as she imagined the headlines. "We all know showbiz revelations sell newspapers, but 'great story' though it may be, for whom and for what? For the film, the actor, the movie machine, possibly. For the two individuals involved, definitely not."

She lifted him from where he had nestled at her feet, his favourite spot when she was working or talking on the landline. Checking she had replaced the receiver

258

fully, Marianne noticed she had an answer phone message. She recognised Sophie's number; her scatterbrained friend had been leaving increasingly anxious messages and she had not responded to any of them. She had heard that Jack had died and Marianne was not to go another day without calling her back or she was going to turn up on the doorstep and camp there with her entire family, until Marianne came out of the house to speak to her and at least tell her she was alright.

Marianne sighed and considered a trip to Sophie's the easier option.

They were catching up over a pot of coffee in Sophie's chaotic kitchen, when Jason, her partner, appeared. He kissed Marianne briefly and, taking a Coke from the fridge, turned to look her over properly.

"You look different Marianne. What is it?"

"Slimmer? Fatter? Older?" Sophie offered.

"No, none of those." He strolled over and, taking Marianne's hands, pulled her off the stool, walking around her slowly. "You're all shiny and glowing. There's a rosiness about you. What is it?"

Marianne just blinked at him.

"You've had sex, wild, unbridled, passionate sex. I'm right, aren't I?"

Sophie gasped.

"Jason, how rude!" And then turning to Marianne, "God, he's right, isn't he? You sly fox, not a mention to me. Who? When? What? How many times? Is he single? No he's married. Do we know him? God Marianne, tell all. I'm getting the wine out."

259

Marianne shrugged.

"Nothing to tell. Jason's never once been right about me and men. He thought George was just my solicitor until I moved in with him."

Jason shook his head.

"Nah. I'm right. I know I am and he's a bigwig, I'll be bound. Someone you can't tell us about but ties you up and screws you senseless every other weekend."

He winked, pinching her bottom theatrically as he left to attend to their children screaming in another room. Sophie went to close the door, she scanned the kitchen, the chaos, and stopped to slump against the fridge freezer, sighing dramatically.

"I'm so tired, I'm worn to a thread. I want my life back." Sophie was a blatant emotional blackmailer. "You could fill me in a little, just to brighten my day."

"This is your life, there's nothing to have back." Marianne started picking things up, putting them in the dishwasher, drawers, bin. She could hear Jason calming the storm in the sitting room, she spied him through the door, his arms around the children, a rug pulled around them as he started to read a story.

"You're so lucky," she said, handing her friend a clean glass, "you'll never know how lucky you are."

"If he's right and there is something you are not telling me, you're dead." Sophie said.

"If he's right and I tell you, mouth almighty, we'll both be dead."

The fact that Sophie freelanced for some of the more salacious women's weeklies meant that she really was going to be kept in the dark, whatever she hoped, as she opened the wine. Marianne knew Sophie's ploy and barely touched a drop, until Sophie eventually waved her friend a slurry goodbye, the bottle empty, and she none the wiser.

Keeping her clandestine meeting with Ryan from both Oonagh and Sophie did not rest easy with Marianne. She pulled on pyjamas grumpily, having barely said goodnight to Monty, whose only outing that evening had been a turn around the garden. She was annoyed, irritated with Ryan and angry with herself. She was a fully grown, single woman; she had every right to a sex life, a fleeting affair, a romantic encounter and even a passionate coupling in a glamorous location. But not to be able to talk about it, boast about it, revel in it and relive it moment by tantalising moment with another female, who would also have fantasised and longed for such an adventure, well that was the worst of it, that was what really rankled.

She banged about her bedroom, switching things on and off, fiddling with the duvet, books on the bedside table, her spectacles. She finally crawled beneath the sheets and was immediately wide awake. A bad night beckoned. When she finally dropped off, she tossed and turned fitfully. She dreamt of Ryan, she was laughing, falling backwards and, just as her heart started to flutter in fear that she would fall into nothingness, she felt his arms around her, strong and warm as if she was falling into a soft, safe armchair.

The Hollow Heart

She woke, shook her head, took a large slurp of
water from her glass and settled back, turning on her side,
closing her eyes tight shut, pushing the images away.
Yet, as she drifted off to sleep, he seeped back into her
dreams, this time pervading her subconscious with short,
vivid recollections of his touch, his lips, his tongue. She
woke again, the more she tried to blank him out, the more
his memory persisted, lighting her up from inside. She
groaned, racked with a longing that glowed like an ember
inside her, growing hot and burning until, feeling the heat
build in her chest, she woke suddenly, her heart racing,
her mouth dry. She glared at the bedside clock. It was
two in the morning.

She fell into a restless doze, only to wake again. It
was still dark, the skin between her breasts damp, the
flesh between her legs wet with desire. She licked her
lips, she could taste him, she could feel his hands sliding
down her spine to caress her buttocks with butterfly
strokes and, with her hand against her ear, she could hear
him breathing, soft heat from his whispering breath.

"Oh God," she pleaded, "make it stop." She
jumped and sat bolt upright, "Who's that? Who is it?"
The sound of her own voice in the darkness had startled
her. She snapped on the light and, glancing quickly round
the room, stuffed her feet in her slippers and went to the
bathroom, staring wide-eyed in the mirror. She shook her
head to clear it, but the memory of their passion draped
her like a cloak, it echoed through her, the longing so raw
it was painful. She pushed her shoulders back, strode
purposefully to bed and, grabbing the closest tome to

hand, read a mind-numbing computer textbook till dawn.

As if to compound her agony, the relentless publicity campaign that is the lifeblood of a global blockbuster, had commenced. Posters of the leading man in various poses were everywhere: bloodied and unshaven toting a rifle; eyes twinkling over a cocktail; hands gripping the steering wheel of the latest super car; or bare chested, the blonde curls of a beautiful girl, supine on his shoulder. Every time Marianne flicked on the TV, tuned in the radio, opened a newspaper or magazine, even watched a bus pass at the bottom of the avenue, Ryan was either on it, in it or being discussed. He pervaded her every waking moment. She was being haunted. Haunted, yet abandoned.

Marianne allowed her gloomy mood to envelop her. She went back to bed, pulling the duvet over her head, blocking out the daylight. Monty snuffled about the kitchen, then popped himself back in his basket. No walk today then. He eyed his lead hanging on the coat hook in the hall and buried his nose in his paws.

Developing the habits of a hermit, Marianne spent the next few months holed up in George's study, working on her project to reunite as many mothers and babies as she could. The files from the so-called charity she had uncovered in her award-winning report had been released, and the notorious Sister Mary May and her associates were serving prison sentences. She had hundreds of names and addresses to put on the website in the hope that those who were robbed of their children would come forward and discover they had not died at all. It was a time-consuming and emotionally draining task. She only left her desk to walk Monty or to act as an unpaid babysitter for Sophie and Sharon, deciding that helping them have a social life was a vague counter to having none of her own.

Oonagh kept her appraised of her condition, alternating between emails filled with riotous joy and paranoid anxiety. Ryan, it seemed, had abandoned her totally, despite his promise to stay in touch. For her part, she made no attempt to contact him: pride, foolhardiness, a naïve notion it is the female who should be pursued, or just fear of rejection, she did not know which, but what she did know was, she missed him more than she dare admit, especially to herself.

Apart from quietly acknowledging George's anniversary in June with a picnic in the park, where she and Monty had scattered his ashes the year before, the uneventful suburban summer was merging into what looked being an equally dull autumn. Marianne was becoming accustomed to a condition she had never encountered in her entire life – boredom. She was arranging knickers in order of wornness, when the land line rang. It was Miss MacReady. Her shrill tone reverberated along the wire.

"Marianne, is that you?" she hissed. She always sounded conspiratorial. "Look, what are you at? Have you a big job on, or what? Oonagh said you've left the newspaper, doing some freelancing. Well, could you consider this, a bit of freelancing for us, here?"

"Er, well, I have quite a bit on." She went quiet.

"Anything that can't be shelved?"

Marianne thought for a minute and then it hit her like a slap in the face. She realised what she had been doing, she had spent the best part of three months waiting for the phone to ring or an email to arrive. She had been waiting to hear from Ryan. This was more than disturbing. This was shocking. It was time to make some life-changing decisions, the rut had deepened, it was time to climb out. She slammed the knicker drawer shut.

The very next day was momentous for two reasons; firstly Marianne put seventy four Oakwood Avenue on the market, barely registering a quiver of regret as the For Sale sign was hammered into the lawn and, secondly, the invitation to the anniversary of the 'Power 2 The People' event arrived. Marianne stared at the white embossed card for some time. Re-named 'The Phoenix Fights Back' the whole event was to be a celebration in defiance of the terrorist attack, which had brought devastation to the capital and sent shock waves around the globe only twelve months before. The initiative would re-launch the worldwide charity the Baroness, who had tragically died in the attack, had founded, raising funds for impoverished people everywhere.

In keeping with the spirit of the re-launch, the survivors of the original event had all been invited as guests of honour. And to avoid sabotage, everything had been planned in secret right up to the invitations being sent out. Marianne was intrigued. She read and re-read the invitation with mounting excitement; all the survivors would have been contacted. Oonagh had told her Ryan was back in England. Would he be there? And if so, would she see him, talk to him, touch him? Or would she blank him, ignore him, pretend they had never met, never kissed, never been lovers?

She started humming *Cry Me A River*, the theme to the spy film, tapping the invitation along the mantelpiece in time with the tune. Monty, sensing a change of mood, trotted to the door, swishing his tail gently. She smiled at him, grabbing his lead, as she pulled on an ageing gilet. He yapped at her, spinning round like a puppy. She checked her lacklustre locks in the mirror, pale face, neglected nails.

"Right, let's get to the salon and book myself in. Time for a bit of a makeover," she told the excited terrier. "A new phase beckons. Who knows, a new me? A new life? A new everything? Let's go, Toto," she said, in her dreadful *Wizard of Oz* impersonation.

Professionally preened and polished, Marianne donned the dark green velvet gown she had worn that first evening at Meredith Lodge. In a mist of perfume, she rushed out of the house before realising she had left her mobile on the dresser. The taxi driver revved his engine. She jumped in. The abandoned mobile vibrated. The driver was playing a soccer match commentary loudly on the radio. Marianne chewed her manicure all the way there.

Hundreds of people were gathered around the red carpet entrance. The cabbie dropped her as close as he could, having only second-level security clearance.

"You'll be alright, love." He nodded towards the police cordon as she paid him. "I mean, you ain't no celebrity, so you'll get in dead easy, no paparazzi, I mean."

She looked up as a battery of flash bulbs heralded the entrance of yet another *A-lister*.

She smiled. He was tense, eager to be gone.

"It will be alright tonight."

He shrugged. "It will or it won't. Those bastards never give up in my opinion." A goal scored, he tuned the radio, and turned the wheel. "Have a good night, love."

He sped quickly away.

Marianne pulled her hood around her, more against the flash bulbs than the weather. She passed through security easily, the invitation had an indelible watermark according her special status as a survivor of the bombing. A tall man in a black tuxedo directed her into the VIP area. She walked straight into Paul Osborne with his latest squeeze; a singer from an all-girl rock band.

"Marianne," he boomed. She immediately noticed his teeth had been fixed. He flashed her a smile, "Stunning as ever."

"Paul," she said coolly, offering her hand.

He introduced the singer, a mere teenager beneath the false eyelashes and spray tan.

"What are you doing now?" he gushed, "working, writing, travelling, what?"

"Resting." She eyed him icily. "Though your

career seems to be going from strength to strength."

"Thank you."

"It wasn't a compliment."

"What do you mean?"

"Another time." Marianne took a glass of champagne from a tray.

"Ah, you mean Jack."

"I mean everything. You were good Paul, looks to me like you sold out."

"Principles are expensive, Marianne, I was broke." He pulled his puppy-dog face.

"Principles are priceless, Paul. We were a good team you, Jack and I."

He shrugged and turned to gaze across the room. He nodded as a flurry of activity signalled the arrival of the world's most popular film star. Marianne's heart leapt, she longed yet dreaded seeing him. She turned away, praying this would prevent her from melting into a pool of desire, right there on the carpet in front of them all.

"Well, he's here at last," Paul's tone was disparaging, "shame we're not good enough to sit with him this time."

Checking the table plan, Marianne saw the organisers had re-seated guests in their original groups, although Ryan had been seated with the hostess and other lumini. Angelique de Marcos was not on the list. Heart beating uncontrollably, Marianne was relieved to see Ryan's son Mike and wife Zara heading towards her. They greeted each other warmly as they were called to their seats.

"I believe you'd a wild old time over in Ireland, with the storm and everything. Pa said you were a great help through the worst of it and that you helped him with his script. Which was the more testing I wonder?" Mike smiled then asked quietly, "Is it a dreadful load of old dross?" He gave her an exact replica of his father's unmistakable twinkle.

"Not now Marianne's had a go at it," Zara interjected, and they laughed.

"The merest tweak," Marianne offered.

"God he could do with someone like you giving lots of things in his life the merest tweak," Mike whispered.

"It'll be alright," Zara patted Mike's hand, "it won't last forever."

As Paul Osborne took his seat beside Marianne, the conversation stopped. Mike and Zara nodded at his companion but both chose to ignore Paul.

The stage burst into light and the atmosphere which had been surprisingly relaxed was instantly electric. The show began. The auditorium held its breath, in unison with the worldwide audience of millions. They were not to be disappointed.

As the crescendo of the first act came to a close, Marianne, desperate for the loo through nerves and too much wine on an empty stomach, left the table, making for the lift and a not-too-crowded restroom on an upper floor.

Heading along a quiet corridor to return to her

seat, a hand flew out of a doorway, grabbed her by the elbow and pulled her inside. The door slammed behind her. She gasped as she was spun round. It was pitch black. She could smell mechanical oil mixed with expensive aftershave; she could hear the whir of the lift, a soft chime at each floor. She felt breath on her cheek. She inhaled to scream. A hand covered her mouth. As a cigarette lighter streaked a flash across a face, he took his hand from her mouth.

"Shit, you scared me half to death!" She thumped him in the chest.

"I was scared I wouldn't see you. Didn't you get my message?"

"Oh, please."

"Seriously? Asking you to join me tonight."

"It's been months."

"Well, whose fault is that?"

"What?"

"I called you. No reply. I left umpteen messages. I texted. No response."

"Oh, stop it, Ryan."

"No, listen, Lisa rang the newspaper and you got them to tell her you'd left."

"I have left."

"And the phone?"

"Went with the job. I changed it."

"Didn't think to let me know then? How do you think I felt, a romantic weekend in a beautiful hotel and then dumped?"

"Oh."

"I kept thinking, maybe she doesn't like me at all, maybe she is going to write a story about my bedroom prowess or lack of it. After what we shared? I said to myself, no, there's no way you could fake that."

"Ryan I am not that kind of journalist, and not that kind of person!"

"I know, I'm sorry, Marie..." He held her tightly.

"Maybe it was just a romantic weekend, maybe we should leave it at that," she heard herself saying.

"I can't. I can't get you out of my mind."

He pulled her to him and kissed her, missing her lips in the dark, his mouth somewhere between her cheekbone and ear. She freed herself.

"You could have found me if you really wanted to."

"I tried, I tell you, and I did find you, finally got your new number from Miss MacReady. I left you a message about tonight. Still no response, how do you think I felt? You could have contacted me, through Lisa. When you didn't, I guessed I'd been had, literally. I kept waiting for the story to be published."

"I've told you, I'm not interested in the story."

"Interested in me, the person?"

"I have missed you," she said, softening.

"And I you, so much."

"I kept thinking, if it's a fling, I can deal with that, you go back to your life and I'll go back to mine." She forced steel into her tone. "If it's to be more than that, he'll be in touch and we'll work something out, if that's what we both want." She was quiet for a moment. "I did feel abandoned."

He stepped back.

"I can see that, I'm sorry," he said, softly into the dark, "so did I."

The bell rang for them to return to their seats. He opened the door. They were caught in a sliver of light from the corridor. They looked at each other, two pairs of eyes, bright with tears and fear.

"I just want you to know, through all of this there's you. Only you," he whispered, as he stood back to let her pass.

She spun round, closing the door abruptly behind her. She pulled him to her, taking his head in her hands, pushing her fingers through his hair as she repeatedly kissed his face. He responded, pressing her against him, his hands all over her, trying to absorb every inch of her body as their mouths sought each other. They wrestled in the tiny space. She could feel him hard against her thigh. She unzipped and released him as they slid to the floor. He ran his hands up her thighs, pulling her underwear aside as she knelt to straddle him. He dragged the fabric down past her shoulders to reveal her breasts, clad in lace, and biting through it, licked and teased her nipples with his tongue until they were wet and hard. She lifted herself onto him and sighed with pleasure as she felt him push deep inside her. They moved together slowly. He kneaded her breasts, pulling at them, pinching and tweaking. She moved rhythmically, her fingers pushing through his hair, then faster and faster, harder and harder, he thrust his hips up into her, pounding and pounding against her. Until, grinding their bodies together in tiny rapid movements, she arched her back and they came in a huge, stuttering shudder, barely able to breathe, let alone speak. They stopped, silently suspended in ecstasy. Ryan sat up slowly and, clamping her to him, rocked her gently in his arms, as their pounding hearts stilled. She wrapped her arms around his head, kissing his hair. He stroked her throat with his fingers.

"I've missed you so much," he told her.

They were quiet for a long moment. Finally she stood up, rearranging her gown. He zipped his fly. She opened the door to let in enough light to re-tie his tie and find her hairbrush.

"When this is over..."

"I'm not waiting for you. I won't play second fiddle," she said evenly.

"I'm not asking you to. I'm not with anyone."

"Well whoever you are not with, is soon to have a child, I hear."

"Angelique's pregnant, there's no denying that, but we're not together and haven't been for months. Who's to say it's mine? It's like I said, it's messy."

"Un-mess it."

"It's complicated."

"Uncomplicate it."

"As flexible as ever," he sulked, "lots of women would love the chance to have an affair with me." And for a second, she heard the old arrogance in his words, but his eyes were burning into hers with love. She laughed and flung open the door. People were returning to their seats.

273

The Hollow Heart

"You're only an actor, Ryan, you don't even say your own lines. You're not such a brilliant catch, you eejit," she teased, striding out.

"Marie." He caught her hand, his eyes were full.

"Ryan," she said, and touched the tip of his nose with her forefinger. She hurried to find her seat, not looking back, suddenly lonely amid the throng.

Paul and Mike rose as she arrived.

"Where've you been? You nearly missed it?" Mike whispered, as the second act began. Paul noticed the red rash of excitement on her chest. He looked across to the top table, where Ryan O'Gorman, smoothing his hair back with his fingers, was also late back to his seat. Marianne put her hand to her throat. It flashed through her mind, had she properly disabled the mobile she sent back to the newspaper? If Ryan had been leaving her messages, had they been found?

"You were gone a while," Paul said, pointedly.

"Unfinished business," she replied, smiling broadly as she reached for her glass and gulped back her wine.

The news reports following the event were unanimous, a spectacular beyond compare. The amount of money raised was vast. Terrorism was for one night obliterated; for one night the world was a good place; to be human, a good thing.

For Marianne, the whole event had confirmed one thing. Ryan O'Gorman was the love of her life, gloriously so, but love of her life, or not, she would never play second fiddle to Hollywood, his career or anyone else besides. She had her own life to live, with or without him, and as Miss MacReady had said, a child changes everything, especially if the child is your own.

Chapter Nineteen – Moving Mountains

Marianne was not altogether surprised to see Paul Osborne at her door the next day, but he was far from welcome.

"What do you want?" she demanded.

"To talk, explain." He gave her a dopey, schoolboy grin.

"Save it. I'm not interested." She went to close the door. He placed an expensive boot in the gap.

"We can't all be as altruistic as you, you know?" The smile fixed on his face.

"What do you mean?" She stood in the doorway, barring his entrance.

"Well for one thing, we didn't all have a George." He glanced over the front of the building, referring to her inheritance. "Please Marianne, hear me out."

Marianne shrugged and let him in. Monty leapt around him, pleased to see his old friend. Paul tugged at his ears, Monty rolled onto his back.

"Paul, make it quick I have a lot to do." She stood, arms folded, glaring at Monty for the traitor he was. Paul sat on the stairs with Monty on his lap.

"We were so close once," he began.

"Cut to the chase, Paul."

"I've been commissioned to write another book, well a series of articles that will become a book; Ryan O'Gorman's biography, the making of a movie star, that sort of thing."

"And why would I be remotely interested?"

"Because I know you're having an affair with him. You were together in Ireland, you had a romantic weekend in Berkshire and I'm pretty sure you had a liaison the other night at the 'Phoenix Fights Back' dinner."

Marianne did not flinch, she just looked at him coldly.

"And now your house is up for sale. Where are you running away to, I wonder?"

"Listen to yourself, Paul. You even sound like tabloid trash." She took Monty from his lap. "Please leave."

"Marianne, don't be a fool, you could give me your side of the story. That way you know it will be told the way you want it."

She opened the door.

"You'd be well paid. Name your price?"

"Out! And take your thirty pieces of silver with you." She nodded to the street.

He stood up to go.

"You're not denying it, then?"

"Go! And if we ever have the misfortune of meeting again, for the sake of Jack's memory, do me a favour and pretend you don't know me."

"I could never do that, Marianne. After all, I know

you better than anyone. Better than you know yourself."

"What absolute crap," she hissed. "Now, get out!"

She could not bear to look at him. She slammed the door behind him and, with Monty still in her arms, rushed to the study to call Ryan's personal assistant to warn of Paul's plans. She stopped. Who could she trust? Someone was leaking all sorts of information to Paul. She went instead to her computer and emailed Oonagh, asking her to send an urgent message to Ryan via his fan club.

Subject: Little White Dog

Message: I've been working on a script. It's a romantic comedy. The lead roles feature an actor and a West Highland terrier. The story is a bit stuck and someone has threatened to expose the plot and spoil the ending. Don't trust anyone.

Signed, Monty Weathervane.

"What does all that mean?" Oonagh pinged back immediately. Marianne speed dialled Oonagh from her mobile.

"Can you make sure he gets it? I have to trust you Oonagh, there's no-one else."

"I'm a gold star, platinum plated member of his fan club. Our messages are blogged daily, and he responds - all part of his contract."

Marianne laughed out loud, but at least she was reassured. Trust Oonagh to be appraised of the detail of Ryan's contract.

"You can't tell anyone where this came from. You have to keep this secret for me. It would serve no purpose to blow this wide open, no purpose at all."

Oonagh was quiet for a moment.

"You've seen him, then?"

Marianne did not respond.

"You two are an item, aren't you? I knew it, knew it all along," Oonagh staged-whispered down the phone.

"Will you help me? Help me warn him?" Marianne pleaded.

"Of course I will. Aren't we as close as sisters? You have my word. I won't let you down."

"You're an angel. Thank you."

"On one condition, you two are godparents to this little one when it arrives."

Marianne was touched by her friend's request.

"I can't answer for *him*, but try and stop me."

The next day an extravagant bouquet arrived, arranged in a vase the shape of a martini glass. A note in Ryan's loopy hand read: *'Message received. Already tricky. Whatever happens, wait for me. Trust me. My love, always.'*

Marianne placed the vase on the dining room table and tore the note into tiny pieces, tossing the shards of paper one by one on the fire.

"Sorry boyo," she told the burning embers, "I'm not waiting around for anyone. I've places to go, people to see."

She poured a whiskey and took it into the study. She needed to commune with George. She needed him to know how she felt. She needed him to understand. She needed him with her. Sitting in the chair at his desk, she reflected that for some time, she had felt strangely detached and hollow, as if Oakwood Avenue were no longer her home, and Chesterford no longer where she wished to be. In a very short space of time she had been through a series of major traumas: George's death; the bomb attack; the storm on Innishmahon. And she had survived. Surely she had been spared for a reason? Surely she was still around for some purpose?

Sipping her drink, she considered her friends, Sophie and Sharon, ex-colleagues more than friends, both busy with babies and all the changes new lives bring. And what of Paul? Once a dear friend, now someone she did not like and could no longer trust. She sighed. She found it hard to believe he had changed so fundamentally. Was it avarice? Jealousy? Ambition? They had been so close once, too close, perhaps. Then she thought about Isabelle, Jack's stoical wife, who had chosen to remain in Scotland. Her homeland, she called it, with or without Jack. None of them needed her, they all had their own lives.

It was time for change, time to forge a new life for herself. She had done it before and she could do it again, maybe this time with a happier outcome. She pulled a tight smile at the framed photograph of herself and George at the awards ceremony, still in pride of place on the desk where he had placed it. She had never made particularly good choices where men were concerned, George being the only exception, and he very definitely had chosen her, not the other way round. Ryan? Well, Ryan would have to be the one that got away, just a fling with a being from another planet; a gorgeous dalliance with someone from another world. It was all just a huge crush and though it hurt, her heart would heal. It was time to take stock, take charge. She nodded at George, as he grinned back from the photo, and drained her glass.

Marianne accepted the first offer on the house, put her best pieces of furniture into storage, and sold the rest. She bought a second-hand 4x4 and booked a crossing to Dun Laoghaire. A cause needed a fundraiser; an unborn child needed a godmother; She would let everyone know where she was, once she was settled. She was on a deadline, her own deadline, for a change.

Monty spotted the walking boots, soles stuck with sand from their last Irish adventure, as they were slung into an old sailing bag with his bowls, rugs and half-chewed toys. He yapped at the bag, then whimpered gently, as the door of his newly purchased travel cage was clipped shut.

"Sorry Monty, long journey, you'll be more comfortable in here."

He gave her a doubtful look but settled down, none the less. Marianne wondered if he knew they were going back to Innishmahon, if he knew they were going for good, and then she smiled, this was the first time she had admitted as much to herself. She pulled the heavy Georgian door closed behind her, clutching the glass paperweight she had redeemed from George's desk before it went into storage. She jumped into the truck and swung out into the avenue.

"Don't look back, Monty," she called, adjusting

her spectacles at the same time as the rear-view mirror, narrowly missing a double-decker bus. "Never look back," she murmured, accidently swishing the windscreen wipers as she drove.

Chapter Twenty – A Proposal

Ryan O'Gorman was both pleased and intrigued to find his agent and friend, Larry Leeson, sitting in his trailer sipping a chilled soda, when he returned from shooting his latest escapade as the daredevil secret agent, Thomas Bentley. He greeted him warmly.

"Hey, nice surprise. Good to see you." He stopped, letting his arms drop. Larry looked in no mood for a hug. He gave Ryan a vague smile and mopped his brow with a crisp, white handkerchief, unnecessary with the air conditioning on full blast. Ryan waited, he knew Larry hated travelling, rarely left his New York office these days, claiming to be incalculably busy. He had even employed another PA to help with the workload, which was indicative of the pressure he was under. Being an inflexible perfectionist, Larry preferred to do everything himself.

Pouring himself an ice cold mineral water, Ryan waited for his visitor to speak.

"How's it going?" Larry's gaze swept over his friend appreciatively; he looked fit, tanned, groomed, yet beneath the makeup, tired. Ryan shrugged. Larry knew how it was going; he received daily reports from his contacts on the set, if not from Ryan himself.

The Hollow Heart

"Is it Angelique?"

Larry nodded gravely.

"The old habit?"

Larry sighed, gazing out of the trailer window across the windblown desert, towards the set which had been created to look like a lunar landscape. Thomas Bentley was displaying his skills as an astronaut in this particular scene.

"She's been partying rather heavily since you guys split. I've had reports of some pretty wild stuff, so I put a private eye on her tail for the last few weeks and some of the photographs... Christ, if the press ever got hold of them!"

Ryan pulled out the chair at his dressing table. He sat heavily, unscrewing the lid off the cold cream, smearing it carelessly over his face, glaring back at Larry through the mirror, his eyes burning through the whiteness slashed across his brown skin.

"Well?"

"She's still pregnant, but only just, I reckon. Anyway, I've seen her, spoken to her, and I'm sorry, Ryan, but if you want to save that baby, if you really believe it's yours, you're gonna have to take a break from filming; get back over there and try and sort her out. Even if you just do what has to be done until the kid is born, and then it's up to you."

"Couldn't you persuade her to go into a clinic, if not for her sake, for the sake of the child?"

"She ain't making any sense, Ryan. It's worse than ever. She's hanging around with a bad crowd, and there's this young rock star. Well, what they're not taking, snorting or drinking is only because it ain't been invented yet and…" Larry was striding about the trailer, twisting and untwisting the handkerchief in his fingers.

"Stop!" Ryan shouted, jumping up and lunging at Larry. He pinned his arms to his sides. "You know it's mine. She was straight enough to calculate that correctly, the last time we made love, to the minute. God knows she knew what she was doing, that's the truth of it."

Freeing himself, Larry handed Ryan a box of tissues to clean his face, then went into the galley kitchen and started making tea.

"Well, I've thought this through, so hear me out," he said, pouring the now-fresh-faced Ryan a cup. "I've negotiated a break with the director. We don't want Angelique's beloved Uncle Franco to know what's really going on, so we'll say it's for personal and medical reasons; she's having a difficult pregnancy, and you need to be with her. Just till the obstetrician says things have stabilised."

Ryan nodded, sipping his tea gratefully.

"You get married, get her into the clinic, finish filming and, by then, the baby should be born and you'll be back home and we can sort things from there."

Ryan gave Larry a wry smile. Larry continued to look him straight in the eye.

"What?!" Ryan yelled, putting his cup down with a clatter. "You're serious? Are you mad? I can't marry that woman…it's, it's a crazy idea. I don't even like her, let alone love her. Come on Larry, I've been trying to sort

Angelique out for ages, but you and I know she's her own
worst enemy. She'll take everyone down with
her…you've got to come up with something else, you've
just got to, please, I beg you."

Larry shook his head slowly.

"I've checked things out. When Angelique has the
baby, and let's face it, unless some sort of miracle occurs,
she ain't gonna make 'Mother of the Year', you will no
doubt want custody of the child. If you're not married, it's
going to cause all sorts of problems and, dare I say it, a
fortune to sort out. Particularly if you want to take the
child out of the US. Believe me, it looks complicated
now, but it really is the simplest way in the long term."

Ryan had, by now, forsaken tea for a very large
bourbon. He took a deep draught.

"But I'm in love with someone else," he said, in a
small voice.

Larry softened.

"I think I know that." He smiled at his client
pityingly. "And if she loves you, you'll work it out. I
know you, you ain't nothing, if not tenacious."

"When has all this got to happen?" Ryan was pale
beneath the tan.

"Right now, my friend." Larry went to the
bedroom to locate an overnight bag to start packing. "And
in secret, no communication, you hear? Don't email, use
your cell phone, nothing. If Angelique gets wind you're
on your way home to break up the party, she'll go to
ground. Lena's on the case, sorting out the wedding
arrangements as we speak. This time next week, it will all

be over, and Angelique will be safely ensconced in the clinic for the remainder of her pregnancy. So, not a word to anyone. We'll surprise her."

"We'll surprise more than her," Ryan said flatly, draining the remains of his drink.

Chapter Twenty One – The Power Of The Pen

The road from Dun Laoghaire to Innishmahon is a long one. Marianne and Monty stopped overnight at a roadside hotel and made good time to Knock the next day. It was unheard of for Marianne to travel to Ireland and not have her fix of Dublin, the playground of her college days, but something was driving her on. She needed to be further away. She needed to be somewhere else. She needed to be in Innishmahon.

She burst through the doors of Maguire's, having driven straight off the ferry and into the car park. Padar was polishing glasses ahead of the lunchtime trade. He dropped the cloth, hurrying towards her with open arms.

"Marie, heavens above, where have you sprung from? I'd no idea. Did you tell Oonagh you were coming?" laughed the landlord, embracing her heartily, as he rubbed Monty briskly under the chin.

"What can I get you? *Oonagh! Oonagh!*" he called up the stairs.

A heavily pregnant figure appeared, clad in a swirling purple kaftan.

"Okay, I'm coming, where's the fire, for god

288

sake?"

Padar oiked a finger at the figure in the shadows.

"She's here. Marie. She, and the little fella with her."

Oonagh was upon them in seconds, tears of joy running down her plump cheeks.

"Hey, hey what's all this?" Marianne hugged her friend.

"Ah, hormones, only. How long are you here for? Come in, come in. Padar, did you get Marie a drink? She's had a woeful journey altogether." Oonagh busied herself behind the bar, pouring a drink for Marie. "Padar, fetch Monty some warm milk. God love them, they're half-starved. Look at them!"

Marianne smiled broadly as she watched the usual scenario unfold.

"There is food in England you know, Oonagh. The war is over."

"Shut up," Oonagh said, eyes twinkling, "well if there is, you eat none of it, and look at the poor little fella." Monty wagged up at her. He loved Oonagh and Padar.

"Well, you're in luck. The people in Weathervane left yesterday and I don't have another booking until next month."

"That's good, but you'll have to put the next lot off too." Marianne sipped her drink.

"Will I? Why? Are you staying for a good while?"

"Put it this way. Is it for sale?"

"At the right price," Padar interjected, returning

with the milk.

"Ah, stop it, Padar," Oonagh chided. "But not a holiday home, surely? Surely you'll come and live among us?"

"That's the plan." Marianne grinned at the couple.

"I knew it. I knew you'd come home. Welcome, welcome, Marie. My heart is lifted. I'm delighted. Thanks be to God." Oonagh was waddling gleefully towards Marianne.

"She'll have the Rosary out in a minute," Miss MacReady strode through the bar, tartan poncho flying, wellington boots thwacking on the stone flags. She stopped and took Marianne's hands in hers; birdlike eyes scanning her face.

"I'm not a bit surprised to see you and, I too, am delighted if you've decided to make Innishmahon your home. We need women like you. We've a few battles to fight."

"Well, I'm here to help."

"Good. And no doubt you're well out of this?" She slapped a magazine on the bar, stabbing at the cover with a blood red finger nail. The main photograph was Ryan O'Gorman and Angelique de Marcos, smiling in the sunshine. Angelique wore a flowing wedding gown, twists of orange blossom in her hair. She was wreathed in smiles, and holding her bouquet aloft. She was obviously pregnant. Ryan wore a crisp Asian style collarless shirt; they were both covered in rose petals and the headline read: 'Superspy Star Weds Actress in Secret Ceremony.'

Oonagh picked the magazine up slowly and then

dropped it back on the bar as if it had bit her.

"I knew nothing of this," she exclaimed, "and I was on the website only yesterday. They certainly kept this under wraps."

Miss MacReady handed Marianne the magazine. Marianne scanned the cover, desperately trying not to appear shocked, hoping it was only she who heard the brittle crack as her heart shattered. She placed her feet slightly apart to prevent the ground from shifting any further. There was a loud whooshing in her ears. Her throat went dry.

Miss MacReady retrieved the magazine from Marianne's tightened fingers.

"I'll have a large whiskey, Padar, and so will Marie."

Padar ferreted under the bar and plonked a new litre bottle on the counter. He unscrewed the top and threw it on the fire, pouring them all large whiskeys. As if he smelled the free drink, Sean Grogan slid through the door. He cocked the one good eye at Marianne, and addressed Miss MacReady.

"It's back then, is it?"

"For good. Buying the cottage next door."

"Didn't know it was for sale."

"Sure everything's for sale, Sean. Especially since the storm. Who wants to come here with no bridge?"

"We're better off without a bridge, only brought trouble."

"You do talk through your arse, Sean," Padar poured them all another good measure of whiskey.

The Hollow Heart

In a matter of hours, news of Marianne's return whipped round the island, and the next day, Father Gregory called at the cottage, quickly followed by Sinead and Phileas from the pharmacy, bearing apple cake and wine to add to Father Gregory's gift of a potted aloe vera; renowned, he said, for both healing and survival.

Marianne busied herself with repairs and renewals for her new home, which seemed sadly neglected in the few short months she had been away. She agreed what was a fair price with the Quinns, and promised to have the funds transferred swiftly from her Dublin bank account, once the sale had been completed on Oakwood Avenue. Oonagh said she was pleased the cottage had gone to a good home, laughing almost hysterically at her own joke, and then bursting into tears of gratitude, telling Marianne she did not know how she would have managed with the baby coming and business so dire. They were sitting in the deserted pub, looking at curtain fabrics.

"I think we've saved each other," Marianne said quietly, returning the latest copy of *The Biz*, Global Communications newly launched celebrity magazine, featuring yet another 'world exclusive' of Ryan's wedding. She noted the author of the piece was none other than her erstwhile colleague, Paul Osborne. She had also noted Larry Leeson and his sister Lena Leeson were among the guests, together with Franco Rossini, the bride's 'beloved' uncle, and producer, of Ryan's film. Speculation regarding the unborn child's parentage had also been resolved for the purposes of the eight-page full colour photo-spread.

It read… *'the bride and groom (twelve years older than his beautiful new spouse) are both happily awaiting the birth of their first child. Ryan has one son, the musician, Mike O'Gorman, from a previous relationship, who, with his model wife Zara, is said to be delighted that his father has found true love at last. Mike and Zara have a baby daughter, a ready-made playmate for the newest member of their extended family.'*

"You've read it, then?" Oonagh noted her friend's empty look.

"Hey, I have a new home, new life, and a hell of a bridge to help build."

"You're throwing your weight behind it then?" shouted Padar from the cellar.

"Yep! All eight stone of it."

"Don't forget the power of the pen!" He smiled, head popping up through the trap door.

"Good woman," called Miss MacReady from the doorway, where she was hammering in a notice with a gold platform boot. "There's a committee meeting this evening. I'll see you there, so." And she left, hopping into the street on the one boot, the other still in her hand.

"Must be a very important meeting tonight, she didn't even have a drink," Padar bemoaned, as Marianne read the notice and announced she was off too. "The meeting had better be here, or we'll all be out the door with the poverty."

Oonagh did not comment, deciding instead, to take

a nap, rather than make lunches that nobody wanted.

All the great and the good were on the committee. Father Gregory was Chairman, with Vice Chairman, Padar Quinn, secretary, Miss MacReady, and newly-appointed communications officer, Marianne Coltrane. The initial ten-million euro allocated by the Dublin Government for the reconstruction of the bridge and repairs to the roads, had been halved, due to the economic climate, leaving little enough to reinstate the roads, let alone the bridge. Father Gregory explained that the committee would have to apply to the EU for top-up funding, and this would not be easy. With the ferry access reinstated, Innishmahon was no longer considered a priority case.

"The few hundred islanders here are hardly a swayable force in the scheme of things," he told them in his pulpit voice, "with so much of the storm damage affecting areas with large populations where allegiance will make a difference to a political party, we have little voice and if we can't come up with something radical our small community won't even be heard, let alone listened to."

Marianne was fully aware that Father Gregory and Miss MacReady had already done the best they could with limited funds and even less experience, but once the imminent danger had passed, the media spotlight had moved away from the island. There was no hope of raising the cash, without raising the island's profile.

After the meeting, which to Padar's relief, was in the pub, the inhabitants of Weathervane cottage lit the fire and settled in for the night. The sea mist, sitting off shore all day, had come in quickly at dusk, and now rain swirled restlessly against the window.

Marianne worked late into the night, tapping away at her laptop, Monty snoozing peacefully at her feet. She was just putting the finishing touches to her ten-point proactive PR strategy, when there was a loud rap on the cottage door. It made Marianne jump, and Monty growl. It was late for callers, even on Innishmahon. Miss MacReady stood in the porch, a leopard print turban rammed on her head, crystal earrings shimmering in the lamplight. Marianne beckoned her in, shutting the door quickly behind her.

"I'm sorry to disturb you so late, Marie, but this came today, and I didn't want to give it to the postman. Thought it best if no-one but you saw it." Miss MacReady drew a long, thin airmail envelope from inside her floor-length wax coat. Marianne caught her breath, the writing on the front was a splodgy mess; she could barely make out her own name.

"It's been forwarded from England but the postmark is Mauritius." Miss MacReady gripped Marianne's hand as she handed her the letter. "There's many a slip twixt the cup and the lip, as the old saying goes, Marie."

Marianne looked at the older woman quizzically.

"Meaning there can be many ups and downs before the final outcome is reached, and sometimes you think something is over when it's really just beginning, but in a different way."

Marianne stared at the envelope, dying to rip it open, yet dreading to. She heard the door close as Miss MacReady left. Taking a deep breath, she began to read.

'My darling Marianne,

This is the only way I could think to let you know what's happening, my emails and mobile are constantly monitored. There's no other way to say this except to come straight to the point. I am writing to let you know I'm marrying Angelique, quickly and in secret. It is, without doubt, a marriage of pure and utter convenience and, believe me, if there was any other way I could deal with this dreadful set of circumstances, I most certainly would. Suffice to say, I have no choice, there's more than myself and my feelings to consider at this point. And then there are your feelings, my darling. I don't know what to say, or what to write, or how to express my sorrow at dragging you into this mire. I'm not even sure of your feelings, our time together has been so fleeting, yet so precious. Rest assured, plans to extricate me from this are in place and, as soon as I possibly can, I'll be with you to explain everything, please, please trust me. I'm praying this reaches you before the story breaks, but if it has, you most probably loathe and detest me and would prefer never to have anything to do with me ever again. Please believe me, it was never my intention to hurt you and, whatever happens, I love you, and when all this madness is over, I want to be with you more than anything, and I am hoping against all hope you will still feel the same. Yours for ever, Ryan.'

Marianne's knees buckled. She felt as if someone

had punched her in the stomach. Sinking to the sofa, Monty jumped up beside her, his inquisitive nose snuffling the discarded sheets. She stood up, folded her arms, walked across the room, came back to the sofa and sat down. Picking up the letter, she read it again more slowly. Monty was watching her intently. Suddenly, she wrapped her arms around the little bundle of fur, squeezing him till he squirmed to be released. She let him down and caught sight of herself in the mirror. She stopped, surprised at her reflection, because despite everything she had just read, and was desperately trying to assimilate, she found herself with a strange look on her face, a crooked half-smile, her eyes bright.

"Well, you never know, Miss MacReady could be right, and you know what they say, it ain't over till it's over," she told her bizarre reflection.

Chapter Twenty Two – Cause Célèbre

It was a beautiful morning. Marianne made a breakfast of sausage and white pudding sandwiches, followed by a brisk walk along the sunlit cove as gulls glided through the air, the waves hardly breaking. The woman and the little dog stood still for a long minute, taking it all in.

"Let's never take all this for granted, Monty. Let's make that promise to each other right now and forever." She bent down and ruffled his fur. He wagged his tail, intelligent eyes looked straight into hers, before he trotted off to continue his usual diligent beachcombing. She had worked through the night on plans for the campaign to reinstate the bridge to the island. Fired with passion, having read Ryan's letter, or a desire to make a mark in this, her newly chosen homeland, she was not sure which, but something had ignited deep within her and it felt positive and powerful. As a journalist, Marianne had always been a campaigner. It felt good to have a new campaign to feel passionate about.

Marianne needed to run her proposal past Father Gregory and Miss MacReady at lunch. There was no time to lose. The deadline for the first bid for funding was approaching, and they had to have a strategy in place to even be considered for the match fund programme being offered by the EU. Despite some enthusiastic bucket-rattling and badge-selling to any visitors who had made the trip to the island since the storm, the 'Reinstate the Bridge' fighting fund, invested safely in the Post Office, was so meagre it would make little impact on the huge task they had set themselves. Major investment was needed; a carefully planned campaign, the only way forward.

She marched back to the cottage, so absorbed she did not notice the figure on the cliff, camera lens trained upon her. Monty looked up and twitched his nose, he had picked up that scent before. He eyed his mistress. She did not break her stride. He had to canter to catch up.

The news they had crossed the first hurdle and the 'Bridge Too Far' campaign had been added to the list for European funding, was celebrated in true Innishmahon style, with a proper hooley in Maguire's. Father Gregory made a speech, praising the committee and, Marianne, in particular. The campaign had begun in earnest. Phase Two was to invite everyone who had been born on the island or who had ever visited for whatever reason, to return for one weekend, to start the foundations of the bridge-building by hand. Marianne had been inspired by the church at her childhood convent. The nuns had longed for a replica of the Grotto at Lourdes. It was during 'the emergency', as the second world war had been referred to by some in the Republic; there was no money or materials for so-unnecessary a building project, but the local men, came together as a working party and, barrowing the stone from nearby mountains, hand-built a grotto for the community. The Bishop had been so impressed by their efforts he had sent beautiful life-sized statues of the Holy Virgin and Saint Bernadette. They had even replicated the spring at Our Lady's feet, with some ingenious and discreet plumbing.

"We'll start the bridge-building the way they built the grotto back then," she explained to the committee, handing out leaflets, calling for volunteers. "We'll lay the foundations ourselves, with our own bare hands, then they'll see we mean business and, if anyone who has ever visited the island volunteers to help, just for one weekend, it will demonstrate how badly we need the bridge to survive."

Marianne issued press releases; they launched a 'Bridge Too Far' website and Oonagh started a daily blog clocking up the numbers of respondents, highlighting writers, artists and other celebrities who had promised to come and join the working party. For those who could not attend, foundation stones were being 'sold' at one hundred euro a time. Cash was beginning to roll in.

"I'm trying to get loads of superstars, boy bands and the rest of their pals to come. I'm on their websites and tweeting like mad," Oonagh announced at the committee meeting prior to the 'Bridge Too Far' festival weekend, delighted with her role of adding celebrities to the guest list.

"Will they take to the stage, do you think?" Miss MacReady was beside herself; she had a particular passion for boy bands.

"Sure a session here would be the best of all worlds, and Father Gregory does a great version of *'I don't like Mondays'* except he sings Sundays," laughed Padar, as the excitement began to take hold.

Oonagh followed Marianne into the loo. Over the last few weeks, her friend had spoken of nothing except the campaign. It had absorbed her entirely. Oonagh thought she looked pale, despite the fire in her eyes. Marianne was dragging a brush through her hair.

"Any news?" Oonagh asked, nonchalantly.

Marianne shrugged. "Sure I'm well off the radar. He's married to Angelique, they are expecting a child, he's made his choice and I've made mine. We won't see him again, and that's for the best."

Oonagh raised an eyebrow. Marianne had done a fantastic job; and all the TV channels were running the story, reporting updates as the campaign progressed. Oonagh blogged news online and Miss MacReady was negotiating exclusive rights with a celebrity magazine and a Sunday newspaper from her newly purchased laptop. Someone would need to be living on another planet to be unaware of what was happening on the small island off the west coast of Ireland. Even if Ryan had missed any of the news bulletins, which was unlikely, Oonagh had kept him up to speed via her special status as one of his most fervent fans. Although disappointingly, she had not had one email acknowledging her pleas for him to help with the campaign. But Oonagh was not prepared to give up on him, she could not believe he had abandoned them. He had been a real life hero in their darkest hour. He was one of their own.

Back in the bar, Oonagh was not going to let the subject drop.

"If you want my advice," she said, gazing sagely at her tea towel.

"It seems I always receive your advice whether I want it or not." Marianne was smiling.

Oonagh continued polishing glasses, "I'd wait for the stallion to return."

"What?"

"Hear it from the horse's mouth, you know, ask Ryan straight out, is he with Angelique or not. Was the marriage a publicity stunt, or something more sinister. Did he have to do it; was he blackmailed. I mean, what do you feel in your heart of hearts?"

"I don't know what I feel if I'm honest, or which way to turn. Sometimes I feel like I'm in the eye of a storm too, blown from pillar to post, homeless, heartless, loveless, oh I dunno." Two huge tears slid unexpectedly down Marianne's cheeks.

Oonagh ran from behind the bar as fast as her bulk would allow. She gripped Marianne by the arms, staring in mock horror into her face.

"Dear God, was that you speaking Marianne? Did you just talk about your feelings? You know, articulate how you actually feel?"

"What do mean?" Marianne sniffed, incredulous, "I'm very open about my feelings, people know exactly where they stand with me."

"Really? Ever told him you're in love with him?" Oonagh released Marianne, and folded her arms.

"Well, of course." Marianne looked out of the window. "You have customers coming."

"Ever?" Oonagh was rooted to the spot.

"Well, probably not precisely in those words, no."

"So he doesn't know where he stands either. Poor fella, trailing halfway round the world in the hope the woman he loves will tell him she loves him, demand he stays with her, or never darken her door again; living in hope she'll make a home for him, so he can, at last, stop flitting around the globe, like a homeless will o'the wisp."

The small area around the bar was suddenly full. The next time Oonagh checked the corner where Marianne and Monty had been sitting, it was empty.

The very next day Miss MacReady charged through the door of Weathervane, brandishing a letter, stamped airmail, from Australia. She and Marianne both recognised the handwriting.

"Well?" Miss MacReady pushed the envelope across the table towards her. Marianne opened it. A cheque for fifty-thousand euro fluttered to the surface.

"Mother of God!" Miss MacReady exclaimed. No note, no explanation.

She handed it to the postmistress.

"Lodge it."

"Good enough." Miss MacReady left, bursting with the news for Oonagh to blog.

Marianne sat down, winded. Monty, always the

opportunist, jumped onto her lap. She put her arms around him and let the tears drip slowly into his fur, till he shook his ears free of the wetness. Sometimes, maintaining this stiff upper lip was bloody hard work.

Chapter Twenty Three - A Double Blessing

Marianne spoke into the receiver. "Love? Are you drunk? Stoned?"

"No way. I only said ..."

"I know what you said. How much is asked of that little word? I mean, really? How can I possibly know if what it means for you is what it means for me?"

"Ah ..."

"Is it a sweet fondness that makes you smile when you hear my voice or see me enter a room, I wonder? Or an all-consuming passion that means you can't think of anything else, food is abandoned, and the night is endless?"

"Er...I think you're the one who's been drinking."

She ignored him. "I mean, I love baked beans, sunshine, Christmas, clean hair, airports. How can that tiny word apply to so much?"

"Well..."

"So no, I don't know you love me and I certainly don't know how much. There's your answer."

"And they say romance is dead." He was laughing, the line crackling.

"I just thanked you for your generous donation to the campaign, I did not expect the response to be 'but you know how much I love you.'" She twisted the frayed cord in her free hand.

"Well I do, and whatever the word means to you, it means an awful lot to me."

"Really, how's your new wife?" She bit her lip.

"Impossible. But that's another story. A story I want to tell you face to face."

"Not sure if I want to listen."

"For fifty grand, you'll listen."

"Don't make me feel cheap."

"Fifty grand is not cheap. Anyway, I genuinely want to help. Innishmahon means a lot to me too, it feels like roots."

"I know what you mean." She softened.

"I know you do, sure we're the same soul."

"*Wuthering Heights* has been done."

"That's the other thing; I'll bring the latest draft of the script with me."

"You're coming, then?"

"Try and stop me."

"I'll tell Oonagh, and she..."

"No. No publicity till after I've been. I'll be incognito."

"I've told you before, Ryan, this super-spy thing is just a role. Might you be taking the method acting too far?"

The line went dead. He had called on the landline from a public telephone in New Mexico. She was thrilled to hear his voice. She dared not admit, even to herself, how much she longed to see him. She shook her head sadly, she probably had drunk a little too much wine with her solitary dinner, but she had been working all hours helping to co-ordinate what was going to be a mammoth weekend. She stood looking at herself in the mirror in the hallway of the cottage, holding the heavy *Bakelite* hand piece aloft. How did she feel now? Exasperated, exhilarated and excited. She replaced the receiver, missing the almost imperceptible click of someone else listening on the line.

'The 'Bridge Too Far' Festival was planned for the Bank Holiday weekend at the end of October. Preparations were in full swing. All the holiday cottages had been let; a special caravan and camping village erected with a huge stage, seating, toilets, showers and canteen facilities all in place. People were arriving by the boatload. Oonagh had emptied Maguire's storerooms to turn them into makeshift guest suites; Father Gregory had given over the Priest's house to invading celebrities and their entourages, and even the abandoned Georgian mansion, positioned on the highest cliff facing seaward, had been made ready for visitors. It was rumoured some young Royals were staying there, bringing friends from the world of sport, stage and screen. Miss MacReady was rather proud of that particular rumour.

A starting gun would sound the commencement of building works at eight o'clock on Friday morning and a siren would cease production at dusk on Monday evening. For entertainment, an open mic session was scheduled for Friday night at Maguire's, a full blown rock concert on Saturday, and a ceilidh on Sunday. The island was to play host to three and a half thousand revellers, most of whom would work for at least a couple of hours on the foundations of the bridge. Some of Ireland's biggest building firms were supplying materials free of charge, and by Friday evening, the concrete for the foundations had been poured into the footings. Everyone was invited to sign their name in the still-wet cement, quickly followed by the laying of blocks bearing the names of the one hundred euro benefactors. Even though only an eighth of the project would be completed by the end of the festival, it was an eighth that could not be torn down, destroyed or blown away. It was a great start.

As the weekend drew to a close, Father Gregory announced word from Brussels was positive. There was every indication, due to the community's dogged determination to help itself, that the match funding would be granted. The news was greeted with rapture. Miss MacReady, resplendent in a red satin cocktail gown, pirouetted into Maguire's, clasping a print of an email.

"We've done it! We've done it! It only needs rubber stamping but we're there. This is confirmation from Nuala, good girl she is." Nuala O'Shaugnessy was the MEP for the area.

"Well done, Miss MacReady. I'm proud of you, proud of all of you," rejoined a distinctive accent from the shadows. Miss MacReady flurried bird-like towards the voice.

"You made it! Fair play to you. What are you doing hiding here in the corner?"

"Waiting for the fuss to die down a bit. You know the press."

"Sure there's plenty bigger names than you here. You'll hardly be noticed in that crowd," she tried to reassure him, indicating the hordes drifting by the window, heading for the extra ferries laid on to see the revellers home in time for work, college or school.

Miss MacReady gratefully sipped the drink he handed her.

"I've a fierce dry throat with all the talking. God, I've been interviewed by everyone, even that lovely fella off the telly. I'd have him on my dance card any Saturday night."

"Sure that would leave anyone thirsty," laughed Ryan.

There was a struggle at the door. Father Gregory appeared with Marianne, supporting Oonagh. Marianne stumbled under the weight of her friend. Ryan was there instantly, taking Oonagh from her. Marianne was so consumed with anxiety, she did not even notice him.

"She's exhausted, taken on far too much," Father Gregory indicated the stairs. The colour was draining away from Oonagh's usually russet complexion.

"Let me." Ryan took over from Marianne. Miss MacReady put her pint down.

"I'm going for Sinead. The baby's coming." She indicated Oonagh's bump, and flew out the door.

Less than an hour later, Padar announced the

premature arrival of his baby daughter, Bridget Marianne, to a subdued gathering of regulars at the bar.

"All's well, all's well," he repeated, not quite convincingly, but as Sinead was not allowing any visitors for at least twenty-four hours, they would have to take his word for it.

"We'll wet the baby's head tomorrow then," Father Gregory confirmed as the crowd started to disperse. The fact he had been asked to stay to conduct the Baptism had not gone unnoticed.

"Can I walk you home?" It was the first time Ryan had addressed Marianne directly. She nodded and, taking her coat off the hook, he placed it around her shoulders. She could feel the imprint of his touch long after he had taken his hand away. Monty padded out behind them. They walked in silence. He took her arm and they strolled down towards the beach and the opening in the cliff leading down to the cove. The last of the festival-goers were leaving, the lights of their cars disappearing as the ferry set sail. Marianne and Ryan stood on the beach and watched, as it left the pontoon, Monty sniffing along the water's edge. Ryan put his arms around her. She returned his embrace. They held each other tightly.

"It will be alright," he said into her hair.

"Are you staying?"

"If I may?"

"Still married?"

"At the moment? Yes."

"You'll have to sleep on the sofa then. I won't be a mistress."

"I know." The reflection of the sea made his eyes glitter, but his mouth turned down at the edges.

"Let's go home," she said. The three turned into the wind and walked briskly back to Weathervane.

The next day dawned bright and blustery. The sea had whipped itself into a swirl of sparkling grey. Cloud streaked across a pale blue sky as the soft sun tried in vain to warm the land. Marianne stumbled down to the kitchen to find Ryan and Monty both missing. By the time she had made coffee, they reappeared sandy, damp and smiling.

"We saw the baby. They're fine, she's beautiful. They had a good night. Padar says the doctor will be here this morning just to check them over, but they're okay. It's looking good."

Marianne sank into a chair.

"Thank God." The word God turned into a sob. Ryan was holding her in an instant. She tried to pull away.

"Hey, hey, you've been awake half the night. You're worn out. Let me take care of you, just for a little while."

She wiped her nose on his shoulder.

"Is that all I have you for, a little while?"

"This time. Can that be enough for now?"

"I suppose it will have to be." She searched his face, it was full of love and disappointment. She thought of George and felt his loss. She took Ryan's face in her hands and kissed him. Love is love, take it when you find it, she told herself.

"This is awful, Ryan. I can hardly bear it."

"I know, but it's not forever. I will sort it, please believe me. I truly do love you and I want to be with you."

"Well, you've some explaining to do, that's for sure."

"I know I have." He handed her a tissue. "Please don't cry, my love, all is not as it appears, but what I'm about to tell you is so screwed, you couldn't make it up." And so Ryan told the woman he loved, why he had just married a woman he did not. Right from the beginning of his and Angelique's wild and wonderful romance, through their turbulent break up, Angelique's addiction, pregnancy and the forthcoming birth of their child. He told her how Larry turned up on set to tell him he had thought it all through, and that the only way he would have the right to custody of his baby, was to marry Angelique, and despite this being the last thing he wanted to do, he saw it was the only thing he could do.

Monty had a long wait for breakfast and, after more tears, recriminations and reconciliation. Ryan wrapped Marianne in a blanket, lit the fire, and held her till she fell asleep, never taking his eyes off her for a minute.

Stateside, Larry Leeson was about to have a coronary, albeit self-induced. Suspecting her estranged husband of infidelity, Angelique de Marcos had booked herself into the Beverley Hills Maternity Clinic for a pre-arranged Caesarean section. The hospital had just telephoned, she had been successfully delivered of a baby boy. Mother and baby were doing well. Father was away without leave, as Larry put it.

"What's the point of having a cell phone if it's never switched on!" the exasperated agent told Ryan's voicemail. Lena was on the other line.

"You know where he is Larry, you always do," she said, "now find him and get him to contact his wife urgently, then at least I can put out some sort of press statement. The uncaring, self-obsessed bastard!"

"Hey, he didn't know she was doing this. The baby is barely due."

"He knows Angelique well enough to figure she is not going to sit around and wait for a natural birth, especially with him disappearing again. C'mon Larry, get real."

"He's due back the day after tomorrow."

"Not good enough, he should be here now."

"I'm doing my best."

"I repeat. Not good enough." The line went dead.

Larry trawled his contacts book to find the selection of numbers he had collected during his visit to Ireland. He was aware the 'Bridge Too Far' Festival had taken place that weekend. He knew of Ryan's donation to the campaign. He had made a not-ungenerous donation himself, but when he pleaded with his client not to attend the event, being so close to the birth of his own child, even if he was estranged from his new wife, Ryan's refusal to even acknowledge the plea gave Larry his answer. He knew where Ryan was, alright, he also knew if Lena had an inkling of how much he did know, she would eat him alive.

He dialled the postmistress. Miss MacReady recognised his voice immediately. She had developed a huge crush on the immaculately groomed New Yorker when he had visited the island.

"Is he supposed to be here?" she asked cautiously, after an ebullient greeting.

"Reckon so."

"And where do you think he might be?"

"Working on that goddamn script with Marianne, I suppose." He laughed at the euphemism. Miss MacReady ignored the inference.

"Is she supposed to be here?"

"No suppose about it. She's like a damn magnet, that woman. No offence ma'am, but this relationship is driving a coach and horses through a number of very important people's schedules."

"Is it now?" Miss MacReady was unimpressed.

"Well is he there, or not?"

"Sure, there's been over three thousand people here this weekend."

Larry sighed. Why were the Irish so damned obtuse?

"Ma'am, could you please just get a message to him? His wife had a baby boy yesterday. Both fine. Can he please get his ass back here PDQ. Have you got that?"

"Oh, how lovely, two babies in the one weekend. A great omen for the future, I'm sure of it."

"If you see my client ma'am, please give him the

message, or he'll have no future!"

"Ah, Mr Leeson, you're very dramatic. I thought Ryan was the actor."

Larry hung up and, not for the first time, tried to fathom out what was going on in the seemingly deranged brain of his long-time-buddy and errant client. Ryan had everything they had been working for all these years, a fantastic career and all that went with it. Okay, his relationship with Angelique was tricky and needed to be handled delicately, but that could be managed, and Ryan could once again be free to enjoy the fame and fortune he had always craved. Yet in those quiet moments during a break on set, or in the back of a limo en route to a press conference, Larry knew Ryan was somewhere else, with someone else, probably being the most important thing of all - himself. He shrugged at the New York skyline through the office window. Well, if that is what love does to you, you can keep it. And forgoing his diet, he decided to treat himself to a very large lunch.

Despite Larry's cynicism, Ryan and Marianne were, indeed, working on the script. Ryan had persuaded an editor friend in Hollywood to look over the first draft and put it on a memory stick. He was having problems with some of the dialogue.

"It's the love scenes. It sounds false. He comes over as a right gobshite."

"The less dialogue in a love scene, the better, I reckon." She turned a few pages, distracted. Ryan cartoon-tip-toed away, then turning back, did a silent movie double-take and threw himself at her, fumbling at her clothes, pulling down her collar to slobber over her throat. She beat him back with a cushion. Monty, now yapping wildly, decided to join in, tugging at the hems of their jeans as Marianne fought back. Ryan started to tie Marianne up in a throw and, as she tried to escape, they all fell writhing to the floor. Miss MacReady nearly collapsed on the swirling mass as she came in through the back door. She was dressed from head to toe in grey flannel. No time for frivolity today.

"What are ye at?" she snapped, "you crowd are always rolling around on the floor together. You're like a gaggle of gypsies."

They broke free, breathless and laughing. Monty greeted her enthusiastically. Miss MacReady always smelled wonderfully exotic.

"Mr Leeson's been on. I have news." She gave them a minute to gather themselves. "Your wife had a little boy yesterday. You're needed elsewhere."

Ryan gasped. Marianne stood up slowly, brushing herself down.

"They're both fine. But you'd better call him, he's very agitated as you can imagine."

Ryan took Marianne's hand. She was staring at her feet.

"I didn't say I'd seen you, either of you. Goodbye now," Miss MacReady called back as she left.

"Goodbye now," Ryan echoed. Marianne let his hand drop. She folded the throw, put the cushions back on the sofa. She gave Ryan a half-smile.

"I'm glad your baby is okay. It's lovely news that you have a little boy. I know you have to be with them," she said.

"I want to be with *him*, not them, and I don't want to leave you, but I do have go back now. Can you understand that?"

"I'll have a look at the script, see what I can do, but no promises. *Gone with the Wind*, it ain't." She straightened some papers on the kitchen table, fiddled with the tap at the sink.

"I'll get going then," he said very quietly, picking up the overnight bag. Pulling his jacket from the back of the chair, he took a small box from the pocket and, opening it, held something glistening on a chain towards her. "For you, a love token." It was a platinum pendant, a tiny replica of a Weathervane with each moving part set with diamonds. He held it aloft and spun the arrow. "Wherever you are, part of me, the best part of me, is with you, and wherever you are, that's where I want to be. It's where I'm meant to be."

His smile was lopsided. He put the pendant around her throat, kissing the downy skin of her neck as he fastened the clasp.

"It's beautiful," she said, silent tears sliding down her cheeks. "You'd better go." She touched the gift and sat down at the table. He patted Monty, kissed the top of Marianne's head, and left.

Chapter Twenty Four – Doing The Right Thing

The photograph of a barely identifiable couple embracing on a wintry beach with a small white dog at their ankles first appeared in an Irish Sunday newspaper. Within a week it had gone global in celebrity gossip magazines; TV showbiz news and online, the story was everywhere. Headlines screamed, 'Super spy love-rat abandons pregnant wife' 'Wife in labour as Ryan labours under another love' 'Star misses birth to be with Irish lover.'

Miss MacReady was straight down to Weathervane when the story broke, bringing copies of newspapers and magazines. Shocked, Marianne immediately prepared a statement to refute the claims but, as the story took hold, she, the experienced media manipulator, felt powerless against the onslaught of gossip and conjecture. The same question kept ringing round in her head. Who had taken the photographs, who had betrayed them, here, where they felt safe, where they could be themselves? Marianne switched off her mobile and unplugged the laptop. Miss MacReady promised to keep her abreast of any significant developments via the landline.

The warning of the small huddle of paparazzi

hiding in the lane behind the cottage, came too late. Marianne and Monty walked straight into them on their way to see Oonagh and the baby.

"How long have you been seeing Ryan O'Gorman, Miss Coltrane?" called one.

"Did you know he abandoned his pregnant wife to be with you?" shouted another.

"It's been said you're an ambitious home-wrecker. What do you say to that?"

Marianne scooped Monty up and side-stepped into Maguire's. Padar slammed and bolted the door behind her. She pushed the hood of her jacket back.

"Miss MacReady phoned here when she couldn't get you up at the cottage."

Marianne sighed heavily. Padar put a hand on her shoulder.

"Can we go up?"

He nodded.

She flew up the stairs to greet a glowing Oonagh and a tiny, bluish baby Bridget. She clasped her sweet smelling friend to her. Oonagh was propped on pillows and cushions, a collection of pink and white gifts already amassing in a corner of the room. Marianne spied the clutter of magazines and newspapers on the floor. Oonagh's laptop was snoozing on her dressing table; her addiction to celebrity gossip barely on hold.

"I believe there's swathes of paparazzi on the island," Oonagh stated eventually, sipping tea Padar had delivered, as Marianne sat in the armchair, nursing Bridget.

"Hardly swathes. They'll soon get bored and bugger off."

"You're very stoical about the whole affair."

"And that's what it is, an affair, or what it *was*."

Oonagh spotted the trinket, glistening at Marianne's usually unadorned throat.

"It's over?"

Marianne did not answer. She turned her attention to Bridget, telling her how beautiful she was and how lucky her parents were to have her. Monty endorsed this from a polite distance, slowly shifting his tail from side to side.

"Did you see the double-page spread in *The Biz*?"

"The new show business magazine, under the editorial direction of one, Paul Osborne?" Marianne raised an eyebrow at her friend.

"A series of pictures going way back, starting with the 'Power 2 The People' Awards. You're holding hands."

"He was leading me out of a bomb site, as I recall."

"Then there are pictures here on the island and, together, having a quiet dinner at a Tudor lodge in Berkshire, more than just an affair, anyway."

"Oonagh, drop it."

"One of the newspaper supplements ran a really unflattering photo of you next to one of Angelique at a red carpet event, with the headline: 'Who would you want to wake up with?' But then another celebrity mag dug out a lovely one of you at the anniversary celebrations, saying you were a highly talented, award-winning journalist and stunning looking as well, in fairness to them." Oonagh always liked to highlight the good points of the publications she was so addicted to.

Marianne asked Bridget when she hoped her official christening would be. Oonagh finally took the hint.

"The eighth of December, Feast of the Immaculate Conception. What do you think?"

"Highly appropriate." They both laughed.

While Oonagh recovered from her traumatic, yet triumphant, pregnancy, Marianne set to work splitting her time between helping Padar run the pub, and editing and rewriting Ryan's script. Not six weeks after the 'Bridge Too Far' weekend, some semblance of normality had returned to Innishmahon. EU funds were allocated, and work on the bridge was scheduled to recommence in the New Year, with everything on track for the beginning of the next tourist season.

Miss MacReady, taking a brief respite in her role as the island's communications mogul, was thrilled to be asked to make Bridget's christening gown, and was working on a concoction of cream satin and antique lace, with hand sewn crystals from a wedding tiara she never had occasion to wear. Legend had it; the treasure belonged to one of the Romanov princesses, who had escaped slaughter at the hands of Russian revolutionaries in 1918. How Miss MacReady had come by it was another story altogether. And oddly for her, one that she would only hint at, as the three women sat sipping Prosecco, making plans for the christening in the room Oonagh had turned into a boudoir suite for herself and the baby.

"Oh, I might have needed it for a wedding myself once, but it wasn't to be." She was puffing on a plastic cigarette, an aid to giving up, she had been struggling with ever since Bridget had been born.

"Not like Miss Haversham, Miss MacReady, you weren't left at the altar, were you?" Oonagh was teasing, but Marianne saw Miss MacReady draw her lips into a crimson slash. She had hit a nerve.

"I'm sure that would never be the case," Marianne offered quickly, "sure women like Miss MacReady lead armies and build empires. You're way ahead of your time, Miss MacReady, an independent, educated, career woman. What man could keep up with you?"

Miss MacReady blinked and was smiling again.

"You're very earnest, aren't you, Marianne?" Oonagh slurred, not able to drink half as much as she could before Bridget arrived.

"Am I?" asked Marianne, and then realising this was not quite the compliment she assumed, "I think I'm sincere."

"Odd trait for a journalist," Oonagh observed.

Marianne nudged her. "Oi, cheeky!"

"You strike me as all those things," concurred Miss MacReady, nibbling a cheese thin. "Ever tried living a bit dangerously?"

"In my own way, at times," laughed Marianne.

"Why have you, Miss MacReady, ever?"

Miss MacReady gazed over their heads.

"Ah sure, what would I know about dangerous living, a meek-mannered spinster like myself. No never!" she said, as she tugged her sparkly vest down to reveal an exquisite tattoo on her left breast. It read, *"My Baby"* in a love heart of roses and barbed wire.

The other two stared first at Miss MacReady, and then at each other, speechless, and then all three of them roared with laughter, rocking the bed with their mirth.

The Quinns invited over eighty guests to celebrate their daughter's arrival into the world. Father Gregory was officiating at the service, which was to encompass Bridget Marianne's formal baptism; a renewal of Oonagh and Padar's marriage vows; a Mass in thanksgiving for the survival of the devastation wrought by the storm, and a general blessing of all souls gathered regardless of race, religion, creed or sexual orientation. As the priest put it, "Sure while I have a captive audience, I may as well throw the whole lot at them."

A feast in honour of the occasion was being prepared in the now highly-organised kitchen at the pub. Marianne and Padar worked well together, despite Oonagh's fierce criticism and disparaging tastings. Padar had become an excellent cook, styling himself on a number of celebrity chefs but with less bad language. Marianne, who had basked in George's encyclopaedic knowledge of food and wine, had never been particularly interested in cooking and only started taking an interest in the kitchen when it was necessary, helping Oonagh and her 'storm troopers' during the typhoon. But as her culinary interest awakened, she too, was having a beneficial effect, choosing a selection of new and old world wines to complement Padar's developing menu. They had even enjoyed a highly favourable review in one of the Sunday supplements, now framed and hung in pride of place above the bar.

Oonagh was, on the one hand, delighted, and on the other, slightly put out that her husband and best friend made such an excellent team, but for the most part, she was happy to leave them to it. Still not in the best of health, she was far too busy with christening plans. She was under no illusion though, Marianne's tireless dedication to duty and interminable workload, was a dogged attempt to wipe Ryan from her consciousness and, if circumstances were different, and Marianne had her own commitments, the Quinns would be the poorer for her lack of devotion. Despite Marianne's evasion of the subject, Oonagh was determined to find the elusive film star and made numerous attempts to contact him, requesting he confirm his attendance at her daughter's christening, as he had promised. Ever hopeful, she checked her emails but there was no response or even acknowledgement from Ryan. As time passed, Oonagh increasingly considered his treatment of her friend and the Innishmahon community, tawdry to say the least, but for once she kept her own counsel.

Meanwhile, on the other side of the Atlantic, an

emotionally-battered man was kissing his baby son goodbye, and grabbing a hastily packed bag to board yet another flight. Ryan was very aware he would miss the little boy desperately whilst on this particular 'low profile' trip. He was, however, totally unaware the child's Nanny had started to telephone her paparazzi contact before his taxi had even swung out of the gates of the rented Los Angeles mansion.

The Virgin's feast day was a great excuse to commence pre-Christmas festivities, and the fact the whole village was invited to a party, meant everyone had a reason to dress up, buck up and perk up. Padar had roped in an army of cousins to assist with the preparations. Oonagh had ordered matching faux fur capes and hats for herself and Bridget, while Miss MacReady was simultaneously putting finishing touches to a formal sari and christening cake. Marianne, clearing out Weathervane's neglected attic, had unearthed a large, grubby Holy Grail affair, which, after a tin of polish, revealed a glorious Georgian punch bowl, complete with stags-head handles and horseshoe feet. Miss MacReady suggested it was part of a haul stolen from the 'big house' at the time of the troubles in 1916, and she and Marianne vowed to attack the attic in earnest once the demands of the festivities were over. Marianne decided to put the punch bowl to work at the party, delving into one of George's tomes for a suitable concoction for a celebratory tipple.

"I shall leave the punch bowl to Bridget in my Will," she told the postmistress.

"She's a lucky girl."

"We're lucky to have her," Marianne replied. Miss MacReady agreed. The bonny child was a delight to all she encountered, being the embodiment of both parents and yet, day by day, very definitely more herself, Miss MacReady confirmed, every time she saw her.

"Oh, she's a lovely child, alright. I always think baby girls are just the best thing in world, don't you, Marie?" Miss MacReady was polishing the punch bowl.

"You never wanted your own?" Marianne asked gently.

Miss MacReady was on her guard.

"I could ask the same of you?"

"I can't have children, so not an issue for me. I just accepted a family is not mapped out for me. Don't have brothers or sisters, either. Just the way it was; it is."

"There's still time for you."

"No, no way, not now." Marianne pushed her hair back from her face. "Perhaps that's why we're so wrapped up in Bridget; she's making up for something neither of us had," she said with forced lightness.

"Not having children isn't the issue," Miss MacReady said, "it's not having a family that's the sad thing. And families can be made up of anyone, anything. You just have to believe love will find a way, whatever happens, whatever life throws at you. And when you find it, bind your loved one to you with bonds of love, keep it together, that's the way." She was polishing feverishly now.

The evocative aroma of incense filled the air. The Innishmahon combined Junior and Senior choirs, all ten of them, set the scene with an impressive descant rendition of *Bone Jesu,* and the Finnigan twins concluded the procession of the extended Quinn family, with a couple of bars of *Riverdance.*

Stillness descended as Father Gregory clattered onto the altar, his shooting boots protruding beneath his cassock. He stood in silence for a moment, taking in the church adorned with wreaths of poinsettia, cyclamen and glossy holly, and filled with bodies clad in tweed, satin and fur. The Quinn family glowed in the candlelight. Wedding vows re-taken to sniffs and watery eyes, were swiftly followed with nods and smiles, as the priest, child and parents swished towards the fount. A door swung closed. A murmur started at the back of the church and fluttered along the pews. A shadow passed beneath the Stations of the Cross, a figure in a dark coat. Father Gregory's voice boomed, bouncing off the marble.

"Do you, Bridget Marianne Quinn, renounce the Devil and all his works?"

Ryan slipped his hand into Marianne's. They clasped their fingers together, firmly.

"I do," they said, together.

Oonagh caught her breath. Bridget burped, and the whole place erupted in laughter.

It was a fantastic party in the grand tradition of Maguire's; singing, dancing, hearty food and generous drinks, hilarity, shenanigans and general unabated craic.

The Hollow Heart

The blessing of a new baby is a glorious occasion and, of one so hoped and longed for, a rare and wondrous event. That special night, everyone was everything to everybody. It was a time for a celebration of new life; a thanksgiving for so many gifts and favours; a time to forgive and forget; a time to love and be loved.

They were sitting in Weathervane's cosy sitting room. Marianne had decorated it in the colours of the island, teal, turquoise and emerald with splashes of ochre; pale lamplight cast a soft glow in pools around the room. She watched him as he sipped his tea. He look jaded; tiredness far beyond any jet lag. Monty sat at his feet, his chin on Ryan's knees, the huge brown eyes staring at him unblinkingly.

"Angelique's in the clinic again," he said to his cup, "I don't know for how long this time. I went to see her to talk about our son, but she wasn't making any sense. There was a young man with her, a musician or some such, he told me they're going away as soon as she's well enough to travel. They're in love, apparently. She said she's taking our son with her, she said after all I've put her through, I'll never see him again."

Marianne moved quietly from her chair to sit beside him on the sofa. She took the cup away and put it on the floor. She took his hands in hers, his head was bowed, shoulders hunched.

"It was over Marianne, long over, but we did that stupid thing people do, we slept together one last time, thinking it might work out but knowing it never would. And that one time she fell pregnant. Now the woman I don't want, could never live with, has the one thing I've wanted all my adult life. A child, a beautiful baby son, to love and care for, and oh I don't know, maybe make up for the son I was too young and foolish to appreciate all those years ago." His voice trailed off. She caught his pain and squeezed his fingers in hers. Two huge tears splashed onto her hand.

"Let's go to bed and sleep awhile and see what tomorrow brings." She took his face in her hands. "Things always look better in the morning, particularly here, you know that." She kissed the top of his head and he followed her slowly upstairs.

The sun was shining through the gap in the curtains as she lay in his arms beneath the faded patchwork quilt which had adorned the bedroom in Weathervane for as long as anyone could remember. He absentmindedly spun the arrow on the trinket she wore at her throat, the gift before his last parting. He had fallen asleep immediately his head hit the pillow, but not before they had kissed gently and he had told her how proud he was of her, and how pleased he was that they were now baby Bridget's official godparents. And how just knowing that, seemed to make them more of a couple. As the sun continued to rise, they held each other tightly for as long as Monty could keep his legs crossed, until finally he whined to be let out, and Marianne wriggled free of Ryan's arms.

After a breakfast of scrambled eggs and toasted soda bread slathered with yellow butter, they sat at the kitchen table drinking coffee, as he showed her pictures of his baby son Joey; a dark-eyed, olive-skinned boy with a shock of blue-black curls. A child the same age as Bridget, who despite his darkness, appeared more fragile when compared with the robust little girl, for all her translucent auburn-ness. Ryan explained that Angelique had been re-admitted to the clinic she regularly attended to help her deal with her 'habits'. He, trying to balance his work, and keep his promise to attend Bridget's christening, had left the child in the care of a professional Nanny. The Nanny had called her media contacts as soon as he left. He started going over the story again, trying to fill in the gaps, hoping Marianne would understand how it had come to this. This tangled mess.

"When we first got together, I was as wild as she was. But I'm older than Angelique, and someone had to keep their feet on the ground. Although she was hugely successful, we lived way beyond our means and she was spending so much money on 'relaxation' as she called it, we were in serious debt. I didn't know the half of it until we started getting threats from all sorts of unsavoury characters for money she owed them."

Marianne was staring at a picture of Joey in Ryan's arms. She had never seen him look so happy. Her heart plummeted.

"I really believed I could make it work, help sort her out, but it was getting worse, so we parted, and that's when she told me she was pregnant, and that's when you first saw me again, lying in the water on the beach. I'd come here to think it through, sort my head out. Landing the biggest role in movie history was not part of the plan." He looked deep into her eyes. "Falling in love with you, wasn't either, but the unintentionals, you and Joey, have turned out to be the best bits."

Marianne turned away and opened the door to let Monty in, who immediately pushed his nose into Ryan's legs, in the hope he would feed him the crusts of toast he knew he always left, off his plate. He was not disappointed. Marianne stood at the little sink, looking out to the yard. The sun had disappeared behind a mass of grey clouds. It would be raining soon.

"Did you have to marry her, though? Aren't things complicated enough?" Her tone was even, she was not accusing him of anything other than making things worse, for all of them.

"I had no choice. I was away on location and Angelique was in full-on party mode. Larry tried to reason with her but he was getting nowhere. He took legal advice and told me I needed to marry her as quickly as possible. I'm not a US citizen and if I ever wanted custody of my son, or needed to take him out of the country, I would stand a better chance if I was married to his mother. It was the lesser of so many evils at the time, and Lena being Lena, made the most of it, because rightly or wrongly, she reasoned whatever legal battles lay ahead, a war chest of a few dollars would help. So she sorted out various deals with the magazines, very lucratively, as it turned out."

Marianne was folding and refolding the tea towel at the draining board.

"The magazine covers were a bit hard to take," she

said.

"I know, but it just demonstrates what a dangerous myth all this fairytale stuff is. Straight after the ceremony, we took Angelique to hospital to have her stomach pumped. The new boyfriend, who she had spent the previous night with, had given her a pretty lethal cocktail of 'relaxants' that morning."

"But the wedding, why did she go through with it, what was in it for her?"

"Money of course, money and publicity, simple as that. She hasn't been fit to work for some time. The cash from the wedding publicity meant she and lover boy could make a fresh start. Should have known, she'd go back on her word about the baby. The deal was, I would be granted custody. She changed her mind as soon as Joey was born." He started gathering up the photographs, putting them back in his wallet. "I was all over the place, Marie. I kept thinking you'd be better off without me coming and going, flying in and out of your life. But even with Joey, nothing changed. I just missed you more, not less, great job, crap life. I seem to always end up doing the right thing for the wrong reasons or vice versa, I don't know."

Marianne cleared the cups away.

"A child is never a wrong reason. You can't be responsible for how Angelique lives her life. Couples are still individuals."

"All the stuff about you and I hasn't helped. Some of it such rubbish."

"It is what it is. It's the world that's wrong, not us,

and let's not forget I'm the one who is single, and I'm the one who keeps being abandoned for your career, wife, child, your other life. I hurt too." Her voice was soft, even.

He nodded gravely and got up to stand at the window, staring down the lane towards the cove and the Atlantic.

"And would you come with me if I asked you to? If I said come now, pack up, let's be together, wherever I have to be." The gate at the end of the little lawn creaked as it blew shut.

"No. I belong here now. We belong here. This is where we can be us, as a couple."

He turned and smiled at her. "You've great faith," he said, gently.

"I've already lost one love, I'm not prepared to lose another just because he has a sick wife, a broken marriage, a film contract, an agent, another life…shall I go on?"

"A baby son?"

"He's the least of our worries; he's the one thing that could help make this work."

"Really?"

"You'll do what's best for him in the end. You're basically one of the good guys. I can't imagine 'Tinseltown' and a drug-dependent mother is the best grounding for a youngster in the twenty-first century. You had very little to do with your eldest son's upbringing. I can't see you letting that happen again."

"If only it were that easy."

The Hollow Heart

"I understand about the film contract, you're a professional doing a job, you must finish the job. But the rest of your life? Making the decision to change things, that's the hard part."

The cloud had thinned a little. Faint rays of light haloed her hair as she stood before him, her eyes filled with all the love and pain in her heart.

"I think I'll walk a while." He could barely look at her.

"Take Monty, he's a great listener." Marianne took herself back to bed, waiting, wide-eyed, the couple of hours he and Monty were away.

She feigned sleep when he returned and, as he held her, he spun the weathervane at her throat, before kissing her cheek softly, wrapping the duvet round her as he rose. She heard him shower, clean his teeth and leave. The time for talking had passed. It was December the ninth, the last time she had seen him was the end of October. Who knows when she would see him again; *if* she would ever see him again. She had given her ultimatum, gently, but it was there nonetheless, this is the last time he leaves, next time he returns, if there is a next time, he stays for good. She would not cry out, beg him to stay or plead with him to take her with him, say she had changed her mind, and that she would go. No, deep in her heart, she knew she was right. Weathervane was their safe harbour, their haven. She had to stay anchored there, no matter how hard the winds of change blew and, for his part, Ryan had to come back to her on his own terms, in his own time, with no regrets. She hoped he would not leave it too long. She had waited for someone to be true to their word before.

Chapter Twenty Five – Close As Sisters

As the twinkling warmth of the Christmas festival faded, the weather took a severe turn, and a bitter wind driving straight off the Atlantic, brought the New Year in with an icy bite. With work on the bridge suspended until the climate improved, and with Ryan filming in deepest Africa, Marianne kept herself busy refurbishing Weathervane, now she had resolved to make the island her home.

Oonagh and Miss MacReady called regularly to check on progress, vehemently disagreeing, as they examined wallpaper samples, colour swatches and cuttings from magazines. Marianne would smile and hand them either tea or whiskey, depending on the hour of the day, always bearing in mind that if it was Monday, Miss MacReady insisted on cocktails, whatever the hour.

Ryan had been in regular contact since his departure in December, always from a payphone landline to foil the hackers, and although Marianne knew he was desperately maintaining a balancing act between filming and child care, Lena had managed to keep the real story of his and Angelique's estrangement under wraps. So for now, reports stuck to the press release. Ryan the actor, working hard on location, while his wife and child lived quietly in suburban Los Angeles, awaiting his return.

Since Ryan's surprise appearance at baby Bridget's christening, Marianne had laid down some new rules, particularly regarding her friends' opinions of their relationship. While she was happy to let them know what Ryan was up to career-wise, details beyond these were taboo. She explained on more than one occasion, rumours and tittle-tattle reported in magazines and online, were precisely that, and bore no relation to what was actually happening in Ryan's life or, indeed, any other '*A-lister*' for that matter.

Miss MacReady seemed happy enough with this arrangement and, a romantic at heart, firmly believed the star-crossed lovers would be together eventually, no matter what the tabloids said.

Oonagh, on the other hand, remained unconvinced, fearing Angelique's hold over the child, as his mother, would keep Ryan dancing to her tune for many years to come. With this scenario in mind, she had taken to matchmaking, recommending unsuspecting bachelors and, not too decrepit, widowers as possible love interests for her friend at every opportunity. When these suggestions, combined with Oonagh's blunt-edged opinions, were aired once too often for Marianne's strained sensibility, Marianne had to ban Oonagh from the cottage completely. It was the nearest the friends had ever come to a real argument. Miss MacReady finally stepped in, and a compromise was reached, with the ruling of no gossip or comments about Ryan, Angelique or the baby, at least not in earshot, and absolutely no matchmaking, even if the possible candidate did have all his own hair and a small fishing boat, paid for!

Monty lodged with Miss MacReady during major works at the cottage, the perfect excuse for the postmistress to don full dog walking ensemble, complete with whistle. She had taken to trudging Monty up and down the main street in a creaky old-fashioned pram, stating that while in her care, he was regularly shampooed and conditioned, so walking was strictly limited to clean floors and carpeted areas. Monty, who had been assured this was a temporary arrangement, fixed Marianne with a baleful eye whenever Miss MacReady announced she would have to leave soon, as it was Monty's bath night. Marianne had to promise his sojourn at the Post Office would last only a few more days, after he finally leapt from the pram into her arms during tea with Oonagh and the baby at Maguire's.

Bridget Quinn was quickly growing into the most beautiful baby in the west of Ireland. A giggler and a flirt like her mother, busy and thoughtful like her father. And yet there were moments when her huge eyes clouded over and she seemed to be somewhere else entirely, wearing a mystical and very un-childlike look entirely her own. Marianne, Monty and, indeed, most of Innishmahon, were entirely besotted. Father Gregory, joining them in the bar after spending a happy hour in her company, allowed himself to wish she would hurry and grow up a bit.

"Whatever for, Father?" Oonagh was shocked.

"So you can claim another soul for Rome?" sneered Sean Grogan, over his pint.

"Not at all," snapped the Priest. "So I can take her hunting. I have my eye on the loveliest little mare for her."

"Oh, I don't know about that." Oonagh was cautious.

"We'll let her make her own mind up, about everything!" Father Gregory replied, seeing Sean off with a scowl.

Marianne was planning a trip to Galway when Oonagh announced she would go with her to help shop for the refurbished cottage, possibly slipping into a couple of antique dealers on the way back. Marianne was delighted to have her friend as company but, as she drove off the ferry onto the mainland, she noticed Oonagh was far from relaxed.

"Okay?"

"Fine, not a bother."

"You seem a bit quiet?"

"No, no, grand altogether."

"Anything you want to talk about?"

"No, not specially."

"You haven't been reading more gossip about Ryan and Angelique, have you? Seriously, Oonagh, everything will be okay, honest it will."

"No, nothing like that, but I was wondering, will all your time be taken up with shopping and such?"

"Not necessarily, is there something you

particularly want to do while we're there?"

"Only if we have time."

Marianne wondered what unlikely gem Oonagh, the queen of the internet, had unearthed to visit in Galway, one of the busiest cities in the West. A fashion show, a beauty spa or showbiz soiree?

"Sure we'll have time, what is it?"

"I need to see a specialist. Some tests have to be done. Since the baby, you know."

It was Marianne's turn to be quiet. She tried to remember Oonagh before Bridget. Admittedly, Oonagh had always been on the plump side but her figure had not returned, despite countless diets and intermittent, yet gruelling, fitness regimes. Her personality had changed too, she was more edgy and impatient, and had lost some of her bounce. But surely that was just depleted energy levels, the result of being an older first time mother?

"What do they think is wrong?" Marianne asked gently, once they were well on the road.

"They don't know yet, but I think it's serious or they wouldn't be sending me for these scans."

"We'll go straight there then and get that out of the way first. Sure we can't enjoy ourselves with that hanging over us. It'll be fine, you see."

"Thanks, Marie, that's great."

"Did you not want Padar with you?"

Oonagh did not reply.

Marianne put a little more pressure on the accelerator.

A fortnight later, the world looked a very different and uncertain place. Oonagh was in hospital in Galway, and Padar was staying at a friend's pub close by, just until she was over the operation. The Quinn clan had been called upon to take over the pub, with Marianne in charge of her goddaughter. If circumstances were different, she would be thoroughly enjoying her new role, but the pleasure was tinged with worry.

Researching ovarian cancer on the internet did little to reassure Marianne. The research stated, although rare in females under the age of fifty, only forty per cent of women diagnosed with the disease survived beyond five years. Marianne pondered the statistics. Padar and Oonagh had found it difficult to conceive. When Oonagh did fall pregnant, she had never been able to take a baby to full term, until Bridget. With Oonagh currently in hospital undergoing surgery, it was surely no coincidence she should be one of the small percentage of younger women to succumb to such a serious illness. Marianne felt sure Oonagh's illness had some bearing on the problems she had experienced trying to conceive, it seemed perfectly logical to her that it was connected. How long had her beloved friend been harbouring this insidious disease?

Marianne grew increasingly frustrated because no matter how many times she typed 'cure' into the computer, she could not find a definitive answer. She sat staring at the screen for some time. Everything she had read just made Bridget more special, even more of a miracle. She sighed heavily, turning the machine off. It would all be alright. Oonagh would recover fully and, appreciate more than ever, the blessing that was her precious little family.

Marianne could hear noises coming from the next room. She closed the laptop and crept across the landing to find Bridget in her cot, gurgling in animated conversation with Monty, who, with his paws on the rails, was making a soft gravelly noise back at her. Marianne stood in the doorway, marvelling. Two completely different species communicating contentedly with each other in a language they both fully understood; a pair of precious souls sharing a moment of communion in their own private corner of a very crowded planet. She had never felt the weight of responsibility so acutely.

Sending Monty to his basket and settling Bridget down for the night, Marianne did something she had not done since she was a child. She knelt by her bed and prayed. Not to a God she had seen in holy pictures or on a cross, or to any of the deities man had conjured up to worship or fight for. But to whatever was out there; holding things together; keeping the gifts of love, life and hope coming at her. To whatever was giving her the strength, will and determination not to give in, not to crumble, not to let the side down. Because this was her side, the side she was on and she was damn well here to stay.

"Amen to that!" she said out loud, before hopping under the duvet.

Miss MacReady had lovingly washed and styled a variety

of wigs for Oonagh's homecoming. Marianne and a cluster of Quinn cousins had polished the pub until it shone. Padar filled every receptacle he could with flowers; lilies and roses, Oonagh's favourites. He had cooked a huge paella, just the way she liked it, so she could share a bite with family and friends before retiring to her boudoir, freshly cleaned, and now home to the aforementioned wigs, grotesquely displayed on a selection of decapitated mannequins, Miss MacReady had collected over the years.

The woman who stepped gingerly from the vehicle was hardly recognisable as the colourful, robust Oonagh Quinn they had all been waiting to welcome. She moved slowly, stooping slightly, her well-loved lilac leisure-suit hanging off her and, what remained of her lustrous hair, hidden beneath a towelling turban; the whiteness of it, stark, against the blotchiness of her skin, despite the makeup. There was nothing frail about her smile though. She beamed when she saw them crowding in the doorway of the pub. Taking Bridget from Marianne, she smothered her shining little face with kisses.

"Mama Ooo-ah," Bridget said loudly, eyeing Marianne to check if this was correct, hugging Oonagh happily. Padar bustled them inside, showing Oonagh to an armchair near the fire, which had been lit, even though it was a beautiful spring day. No-one needed to tell Oonagh it was great to have her home, nor did Oonagh need to say it was wonderful to be back, the sheer joy and delight of the whole occasion trickled into every corner of the room.

The Hollow Heart

Marianne was just getting used to Oonagh in the blonde Dolly Parton, when Oonagh announced two items of news. The good news was, her hair was growing back. The bad news, the Oncology Unit wanted to see her as soon as possible. Oonagh was very matter of fact about the situation. She assumed they had found secondary tumours and, although new battle lines were being drawn and the war was not yet over, just the thought of having to pull together every dilapidated fibre of her being to face another fight, completely exhausted her.

Marianne took her friend's hand. They were sitting together in one of their favourite places, a small clearing halfway up the cliff, just off the new road. It was where they brought Bridget and Monty on picnics as the days grew longer and summer started to stretch ahead. The Atlantic glistened below, a shimmer of diamonds, gentle and calm on today, of all days, when all Marianne could hear was a crashing in her chest and roaring in her ears.

"You'll be grand," she said, unsmiling, to Oonagh.

"Ah sure." Oonagh's universal response when things were too difficult or complex to be aired. She nodded over at the baby sitting beside the terrier, sharing her sandwich, diligently checking the halves were equal so neither would be deprived of sustenance. Monty waited to take the bread daintily as Bridget gurgled at him, deep in discussion about whatever was on the infant's mind.

"I just wanted to ask, Marie, if it's not good, you

know, at the hospital, well I'd feel better if I knew you'd be there, afterwards, when I'm not around. I know it's a lot to ask but..."

"Stop it Oonagh, don't talk like that."

"I'm being serious. I will need to make arrangements, need things sorted."

Marianne closed her eyes briefly. "Of course, you can depend on me, whatever you need."

"Or whatever *she* needs." Oonagh's eyes filled with tears as she watched her little daughter. She wiped her nose on her sleeve. "You're so good with her, the little one. You never wanted your own, Marie? Were you always the career woman?"

"It wasn't through choice."

"Really?"

"No. I had a miscarriage, years ago. It made a bit of a mess of me, so they had to operate. It left me unable to have my own."

"Oh God, that's terrible. I never thought... and all through this, me and my problems you never said a word. What happened?"

Marianne looked out to sea, plucking at the grass, "Ah, it was a long time ago..."

Oonagh was quiet for a moment and then asked, "And was this before George?"

"Yes before George. A bad relationship, I was very young. A mistake."

Oonagh took Marianne's hand, her pale face even whiter. "Tell me, Marie, you shouldn't keep things like that to yourself."

Marianne took a deep breath.

"Not long after my parents died, I had a mad fling with a well-known photographer in Paris. I was crazy about him, when he said we'd get married, I believed him. It was great to begin with; we partied as hard as we could, for as long as we could. Anyway, it turned out he'd always been a womaniser, and though I had a feeling there had been a few affairs, when I found out his young assistant was pregnant by him, well that was the last straw."

Oonagh gasped, nodding Marianne to continue. "I confronted him, he flew into a rage, denied everything, we had a huge row and he said he was leaving. I was distraught, we'd both been drinking. I ran out of the apartment after him, he was in the car, the engine was running, and I jumped in front of it as he pulled away. I flipped over the bonnet, like a rag doll, splat on the road, unconscious."

"God!" Oonagh exclaimed. "Did he not see you?"

"He said not, but who knows, he was out of his head anyway. When I woke up in hospital, they told me I'd lost the baby – I hadn't even known I was pregnant – I was bleeding internally, it was very serious and they had no choice but to operate."

Oonagh blessed herself.

"Oh Marie, I'm so sorry. I never even thought you might have wanted children. Though you did seem to want Padar and I to have a child almost as much as we did. You never said a word though."

Marianne squeezed her friend's hand.

"It's weird you know, everyone makes that assumption, if a woman doesn't have children, particularly a career woman, they assume it's by choice, when it's usually the other way round. She has the career because she has no choice. It's like being an amputee, everyone can see a limb is missing, but no-one dare ask how it happened."

"Marie, that's just awful." Oonagh's eyes filled with tears. "And what happened to the father?"

"We never told anyone the real story about my accident. The police would have been called and it would have been an awful mess. He took me in a taxi to the hospital so the emergency services weren't involved, and no-one knew about the baby but us; it was our terrible secret." Marianne looked out at the Atlantic, the flat horizon in the distance. "He married the assistant soon after. I moved back to England...made a new life."

"And did he get his happy ever after?"

"Oonagh, life isn't a film, I keep telling you that. I don't know if he did, I hope he did. He's not around now, anyway." Marianne chose not to mention how Claude's life ended.

"The bastard, good riddance," Oonagh hissed.

"Don't feel anger on my part, Oonagh. I let it go, ages ago. I didn't think I could and then, I felt different and all the bitterness and pain was gone and I hadn't even noticed. It wasn't to be, it wouldn't have been right. If we'd had a baby, I'd have stayed for the wrong reasons. That's no way to raise a child, ending up blaming them for staying in a bad relationship. No, it was for the best."

347

She took Oonagh's hands, looking her straight in the eye. "And there is more than one way to have a family, more than one way to be cocooned in love. It comes in many guises, I find. I mean, I would never have met George, you, Padar, Miss MacReady, Ryan – I wouldn't have Bridget or Monty in my life." She smiled across at the pair on the tartan rug, snuggled together in the sunshine.

"And that's a good thing? Have we brought you happiness, real love?"

Marianne was shocked. "Are you joking? I love you. All of you. Okay, things aren't perfect, but I wouldn't swap any of you, change anything. I love every hair on your baldy head, you silly woman."

Oonagh smiled, wiping her eyes.

"We're more like sisters than ever now, that's why I want you to mind Bridget, and Padar too, if you were able, I'd worry less when I'm over the other side." Oonagh's grey eyes were piercing. Marianne stared back at her.

"The other side? What side is that you're going to? Hey, they're not holding a pair of white feathery wings in readiness for you, Mrs Quinn. George is on angel duty maybe, but you and I have no chance." Grinning, Marianne tugged the blonde bouffant from Oonagh's head to reveal her patchy pink, sprouting scalp. "You're looking loads better these days; you're on the mend, make no mistake about that. You're just a bit too attached to this fecking wig!"

Oonagh lunged at her to grab it back and, laughing, they hugged each other, a long rocking-together

348

hug, high on the cliff, with the Atlantic swirling below
and the gulls chorusing their tuneless, summer song above
them.

Chapter Twenty Six– A Smack In The Eye

R yan was speaking from his hotel room in Mayfair. "I was going to organise this as a surprise for you, but what about bringing Oonagh along for the ride?" Filming had finally finished and the round of publicity interviews was about to begin. After interviews in London and Belfast, next stop Dublin and a late night chat show.

"Organise what?" Marianne was intrigued.

"I'm sending a helicopter so you can come to the press reception and the TV show if you'd like?"

"What do you mean, if I'd like? Try and stop me! A helicopter, wow, I've never ridden in a helicopter. Are you serious?"

"Well, your fella is a famous movie star, what's a trapping or two for my gorgeous girl and our lovely friend. So, what do you say?"

Marianne whooped.

"Wait till I tell Oonagh, she'll freak. Your biggest fan, going to a real celebrity bash. Ryan, you're an angel. She's going to just love it, we both will; it will be a real tonic, honest it will!"

"Great that's all set, I'll send the chopper on Friday morning. The press reception is that evening. We record the TV show live after that. You and Oonagh can enjoy Grafton Street together before I head to the airport for Paris and you go back to Innishmahon."

"Paris? You're not coming back with us?"

"Not this time, love. Coming to the end though, it won't be too long now."

Marianne let it go. The excitement of the news of the helicopter trip would not be spoiled with a row.

"I can't wait to tell Oonagh, and I can't wait to see you. Are we incognito or what?"

"No way, come as yourself. I've fulfilled my part of the contract, the movie's finished and I'm promoting it. After Paris I'm done, it's time to get my life back!"

"It's a three-film deal, don't forget?" Marianne reminded him, and herself.

"I haven't forgotten. Now go and tell the Queen of my Innishmahon fan club she can go to the ball, and I'll see you the day after tomorrow." They were just about to say their goodbyes when a small voice interrupted.

"Sorry Marie, Ryan, apologies for the intrusion, but I couldn't help overhearing..."

There were gasps and muffled laughter down the line.

"Ahem, what couldn't you help, Miss MacReady?" You could hear the smile in Ryan's voice.

"The helicopter trip; the jaunt to Dublin for the press party; the TV show and all?"

"And?"

"Well, I was only thinking, if you and Marie are together, Oonagh might be left on her own, and she's a lot better, but she's not altogether well, and it's years since I was in Dublin's fair city. Sure I may never get the opportunity to go again."
Silence. The line crackled.

"I've never been in a helicopter either."

"Marianne, any room for a little one?" Ryan asked.

"Only if she promises not to cause any trouble. No flaunting herself and breaking hearts up there in the big city!"

"Okay, I'll sort things this end. That's my three favourite women in the world coming to spend a couple of days with me, couldn't be better. Have to go, love you." Ryan clicked off.

"Oh, Marie, that's fantastic, amazing," said Miss MacReady, "I'm thrilled, delighted, he thought to ask me. He's a darling man. Now I must go and plan my ensembles, there'll be at least three changes a day with that film crowd, I bet."

"Miss MacReady, you really are incorrigible." The line went dead and Marianne had no time to bask in the glorious anticipation of the forthcoming sojourn into the five star world of her movie star lover. If she did not get her skates on and rush round to Maguire's immediately, Miss MacReady would telephone Oonagh and spoil the surprise.

"Don't answer that!" shrieked Marianne, as she charged

behind the bar and snatched the phone from Oonagh's hand. "Thanks, Miss MacReady, I'm here now, no worries, I'll fill Oonagh in on all the details. Leave it with me. Phew!" she exclaimed as she replaced the receiver, giving Oonagh her broadest grin.

Padar stood holding Bridget under one arm and Monty under the other, so was incapacitated in the waving-off department. However, Pat MacReady the taxi man, made up for any lack of adieu, the three female incumbents of the helicopter may have been experiencing, by leaping up and down, flapping his arms repeatedly and making loud, whooping noises. Marianne glanced back through the helicopter window and laughed, looking from Pat to his elder sister, Kathleen, seated as close to the young pilot as she could possibly be without landing in his lap. She wondered if any of the MacReadys were normal. They seemed to range from slightly eccentric to barking mad. Miss MacReady immediately engaged the pilot in conversation and, by the time they had crossed the little stretch of water to the mainland, knew all about him, where he was from, marital status, the lot.

"Single!" She nudged Marianne indiscreetly. Marianne took no notice; she was wallowing in the familiar, fabulous deep down rumble of excitement she felt whenever a reunion with Ryan was on the horizon. After a while, she noticed Oonagh was unusually quiet, strapped in behind them. She turned to find her face pink with heat despite her cream linen tunic and silk blouse, purchased online for the trip. When Marianne gave her a quizzical look, she expelled the breath she had been holding, explaining she hated flying, particularly over water for some bizarre reason. She did not know why.

"Why didn't you say?" Marianne asked.

"What, and miss the trip of a lifetime. Are you mad? Not only Dublin; not only a live TV show; not only a press reception but *THE* film of the decade, stars, celebrities, media, paparazzi. Oh it's almost too much!" She fake-fainted back into her seat.

"Do you think there'll be a red carpet?" Miss MacReady wanted to know, as she painted on a beauty spot with an eyebrow pencil in one hand, a jewel encrusted compact in the other.

"Bound to be," Oonagh nodded, the pinkness calming as they passed over the fields below.

"Ladies, here's the schedule and there are some drinks and snacks in the cooler box behind your seat," the pilot indicated to Oonagh, who immediately dived into the box and emerged exclaiming,

"Look! Champagne, strawberries, croissants and chocolate, happy days!" Her eyes sparkled, and Marianne felt an inner warmth and deep gratitude.

"I love Ryan O'Gorman," she said loudly.

"We know," Oonagh and Miss MacReady shouted back.

Miss MacReady donned glasses to read out the schedule bearing the studio's logo. It was very official and timed to the last minute.

*"Arrival Dublin 14:00 hours: Helicopter lands on
rooftop of hotel
14.30 – 15.00 hours: Private lunch with Mr O'Gorman
15.15 hours: Check-in
15.30 hours: Guests meet in foyer for informal photo-call
16.00 hours: Press reception
18.00 hours: Cars to the TV studio
19.00 hours: Guests reception
21.00 hours: Guests take seats in the audience
22.00 hours: Show goes Live
23.15 hours: Green Room reception
01.30 hours: Cars depart for the hotel
02.00 hours: Light supper and drinks served privately for
Mr O'Gorman's guests"*

"How lovely," Oonagh cooed, "it all sounds just
perfect."
Marianne could not resist taking the schedule from Miss
MacReady and scan-read the rest.

"Brilliant! Champagne breakfast the next
morning, followed by a preview of the film, shopping,
sightseeing and, at half past two, the helicopter flight
home."

"Gosh! Dublin, Grafton Street, St Stephen's
Green, I haven't been there in an age." Miss MacReady
was wistful.

"We'll even have time to hit the shops, I'm dying
to buy Bridget lots of lovely things. It really is the perfect
trip." Oonagh was beginning to relax.

In just over an hour, the helicopter swooped over
the Dublin mountains as the city, sitting neatly in its

perfect curving bay, lay glimmering in the sunshine before them. Beyond it, the Irish sea, a sparkling wrap around the coast.

Marianne gasped, "I've never seen it like this. It's glorious."

Miss MacReady, who had been dozing slightly from a little too much champagne, was suddenly alert. "Will you fly us in along the Liffey and over the Bank and Trinity College, just so I can get my bearings and make a proper entrance?" she asked the pilot

"Sorry Ma'am, I'll come in from the North West and head straight to the landing zone. Mr O'Gorman wants to see Miss Coltrane as soon as possible. They're my instructions."

"I bet he does," chortled Oonagh. Marianne looked knowingly at her friend, who was beaming out of the window. She looked better than she had in months. Marianne felt sure that, at the very least, the disease was in remission, and they could look forward to a string of happy times together.

Nipping over the treetops of St Stephen's Green, Marianne spotted the large H on the roof of the hotel and, if she was not mistaken, as they drew closer, a man in faded jeans and an Irish rugby shirt, standing with his face craned upwards, clutching the rails of the safety zone just beyond the helicopter landing pad. Her heart leapt, her insides turned to slush, and she could feel tears behind her eyes. She never missed him as much as when she first saw him again, the longing to be with him so raw, it hurt. As if sensing the emotion, Miss MacReady gripped her hand.

"There he is love, there he is waiting, not long now."

Marianne abandoned everyone and everything as she scrabbled out of the helicopter. Blades barely slowing, she charged across the tarmac. The man dived under the railings as soon as he spotted her, and ran towards her, arms outstretched, the draught from the blades making their clothes flap and their eyes water. They flew into each other's arms and held on tightly. Marianne buried her face in his chest, breathing him in. He wrapped his arms around her head, protecting her ears from the noise, turning her face upwards to kiss her forehead, nose, mouth. Suddenly, all was quiet, all was still, everything stopped. She was in his arms, lost in his kiss and, together, they were suspended in an exquisitely perfect moment in time. He broke away from her lips, hugging her to him.

"God I could eat you," he said, into her hair.

"And I could eat a horse," laughed Oonagh, sashaying behind them as best she could, given the amount of luggage she was carrying. The poor pilot was still unloading under Miss MacReady's beady eye. Releasing Marianne with one arm, Ryan scooped Oonagh to him with the other, kissing both cheeks and grinning at her.

"You look good, Oonagh. Are you well enough for this? If you want to stop at any stage, take a break, bow out, no worries, give me the nod."

"Are you out of your mind? I'm not missing one

second of this. This is a dream come true. Bring it on, Mr O'Gorman, bring on as much of the ritzy, glitzy, showbiz razzmatazz as you like. I'm ready for it."

"And so am I!" Miss MacReady joined them, tripping over the roof in red, frou-frou mules, as the helicopter pilot buckled under the baggage behind her. Ryan looked at Marianne and raised his eyebrows.

"I know." She laughed. "We never did do normal!"

After a delicious lunch of Dublin Bay Prawns, fresh salad and baby new potatoes in butter and chives, devoured ravenously by all, Marianne, who had been grinning inanely at all three, relaxed back into one of the restaurant's sumptuous sofas. She unashamedly allowed herself to gaze adoringly at Ryan, who was strutting his stuff, entertaining them with snippets of showbiz gossip and a roundup of the latest happenings on set. He looked well, better than she had seen him look in a long time. Calm yet excited, animated and charming, groomed yet just a little ruffled, taking the edge off the smoothness.

"God but you're gorgeous," she said to herself, dreamily imagining them making love later on, and then realising she had actually said the words out loud, she joined the others in laughter, as Ryan twirled like a mannequin, giving them the benefit of a wiggle of his neat bottom in faded jeans. Lisa arrived, clipboard in hand, mobile phone glued to her ear, and Ryan indicated it was time to get the show on the road.

"Your luggage has gone ahead. There's a car

outside." Lisa nodded down the sweeping staircase to the hotel entrance.

Once outside, Oonagh and Miss MacReady bundled into the discreet grey Mercedes to take the short journey to the luxury hotel where they were staying. Ryan took Marianne's arm.

"Let's walk."

"I was just about to suggest the same." She smiled.

Within minutes, they were strolling hand in hand along Grafton Street, amid bustling shoppers and buskers on every corner. Marianne noticed that, although Ryan was recognised as they passed along the busiest thoroughfare in the city, no-one bothered them. Dubliners had always been at ease with celebrity, she surmised. The famous had always found sanctuary in the city's bars and restaurants. The natives liked it that way, letting the great and good rub shoulders with them. Besides, they were usually so busy with their own colourful lives, the transience of celebrity was accepted for what it was.

"I love this city," she said. They slowed as they passed a famous coffee house, to inhale the pungent fragrance of freshly ground beans. Turning right, the heady scent of lilies and roses filled the air, together with the flower seller's shrill cry of bargains to be had. Despite her protests, Ryan stopped to buy an armful of blooms, randomly selecting from the buckets on display and, once happy she could, in fact, carry no more, spun her through the door and into the snug of her, and as it turned out, his, favourite bar. The very pub where he had spotted her all those months ago and had assumed she was stalking him for a story.

"Let's lay a few ghosts to rest," he said, settling beside her and taking her hands. "I remember when I saw you here. Despite thinking you were on my tail for some sort of sordid expose, I also remember thinking how stunningly beautiful you were, and wishing you were on my tail for whatever reason."

"I didn't even see you that day." She pushed his hair back from his forehead. "Probably wouldn't have registered anyway. I was pretty frazzled at the time. No, flat out on the beach, that was the first time I saw you again, properly. God, you looked rough. I really did think you were drowning." They laughed and then he was suddenly serious.

"I was pretty frazzled myself, 'til I met you. You seem to smooth that bit out." He looked at her intently.

"Which bit?"

"The bit that keeps churning away inside. It kind of stops when I'm with you, it all feels calmer, smoother, safer."

She held his hand to her cheek and kissed his palm. "Me too."

And then a man with a camera appeared from nowhere and stuck his head around the glass partition. The flash popped and he was gone. There was a commotion as a barman leapt over the counter, chasing after the photographer, shouting.

"Hey, none of that in here, this is where people

relax, for fuck's sake."

"Indeed," came a familiar voice from behind them. "A place where people can relax, be together, in private." Paul Osborne was perched on a bar stool, pint in hand. "Slainté," he said, grinning like a Cheshire cat.

"What the hell are you doing here?" Ryan snapped.

"I'm press, remember? There's a press reception." Marianne jumped out of her seat.

"How dare you, you're a disgrace to the profession!"
Ryan stood up beside her.

"Anyway, you're out of touch Osborne. There's no story here."

"Are you sure?" Paul sneered, "seems the goodie, goodie Hollywood movie star, has yet again abandoned wife and child, for a little grope under the duvet with his favourite colleen."

"There's no story, Osborne. I've told you. Not that it's any of your business, but Marianne and I are together, and arrangements relating to our private lives are exactly that. Private."

Marianne saw a flicker cross Paul's eyes. Ryan looked from Paul to Marianne and back. They were all standing now, the barman was hovering close by. The pub grew quiet.

"It's not about you, arsehole," Paul snarled.
Marianne stepped between the men.
"What do you want, Paul?"
Paul moved closer. Towering over her, he bent his head

361

to hers, his forehead grazing her hair.

"He doesn't deserve you. He's a liar and a cheat and basically an arrogant, vain tosser, who keeps dangling you on a string so he can drop by for a decent meal and a good shag every now and…"

There was a faint whistling sound as Ryan landed a left hook to Paul's jaw. The crowd gasped as one.

"Owww!" Paul put his hand to his chin, turning away from his assailant slowly, then, in a flash, he whipped back and landed Ryan a full punch to the stomach.

"Ugh!" Ryan bent double, winded. As he went down, Paul smacked him on the back of the head. Ryan lost his balance and fell to his knees.

"Stop!" Marianne screamed, lunging at Paul. At the same time the barman expertly scooped her up, placing her neatly behind the bar out of harm's way, as the usually genteel and rarefied atmosphere exploded, and a full-on brawl ensued.

A drinker from a neighbouring table walloped Paul across the shoulders with an umbrella. Ryan, regaining his composure, used Paul's distracted state to climb onto a chair, leaping onto his back and securing him in a headlock. Paul relieved the man of the umbrella and was using it to fend off Ryan's attack. As Paul twirled round trying to free himself of Ryan, the barman tripped him up and they all fell to the floor in a swirling squirm on the dark, red Turkish carpet.

"Doesn't show the blood," the barman told Marianne, helpfully. Horrified, she broke free and was just about to join the writhing mass in an attempt to knock some sense into her lover and former colleague, when a long shadow fell across the room and, bit by bit, the warring factions quietened, gradually peeling away to the walls. Even the tall, brass gas lights standing on the marble bar seemed to quiver as an eerie silence descended.

"Well, well, well, what in heaven's name is going on here? This is usually such a civilised part of the city. I mean, really!" The words hung in the air, the soft Cork accent menacing in its lightness. Ryan and Paul staggered to their feet. Ryan's right eye was half-closed and there was a bloody gash above his brow. Paul's nose was bleeding and his bottom lip had split. Marianne groaned as she surveyed them, and the devastated snug. She glanced nervously at the huge, dark figure filling the doorway. The man in uniform gave her a slight salute, as shrewd bright eyes flashed around the room. *"Well?"*

"A minor disagreement, Inspector. Is all it was. All over now, forgotten," offered the barman, busily wiping the marble top and setting a couple of glasses under the taps.

Ryan pushed his shoulders back, stood forward, hand extended.

"No harm done, sorry to trouble you, Inspector." The Garda eyed him suspiciously, not moving, and then, "Well lookat, it's yourself, Ryan. Ryan O'Gorman, how the divil are you? Sure I'd no idea it was you." The inspector shook his hand heartily. Ryan winced, and then as recognition dawned, grinned as the officer removed his hat.

"It's me, Dermot. I always liked dressing up, so opted for a uniform when the acting offers dried up." They hugged like long lost brothers, and the whole pub breathed a sigh of relief.

"Marianne, meet Dermot Finnegan, he was in drama school with me. Better actor than I ever was." Ryan saluted the Garda.

"Yeah true enough. Trouble was, he was better looking than all of us. Some break!"

Marianne, bemused by the whole episode, was irritated Ryan and Dermot seemed suddenly so relaxed about everything. She turned to go and freshen up and found Paul standing beside her. He wiped his bloody nose with the back of his hand and gave her a sheepish glance. She sighed.

"Sorry," he mouthed, then put his hand urgently to his lip. She rolled her eyes and shrugged. The inspector resumed his authoritative stance.

"Now." He took his notebook out of his pocket, pencil poised. "Anything to report?" The incumbents of the bar mumbled and shuffled back to their seats. The Inspector looked at Paul.

"You sir, what's your name?"
Paul looked anxiously from Marianne to Ryan.

"It's alright, Inspector, it genuinely was a misunderstanding," Marianne said softly, praying this would be the end of the matter. Inspector Finnegan looked from one to the other. Ryan gave him a nod.

"Ah, fair enough so." The Garda put his pencil

and pad away. "Any apologies required?" Silence. "If we're drawing a line under this, I think the air should be cleared once and for all," he said wisely.

Ryan looked at Paul. Paul looked back. Their faces were bloodied and bruised, hair standing on end, clothes torn. Paul held out a hand. He was trembling. Ryan stared at it for a long moment, then he took it.

"Behind us?" Ryan asked.

"Yes." Paul held his gaze.

"All of it? Everything?"

"Finished. End of."

"I have your word?"

"You have my word."

They shook hands, both wincing in pain, as Marianne blinked away tears.

The door flew open and a flurry of colour burst into the room. Oonagh and Miss MacReady were dressed to the nines, and breathless.

"I told you there'd been trouble." Miss MacReady nudged Oonagh as they surveyed the scene. Oonagh beamed at the officer.

"Alright?"

"All sorted here, Madam. No bother." He beamed back.

"The cars are waiting to take us to the studio. Lisa's put the press reception back until after the show, said you'd been unavoidably delayed. No-one was that bothered, they'd all had champagne and were going to the show anyway," Miss MacReady told them.

"Ah, yes, the TV show, you're on this evening."

Dermot reminded Ryan.

"Inspector, if we get these guys cleaned up and ready, would you mind escorting us?" Marianne asked, all eyes on the Garda. A police convoy would surely speed things up.

"Just about to suggest that myself," grinned Dermot.

The makeup team did a superb job disguising evidence of Ryan's brawl. The bruising hardly showed, and the floor manager thoughtfully turned his chair sideways on, so that his gently-swelling left eyelid could not be seen by the camera.

Paul had also been skilfully patched up by Oonagh and Miss MacReady, using a combination of their makeup bags. To Paul's relief, Ryan issued instructions for him to travel to the studios with the rest of his party and, although Marianne knew Paul wanted to talk, she was not quite ready for a conversation with him, and had been happy to leave him to the care of the 'Innishmahon' fan club.

"What on earth were you fighting about?" Miss MacReady asked as they settled into the back of the car. She had insisted Paul sit between herself and Oonagh. Although Oonagh was uncomfortable, she had not minded patching the poor man up but she was unsure if he was to be treated as a fellow guest on their trip. Had Ryan and Marianne forgiven him, made friends, even?

"Something and nothing I suppose," Miss MacReady continued.

"Probably more like everything," Oonagh interjected. Paul looked out of the window in silence.

Meanwhile, Marianne's fury with Paul and, indeed, Ryan, had subsided slightly, as she bathed the gash above Ryan's eye in the bathroom of their suite. Particularly when he had given her his mournful, gooey-eyed pity-me face. She looked away, amused that he imagined for one second, she would fall for his awful performance. She pretended to ignore him, tutting loudly, as she dabbed his brow with a makeup pad drenched in face tonic. The astringent made him whine. She resisted the urge to kiss it better.

"Not very clever, eh?" he whispered. She carried on without comment. He was sitting on the loo, she reached over to find a tissue to dry the wound off and, needing more attention than he was receiving, Ryan threw his arms out to grab her and pull her to him. Marianne made a skilful swerve to avoid him, tripped over the toilet brush and, as he lunged to save her, they both ended up in an inevitable pile on the bathroom floor.

"Ugh!" Ryan was winded. Marianne was sitting on top of him. She gave him a scathing look.

"You're making it up, it's not that bad."

"I'm not. I really hurt, honestly."

"Your own stupid fault."

"Hey, I was provoked."

"You're not in the playground."

Marianne squirmed about a bit, deliberately.

"Ach, ouch." His eyes were watering. She relented.

367

"Looks like our night of passion is out of the question then." She took hold of the side of the bath and hauled herself up. He took a deep breath.

"No way, I'll take loads of painkillers, I'll be fine." He struggled to his feet.

"I could exchange it for a hot bath and a nice head massage until you feel better?"

"Oh that sounds grand." He had trouble straightening up. She threw a towel at him.

"For me, ya eejit!" They started to laugh, Ryan holding his ribs, clearly in agony.

Smiling at the recollection, Marianne found Paul watching her in the rear-view mirror of the limousine. He smiled back, then put his hand to his lip, trying to prevent it from bleeding again. She shook her head despairingly, dropping her chin to her chest so he could not see her chuckling. She could not remember the last time two boys had fought over her. Grown up boys, at that.

Not unsurprisingly, Oonagh and Miss MacReady knew everybody they encountered at the TV studios. Miss MacReady introduced herself as the Director of Telecommunications for Innishmahon, and Oonagh flirtingly described herself as a close personal friend of Ryan O'Gorman's, and his other close personal friend, Marianne Coltrane. As is the way in Dublin, no-one really cared who they were, they were there and were made welcome whoever they were, and the two ladies made the most of it.

The chat show went according to plan, the

conversation was totally focused on the movie and related anecdotes as decreed by Lisa courtesy of the PR machine. But then a surprise was sprung. There was an extra guest on the show. A home coming gift for Ryan. And to a full musical fanfare, his old showbiz touring companion, Inspector Dermot Finnegan, took to the stage. They all laughed and chatted about the old days when they were in the band with George, and then Dermot persuaded Ryan to join him for a rousing rendition of '*You're Such A Good Looking Woman*'. It took only the opening bars, and the audience, led by Oonagh and Miss MacReady, twirling with gay abandon in the aisles, was on its feet as one. Marianne was particularly enjoying the performance, because, although Ryan was a great singer, his dancing was hilarious and he and Dermot were having so much fun it lifted her heart. Especially as he touchingly singled her out whenever he came to the rousing chorus.

Oonagh kept nudging her and nodding at Ryan as she danced. Miss MacReady, meanwhile, had the floor manager clamped to her, in an excruciatingly intimate version of the tango. He just managed to shout 'Roll the credits' before she threw her lips at his mouth in an almighty smacker. It had been a wonderful evening.

Marianne spotted Ryan and Paul having a pint together in the corner of the Green Room after the show. She joined them. Paul offered his right hand. She just looked at it.

"Go on," Ryan said, "make your peace now. It's over, well nearly, anyway."

"Ryan, will you excuse us?" She kept her tone light, flashing him a glance.

"Good luck," he said to Paul, patting him on the shoulder as he left.

"Marianne," Paul began. She dismissed him with a wave.

"Can you tell me why? That's all. I just want to know, why?"

"You know why."

She shook her head. "Words of one syllable please."

"It seemed like a good idea at the time. Doing a follow-up on the terrorist attack, particularly as Ryan was central to masterminding our escape, and then he landed the part of Thomas Bentley. It was like art imitating life, and there was my first inside take on a superstar, giving me the perfect opportunity to make a name for myself."

"Opportunistic, more like. But how you did it was so crass, Paul. More like a bounty hunter than a biographer and, why? I still don't know why?"

"You had abandoned me. Jack was gone."

"Abandoned? You sound like a child I was somehow responsible for. I think I did my bit by you, Paul. I don't owe you anything."

"I see that now, but that's not how it felt at the time." He took a sip of his drink. She folded her arms.

"I loved you, Marianne. I was hurt and then when I saw I could stir up some shit for Ryan and get paid for it, I went for it. What was the worst that could happen? Once you found out all about him and his carrying on,

370

you'd get pissed off and come back to me and we could be together."

"But there was no us, together."

"I know that now, but I hoped, deluded myself. I thought if I had a glittering career and money too, it would help. Put us on the same footing; make you want me as an equal, a lover, not just a friend."

Marianne could see Ryan looking back at them anxiously. She nodded to show everything was alright.

"I'm really sorry," Paul offered, and they looked into each other's faces.

"So am I," she replied.

"Forgiven?" He gave her his puppy dog eyes.

"Maybe one day. Not yet though, too raw."

He touched her arm as she turned to go.

"He's told me what he's going to do. He's told me he's going to make you happy. I hope it's true, but if..."

She gave him a half-smile.

"We'll be fine. If you would only promise me you'll go off and do some decent work, right a few wrongs, shake things up a bit, make me proud, that would make me happy too."

He grinned back at her, his big, open-faced boyish grin.

"Okay, it's a deal. You have my word."

"I'll keep you to that." And finally she kissed him, swiftly, on the cheek.

It had been hard to unravel herself from Ryan's

sprawling embrace in the huge bed that took centre stage in their suite. Their lovemaking the night before had been excruciatingly gentle, due to Ryan's abundant bruising, and she was sorely tempted to see what tantalisingly new techniques they could pursue for their pleasure this morning. But Oonagh had already texted that she and Miss MacReady were ready and waiting to hit the shops, and she knew Ryan had a full schedule before they all met for lunch, ahead of taking their leave of each other.

She was just squirming free, when the telephone buzzed. Lisa confirmed the media had reported only rave reviews of the film following the press showing, and glowing reports of the impromptu performances on last night's TV show. There was no mention of the unseemly brawl in the hostelry. No doubt Inspector Finnegan had something to do with that happy outcome.

Buoyed by all this good news, Marianne was showered, dressed and ready in minutes. Kissing her still-dozing movie star goodbye, she flew down the grand staircase to reception. It was only nine thirty, which by Dublin standards, is early on a Saturday morning. Oonagh was in deep 'fan club' conversation with Lisa, as they sat on lavish sofas either side of the huge fireplace; the grate spilling lilies and roses onto the hearth in acknowledgement of the height of summer.

Marianne scanned the room for Miss MacReady, as liveried porters swished effortlessly through the rotating door; glass, brass and buckles glinting in the sunlight, the scent of the stirring city drifting in from the street. She looked to the left through a large open doorway and caught sight of a silver gladiator sandal swinging from a stool in the hotel's famous bar. Tiptoeing across the carpet to the marble floor, she found Miss MacReady, dressed in an aquamarine trouser suit, beneath a full length matching trench coat, hair pinned with diamante clips. She was sipping the inevitable cocktail. Marianne slid onto a stool beside her. The glittering art deco room was deserted. A lone barman polished glasses, discreetly.

Miss MacReady did not look up, but sniffed loudly, as a large tear plopped from the tip of her nose into the glass.

"What's wrong?" Marianne asked softly, touching the woman's hand. It was ice-cold despite the warmth in the room, the purple fingernails trembled. Miss MacReady wiped her nose with the tissue Marianne offered.

"Nothing, I'm grand." She gave Marianne a watery smile.

"It's very early for a cocktail and it's not even Monday."

Miss MacReady nodded. "Special occasion."

"I'll join you then if I may?" Marianne nodded to the barman who swiftly produced two more Bloody Marys. Miss MacReady took a large swig and wiped another tear away.

"We came to Dublin once, we stayed here. It was heavenly, divine, the most glorious time of my life." She looked wistfully into her glass.

"You never said you'd stayed here before."

Marianne waited for an explanation of the 'we'. Miss MacReady blew her nose, stirred her drink and sighed.

"He started the tradition, the Monday cocktails. He knew I loved to dress up, so we made it our special day, because people tend to dislike Mondays and we were different, he said, in so many ways. So we had it as our special day and Dublin was our special time. Away from the island, away from everyone who would have disapproved. Just us, lovers in the city, the city that hid us, held us, loved us too." She smiled at the memory and squeezed Marianne's hand as it rested on the bar rail,

"I can see when Ryan is away from you, the hollowness of your heart and how it echoes with pain until he returns. I've held a hollowness such as that all my adult life. It's far worse than any heartbreak, that empty love-lost fog. I can see it every time you look at him, your heart bursts with love, and when he is not with you, you carry it around aching and empty. I can see it breaking, tiny little slivers chipping off, when they say things about him in the press. I can feel it all again, as livid an agony as if it were myself, every time I see you together and apart." She wiped her eyes and drew breath.

"Be with him, Marianne, whatever it takes, be with him. He is your love, your life, don't miss your chance, don't lose what's yours. Make it happen, fill that hollow heart with love, because try as you might, nothing else will ever take the emptiness away." And with that, she swung her knees round and jumped off the stool. "Come now." She grabbed her bag, "Let's get moving, places to go, a movie to watch, helicopters to catch." She beamed at the barman, collecting Oonagh from reception as they left.

Ryan commented they needed another helicopter for all the shopping bags as they made ready to leave. He took Marianne in his arms at the safety rail, lifting her chin with his fingers as his eyes scanned her face.

"Nearly there my love, nearly there." He kissed her firmly.

"I hope so, Ryan. I'm tired of waiting, tired of being understanding. I know all the reasons why and why not, but I just want to be with you and we should be together." She said it with a smile on her face, but tears were brimming. She blinked them away, touched his face with her fingertips, and headed off towards the helicopter. The blades started up, the draught whipped at her hair, pushing her back. She strode on.

Chapter Twenty Seven – All The Nice Girls...

O nly two weeks later, Ryan picked up an urgent message from Marianne on his new mobile. He was in South America, nearing the end of the publicity tour. He dialled the cottage. He knew if there was no reply, Miss MacReady usually intervened to check who was calling and would see if she could locate the absentee.

"It's yourself, is it?" Her voice was tense. "Looking for herself, I suppose? Well, I've no idea where she is. Headed off with Oonagh and the baby. They were having a picnic. Oonagh had news from the hospital a couple of days ago. No-one's saying very much but I'm not convinced it was positive."

"Ah." He went quiet. Miss MacReady always knew everybody's business.

"Are you still there? Where in the world are you, for heaven's sake? Are you still on the publicity tour for the film? Goodness knows, between the making and the selling of it, it takes an inordinate amount of time. Sure it only ends up an hour and a half. Be quicker just to sit there and read the book."

Ryan was in no mood for the postmistress's

philosophical ramblings.

"Just say I'll be there, day after tomorrow. Just say I'm on my way." He disconnected.

He did not sound in the best of form either, Miss MacReady surmised. Trouble brewing in his life too, she did not wonder. There was quite a bit of trouble stirring between one thing and another. The planets were out of sync, weather patterns disturbed and the wind kept changing direction at random, every hour or so. Miss MacReady took some deep breaths and went to light candles at her Buddhist altar, tracing the outline of the crystal wind chimes as she passed from the telephone exchange to her inner sanctum.

The couple stood in the freshly painted hallway of the cottage. He let his bag slide from his shoulder to the floor with a thud. She dropped the tea towel she had been using to dry her hands. They did not move for what seemed an age, the only sound the ticking of the newly restored Grandfather clock she had brought out of storage from England. Picking up his scent, Monty bounded in from the garden to greet him. Breaking the trance, he bent to lift the little dog into his arms, nuzzling him in welcome.

"Well, at least you're pleased to see me."

She ran the short distance, throwing her arms around them both.

"I've never been so pleased to see anyone in my life." She buried her face in the collar of his old jacket. He smelled of another place.

"Nor I." He kissed her on the nose, the forehead,

then on the mouth. Monty squirmed to be released; they were squashing him.

Ryan did not display even the merest flicker of shock when he and Marianne joined Oonagh and Padar for supper that evening in Maguire's. He was an actor, after all, but he had never witnessed such a dramatic change in the physical appearance of a human being. Oonagh had not only become shrunken and frail, and half the size she had been the last time he had seen her, but she was now 'Grand Ol Oprey' blonde with a husky new voice three octaves deeper than he remembered. Though nothing could diminish the light in her eyes when she caught sight of him, or the brightness of her smile as she stood with her arms wide open to welcome him.

"Ryan O'Gorman, as I live and breathe, come here to me, me favourite film star, gorgeous as ever." They hugged for a long moment. Padar busied himself behind the bar pouring drinks. Marianne lifted Bridget onto her hip as Ryan, freed from Oonagh's grip, presented trinkets from his travels for his godchild and her mother.

"We'll take the boat out tomorrow," Padar announced, putting a pint before Ryan on the table.

"Boat?"

"Did Marie not tell you? Oh, it's a fine boat, second-hand, but you'd never know it. Weather's set fair, would be a grand day for it."

Despite living on the island all his life and sailing since a child, Padar had never really owned a boat. He had a share in a couple of dinghies as a child and a small fishing boat once, but never owned a real boat. Last month he and Father Gregory had travelled to the mainland to return two days later, sailing triumphantly into Innishmahon aboard a forty-foot Moody; instantly the grandest yacht in the harbour. The waiting land lubbers, Oonagh, Marianne and Miss MacReady had waved at them with delight, eagerly directing the Captain and his crewmate to a berth in the newly created marina. All part of the island's development programme.

The two men jumped from the vessel to proudly welcome the ladies on board and, hardly able to stop grinning, Padar guided Oonagh around every inch of the yacht, laughing at her exclamations of surprise and approval, as she flicked switches and opened doors, running her hands along the gleaming galley and chart table, to finally stretch out like a starfish on the double berth in the oak panelled sleeping quarters beneath the cockpit.

"God, Padar it's like something off a film." She smiled, chinking plastic glasses with the others as they sipped champagne on deck. "And a real bargain."

He nodded. He had lied about the price, choosing not to tell her he had re-mortgaged the pub to buy his dream. She knew he had lied. She had a dream of her own to fulfil and she needed Padar onside if events were to unfold according to her wishes. Oonagh sat back and watched as he took Marianne and Miss MacReady on his far-too-technical guided tour. The only other time she had seen him this happy was at Bridget's christening, when all seemed well and the future looked bright.

379

Father Gregory was fiddling with the jib. He caught her eye.

"He's thrilled, isn't he?" Oonagh asked.

The Priest nodded. "He needs it, or *her* I should say."

"Yes, another woman in his life for when this one is gone."

"I don't believe we go, Oonagh."

"Gregory, this isn't the time or place for a debate on the afterlife, but I never took you for a fecking eejit."

"Didn't you? Well, I'm the bloke who wears a dress to the office, that should have given you a clue!"

Oonagh nearly spilled her drink, laughing.

The next day dawned fresh and bright, a light south-westerly wind scudded puff ball clouds across the early sun. The incumbents of Weathervane were already up and about. Marianne was busy putting finishing touches to smoked salmon and cream cheese brioche, chunky cucumber and feta cheese salad and a hearty seafood chowder, all planned for supper, should they decide, depending on how Oonagh was feeling, to spend the night on the water. Ryan had gathered together the ingredients for a number of cocktails and had stuffed candles, a silver candelabra and a box of matches into a kit bag, having told Oonagh and Marianne to bring a change of clothes for dinner. It was going to be a grandiose affair.

By the time they had loaded the 4x4, fitted Monty into his life vest, collected Oonagh and the baggage of drugs, lotions and potions which seemed to follow her everywhere, kissed Bridget and Miss MacReady farewell, Padar and Father Gregory had the boat shipshape and ready to sail. The sun was blazing as they clambered on board, Padar helping Oonagh as she struggled with the two walking sticks she had come to rely on, refusing point blank the wheelchair he had tried to insist she used, at least around the village. He settled her on cushions in the shade just inside the cockpit. Swathed in layers of purple and magenta, she was wigless and had taken to wearing a turban studded with crystals, and huge, 1960s-style sunglasses, refusing the lifejacket he proffered. She tugged off her pink deck shoes to reveal scarlet toenails, stark against her thin, white feet.

Marianne took up position opposite her. She had not sailed since she was a youngster, so would await instruction from the helmsman. Slightly apprehensive, she was relieved all the men were competent sailors. As this was a big boat and new to them all, she did not want anything to spoil what was to be a glorious and unforgettable maiden voyage. She glanced upwards, not a cloud in the sky. Monty, having completed his inspection of the deck, trotted back to the cockpit to nestle beside Oonagh, his chin on her lap.

"Fenders in," Padar shouted.

"Fenders in," Ryan replied.

"Cast off."

"Cast off." Father Gregory jumped from the quayside, onto the boat.

The engine purred as Padar swung the gleaming

vessel away from shore, heading boldly out to sea.

Marianne watched Innishmahon slide into the distance. She leaned across and squeezed Oonagh's knee. Oonagh looked odd, makeup streaked with tears she had shed uncontrollably on leaving Bridget and Miss MacReady, and now she seemed both excited and anxious.

"Right, me hearties," called Ryan from below deck. "Let's have a drink."

"Thank God for that," whispered Oonagh, "I'm terrified of the water."

"Bullshit!" laughed Padar. "The only water you're terrified of, is if there's too much in your whiskey."

"Let's hoist sail, then we'll have a drink." Father Gregory strode the deck, taking charge of the mast. "Ryan, grab that foresheet, let's get out there and see what this baby can do."

There is no experience so sublime as creaming through the water, wind billowing the sail with a fragrant breeze kissing your face, as you turn to watch sparkling waves part in your wake, Marianne considered, as she stretched out on the deck, basking in the bubble of tranquillity that accompanies a blistering sail on a hot summer's day. She could hear the soft murmur of the men discussing charts and equipment behind her in the cockpit, Oonagh snoozing with Monty in her arms, the shrouds at the mast clanking a tuneless lullaby as gulls called overhead, swirling through the cloudless sky. For all the movement and sounds about her, she recalled it was sailing with her parents that she loved more than anything else. The moment the sail took the wind and the boat with it, only then would she become perfectly still and in one of the quietest, safest places she had ever found.

Oonagh's sleep, combined with the salt air, had revived her and she refused to sail back on such a fabulous afternoon.

"Let's drop anchor and have our little dinner party. It's perfect Padar," she reassured her Captain.

And so they did, taking in the sails and lighting lamps along the deck as Marianne and Ryan set to work in the galley, preparing cocktails and food; laying the chart table with olives and stuffed peppers and then the grand table in the salon with silverware, crystal and the candelabra. The women giggled together as they donned jewellery and lipstick to join the men for drinks, Marianne having pinned Oonagh into a party dress, now at least two sizes too big. She said it was Padar's favourite.

After Ryan's horrendously strong cocktails, taken on deck as the sun slipped slowly beneath the horizon, the five nestled comfortably around the table while Monty slept, happily ensconced in a sail cover beneath the cockpit. The meal could not have been more eagerly relished and once replete, port and brandy were produced with cheese, and the obligatory tales of heroic sea adventures ensued. Visibly tiring, Oonagh insisted they all hush up as she begged Ryan to regale them with blow-by-blow accounts of his film making and Hollywood hobnobbing.

"And what about Serene La Blanc, is she

absolutely fabulous in the flesh?"

Ryan glanced at Marianne who knew full well he had never met the starlet. "Indeed."

"And Rocky Vegas, how tall is he in real life?"

"So big," Ryan demonstrated.

"And Vienna Ventura, how does she look these days?"

"Ah, much better."

And on she went, barely able to keep her eyes open, her husky voice no more than a harsh whisper as the candles burned and the night wore on.

Father Gregory was the first to leave the table, weary and slurring but able to kiss them all goodnight before he headed to his bunk.

"Terrible waste of a good looking man," Oonagh told him as he left.

"I've had my moments." His eyes twinkled.

"I don't think God expects us to be celebrate at all," she said, and they laughed at her misnomer.

"Looking at the human race, God's expectations must be pretty well shattered at this stage anyway," Gregory told her.

"But not to have sex. Not to fall in love."

"Who said anything about not falling in love? Sure that's the easy bit, it's relationships that are the problem. I couldn't do that and my job. I leave stuff like that to you guys." He kissed her again and she blushed, closing her eyes until he had gone.

"Now," she said, hauling herself upright at the table. "You two, what's the story?"

"Ah, Oonagh…"

"Padar quiet, I need to know."

"I could say mind your own business." Marianne placed her hand over her friend's.

"We love each other, Oonagh, we'll work it out," Ryan interjected.

"When? Time's moving on. Neither of you are spring chickens. You don't want a life wasted with regrets and 'maybe ifs'. You have responsibilities; you have a young son, a godchild, each other. You'll all need each other, that's all I'm saying." She struggled on the last words. Padar passed her some water.

"C'mon to bed love, you'll have a lovely rest in that big bed, the sea rocking you to sleep."

Oonagh did not argue. She pulled herself up and, after kissing both Ryan and Marianne as hard as she could, Padar helped her down the corridor and into bed.

Once they had cleared away, Marianne and Ryan moved the table and made their bed up in the salon. Exhausted, they curled up together and let the movement of the big boat slide them to slumber.

Dawn was breaking when Marianne, turning in Ryan's arms, thought she heard footsteps on the deck above. He stirred and all went quiet. She did not hear the barefooted shuffle of two pairs of feet heading towards the bow, or the anchor stealthily lifted. The key to the engine was waiting to be turned, to purr into life and push them away. If she had followed her instinct, she would have crept to the cockpit and, looking out along the deck, would have seen two people embracing and then, one helping the other crouch down onto the side, lowering them gently into the water. But she was warm and comfortable, so she stayed where she was.

The engine started, the boat was moving, swinging about, turning back to face the land, away from the swimmer; the person in the water. But the person in the water was not swimming. Instead she was quite still, bobbing calmly up and down. She lifted her arm and waved at the man standing at the bow, his face wet with tears, his heart breaking behind his eyes. She lifted her arm once more, a silver christening bangle glinted in her hand and then, completely still, she slid softly beneath the surface, a halo of bubbles bursting on the water as she disappeared from view.

Now fully turned about, the boat with the engine at full throttle, sliced through the waves heading back to shore. The man at the helm quickly blessed himself as the dog, aware of someone in the water, starting running the length of the boat, barking a frantic warning back into the black sea. Ryan was awake and up in an instant, taking the steps in two strides and, as Monty neared the edge of the boat in a frenzy of panic, Ryan lunged and lifted him up and back to safety. The sky was brightening. He looked from one end of the boat to the other. Padar was standing at the bow, gripping the handrail, rigid. Father Gregory's face set grim at the helm, concentrating on getting them all back as quickly as the engine would allow.

Marianne surfaced, and climbing on deck, took

Monty from Ryan. Still groggy with sleep, she was unable to take it all in at first. Then an icy realisation began to creep along her spine, the hairs on her skin lifting in horror. Her voice trapped at the top of her throat, came out as a strangled squeak.

"What is it? Is it Oonagh?"

Ryan grasped her shoulders and turned her round, guiding her back to the lower deck. She stopped, refusing to move.

"Padar, Padar, is it Oonagh?" she shouted, the wind whipping her words away. She looked from one to the other. "Where's Oonagh?"

The man standing at the bow of the boat did not hear, or if he did, did not answer. He just looked down at the water; the water that had taken his wife. Marianne turned to Ryan. He turned away, staring straight ahead at the island. She sought out Father Gregory at the wheel. He too was stony-faced, his gaze fixed on their destination.

"Will you not even tell me what happened?" she screeched at them. *"Any of you, tell me what happened, tell me the truth!"*

"She's gone Marie, her way, her choice," Ryan answered.

"Oh God." Marianne pushed her hand into her mouth to stop the scream.

The village closed ranks following Oonagh's disappearance. Official reports had been fudged, few questions asked. There was a small memorial service in the church, conducted by the priest who had been at the helm when it happened. A tragic accident, a blessing in some ways, the poor girl was terminally ill anyway, the husband devastated.

Marianne and Ryan returned to Weathervane after the service. Bereft, they had eaten in silence, there was so much to talk through and yet they had nothing to say. The air was filled with the slightly chemical smell of softly burning peat – it mingled with the smoke from the single French cigarette Ryan still allowed himself after dinner.

Marianne had just settled Monty in his basket for the night. Making her way back to the sitting room, her pumps shuffled across the quarry tiles, until the sound was muffled by the hearth rug and she sank to the floor at Ryan's knees. He struck at the peat with the poker, passing a squat glass of amber to her over her shoulder. '*Lover Man*' played achingly in the other room. Monty stretched and made a little puppy sound which belied his years.

Ryan put the poker down and twirled a strand of Marianne's hair idly through his fingers, watching the lazy flames from the fire soothe the highlights of coppery brown. She turned a page of the magazine on the floor, not really reading. The page brushed his foot. She followed the stroke of the page with her hand along his bare brown skin, tanned by far sunnier climes than this. His toes were long and straight, the nails white, hard and shiny, the feet of a young boy. She put her fingers to her lips and then pressed them against his toes in a kiss.

The telephone shrilled. The peace shattered like

glass. Monty lifted his head, and growled. It shrilled again, an old-fashioned ring, urgent, demanding. Marianne grunted, pulling herself up.

"Who the..?" Ryan asked uselessly, as she padded out to the hallway, where, despite all the modernisation, the black *Bakelite* link to the outside world lay rattling in its lair.

"Hello, Miss MacReady, what can I do for you? I see. Wait. I'll fetch him." Marianne was terse. It was cold out in the hallway away from the fire. The wind threw a handful of hard raindrops against the solitary pane in the hall door. He was standing when she went back to the room, head tilted, listening.

"It's for you. Long distance," Marianne glared at him. He frowned, touched her hand as he passed.

"Be careful, Miss MacReady will be listening on the line." She hissed, in warning.

"Yes, thank you Miss MacReady. Angelique, hi, yeah fine. What's wrong?" Ryan sounded angry.

Marianne moved away from the doorway. Her stomach caught in a clamp. She picked up the magazine, threw another briquette on the fire, plumped up the cushions, put their whiskey glasses side by side on the mantel. Ryan's leather jacket slipped off the arm of the chair. She picked it up, something dropped onto the flagstone. His wallet. It lay face down, open. She picked it up and, turning it towards her, a beautifully fragile young face gazed back at her. The clamp tightened. She snapped the wallet shut and rammed it back in his pocket. She took a deep breath. It was not as if she had not seen

389

him before. It was not as if she did not know about him. She moved back towards the door. Monty was listening too.

"I know," Ryan was saying, "but I have things to do here. I will be back next week. We'll sort things out then. No, don't do that..."

A pause and then the obvious softening of the voice. The kinder, loving, missing you tone of a long distance father to child. A plea to the heart.

"Hello my love, are you having a nice visit with your mother? Is Larry there? Good. *Nanny?* Good. I'll be home soon. Be a good boy. Goodnight now." She had never heard that tone before, that love and pain and longing. "Oh God," she thought, "I've lost him."

The phone clumped in its cradle. He moved back into the room, the former haven destroyed by tidiness, the atmosphere dissipated, left clinging to the four corners.

She banged in the kitchen, drowning the dishes in the sink. He picked up a tea towel. Annoyed at his attempt at normality, she whipped it out of his hand.

"What does she want? How did she find you?" She held the tremor out of her voice, her eyes burning.

"To discuss things. Sort things out. I've asked for a divorce, she won't listen, so Larry said he'd go and see her, tell her I'm going for custody. He gave her the number. Marie, I need to go and sort this..."

She scrunched the tea towel in her hands.

"Again, you need to go again...and you'll always need to go again. Wherever we are, whatever we are doing, the phone will ring. She will call, and then the

child or Larry or God knows who else, and you will need
to go, and sort this or that and I will be left, again."

He moved towards her, pleading. She drew back,
glaring.

"Marie, help me."

"Ah, help yourself Ryan," she blazed, "you're not
in a bloody movie now, you spoiled, selfish brat. I was
not put on this planet for your bloody convenience, to
dance attendance on you when you can spare me the time
or inclination. Enough! You're not the only pebble on the
beach, fish in the sea or flea on the dog's back!"

Monty lifted an eyebrow. He had not heard a full
blown rant for ages. But Marianne had been building up
to this, rehearsed it in her head many times. She had just
not expected it to be now, but here it was, and out it
tumbled, for better or worse.

"I've had it. I'm calling it quits, calling it off,
calling time, hasta la vista, auf wiedersehen pet, and
goodnight, Vienna." The tirade was accompanied by
various pokes in the ribs, thumps to the shoulder and,
finally, a sharp kick on the shin. Ryan hopped, clutching
his painful limb.

"Now, Marie." He was half smiling, half wincing.
"Calm yourself. We've had a few drinks, you're grieving.
We both are. You don't mean it."

She drew herself up to her full five foot three.

"How dare you?" she bellowed. "How dare you
even suggest I am drunk, you no-good, two-timing, hairy-
arsed bastard." She charged towards him, arms flailing,
fists clenched. He ducked expertly but caught his much

admired cheekbone on the door jam. "Ouch!"

She smacked him on the other side of his face for good measure. She was on a roll now, her gander up, but she had pushed him too far. Slow to anger, he was one of those brooding Celts who could really lose it on or off screen. He lunged at her, pinning her arms by her sides and then he shook her, hard.

"You're beating me up, for God's sake. Stop it!" He said.

She pulled an arm free and smacked him again. He released her.

"I don't believe this. I don't know why I ever had anything to do with a self-obsessed, screeching, banshee of a harridan like you! Yes it's over, well and truly over, and bloody good riddance." He whirled into the hallway, slamming the hall door behind him and stood, nostrils flaring, in the filthy black night. Cold driving rain lashed into his face.

"Shit!" He swore, as he squished in bare feet and t-shirt to the car. Thank God the keys were in it, he rejoiced begrudgingly. He turned the ignition. The old truck drawled to life. Flinging the steering wheel through his hands, he streaked away.

He drove like a madman for about half a mile, screeching down the main thoroughfare away from Innishmahon. Then, slamming brakes on, he twisted the wheel again, bumping the front of the car off the bank as he struggled to complete a U turn and head back to the cottage. He crashed to a halt, slammed the car door, nearly took the garden gate off its hinges, and banged so hard on the knocker, if it was not for the howling wind and driving rain, it would have been heard by the radar-eared Miss MacReady at the Post Office on the other side of the village.

The door opened a sliver. He kicked it open the rest of the way and stood in the pouring rain, staring at her. She had dragged on the comfort of his jacket, he noticed. Her face was striped with mascara, her mouth turned down at the edges, hair standing on end from running desperate fingers through it. He thought her the most beautiful thing he had ever seen. He grabbed her shoulders and pulled her out to him in the rain. He pressed his mouth, hard and fierce, against her lips, a kiss of passion and possession, no room for argument or discussion. They fell back into the hallway together. He drew the jacket and her top off her shoulders, pulling it down to reveal her breasts, and pushed his wet face into her bosom, gnawing gently at her skin.

"I love your breasts," he whispered, then pressed his mouth to her shoulders. Scars from the bomb attack stretched snail-like to her collarbone. "I love every inch of your flesh, every inch of you." She stood motionless against the wall as he pushed her jog pants to the floor and fell to his knees. He kissed her, again and again, soft, delicate kisses all over her thighs, her groin, her hips. He kissed her belly and held his cheek against her stomach, warming her through.

"I love every scar and every inch of you, and you are, whatever you are, the love of my life." He looked up into her face with so much adoration she began to tremble. She buried her fingers in his sodden hair and sank to the floor beside him. They wrapped their arms around each other and lay there clasped together for a long time. Finally, they climbed the stairs, hand in hand. Monty had long since removed himself from this scene of raw emotion, having put himself quietly to bed in the basket located snugly beneath the stairwell.

Ryan was pushing his toilet bag into his holdall as she handed him a coffee. They had barely said a word to each other since they had woken.

"You off then?" she asked, trying to keep the sarcasm out of her voice.

"I have to sort things out once and for all."

"I have heard that before you know." She handed him his shirt.

"I know, no empty promises this time, I promise."

She took his hand in hers, preventing him from zipping the bag.

"This is the last time, Ryan. If this is goodbye, it's goodbye, but this really is the last time. Go for good, or come back for good, no in between, not anymore. I'm worth more than this. We both are." She released him and zipped the bag, handing it to him. He went to kiss her. She blocked him with hands. He went to speak. She put a finger to her lips. He grabbed his jacket and his keys and was gone.

Adrienne Vaughan

Chapter Twenty Eight – An Act Of Betrayal

The weeks following Oonagh's death were a blur. Padar was, one minute, fully compos mentis, the next, a gibbering wreck. Miss MacReady appeared staunch with sobriety throughout the evenings yet, could be found slumped in a stupor in the sorting room at the Post Office at half eight in the morning. Marianne was wasting away to nothing, alternating between helping at Maguire's and the Post Office and trying to keep Bridget fed, washed and watered in between.

It was Father Gregory who finally put his foot down. He called a meeting of the 'Bridge Too Far' Committee, assembling the grief-stricken adults, in the hope that once gathered, they could discuss how to restore some sense of order into the life of the child, who was suffering due to their pre-occupation with maintaining some semblance of normality. Once they had finished deliberating the slowness of the construction process, the popularity of the new marina and the latest funding report, the Priest called them to order and put the upbringing of young Bridget Quinn under 'Any Other Business'.

Padar was shocked. "We're grand, Father."

"I'm not saying you're not, Padar. But the child needs a routine. Sure you're run ragged with the pub and the holiday lets. It's time to sort something out."

"Sure I'm a great help to them, aren't I, Padar?" Miss MacReady interjected, indignant at the Priest's suggestion the child was being neglected. Padar and Marianne murmured in agreement. The Priest banged the table.

"To put it bluntly, I think she should go and live with her godmother for at least part of the week, if she'll have her. Only two minutes from the pub, Marianne could set up a proper routine for her, while Padar gets on with running the business to provide for them. It's what she needs. It's what we all need."

It was Marianne's turn to be surprised. She knew the situation was less than perfect and, if she was honest, could not continue indefinitely, but she had not considered for a moment, that she could be the person to remedy the situation. Yet thinking about it and putting the child first, she could see what Father Gregory was suggesting made perfect sense, at least for a while.

Padar, who was struggling to keep the business going on his own, initially bridled at the idea of the arrangement and had to be assured his relationship with his daughter would not suffer. Indeed, it could only improve. He saw so little of her at the moment. Father Gregory slammed his clipboard on the table.

"I'll leave it with you then." He left without finishing his drink.

Miss MacReady remained indignant, ramming Oonagh's curly blonde wig a little further back on her head. Marianne could not help wishing she would soon relinquish this particular memorial.

"The Priest has a point, Padar. She's growing up fast; she needs stability in her life. We all do," Marianne offered softly.

Padar said he would think about it, but when Bridget crawled into the doorway in a soiled romper suit with chocolate stains all over her face, he just slumped in his seat.

"I'll take her," Marianne said, and swept the little one and Monty back to Weathervane for a warm bath, supper and a bedtime story.

Two days later, a desperately exhausted Padar asked to see her. They came to an arrangement. Bridget would live with Marianne at Weathervane during the week, ensuring they all ate together at least once a day, before Padar became embroiled in the business of the bar. They would alternate between Weathervane during the week and Maguire's at the weekend, when Padar and Marianne would be at the pub catering for the weekend trade anyway. They agreed to give the arrangement a three-month trial. All parties were satisfied, even Miss MacReady who was to act as on-call babysitter, giving both Padar and Marianne a break when required.

It was on a Thursday night, the week before Halloween, that Miss MacReady stepped into the breach to give them both a night off. It was over two months since Oonagh's death. Ryan had been gone for almost as long, finishing the promotional tour which seemed to be taking him the length and breadth of the planet. He had contacted Marianne on numerous occasions, left phone messages and sent emails but she had forced herself not to respond, telling herself she was far too busy to stress unnecessarily about Ryan and his schedule. If he could compartmentalise his feelings, then so could she. She had other priorities at the moment. Plenty of busyness to fill her hollow heart, Miss MacReady would no doubt agree.

"Marie, I wondered..." Padar was fumbling at the till, straightening the Worcestershire sauce. "Would you come out with me for a bite of supper? There's a new place down at the Marina, a bit of competition. Will we check it out?"

"We would, of course." She smiled at his awkwardness. "I'll be ready in a jiffy, beep the horn and I'll come out to you."

"Not like Oonagh then, she'd take an age to get ready."

"She did. But didn't she always look gorgeous."

He busied himself at the optics. Marianne swung out through the side entrance, missing Miss MacReady arriving to collect Bridget, waving a copy of the celebrity magazine, *The Biz*.

Padar rolled his eyes to heaven.

"More of the same, is it?"

"Worse. It's a scandal. Pictures of you all on the yacht, and then a write-up, saying Oonagh disappeared off

398

the boat, and could there have been an orgy? And was there foul play? No name attached to it though, but they're calling it an exclusive, would you believe?"

"Dear God." Padar slammed the till shut. "Will they not let the dead rest in peace?"

"Not that lot." Sean slid onto his usual bar stool. "Sure that's dancing with the devil, courting favour with that shower." He glowered at Miss MacReady as she took Bridget and Monty away with her for the evening, two of Padar's cousins arriving to take over the bar, as she left.

He sat stony silent over his fish pie.

"Not to your liking?" Marianne broke his reverie.

"Have you seen the latest?"

"I've been warned about it. I'd just love to know where they get the pictures from. Ever since myself and Ryan have been coming here, someone has been taking pictures and sending them to the press. It's someone we know, but who?"

Padar shrugged.

"Is it that Paul Osborne fella dishing the dirt again?"

"No, Paul's moved on, working for an independent TV company in the Gambia, I heard, making a programme about the local people and their struggle to survive." Marianne was thoughtful. " I've always wondered who the traitor is. It's a small island. It must be someone very close to us."

Padar grunted, poking his fork in the pie. Marianne continued,

"Sean Grogan always seems to have money for things like satellite TV and the latest mobile phone, I've never known him sell any livestock, so where does all that come from, I wonder?"

Padar shrugged again.

"Why bring Oonagh into it? Why make up stuff like that?" he said, eyes searching her face.

"It's what they do, Padar. They're very clever you know, always run it past their legal department first. None of you get it. Oonagh was the worst, the most naïve for all her assumed sophistication. It's only about circulation figures, not like the good old days when a decent journalist was highly principled, a campaigner for justice, righting wrongs, exposing evil, fighting good causes."

"Were you one of them?"

"I'd like to think so. Chequebook journalism is what it is. Cheap and nasty. There's enough that's cheap and nasty in the world."

Padar took a large slurp of his drink.

"Do you think he'll come back?" he asked.

"Who?"

"Ah, you know full well who!"

"Ryan? Don't know. We didn't part on the best of terms. The longer he's away the more he becomes engrained in another way of life, another set of values. I don't know."

"Would you have him back?"

"That's a very personal question, Padar?"

"Would you though?"

"Only on a permanent basis, all or nothing, and

that's not going to happen, so I guess it's nothing." She knocked back her wine.

"Sorry." Padar looked baleful.

"Me too."

They ate the rest of their now-cold food in silence.

News that the merchant banker in England had put the Georgian mansion on the market, disturbed Marianne for some reason. It had been refurbished to a very high standard prior to her arrival on the island but she had never even seen its absentee owners, who had only once sent an entourage to air the place ahead of the vagary of celebrities and politicians booked to stay during the 'Bridge Too Far' weekend.

Searching out Father Gregory, she found herself in one of his Confessionals.

"To what do I owe the pleasure?" He smiled through the grille.

"Funny, that's not the Act of Contrition I remember."

"You've never struck me as particularly contrite."

"Ouch!"

"I meant it as a compliment. You always seem pretty comfortable in your own skin. What's up?"

She explained that the former doctor's surgery was on the market and a bit of an idea was germinating in her brain.

"More fundraising, Marie. I think we're all a bit battle-weary on that front, don't you?"

"I have a benefactor in mind but the most

important thing would be reclaiming the house for the island, putting it back to good work. What do you think?"

"They always say there's none as evangelical as a convert. That must go for island converts too. When did the 'we' come into it?"

"Gregory, you've too much about you just to go round hunting, shooting, fishing and throwing Holy Water at people."

He laughed, blessed her in Latin, and closed his side of the grille.

"No penance, then?" she shouted through the shutter.

"Your projects are your penance," he shouted back.

Miss MacReady was enthralled. She sat on a bar stool, legs crossed in fishnet tights, red stilettos on her feet, horn-rimmed spectacles on the end of her nose as she poured over the architectural drawings.

"It doesn't need a lot doing to it," Marianne explained, "It was beautifully restored and here, you can see this would make a playroom; this could be a club room for the older children."

"With computers, DVDs, games consoles and the like," Miss MacReady sipped her Singapore Sling; she did so like to get down with the kids. "But who'd run it?"

"A board of Governors, like a school, with someone qualified doing the day-to-day stuff."

"Someone like Sinead." Father Gregory made a note.

"I've already mooted the idea. She seemed quite interested, said she might be looking for a new challenge." Marianne folded the plans away. Miss MacReady nodded, she had heard Sinead and Phileas were going through another bad patch. Sinead was thinking of moving back to Cork. Island life was not proving to be the idyll she had hoped.

The ubiquitous Sean pulled his coat off the back of his stool.

"Great! A shower of rag-arses down from Dublin for the summer to vandalise and rob us. Great plan. Yet another outsider sticking her nose in and knowing what's best for us, and all she does is bring scandal and disgrace on the place."

"Hey now." Father Gregory stopped him in his tracks. Sean pushed past him.

"Go to hell, Father. Sure we probably all will."

The priest smiled at Marianne.

"Bound to be a winner then if Sean's against it. Hasn't that always been the case?" Miss MacReady agreed wholeheartedly, volunteering to sound Sinead out at the earliest opportunity.

Not two days later, the three women were examining the plans over the kitchen table in Weathervane. Sinead was all for the project and loved the ideas for the house, which they discovered was called Ophiuchus.

"I've researched the name," exclaimed Miss MacReady, who was wildly enthusiastic about the whole thing. "It's the thirteenth constellation in the solar system.

The ancient astronomers called it 'the sign of the wounded healer'. Most appropriate for its new lease of life."

Marianne's original concept was for the house to be turned into a summer retreat for underprivileged children, a special holiday home for kids who did not have holidays; the sort of kids where each day merged into the next because of family circumstances. Sinead took it to the next stage, suggesting the project be specifically for those children who were carers, looking after sick or elderly family members, taking care of the disabled or terminally ill. Everyone considered this an excellent idea, as Marianne set to work pulling together the plan for the purchase of the property, whilst setting the publicity machine in motion.

"I'm pretty well-known these days," she told her contact at the radio station. "Might as well put some of this infamy to good use." The radio interview which followed gave the new campaign a kick-start.

To buy the property quickly and get the project moving, Marianne invested a generous slice of her own funds. When she told Padar she wanted to call it the Oonagh Quinn Foundation, he begrudgingly agreed, handing over a donation following the sale of the yacht he could no longer bring himself to board, let alone sail.

"You're not keen on the children's project are you, Padar?" she asked as he cleared away the dishes following one of their regular weekend meals together in the pub. Bridget slumbered on the sofa with one arm flung across Monty's curled up frame.

"Not really. You've enough to be doing." He nodded towards the little one. "And I'm of the same opinion as Sean. I don't want a shower of roughnecks from the towns here. They'd be a bad influence."

Marianne was disappointed.

"It shouldn't be like that, and Bridget is a very lucky little girl, she has you and all of us who love her. It would do her good to mix with kids less fortunate."

"You mean, put her own situation into perspective."

"In a way." She stood to help.

He put the dishcloth down and was standing beside her, very close. He took her by the shoulders. She could feel his breath, hot on her cheek.

"Padar?"

His eyes were boring into her face, full of longing and desire. He pressed himself up against her. She felt a blush rise from her chest and then a flutter of fear.

"Oh, Marie, say you'll have me. I'm dying for you. We can be a family, that's all we need."

He tried to kiss her, gripping her shoulders tightly. She pushed him away.

"Padar, stop. Stop it!"

Instantly, Monty was at his heels, barking and snarling furiously. Marianne struggled to break free. Monty, now frantic, leapt up and nipped Padar on the wrist. He released her immediately and took a step back, confused. Then he seemed to snap out of it.

"Oh God, Marie, I'm sorry, so sorry." Flustered, he fled the kitchen, dishes abandoned. Shocked, Marianne stood fixed to the spot.

Much later, putting Bridget to bed in her cot adjacent the boudoir the infant had shared with her mother, Marianne could hear Padar weeping softly. She pushed the door ajar. He was standing in a corner, facing the wall, his head in his hands. The room was full of boxes, bearing the logos and slogans of vintners and brewers. The boxes were packed to bursting with Oonagh's possessions, clothes, shoes, handbags, all her worldly belongings. He turned when he heard her at the door, eyes wild with despair.

"I'd have given you a hand with all of this," Marianne said.

"It's a mess." Padar looked away.

"It'll be okay. It's just a bit early Padar, a bit soon."

"I know, Marie. I'm just so lost without her."

She moved to put her arms around him, all his lust gone.

"I know. I'm a bit lost too," she told him.

She scanned the clutter.

"It might help if you didn't have to face this lot whenever you came into your bedroom," she said, checking under the bed to see if she could store anything there, out of the way. She burrowed beneath Oonagh's flamboyant valance, caught hold of what felt like a metal box and dragged it out. She instantly recognised a professional camera case and flicked the clasps to reveal the latest camera, complete with telephoto lens.

"I didn't think you were interested in photo…"

She stopped, holding the camera away from her as if it were a snake. "Oh my God, Padar, it's you! You're the one feeding the media with pictures. You're the bastard working for the paparazzi."

Padar snatched the camera from her.

"It's none of your business!"

"None of my business? How dare you? You've made our business, everyone's business. You absolute bastard. I bet Paul Osborne put you on the payroll the very first day he came here. I thought it was Sean, but there was so much other stuff Sean couldn't have been party to. Now it all makes sense, except the latest bit, the bit about the boat and foul play, that wasn't you, was it?"

He shook his head, the colour had drained from his face.

"I told Paul I'd had enough when we knew Oonagh wouldn't get better. He said he understood, he was thinking of changing direction anyway. But he warned me the publishers wouldn't be very happy. He said they'd try to make it worth my while to stay on, that they might turn nasty. Guess that's why they made up the story about Oonagh and the orgy on the boat, getting their own back."

"How low can they sink? And you, look what it's done to you, turned you into a snide, spying on your friends and using us. Why, Padar, why?"

"How on earth was I supposed to pay for the renovations after the storm? We'd no insurance, sure the pub is hardly worth a light, especially with no tourist trade."

"Did Oonagh know?"

"Of course she didn't know. Oonagh knew more about Hollywood than Innishmahon and then later, she was out of it most of the time on painkillers; living in la-la land; buying anything she wanted off the internet for her and the baby on the credit card. What could I do?"

Marianne slammed closed the lid and kicked the case back under the bed.

"You could have chosen not to let her spend money like water. You could have stayed loyal to us, all of us, instead of using us to earn a fast buck. The anguish you've caused, the irreparable damage and pain." Her eyes filled with angry tears. "You made something beautiful, sordid and dirty, something for all the world to laugh at and deride. I can't believe it was you all along, Padar. You make me sick to my stomach. I'm going home now and I'm taking Bridget with me. I can't leave the child here with you…with a traitor." She slammed the door as she left.

In her usual infuriating way, Miss MacReady did not seem surprised when Marianne, still ashen with rage, told her over coffee that Padar Quinn had been Paul Osborne's undercover photographer.

"I thought maybe it was Padar. Too much cash and credit readily available."

"Not Sean? I thought Sean when he got the flat screen TV and everything."

"Ah, he could have been in on it alright, in the beginning, spying and such. But no, it needed someone a bit more switched on to take the photos. Padar does fit the bill."

"And you're not horrified?" Marianne asked. "Mortified he betrayed us? All of us?"

"I don't think he bargained for the last lot, the made-up reports about Oonagh and the orgy on the yacht. That went too far." Miss MacReady put her cup down, smiling indulgently at Bridget who was conducting one of her many diatribes with Monty. "I don't see it quite like you, though. Oh, it was sneaky alright. It was wrong, no doubt, but everything happens for a reason. We'd not have had the support for the bridge, or the new project without the fascination the media has with yourself and Ryan, hyped up by Padar and his pictures. A double-edged sword, as they say."

Marianne blinked. The postmistress had a point.

"And all the lovely things Oonagh and the baby enjoyed before she died, the fabulous christening and the boat and all. It wasn't all bad. It might end well, after all."

"What on earth do you mean?" Marianne was incredulous.

"Well your fella is on the telly tonight doing the chat show again and a little birdie tells me he has some news of his own to impart."

Marianne was intrigued. Miss MacReady always seemed to know everyone's business, even people thousands of miles away, on another continent.

"Have you anything else to tell me?" Marianne held Miss MacReady's gaze.

"Well, I did overhear Padar confessing to Ryan

about being the secret photographer and I got the distinct impression Ryan wasn't bothered, not bothered at all. As if he'd gone beyond all that, as if it didn't really matter one jot in the overall scheme of things."

Marianne clattered the mugs into the sink.

"By overhear, I take it you mean on the telephone?"

"Of course on the telephone, how else am I to keep track of everybody and their comings and goings? It's my job."

Miss MacReady suddenly decided she needed to be somewhere else, obviously aware she had revealed too much. Irked, Marianne forced herself to completely ignore the fact Ryan was on television that evening. She had never succumbed to a TV in the cottage. Weathervane was her haven. If she did want to watch the box, Maguire's had the latest satellite paraphernalia only a few strides from her door. So after walking Monty along the cove, with Bridget firmly strapped into the baby sling, all three of them devoured a delicious supper of lamb stew and creamed rice pudding and settled down for the night.

Unsurprisingly, Marianne was restless and unable to sleep. She went to her desk to dig out the problematic paperwork relating to the purchase of Ophiuchus; the house she intended to transform into a holiday retreat.

There was a complication relating to the deeds of the property. The merchant banker who owned it had fallen on hard times and had re-mortgaged the property, but no-one knew who with. The new mortgage had never been cleared and it could prove an expensive legal wrangle if not dealt with. Just the sort of mind-numbing distraction she needed to fuddle her brain and prevent her from dwelling on things like self-obsessed celebrities spouting off to millions of viewers on national TV.

Marianne rang Father Gregory. No answer. She tried Miss MacReady. No response there either. She growled to herself, she supposed they were all in the pub watching, mesmerised, as Ryan blathered on about this or that exotic location. Good God, had they not all heard enough of his bullshit over the past couple of years? Suffering a major grump, she pinged off an email outlining the problem relating to the deeds, requesting names of legal contacts and other assistance she could call upon to help resolve it. She copied in the whole Board, the same team who had managed the 'Bridge Too Far' campaign. Then, finally slamming shut the lid of her laptop, took herself off to bed, far too bad-tempered to concentrate on the novel she was reading.

Bridget was unusually fractious the following morning. Monty, too, seemed below par, only giving the sea grass in the garden a cursory sniff before returning to the cottage to sit moodily in his basket. Marianne prepared breakfast in silence, not even switching on the morning radio programme she loved to argue with. Monty growled, indicating a visitor approaching, when Padar poked his head through the top half of the kitchen door. It made her jump. The toast fell to the floor, butter-side down. Her mouth dropped open. She could not believe he had the gall to show his face after all that had happened. Padar was pink and flustered. Marianne continued to glare at him. Bridget, spotting her father, started to squirm in her high chair, reaching out and gurgling a welcome. Monty, sensing trouble, just looked cagily from one to the other. Marianne bent down, picked up the toast and threw it in the sink.

"What the hell do you want?"

"To apologise," Padar said quietly, "for everything."

"Go away, Padar." Marianne busied herself making fresh toast. She could feel a burning rash of anger at her throat. Frustrated at not being picked up by her father, Bridget started to grizzle. Monty was pacing around the table; he hated it when Bridget was upset.

Padar stood at the door like a statue.

"I have to talk to you, Marianne. I've been awake all night. I can't bear it if you leave me too, if I can't call you a friend."

"Ha! I called you a friend, and look what you were doing to me. Us. All of us." She rescued the burning bread from under the grill. Bridget had started to howl. Monty was joining in. "For God's sake, Padar, come in and pick the child up."

He flew through the door, took Bridget in his arms, burying his head in her fluffy, pink romper suit, and started to sob. Marianne sighed loudly but, turning from the sink, felt her heart break as she watched him weeping into his daughter's downy hair.

"Pull yourself together, Padar. Come on now," she said coldly, but her eyes were soft. He sniffed.

"It all got a bit out of control." He turned bloodshot eyes on her. "I really didn't mean to make trouble for you and Ryan. At first I thought it would just be a bit of harmless fun. I'd get paid, pay a few debts and that would be it. But they wouldn't let me stop. They kept demanding more and when they found out how ill Oonagh was, they threatened to tell her everything if I didn't keep the photos coming."

"Ah, Padar," Marianne said dismissively, looking down so he could not see the pity in her eyes.

"I'm sorry I made everything so bad for you, really, really sorry."

Marianne closed the top of the kitchen door. The breeze off the sea was fresh. There was a chill in the air. Padar took a deep breath.

"You probably don't like me anymore, and I don't blame you," he stuttered, "but if we could put this behind us, and if you could just be civil to me, if nothing else for Bridget's sake. I dunno." His eyes filled with tears again. He pushed an envelope across the table towards her.

"More photos?" she asked, and opened it. She gasped. It was a picture taken at Bridget's christening. They were all in a disorganised row. Padar with Monty in his arms, smiling next to Ryan. Ryan with his arm around Oonagh, his hand on Marianne's shoulder as she held Bridget grinning into the camera, the baby looking up at her. It was a picture of everyone she loved in the world, a picture of happiness, heart-breaking happiness. She slumped into a chair and put the photo on the table before her. She pushed her hair back. She was tired, she had hardly slept, and when she finally woke she had come to the conclusion that, like so many people in her life, Padar had been doing all the wrong things for what he thought were the right reasons.

She beckoned him to sit down.

"Tell me this is an end to it and the source of all this inane and hurtful drivel has well and truly dried up?"

"I'm finished with all of that, I promise you."

She turned to face him, arms folded.

"Okay, we can talk and I'll be civil, but I'll have to work on the forgiveness and it could take a while."

He breathed a sigh of relief, placing a now smiling Bridget back in her high chair. Monty emerged from his basket, wagging his tail. Marianne picked him up so he was level with Bridget, who immediately fed him her toast.

"We'd better go back to our original arrangement or Bridget will have him the size of a house," Padar suggested meekly.

Marianne was just about to agree, when Miss MacReady appeared, black PVC raincoat flapping in the wind, collar turned up and an overlarge sou'wester pulled down over her ears against the October squall. Her earrings jangled as she clattered onto the tiles, her bare feet filthy in daisy-adorned flip-flops. She took in the scene in the kitchen with one sweep of her birdlike eyes and declined to comment.

"Well, what do you think?" She poured coffee from the pot, lifting the rim of her hat to drink.

"I think we'll be grand."

"No, not you, Padar. The news, Marie. What do you think of the news?"

Marianne shrugged.

"Did you not hear?" Miss MacReady glanced at the radio. "Last night, on the live chat show, Ryan announced he's jacked it in, resigned, stepped down, given it up. There, live on the telly in front of the whole nation."

"Given what up?"

"The role, the job, the super-hero spy fella. It's all over the radio this morning, be in all the papers tomorrow. They could sue him for breach of contract – he's supposed to do three films – but he said he's not bothered about that, so there you are." She took a mouthful of her drink, while Marianne and Monty watched, bemused. "And what's more, the divorce. That's next. He's filed for divorce and is going for custody of the child."

Marianne put Monty down. As usual, Miss MacReady knew far more than what might have been said during a television interview.

"He'll get it too," Padar surmised. "There's loads more men are getting custody of their kids these days, particularly when the mother is a druggie."

"Substance dependent, Padar. It's not the same," explained Miss MacReady.

"It is so." Padar was adamant.

"Well, anyway, he finished by saying he is coming to live in the West of Ireland to pursue a career as a scriptwriter. It's what he's always wanted to do. Well, what he actually said was, 'revisit my one true love' and then explained he meant scriptwriting. Isn't it great news altogether?"

Marianne raised her eyebrows. "For whom?"

"Everyone. He'll be back now, surely."

"Don't hold your breath," Marianne said, although deep down inside, her breath had been on hold for some time. "Anyway, I have bigger and better things to worry about, there is a problem with the deeds for the children's retreat. A company in England has a charge on the property. It's complicated, and I'll need a hand sorting it out. English and Irish law can be far from compatible. Now, Padar, off you go and open the pub, and if you don't mind, Miss MacReady, I'm very busy and I'm sure you are too," she said, taking Miss MacReady's mug off her and shooing them both out the door.

Chapter Twenty Nine – A Fair Wind

A few days later, word came from Snelgrove and Marshall; they could untangle the charge on the property; it would cost twenty-five thousand pounds to pay off the charge and about three thousand pounds in legal fees. There was enough in the bank account to do this but the lawyers needed proof of identity to be satisfied the sale was legitimate and there was no risk of money laundering. Once all this was in order, the whole thing could be completed in a matter of weeks.

Marianne was relieved, the same legal team had handled George's legacy, the sale of the house in Oakwood Avenue and the purchase of Weathervane. She knew she could trust them. She and Sinead were keen to get the holiday retreat up and running as quickly as possible. They had already planned a packed schedule for the children they hoped would arrive in the summer via the new bridge, if everything went according to plan. But time had a habit of flashing by, and as with all her projects, Marianne became totally immersed in every tiny detail, driving things forward with her usual obsessive ambitiousness. Still refusing to admit, even to herself, that this was the way she always dealt with any prolonged loneliness or grief, obstinately pushing Miss MacReady's revelations about Ryan to the back of her mind and, ignoring the fact that despite his momentous change of plan, he had still not been in touch. To be fair to Ryan, Marianne had been refusing to acknowledge any correspondence from him for some time and was quite proud she had managed to stick to her resolution.

Pulling out the chest where she kept her birth certificate and adoption papers, Marianne could not recall the need for such rigorous proof of identity when she had upped sticks and moved from England to this far-flung western isle. Surmising that times do indeed change, rooting through the chest she came upon a plethora of memorabilia she had not seen for years. Scattering papers and photographs across the desk, she found her old passport, stamped by the French Authorities, acknowledging her arriving and leaving Paris. It was strange, as if it had happened to someone else. She remembered speaking to Claude for the last time on the telephone to the hospice, when he had asked her to forgive him. Forgive him for what? Breaking her heart? She shrugged. There was plenty of tape around her heart, at this stage of the game, anyway.

Then she found a copy of George's death certificate, folded carefully in a velvet purse containing his signet ring and mother of pearl cufflinks. A copy of the picture of them at the Awards Dinner fell onto the desk. She blinked her tears away, smiling at George, who was grinning like a Cheshire cat, then grinning to herself,

she looked smug and a little bit pissed. She laughed out
loud when she came across the handwritten proposal
George had tied to Monty's neck when he had presented
the puppy just before Christmas. The proposal and ribbon
Monty had been wearing were wrapped around his
Kennel Club Certificate – George had been very proud of
the fact he was the offspring of a supreme champion, she
remembered.

Then she found her own birth certificate. This had
always been a mystery. Handwritten in ink, it looked as if
it had been deliberately splashed with water. The
mother's name was indistinguishable, the father's name
only slightly more legible, definitely beginning with a B,
but her mother's was just a splodge with a y at the end.
Her place of birth had not been defaced, but it was just a
squiggle, so again, impossible to decipher, although she
had been told she was born in Galway, but where was the
proof, she sometimes wondered. By comparison, her
Certificate of Adoption was pristine; the Coltranes'
names clear and efficiently entered. Another thing that
had always fascinated her, attached to the certificate, was
a picture of herself as a baby, a tiny black and white
photograph. Fascinating, because she had been a toddler
when the Coltranes had adopted her, although she could
barely remember anything about it. Yet her mother had
treasured this picture of her as a tiny infant, as if she had
wanted to capture her earliest years and share them, as if
she had given birth to her, as if they had always been
together.

Monty, snuffling through some of the papers she

let slip to the floor, brought her back to the task in hand. Quickly putting everything away, she shoved the required paperwork in an envelope and, clipping him onto his lead, walked up to town to make copies and discuss with Miss MacReady, the best way to send off the original documents safely.

Miss MacReady was thrilled to see them. She was wearing one of her favourite purple ensembles, a luxuriant velvet kimono, with bare feet, toenails painted peacock blue.

"Come in, come in, let me get you a drink," she called, turning the closed sign on the door as they passed through. Marianne gave her a broad grin to show the fractiousness of a couple of days ago was long forgotten. Miss MacReady poured them each a large measure of whiskey. Monty had his own dish on the floor of the postmistress's kitchen. She warmed some milk in the microwave for him and he lapped at it leisurely, keeping an eye on Marianne, which Marianne knew was his way of conveying he was not planning to stay. He needed to be clear about that.

Marianne explained the scenario to Miss MacReady.

"I saw from the email you sent round that we had a problem. Will these fellows in England be able to sort it?" she asked.

"I hope so. It's expensive but I don't want the property to go back on the market. We could lose the opportunity to turn this into something useful for the island."

"That's not everyone's opinion," Miss MacReady conceded.

Marianne dismissed the notion.

"We have to make something good out of all that's gone on here; something we can all be proud of, something which will serve as a memorial for Oonagh."

Miss MacReady dropped ice into the whiskey. It cracked.

"We have Bridget, that's our gift from Oonagh and our life's work too, we have to do right by the child. Have we not enough to be doing?" Miss MacReady eyed Marianne closely, sipping her drink.

"But we could do right by so many more," Marianne protested. Miss MacReady pushed her face into the other woman's.

"Have you always been such a pain-in-the-arse do-gooder?"

Marianne burst out laughing.

"Yes. Have you always been such a bloody know-it-all?"

"Of course," grinned Miss MacReady, chinking her glass with Marianne's.

Marianne drew the envelope out of her bag, explaining she had to send the original papers to England, but she needed to take copies just in case anything went awry.

They stood at the photocopier together. Marianne handed Miss MacReady her adoption certificate.

"Ah, if you are adopted, we need your birth certificate as well," she said, matter-of-factly.

"I know," smiled Marianne, "I've brought it." She handed it over.

Miss MacReady unfolded the documents. She glanced at the Birth Certificate and then went back to the Certificate of Adoption. She looked at the fading photograph which had been attached to the piece of paper for over thirty years. She put her glasses on and looked at it again. She held it at arm's length, brought it up to her nose, and then put it very slowly down on the copier. Pointing to the photograph, her voice a whisper, she asked,

"Who's this?"

"Well, me of course," Marianne replied, laughing, "I've changed a bit, I grant you." The room went quiet. She could hear the clock ticking out in the shop front of the Post Office. She turned and watched as the colour drained from Miss MacReady's face. Marianne heard her take a deep breath as the older woman grabbed the birth certificate, rushed to her desk and flicked on the lamp. She held the birth certificate beneath the light, hands shaking.

"What?" Marianne followed her.

Miss MacReady held her hand up for silence. She took a key from a chain around her neck and unlocked the desk drawer. Drawing it open, she took out a slender lacquered casket, placed it on the desktop and lifted the lid slowly. With trembling fingers, she withdrew a small envelope, brown with age. She opened it and placed the Certificate of Adoption with the photograph attached, beside it. She withdrew a piece of paper from the envelope. It was a photograph, an identical photograph to the one attached to the paperwork. She placed them side by side.

Marianne could hear a loud rushing in her ears. She tried to ignore it.

"They look so similar, they could be twins," she offered. Miss MacReady was holding onto the edge of the desk, she had turned very grey. She took another piece of paper out of the casket, unfolded it and laid it on the desk beside the Birth Certificate. It was a copy of the same Birth Certificate, except this copy had not been tampered with. The ink had not been smudged with water. It read: Mother's name; Kathleen Marianne MacReady. Father's name: Brian Joseph Maguire.

Marianne felt a jolt, the whooshing sound was even louder. She thought she heard Miss MacReady say something. She thought she heard her say,

"They told me you died. They told me a lie. I always knew it was a lie."

Marianne tried to speak, but her mouth was so dry her lips were stuck together. She was trying to stand upright but her knees had turned to jelly.

The women just stared at each other. Miss MacReady could see Marianne's eyes were those of her beloved Brian; Marianne looked Miss MacReady up and down slowly, they had the same legs, feet, mouth. This was insane.

"Thank you, thank you," Miss MacReady exclaimed, lifting her arms to the sky. "Thank you, whoever you are?" she called at the top of her voice as she rushed to embrace Marianne. Marianne just stood there, heart pounding, as the older woman, face wet with tears, hugged her.

"No, no you're wrong. I was born in Galway... I was born in..."

"The same hospital Oonagh was treated in, that's the nearest hospital to here, that's where half the island was born. Afterwards, I always thought it was funny there are no illegitimate children on the island. The most natural thing in the world never happened here."

"But…"

Miss MacReady passed Marianne her glass. She gulped it down, taking deep breaths, slowing her heartbeat. Miss MacReady poured them fresh drinks. She had started to weep quietly. She lifted Monty onto Marianne's lap and Marianne cuddled him for warmth, his bright brown eyes searching hers.

"If it's true, why?" she asked, finally finding her voice, "Why were you in that position in the first place?"

"We weren't married. He wanted to marry me, but they were Protestants, his father wouldn't hear of it, said I ruined his life. I had the baby, you, in the hospital in Galway and was sent to the convent in Wicklow to recuperate before I came home, but it was while I was there I fell seriously ill. They took my baby away until I recovered and, though I begged and pleaded to have my baby back, they finally told me she had died." She wiped her eyes at the memory. "They were all very sympathetic and looked after me until I was well again and the Abbess found me a position with the Post Office in Dublin, but I hated it. I couldn't shake the idea that my baby was not dead. She didn't feel dead. I thought I was going mad."

Marianne touched Miss MacReady's hand. It sounded like so many of the terrifying tales she had heard when she was uncovering the 'Babies for sale scam' story for the newspaper. It was too real not to be true. She nodded Miss MacReady to go on.

"I used to go to the bar in that Dublin hotel every Monday night, hoping he would come and fetch me, take me home, but he never did. Some knight in shining armour! Anyway, I was determined to come back to Innishmahon with a career, and I did, and as postmistress, I had a position in society, such as it was. Brian was still here, practising as a GP. He never married and though I tried to get him to talk about it, he never spoke to me again. I think he knew. I think he knew his own child had been 'sold' into the adoption system. I think the Doctors' Maguire had always been part of the baby trade that still happens the world over. It's desperate. It's worse than murder." The older woman was trembling, her makeup streaked with tears as she clasped Marianne's hand in hers.

Marianne put her arms around Miss MacReady, holding her close as she wept. Nothing that had ever happened to her, could compare with her own mother being told her baby had died soon after birth. Gathering herself, Miss MacReady went to her desk and fetched the Death Certificate for her baby girl. Marianne gasped and then nodded as she read it, checking for the signs of forgery she had become aware of whilst investigating the

'Baby Scam'.

"You're right, it looks just like all the others."

"Then you are my baby. You've come home," She looked into Marianne's eyes.

"Do you really think so? It's all a bit of a coincidence isn't it?"

"Not really. The Coltranes came here often enough, they would have known the Maguires. They might even have known about you; who you were. They were childless. The Maguires probably wanted a decent home for one of their own, even though she could not be acknowledged as such, an illegitimate baby girl and from a Catholic mother at that."

Marianne nodded and then shook her head.

"But we're talking about the 1970s for God's sake. This sounds almost Dickensian."

"We may have all the trappings of the twenty-first century, but old bigotries run deep." Miss MacReady took Marianne's hand.

"Did you never wonder, never want to find out about your own mother?"

Marianne shrugged. "I figured she had her reasons for giving me away. What was the point of seeking her out, the reasons wouldn't have changed."

"But times change, and circumstances, too."

"What chance would I have had with that birth certificate anyway, deliberately tampered with so I could never find out." Marianne was surprised at the anger in her voice.

"So you've carried that with you all your life,

given away by your birth mother, no reason, no explanation, no way of finding out who she was?"

"It was fine, it suited me. I had enough to deal with, being adopted, and being an only child. I didn't have a proper family. I didn't need one." Marianne went to pour another drink.

"I think not having any family around you is worse when you can't have your own," Miss MacReady said. "No-one to turn to, no-one to talk it through with, no-one who understood what it felt like not to have your own child."

"It was okay," Marianne said. "I kept busy, I managed."

"Yes you did, and if you are my daughter, and I'm damn sure you are, well I couldn't be more proud." Miss MacReady started to cry again. Marianne knelt beside her and hugged her tightly.

"It's alright, it's alright," Marianne kept repeating, her head full of questions yet her heart beginning to flutter with joy.

"It is now." Miss MacReady smiled into her face, the brightest, most beautiful smile Marianne had ever seen her wear. "You have been sent back to me and I to you. Whoever is taking care of us up there, she's doing a great job."

"It's a he," said Marianne. "His name's George. Oh, and he probably has a bit of help from a terrifying new sidekick called Oonagh." And they laughed together, a very similar sounding laugh when you listened closely.

The Hollow Heart

The following week was one of the most fantastic Marianne had ever experienced. Not only was she delighting in getting used to the revelation that her birth mother was, in fact, the wonderfully eccentric Kathleen MacReady, and Innishmahon was in so many ways, her true spiritual home. She also had notice that the purchase of the Ophiuchus had been agreed and the official papers were being delivered by special courier. There was a distinct possibility the house would be up and running as a respite resort for young carers in time for the new season; coinciding nicely with the opening of the new bridge.

It was a glorious late October morning, almost a year to the day since the 'Bridge Too Far' Festival. There was going to be a small reunion of stalwart supporters over the weekend and the Finnigan Twins were booked for the session that evening in Maguire's.

Deciding to take their constitutional before she became bogged down in arrangements at the pub, Marianne took Monty and Bridget, now too heavy for her carry sling, up to Ophiuchus to inspect the Planning Notice attached to the gatepost, and then down to meet the ferry and take delivery of the official documents being delivered that very day.

The wind was the softest kiss as they climbed the slope to the grandiose gates of the fine Georgian house. Bridget was in her pushchair with Monty helping to haul the contraption along, like a husky. The sun was already warm; it was one of those rare October days masquerading as July. The ferry sounded its arrival, sliding into the harbour on a slipstream of sparkling water. Marianne nodded to herself as she read the Planning Application for the alterations to the house and, turning towards the sea, shielded her eyes from the sun as she watched the ferry passengers make their way along the gangplank. Monty followed her gaze, then spotting something he recognised, pricked his ears, tugged free of his lead and started back down the track. Marianne called him but he paid no heed. She quickly lifted Bridget out of the buggy onto her hip, frightened it would topple over if she attempted to follow her four-legged chum.

"What has he seen?" she asked the child, shielding her eyes again. And then she spotted the subject of Monty's distraction. A man, tall and slim, with dark hair, wearing a battered leather jacket, was standing on the quayside. He had seen her and was waving something at her, an envelope or document of some sort. He was starting to move towards her. The little white dog had almost reached him but he stopped and turning back to the boat, signalled a purser to lift a bulky piece of cargo carefully off the gangplank. It was a child's pushchair and there was a child strapped into it. A child in blue. A little boy.

She hoisted Bridget higher, clamping the little girl tightly to her hip so she could lift her other arm high above her head, giving the watching figure a huge wave of welcome.

He waved back, manically, with both arms, jumping up and down as if he were keep fit training. The purser who had lifted the pushchair was busy piling suitcases and luggage beside the cluster of man, child and dog on the quayside. It looked as if his whole life had arrived with him.

Bridget stretched out her arms towards them. Marianne made a sound as if she had been stabbed. Ears rushing with noise, she could feel her heart beating; the excitement building as she started to stride from the house down the track, holding the little girl close in her embrace, moving faster and faster. The man kept jumping up and down like a lunatic, pointing at the child in the pushchair and back towards her and Bridget. As she drew nearer, she could hear him shouting,

"Look, look, we're here. We're all here."

Monty was running in circles, wagging his tail and yapping wildly. She started to laugh, as she pulled up the collar of her jacket. Despite the sun, the breeze had whipped up, coming from behind her; pushing her down the hill towards the sea, towards where Monty now stood with the little boy in the pushchair and Ryan and all his baggage. Strange, she thought, smiling, the wind has changed.

THE END

Adrienne Vaughan

Can't bear to leave the island? If you would like to stay on Innishmahon and find out what happens to Marianne, Ryan and all the other wonderful characters, A Change of Heart, the sequel to The Hollow Heart, will be available in 2013. Here's a taster...

They were in the largest cellar room, at the very end of the long corridor which ran from the bottom of the stairs the length of the house. There were windows high in the walls, small ones but plenty of them. Painted cream or white instead of gloomy mustard brown, it would transform the place she thought, placing her clipboard on a chest.

"Great breakout area, don't you think? Perfect for a pool table, some sofas, a bit of music." He said. She had her head buried in one of the many wooden chests fixed along the walls. He strode to the far end of the room, pushing back a screen on squeaky wheels.

"Hey, what's this?"

She looked up. Half a dozen steps led up to a pair of narrow doors. The doors were paned with glass but the glass had been blacked out. He tried them.

"Stuck, or locked, or both." He took a crowbar from the tool bag, easing it into the gap, it made a loud crack and as he pushed the doors open, moths and beetles scrabbled for cover. He brushed cobwebs away. The doors led onto a patch of overgrown gravel, then a lower lawn, a grassy slice of beach and then the shore.

"Come and see," he called to her, amazed the house, so high above the village, secretly slid down to the water once you were inside. He looked up. "Hey, I've found a balcony, a tiny little Juliet balcony." He pulled at the strands of ivy, trailing down. "Romantic."

"There hasn't been much romance here in a long time," she said, beating dust off the drapes at the door with her clipboard.

"Come out here," he demanded, taking her hand, pulling her outside to stand on the gravel beside him looking down at the secret beach.

"Oh," she said, surprised. "It's like a little smuggler's cove."

The sun was sliding towards the horizon, the sky cloudless and bleached blue. They stood side by side, arms touching. They could feel the heat. She dropped his hand and stepped back inside.

"Do you want to make a start on the painting, or have we other jobs?" He called after her.

"The first coat's not dry yet, that's tomorrow's job. Let's get stuck into these chests, see what we can sling or recycle."

"Good plan." He agreed, not moving from his lookout post. The bewitching promise of a glorious sunset rooted him to the spot. "Look at this."

She was poking through a pile of files.

"There's so much that should have been thrown away, medical records from years ago."

"Just bin them," he advised. "Come and look at the sunset woman."

She had a headache, her feet hurt. She dropped the bin bag and, kicking off her shoes, went to join him.

"At last," he smiled into her face. A light breeze was coming off the water, the air sweet and clean. They stood shoulder to shoulder looking out. It stretched before them, a smooth of green, a rustle of blond and then the sea; deep, dark and glistening. She shivered. He put an arm around her shoulders. She inhaled deeply and nestled into him, his scent mixing pleasingly with the salt air. She put her head on his shoulder, he leaned down to her, rubbing his cheek briefly on her hair, breathing her in. She lifted her chin to speak, her lips almost touching the small, soft space of skin beneath his ear. The sun had turned into a huge, orange orb.

"This is so beautiful," he whispered, staring straight ahead. "I could stay here, like this, forever."

"Me too," she replied, the breath from her words tickled his skin. He wrapped his arms around her, pulling her in close, a gentle, brotherly embrace she was free to release herself at any point. She looked up at him, his eyes were soft, kind, loving. She was suddenly tearful.

"Hey, hey," he said cupping her chin in his hand. "You're too beautiful to be always so sad."

She blinked the tears away, then standing on tiptoe she kissed him, the lightest kiss, her mouth just brushing his lips and releasing herself, she went back into the house. He turned to follow her and then stopped. Pushing his hands into his pockets he frowned out towards the sea, breathing deeply, willing the desire away. He watched the sun start to sink.

"Come inside," she called out to him, "I've something to show you."

The room was gloomy now the sun had dipped, he went to switch on the lights.

"Don't, come here." She said softly, her voice was coming from behind the screen, near the drapes. He could not see her, he followed her voice, his foot caught in something soft, he kicked it aside.

"Are you hiding?" He asked, with a smile in his voice. He pulled the drapes aside. She stood there in the half light, her hair loose around her shoulders, her blouse open to the waist, her breasts barely covered by a sheer vest top. She had taken off her long chambray skirt and her smooth legs shone like marble against the dark, full length curtains. She raised her arms above her head, leaning back against the wall so he could see all of her, every inch of her from head to toe. She was smiling, a low sweet smile, her lips parted.

He was stunned, too shocked to speak. His eyes flickered as his gaze swept over her. He tried to look away but his body was responding in a way he had not felt for years. Seeing him struggle, she gasped and pulled her blouse closed, stooping to collect her skirt.

"I'm so sorry," she whispered, her voice a rasp in her throat.

"Oh God, don't be." He begged, taking her hand, letting the skirt fall.

Acknowledgements

Literally dozens of fabulous people have put up with me writing this book. I would like to thank you all, especially my fantastic family, the folks, the sis, the other half and one's aunts **Tricia Broome** and **Alice Hall**; those dear friends and colleagues who have listened, trying not to yawn, for your unlimited patience, encouragement and support. Far too many to mention but you know who you are.

A sincere and heartfelt thanks to those who helped make it physically happen...**Jan Brigden**, **Julie Cohen**, Rebecca Connell, Helen Corner and the participants in the 2010 Cornerstones Writing Women's Commercial Fiction Course, **Amanda Grange**, Sue Peebles and the wonderful writers at the Arvon Centre in Inverness, **June Tate**, Michelle Tayton, **Natalie Thew** and not forgetting **David Burton**, a far from token male!

My very special friends and colleagues in the Romantic Novelists' Association, and particularly the Leicester Chapter, including Jean Chapman, Lynda Dunwell, **Margaret Kaine**, Cathy Mansell, Katharine Garbera and Alex Gutteridge, they are one of the most amazing groups of talented and feisty females I have ever encountered.

And last but not least, the New Romantics4, **Mags Cullingford**, **June Kearns** and **Lizzie Lamb** – a force to be reckoned with!

About the Author

Adrienne Vaughan has been making up stories since she could speak; primarily to entertain her sister Reta, who from a very early age never allowed a plot or character to be repeated – *tough audience*. As soon as she could pick up a pen, she started writing them down. It was no surprise she wanted to be a journalist; ideally, the editor of a glossy music and fashion magazine, so she could meet and marry a pop star – *some of that came true* – and in common with so many, still holds the burning ambition to be a *'Bond Girl'*!

She now runs a busy PR practice and writes poems, short stories and ideas for books, in her spare time. She is a member of the Romantic Novelists' Association and a founder member of the indie publishing group The New Romantics4.

Adrienne lives in Leicestershire with her husband, two cocker spaniels and a retired dressage horse called Marco. The Hollow Heart is her debut novel. The sequel, A Change of Heart, is currently being scribbled down at every available moment.

www.adriennevaughan.com

Adrienne Vaughan

Check out the latest novels published by
The New Romantics4

Tall, Dark & Kilted
By Lizzie Lamb

An Englishwoman's Guide
To The Cowboy
By June Kearns

Last Bite Of The Cherry
By Margaret Cullingford

an indie
publisihing group

3130368R00220

Printed in Great Britain
by Amazon.co.uk, Ltd.,
Marston Gate.